ROBERT LOUIS STEVENS̶on was born in Edinburgh in 1850. The son of a prosperous civil engineer, he was expected to follow the family profession but finally was allowed to study law at Edinburgh University. Stevenson reacted violently against the Presbyterian respectability of the city's professional classes and this led to painful clashes with his parents. In his early twenties he became afflicted with a severe respiratory illness from which he was to suffer for the rest of his life; it was at this time that he determined to become a professional writer. The harsh nature of the Scottish climate forced him to spend long periods abroad and he eventually settled in Samoa, where he died on 3 December 1894.

Stevenson's Calvinistic upbringing gave him a preoccupation with predestination and a fascination with the presence of evil. In *Dr Jekyll and Mr Hyde* he explores the darker side of the human psyche, and the character of the Master in *The Master of Ballantrae* (1889) was intended to be 'all I know of the Devil'. Stevenson is well known for his novels of historical adventure, including *Treasure Island* (1883), *Kidnapped* (1886) and *Catriona* (1893). As Walter Allen in *The English Novel* comments, 'His rediscovery of the art of narrative, of conscious and cunning calculation in telling a story so that the maximum effect of clarity and suspense is achieved, meant the birth of the novel of action as we know it.' But these works also reveal his knowledge and feeling for the Scottish cultural past. During the last years of his life Stevenson's creative range developed considerably and *The Beach of Falesá* brought to fiction the kind of scene now associated with Conrad and Maugham. At the time of his death Robert Louis Stevenson was working on his unfinished masterpiece, *Weir of Hermiston*, which is at once a romantic historical novel and an emotional reworking of one of Stevenson's own most distressing experiences, the conflict between father and son.

DONALD MCFARLAN was born in Glasgow in 1952. A 'son of the manse', he was educated at Glasgow Academy and Cambridge University where he read English. In a varied career in publishing he has been, *inter alia*, Editor of the Penguin Classics and of *The*

Guinness Book of Records. He is also the author of *The Guinness Book of 'Why?'*, a book about the science of everyday things.

ALASDAIR GRAY, born in Glasgow in 1934, became jack of several trades, being unable to earn a living by one. He has painted many kinds of pictures and written several kinds of books, designing and illustrating his own and others. In November 2007 Bloomsbury is publishing his novel *Men in Love*; in 2008 Canongate will publish a book about his art, *A Life in Pictures*.

ROBERT LOUIS STEVENSON

Kidnapped

Edited with an Introduction and Notes by
DONALD MCFARLAN
and a Foreword by ALASDAIR GRAY

PENGUIN BOOKS

PENGUIN CLASSICS

Published by the Penguin Group
Penguin Books Ltd, 80 Strand, London WC2R ORL, England
Penguin Group (USA) Inc., 375 Hudson Street, New York, New York 10014, USA
Penguin Group (Canada), 90 Eglinton Avenue East, Suite 700, Toronto, Ontario, Canada M4P 2Y3
(a division of Pearson Penguin Canada Inc.)
Penguin Ireland, 25 St Stephen's Green, Dublin 2, Ireland
(a division of Penguin Books Ltd)
Penguin Group (Australia), 250 Camberwell Road, Camberwell, Victoria 3124, Australia
(a division of Pearson Australia Group Pty Ltd)
Penguin Books India Pvt Ltd, 11 Community Centre, Panchsheel Park, New Delhi – 110 017, India
Penguin Group (NZ), 67 Apollo Drive, Rosedale, North Shore 0632, New Zealand
(a division of Pearson New Zealand Ltd)
Penguin Books (South Africa) (Pty) Ltd, 24 Sturdee Avenue, Rosebank, Johannesburg 2196, South Africa

Penguin Books Ltd, Registered Offices: 80 Strand, London WC2R ORL, England

www.penguin.com

First published 1886
Published in Penguin Classics 1994
This revised edition published with a new foreword 2007

1

Introduction and Notes copyright © Donald McFarlan, 1994
Foreword copyright © Alasdair Gray, 2007
All rights reserved

The moral right of the author has been asserted

Set in 10.25/12.25 pt PostScript Adobe Sabon
Typeset by Rowland Phototypesetting Ltd, Bury St Edmunds, Suffolk
Printed in Great Britain by Clays Ltd, St Ives plc

ISBN: 978-0-141-44179-5

Contents

Foreword

Reader, if *Kidnapped* is new to you do not, by first tackling this foreword, spoil your enjoyment of a good story. Read the novel (with pauses for food, work and sleep) straight to the end. If you then want to know how Robert Louis Stevenson came to write it, return here.

> I was born in Edinburgh, in 1850 [wrote Stevenson], my father Thomas Stevenson, my mother Margaret Isabella Balfour. For near three centuries before my appearance, these Balfours had been judges, advocates, and ministers of the Gospel. It concerns me much that John Balfour of Kinloch, the covenanting fanatic, was an ancestral cousin.

That fanatic helped kill Archbishop Sharp in 1679, for which Walter Scott dramatized him as Balfour of Burleigh in *Old Mortality*. Margaret was a douce, nineteenth-century Kirk of Scotland minister's daughter. Her maternal grandfather had been mocked in Burns's satire *The Holy Fair*. 'Thus', said R.L.S., 'I may call myself connected both with Scott and Burns. My father's family is much more remarkable; this much at least may be said for it, that its history is unparalleled.' The Stevensons were descended from obscure lowland farmers and tradesmen of a sort (said R.L.S.) who had small, decent character parts in Scott's novels. In 1786 a Stevenson widow with a clever young son married an Edinburgh manufacturer of oil lamps who came to design and construct Scotland's first modern lighthouses. That clever son became the firm's leading partner. Scotland had by then overcome the economic damage of the

1707 Union of Parliaments and was a leading world market. At a time when heavy goods could only be moved far in ships it imported raw sugar, tobacco and cotton from across the Atlantic, exporting them repackaged or refined to Europe, the British colonies or back to America. Since Scotland's coastal shipping lanes were more complex, more dangerous than England's the Edinburgh Northern Lights Board was independent of Trinity House, its London equivalent. The widow Stevenson's clever son became one of Scotland's greatest civil engineers when Scotland had several.

> We rose out of obscurity in a clap. My father and uncle David made the third generation who had been engineers to the Board of Northern Lights; there is scarce a deep sea light from the Isle of Man north and around to Berwick, but one of my blood designed it; and I have often thought that to find a family to compare with ours in the promise of immortality we must go back to the Egyptian pharaohs: – upon so many reefs and forelands that not very elegant name of Stevenson is engraved with a pen of iron upon granite.

The Stevensons were also consultant engineers for the building of roads, bridges, harbours, canals and railways. Thomas met Margaret Balfour when she was eighteen and he twelve years older. Their son said, 'I was an only child and, it may be in consequence, both intelligent and sickly.'

The family home was in Edinburgh New Town, the best-designed eighteenth-century town outside Bath. But Bath was made for fashionable invalids and summer holiday-makers; the new half of Edinburgh was built for merchants, lawyers and other folk managing Scotland. Summers could be wet and windy, and after summer sea fogs blew from the Forth, often thickened by soot from the reeking chimneys of Edinburgh Old Town, which had become Europe's tallest slum.

Robert Louis easily caught colds in which he coughed up blood, and sometimes gastric or rheumatic fevers kept him in bed for days, weeks or months. Before learning to read at the age of seven he could often do little but suffer and imagine things. Afterwards he read copiously and began writing. In those days affluent families employed servants to do the inconvenient parts of mothering, sometimes to the child's advantage. Walter Scott, Rudyard Kipling, most nineteenth-century Russian writers and a few southern USA ones owed their social insight to childhood servants. In an essay about nurses R.L.S. hoped that in a better state of things there would be no more nurses and every mother would nurse her own offspring. He wanted that, not for the child's sake, but because most nursemaids had no chance of mothering their own children, so were condemned to a lonely old age. When thirty-five R.L.S. published *A Child's Garden of Verses*, dedicating it to 'Alison Cunningham from her boy', with these lines:

> For the long nights you lay awake / And watched for my
>   unworthy sake:
> For your most comfortable hand / That led me through the
>   uneven land:
> For all the story books you read: / For all the pains you comforted:
> For all you pitied, all you bore, / In sad and happy days of yore: –
> My second Mother, my first Wife, / The angel of my infant life –
> From the sick child, now well and old, / Take, nurse, the little
>   book you hold!

Alison read young Robert stories from the Bible, *The Pilgrim's Progress* and lives of seventeenth-century Presbyterians who had been persecuted or killed for refusing to worship God with English prayer books. She read him tracts about children who, after telling a lie or enjoying something on Sunday which should *not* be enjoyed, were thus struck dead and damned to Hell. Bodily pain and fear of death were thus complicated by dread of worse to follow – for his parents as well as himself! Theirs was a liberal, nineteenth-century Kirk of Scotland faith. Without doubting Hell they thought only unusually bad people went there, so it was not wicked to invite friends for dinner on Sunday and play cards with them after. Alison, like many Scots working-class folk then, held the older, tougher Presbyterian faith that thought these things damnable, so had the wee boy begging God to show his parents the error of their ways.

Many painful, sleepless nights combined with fierce biblical and historical legends would certainly have warped someone less intelligent and less sure of love. By giving him two simultaneous but conflicting Christianities nurse and parents fostered an independence that later led him (after reading Darwin and Herbert Spencer) to disbelieve in the soul's immortality and lose (like David Hume before him) his fear of death. This nurturing also introduced him to a province of the mind sometimes called the *subconscious* because many things too awkward to remember live in it, so most folk only go there in dreams and nightmares. R.L.S., like Yeats and other creators, knew that province better than most so found good ideas for stories in dreams and nightmares. When unsure how a story should continue he learned to leave it with subconscious agents he called his *brownies*, and wait till these returned the material to him in a more useful shape. Unlike Yeats he had no time for spiritualism and the occult, because Stevenson knew the supernatural was an imaginative device, the subconscious an intellectual one. Though not religious he respected stories from which religions grew and said the Garden of Eden and Fall of Man in *Genesis* were a better account of life than even Shakespeare's.

He grew taller than the Victorian average but pale, thin, narrow-chested. His poor health made school attendance sporadic. Private tuition and love of reading educated him more thoroughly than any school. Though coddled at home (without coddling he would likely have died), in healthy intervals he was as adventurous as possible: climbing, fishing, making midnight excursions with other boys and later going on long walking and canoeing holidays. His adventurous spirit and constant need to find a healthier climate eventually made him the most restlessly itinerant of all fine writers with the possible exception of Herman Melville. After much sojourning in France and America he finally died among the Pacific islands, where Melville's writing career started.

R.L.S. enrolled at Edinburgh University but attended few lectures, preferring to mix with poorer folk and prostitutes in the pubs of the Old Town. He rejected the hard hats, stiff collars, waistcoats, frockcoats of nineteenth-century respectability – wore his hair long with soft-collared shirts, floppy bowties, velvet jackets or, in cold weather, the sort of reefer jackets worn by seamen. This rejection of middle-class uniformity came from his hatred of the poverty most respectable people liked to ignore. When many parents could not afford to buy shoes for their children he was sickened by the sight of a child's bare feet on frosty winter pavements. He later described his own situation in the third person:

> My friend had been kept alive through a sickly childhood by constant watchfulness, comforts and change of air, for all of which he was indebted to his father's wealth. At college he met other lads more diligent than himself, who followed the plough in summer-time to pay their college fees in winter; and this inequality struck him with some force. He was at that age of a conversable temper, and insatiably curious in the aspects of life; and he spent much of his time scraping acquaintances with all classes of man- and womankind. In this way he came upon many depressed ambitions, and many intelligences stunted for want of opportunity ... There sat a youth beside him on the college benches, who had only one shirt to his back, and, at intervals sufficiently far apart, must stay at home to have it washed ... My friend began to see that life was a handicap on strange, wrong-sided principles and not, as he had been told, a fair and equal race ... Sometime after this, falling into ill-health, he was sent at great expense to a more favourable climate ... When he thought of all the other young men of singular promise, upright, good, the prop of families, who must remain at home to die, and with all their possibilities be lost to life and mankind; and how he was chosen out from all these others to survive, he saw no justice in this social arrangement. A religious lady, to whom he communicated these reflections, could see no force in them. It was the will of God, said she.

His parents were unworried by his bohemian ways, poor university performance and social conscience. Thomas assumed his son would master engineering, like he and *his* father had done, by practice. When eighteen the boy attended the construction of a harbour wall in east-coast Anstruther, and at Wick on the northern coast he descended in a diving suit. When twenty he was on the western island of Earraid, near Iona, at a camp for workers building a lighthouse on rocks where, fourteen years later, he described the brig *Covenant* being wrecked. Earraid was where David Balfour spent painful days before discovering he could walk off at low tide. R.L.S. learned Scotland's geography through his dad as thoroughly as he had learned history through his nurse and Walter Scott. But by then he was going everywhere with a book to read in one pocket, in the other a notebook to write in. He was studying to become what the Victorians called *a man of letters*.

The most successful had been Joseph Addison, whose poem celebrating the Battle of Blenheim in 1704 led to a Whig cabinet giving him a well-paid government post. After that Addison wrote a successful opera, a blank-verse tragedy and political pamphlets, but was chiefly famous for essays published in the *Spectator*. This was the first periodical magazine to amuse both Whigs and Tories with commentaries on middle and upper-class fashionable life. It was written in a style that flattered the readers by suggesting they too were tolerant, broadminded, well-educated and understood Life. When Britain had no police force – when rapes, stabbings and duels were often unpunished, especially if committed by the nobility – the *Spectator* essays strove to make selfish rowdiness unfashionable, and English readers loved them for it. Its polite literary style, like good manners, was thought civilizing. Dr Johnson's personal manners were often rude but he said that all who wished to write good English should continually study the essays of Addison. Early in the nineteenth century Addison's diction had been joined by the more relaxed styles of Lamb and Hazlitt who, though polite and good-natured, had no interest in fashionable society. Like them R.L.S. described interesting folk he met, chiefly vagabonds. He wrote fables and verses in Scots and conventional English – he started a blank verse tragedy in Webster's Jacobean style then rejigged it as Restoration-style

Congreve. Able to read and speak French like a native, he had a life-long admiration for Dumas's musketeer romances, but the main French influence was in his struggle for a prose uniting description and commentary without obvious joins, a prose behind which the writer would be invisible.

This concern was unusual in a writer of English. Addison's style reads like the polite speech common in his day – he did not want people to think he wrote with conscious effort. When Voltaire tried to discuss writing with him Addison said he did not regard himself as a writer, but as a gentleman who occasionally wrote. Fielding, Scott, Dickens and Herman Melville also mainly used the polite speech commonest in their day, enriching it with suggestions from well-known plays, hammering their styles out in the hurry of getting books quickly written. Thus Dickens and Melville wrote paragraphs equalling great poetry, but their reviewers paid no attention to their styles because before the twentieth century English universities thought novels worthless literature. The historians Macaulay and Carlyle and the art critic Ruskin were admired for unique, emphatic styles that other writers had better not imitate. Stevenson analysed Macaulay's sentences to demonstrate why their famous style was heavy-handed daubing. At that time only in France was good prose publicly, critically debated and novels accepted as important art. This may be why Stevenson was taken seriously by the French when many British critics before the 1980s dismissed him (along with Edgar Allan Poe) as a shallow entertainer.

Many Edinburgh acquaintances thought him a poseur. His conversation quickly convinced intelligent strangers, especially writers, that his mind was considerable. When twenty-three and visiting relatives in England he met and made a fast friend of Sidney Colvin, Cambridge professor of fine art who reviewed books in the *Fortnightly Review*. Through Colvin he met Lesley Stephens, W. E. Henley, Edmund Gosse and Andrew Lang, who were, or soon became, leading British editors and book reviewers. They admired his style and printed his first essays, a good start for a young writer when magazines had replaced pulpit sermons as Britain's main form of broadcasting. But the payment could buy little more than his clothing. His dad thought such writing a mere hobby, because Stevenson's famous literary friends, while inheriting unearned incomes, had university jobs and editorial salaries. Even Walter Scott, the world's most highly paid author, had written fiction while toiling as a High Court lawyer and Midlothian Sheriff until overwork induced premature senile dementia. The elder Stevenson was rich and generous but thought that subsidizing his son as a writer would turn him into a parasite. Since ill health made an engineering career impossible he promised to support Louis if he qualified for the Scottish Bar. R.L.S. studied hard – took his law degree – never practised law – never stopped being supported by the family money, though perhaps in the last five years of his life he could have survived without.

His first books appeared in 1878. *An Inland Voyage* and *Travels with a Donkey in the Cevennes* were travel books describing canoeing and walking excursions abroad. They do not tell how he had lodged in the forest of Fontainebleau at an inn popular with artists and tourists who enjoyed the company of artists. Here he had met Fanny Osbourne, a Californian ten years older than he, who was visiting France with her daughter (often mistaken for her young sister) to escape from an unhappy marriage in the USA. She belonged to that first wave of American women visitors whose independent attitudes shocked, astonished and attracted men in a Europe where women were still expected to be coy admiring helpers of robust males. She was charmed by R.L.S. and before she returned to California he was in love with her. Two years later, hearing her divorce was imminent, he followed her there, making the most of his father's allowance by travelling third-class among the poorest immigrants.

Fanny may have been disconcerted by his arrival – she had an eleven-year-old son besides an older daughter, and for the last time seems to have been trying to make her unsatisfactory marriage work. She did not reject the lover who had come so far for her, though he was an invalid living on a small allowance from a father who would now perhaps cut it off, and whose only other chance of money was a publisher's advance for his account of the voyage out to meet her. She divorced Osbourne, married R.L.S., who was then suffering (said the doctors) from a dose of malaria, and soon after a telegram from his dad told them his monthly allowance was increased. In 1880 the couple and Fanny's son Lloyd crossed the Atlantic and were met at Liverpool by Stevenson's parents. They were at once charmed by Fanny, who had recently nursed their son through illness that had reduced him to (he said) 'a contraption of bones and coughs'. They all went for a holiday at a sanatorium in Strathpeffer.

This was his first experience of the *inner* Highlands. He was surprised to find it much more than the wilderness of bare mountains many tourists had described and that his views from the coast had almost confirmed. Being curious about his immediate surroundings he investigated the culture of Gaeldom in talks with Highlanders he met and in historic documents: a neglected subject despite Scott's *Lady of the Lake* and *Waverley*. Most British histories then and for long after were histories of England, sometimes interrupted by dealings with Scotland until 1707 when the Edinburgh parliament was absorbed by London's, after which Scotland was mainly seen as a useful supplier of men to Britain's armed forces and imperial expansion. Most Lowland Scots viewed the Highlands like that. They thought the clan system barbaric compared with England's military organization, so a proper history of the Highlands had never been written. R.L.S. began making notes for one. The onset of the Scottish winter forced him and his new family to leave for Davos, a sanatorium village in the Swiss Alps where the cold, dry air was good for consumptives. Forty years later Thomas Mann made it the setting for his novel *The Magic Mountain*. Here R.L.S. pondered his notes about Gaeldom and read books his dad had posted from Edinburgh.

He was particularly interested in the murder of Colin Campbell, nicknamed 'the Red Fox', one of the clan headed by the Dukes of Argyll and used by both Stuart and Hanoverian kings to impose their power in the Highlands. The man tried and hanged for that killing at Inverary was certainly not guilty. Alan Breck Stewart was thought a more likely perpetrator.

Unsolved murders generate much speculation, written and verbal. The following summer Stevenson returned to Scotland and made enquiries near the scene of the crime.

At this time Edinburgh University announced the retiral of its Professor of Scottish History and Constitutional Law, a job that would have given R.L.S. a good income for lecturing at Edinburgh during the summer while letting him spend winter in a healthier climate. His law degree qualified him for the Constitutional part of the job, while his interest in history, especially Scotland's, would make him an outstanding professor of it. From his family fortunes – his nurse's Covenanting stories – from Scott, Dumas and extensive reading – he had come to see human history as a mighty adventure, especially when approached through source documents. He distrusted most histories written much later. He wrote:

> It is a pet idea of mine that one gets more truth out of an avowed partisan than out of a dozen of your sham impartialists – wolves in sheep's clothing – simpering honesty as they suppress documents. After all, what one wants to know is not what people did, but why they did it – or why they *thought* they did it; and to learn that, you should go to the men themselves. Their very falsehood is often more than another man's truth.

In a letter to his father he laid out his plan for a Highland history.

> My dear Father, – Here is the scheme as well as I can foresee. I begin the book immediately after the '15 [meaning the Jacobite Rebellion of 1715] as then began the attempt to suppress the Highlands.

I. THIRTY YEARS INTERVAL

(1) Rob Roy.
(2) The Independent Companies: The Watches.
(3) Story of Lady Grange.
(4) The Military Roads, and Disarmament: Wade and
(5) Burt.

II. THE HEROIC AGE

(1) Duncan Forbes of Culloden.
(2) Flora MacDonald.
(3) The Forfeited Estates; including Hereditary Jurisdictions; and the admirable conduct of the tenants.

III. LITERATURE HERE INTERVENES

(1) The Ossianic Controversy.
(2) Boswell and Johnson.
(3) Mrs Grant of Laggan.

IV. ECONOMY

(1) Highland Economics.
(2) The Reinstatement of the Proprietors.
(3) The Evictions.
(4) Emigration.
(5) Present State.

V. RELIGION

(1) The Catholics, Episcopals, and Kirk, and Society for Propagation of Christian Knowledge.
(2) The Men.
(3) The Disruption.

If written as planned this would have been a remarkably valuable history. Rob Roy and Flora MacDonald are legendary names but have a part here because, like Lady Grange, Duncan Forbes and Mrs Grant, their lives illustrate the nature of Highland society in a time of crisis. The absence of Bonnie Prince Charlie's name shows R.L.S. did not attach much importance to his character. The English General Wade and Burt, Wade's engineer, were intelligent and mostly fair-minded observers of the Highland culture they were employed to destroy. Johnson and Boswell would have provided later insights. But note how Stevenson sees that military forces, the law, economics and religion are intertwined, and plans to bring the whole story up to the evictions and Kirk of Scotland Disruption in his own lifetime. Most Scots historians have ignored the Clearances and

Disruption, or dismissed them in very few words, and several
have resented the Canadian John Prebble for his books arousing
interest in the former. A contemporary *Herald* journalist has
said the pain of those whose homes were destroyed should be
forgotten, as they or at least their descendants found better
lives in America or Australia, so the evicting landlords were
really doing good, besides making more money out of sheep.

'It seems to me very much as if I was gingerly embarking on
a *History of Modern Scotland*,' he wrote to his parents. 'And
once I have studied and written these two vols., *The Transfor-
mation of the Scottish Highlands* and *Scotland and the Union*,
I shall have good ground to go upon.' Good ground as a professor of history, he meant. The retiring professor was friendly
to R.L.S. succeeding him, but despite good references from
English professors and critics, the Edinburgh Senate remembered him as a student who dressed funnily and seldom attended
lectures, and they gave the job to someone else.

The great two-volume history of Scotland, from the union
with England to his own time, never got written. His guilt about
living on his father's money drove him to write more sellable
things, especially after dad suppressed his third travel book (*The
Amateur Immigrant*) by paying back the publisher's advance. It
was thought this account of his first transatlantic voyage
described the division between third-class passengers and the
rest in a way that would annoy middle-class readers; Mr
Stevenson was also friendly with an owner of the shipping line.
R.L.S.'s next publications were about his travels inside America
and a collection of essays: *Over the Plains*, *The Silverado
Squatters* and *Virginibus Puerisque*. But over a year of research
into Scotland's eighteenth century underlies his best novels,
Kidnapped, The Master of Ballantrae, Weir of Hermiston.

His companionable nature led him to write in collaboration
with others, especially W.E. Henley and his own stepson Lloyd.
With Henley, who was keen to get a west-end-of-London theat-
rical success, he wrote five plays, only one of which was produced (it was not a success). When a famous author in Samoa
he collaborated with Lloyd on an unsatisfactory novel, *The
Wrecker*. Yet he owed his first great work of fiction to both of

them. Like perhaps too few fathers he enjoyed revisiting his childhood by playing childish games, and when Lloyd was twelve drew for him the map of an island where pirates had buried stolen gold. From the story this suggested grew his first good novel, *Treasure Island*. The character who maintains it is Long John Silver, copied from the one-legged, forceful and sometimes unscrupulous Henley. This was Stevenson's first bestseller and it disconcerted friends who had expected more from him than a boy's adventure story. His following novels, *Prince Otto* and *The Black Arrow*, contained no memorable characters. He knew they were pot-boilers, written as carefully as everything he wrote, but lacking that peculiar excitement called inspiration.

This came in his three years at Skerryvore, a house at Bournemouth he named after a famous lighthouse built by his uncle, a house where (says Colvin) 'he was compelled to lead the life of a chronic invalid and almost chronic prisoner . . . sometimes for whole weeks together, he was forbidden to speak aloud and compelled to carry on conversation with family and friends in whispers or with the help of paper and pencil.' Yet he wrote so much that to evade writer's cramp he learned writing with his left hand. Here he completed and saw through publication six books, half of them truly inspired: *A Child's Garden of Verses*, *The Strange Case of Dr Jekyll and Mr Hyde* and *Kidnapped*. They brought him international fame.

R.L.S. was now halfway through the seventy years of biblical lifespan, the age at which Dante said he found the entrance to Hell. Stevenson wrote to an American fan:

> I have outlived all my chief pleasures, which were active and adventurous, and ran in the open air; and being a person who prefers life to art, and who knows it is a far finer thing to be in love, or to risk a danger, than to paint the finest picture or write the noblest book, I begin to regard what remains to me of my life as very shadowy.

Yet William Archer, a fine critic who regarded Stevenson's work highly, assumed he was a hearty, healthy man who needed experience of life's painful side. Not surprising, when we read the lovely, youthful, spring-morning opening of *Kidnapped*, where a young lad of seventeen sets out with great expectations from the cottage where he was born, wholly unencumbered by the parents who stop most children having adventures.

Like most big things in life, an accident seemed to start it. Fanny had hopes of becoming a crime writer, Stevenson was glad to help. Her plot culminated in an Old Bailey trial, so they ordered a parcel of books about these from London. One was entitled:

THE, TRIAL OF JAMES STUART *in Aucharn in Duror of Appin*
FOR THE Murder of COLIN CAMPBELL of *Glenure*, Efq:
Factor for His Majefty on the forfeited Eftate of *Ardfhiel*.

This called to Stevenson's mind his abandoned plan for a Scottish history containing the '45 revolt. Suddenly the R.L.S. imagination was in that creative state when all occurring to it, from the moment in 1751 when David Balfour takes the key for the last time out of the door of his father's house, is useful. Fanny tells how she interrupted him by reading out a quaint recipe from an old cookery book. '"Just what I wanted!" he exclaimed; and the receipt for the "Lilly of the Valley Water" was instantly incorporated.'

The decent minister, the brisk barber, lead to the ominous old woman with her curse upon the House of Shaws: 'Blood built it; blood stopped the building of it; blood shall bring it down.' This curse is never explained, but what a splendid introduction to the miserly uncle, a stock comic character in earlier fiction, with the added twist of making him a would-be murderer. And before we learn exactly why David Balfour has a claim to his uncle's estate he is kidnapped! The explanation – not a convincing one – is left to the last chapter where we swallow it whole because we have forgotten the need for it. But early in the writing R.L.S. had written to his father:

As far as I have got, I think *David* is on his feet, and (to my mind) a far better story and far sounder at heart than *Treasure*

Island. I have no earthly news, living entirely in my story and only coming out of it to play patience.

To a critic who later suggested that the first chapters including Uncle Ebenezer were separate from what followed Stevenson wrote:

What you say of the two parts in *Kidnapped* was felt by no one more painfully than myself. I began it partly as a lark, partly as a pot-boiler; and suddenly it moved, David and Alan stepped out of the canvas, and suddenly I was in another world.

So is the reader. It is the tough eighteenth-century world of the Scottish Lowlands and Highlands, where lonely people *were* kidnapped, taken across the Atlantic and sold as slaves. One East Coast ship owner and Lord Provost did it with a boy of twelve. I find no painful transition from Uncle Ebenezer to Captain Hoseason of the brig *Covenant*. Stevenson's most valued reading, memories and research went into this book. The old woman and her curse are adapted from Meg Merrilies in Scott's *Guy Mannering*, Uncle Ebenezer from his *Heart of Midlothian*. Years before, Stevenson had written that the Hawes Inn, Queensferry, should be part of a wild adventure. Into David Balfour and Alan Breck Stewart went all his knowledge of Highland and Lowland people in his lifetime and in the crucial years following the 1745 revolt. The landscapes and stormy waters came from his long tramps in Scotland and spells as a trainee lighthouse engineer and of canoeing on the Forth.

In an essay Stevenson tells how daunting he found the idea of writing the kind of three-volume novel that the Victorian reading public loved, and which nowadays, since wood-pulp paper has replaced the woven fibre kind, is printed in a book of a few hundred pages. He noticed with alarm that *David Balfour* (as he then called *Kidnapped*) looked like becoming such a book. In April 1886 he wrote:

My Dear Father, – The *David* problem has today been decided. I am to leave the door open for a sequel if the public take to it and this will save me from butchering a lot of good material to no purpose . . . I am in great spirits about *David*, Colvin agreeing with Henley, Fanny and myself in thinking it by far the most human of my labours hitherto. As to whether the long-eared British public may take to it, all think it more than doubtful: I wish they would, for I could do a second volume with ease and pleasure, and Colvin thinks it sin and folly to throw away David and Alan Breck upon so small a field as this one – Ever your affectionate son, R.L.S.

It is good that R.L.S. stopped *Kidnapped* where he did. After Mr Rankeillor takes over as David's counsellor and guide the story begins to lose its grip. Alan is useful in getting the uncle to admit his guilt – an admission that would never have been allowed in a court of law, as Stevenson points out in another letter. In the last chapter, 'Goodbye', Alan departs and David is left with 'a cold gnawing in my inside like a remorse for something wrong'. But then: 'The hand of Providence brought me in my drifting to the very doors of the British Linen Company's bank' – where he can draw upon a large account. He has left childhood and will now be a tax-paying citizen.

The sequel Stevenson had planned was written four or five years later in Samoa. He meant to call it *David Balfour*, it was eventually published as *Catriona*, and starts with David leaving the bank and almost at once meeting and falling in love with the heroine. It is as beautifully written as all Stevenson's work. In a letter to a friend he said it was almost his favourite novel. In *Narrating Scotland: The Imagination of Robert Louis Stevenson* Professor Barry Menikoff demonstrates that, together with *Kidnapped*, it is historically accurate. I will not say here why I think the love story in *Catriona* tedious and unconvincing. I only hope to have indicated the rare life and intelligence that made *Kidnapped*.

Alasdair Gray
Glasgow
6 April 2006

Significant Dates in Stevenson's Life

1850 13 November: Born, 8 Howard Place, Edinburgh. Grandson of Robert Stevenson (1772–1850) and son of Thomas (1818–87), world-famous lighthouse engineers. Loving father, like them a dedicated Calvinist. Mother was twenty-one. Born Margaret Balfour, the daughter of Revd Lewis Balfour, Church of Scotland Minister at Colinton (where RLS would spend many childhood breaks), she was very loving but subject to nervous troubles and to chest trouble, which she transmitted to her only child. RLS throughout his life was frequently ill, sometimes severely so.

1852 Alison Cunningham, 'Cummy', a hell-fire Calvinist, becomes RLS's nurse – 'My second Mother, my first Wife.'

1856 November–December: RLS dictates to his mother his first composition – *A History of Moses*.

1857 RLS introduced to his brilliant, artistically gifted cousin, Robert Alan Mowbray Stevenson, 'Bob', with whom he forms an imaginative alliance.

1861 In the course of a patchy schooling, attends the famous Edinburgh Academy for a year and a half.

1862 Family trips to London and Hamburg.

1863 Continental tour with family – France, Italy, Switzerland.

1866 Pupil at Mr Thompson's small school for delicate and backward boys in Frederick Street.

November: Father pays to have 100 copies printed of a 16-page account by RLS of the Covenanters' 'Pentland Rising' of 1665.

1867 Thomas Stevenson takes a lease of Swanston College in the Pentland Hills, as a family retreat.

November: RLS begins (desultory) studies at Edinburgh University.

1868 Summer vacation in north-east Scotland, learning trade of lighthouse engineer. Sojourn in Wick (Caithness).

1869 Trip with father to Orkney and Outer Hebrides.

1870 'Affair' with 'Jenny', daughter of a family acquaintance.

Summer: Views early stage of building a lighthouse off Mull. In the Hebrides, meets Edmund Gosse, later a prominent man of letters.

December: Appointed one of four editors of the *Edinburgh University Magazine*.

1871 March: Delivers a successful paper on a new form of intermittent light for lighthouses to the Royal Scottish Society of Arts. Then decides to give up engineering. Turns to law course at Edinburgh University.

1872 May–July: A law clerk under Skene's, solicitors, learning conveyancing.

Summer: Three weeks in Germany with university friend, Walter Simpson.

9 November: Passes preliminary examinations for the Scottish Bar.

Autumn: Under Bob Stevenson's influence, a crisis of belief. Bob founds Liberty Justice and Reverence Club, advocating socialism and atheism.

1873 January: Thomas Stevenson finds a copy of the LJR constitution. Months of conflict between father and son follow – Bob is eventually barred from Heriot Row.

April: RLS is sent to cool off at Cockfield Rectory, Suffolk, where his cousin Maud Babington is a vicar's wife. Meets there Mrs Fanny Sitwell, twelve years older than himself, and falls passionately in love with her. Through her, introduced to Sidney Colvin, young (twenty-eight) Slade Professor of Fine Art at Cambridge University and a curator at the British Museum.

November: To France, ostensibly for his health. Sojourns at Menton.

1874 April: Leaves France.

May–June: Edinburgh and Swanston, London and Hampstead with Colvin. Realizes that his relationship with Fanny Sitwell cannot be physically intimate. Elected to the new Savile Club, 3 June.

July–August: Cruises Inner Hebrides with Simpson.

November: Resumes law classes.

December: London and Cambridge with Colvin.

1875 February: Meets the English poet W. E. Henley, a patient in Edinburgh Infirmary.

March–April: Visits artists' colonies in France with Bob.

July: Admitted – an advocate – to the Scottish Bar. On return to France meets Mrs Fanny Van de Grift Osbourne, ten years older than himself, a student of art with an estranged husband in California, a nearly grown daughter Isobel and small son Lloyd.

September: Back in Edinburgh.

1876 January: Walking tour in south-west Scotland.

April–May: London.

August–October: Canoe trip in Belgium and France with Simpson – 'an inland voyage'.

Autumn: France – Grez and Barbizon.

1877 January–February: London.

June onwards: Almost continuously in France until March 1878.

1878 April–May: Edinburgh. *An Inland Voyage* – first book – published in May.

June: Paris, as secretary to Fleeming Jenkin of Edinburgh University, a juror at the Exposition – the only salaried post RLS ever held.

August: London and Paris. Fanny Osbourne returns to America.

September–October: Walking trip in the Cevennes.

October–December: London. *Edinburgh: Picturesque Notes* published (December).

1879 January: Swanston with Henley, writing *Deacon Brodie*.

February and May: London.

June: Cernay-la-Ville in France. *Travels with a Donkey* published.

July: Edinburgh and London.

August: Embarks for America.

September–December: With Fanny Osbourne and her family in Monterey, California.

December: Till May 1880, living in San Francisco (Fanny in Oakland).

1880 19 May: Marries Fanny in San Francisco.

June–July: Honeymoon in Silverado, Napa County.

August: Returns to Britain with Fanny and Lloyd.

August–September: Strathpeffer (a spa in the north of Scotland) and Edinburgh.

November: Till April, in Davos, Switzerland. Meets poet and man of letters, John Addington Symonds, and his friend H. F. Brown.

1881: April: *Virginibus Puerisque* published.

June–July: Pitlochry (Perthshire).

August–September: Braemar (Aberdeenshire).

October: Again in Davos, till April 1882.

1882 March: *Familiar Studies of Men and Books* published.

April–June: London and Edinburgh.

June–July: Stobo Manse, near Peebles (Scottish Border country).

July–August: Kingussie (Perthshire). *New Arabian Nights* published in August.

September: In France with Bob, looking for a home – joined by Fanny in Marseilles.

October: Campagne Defli, St Marcel, near Marseilles.

December: Marseilles and Nice.

1883 March: Chalet, 'La Solitude', at Hyères, inland from Nice.

July–August: Royat.

December: *The Silverado Squatters* and *Treasure Island* published.

1884 January: RLS, long subject to haemorrhages, very ill in Nice. 'For the next five years, until he reached southern Pacific waters, Louis was liable to sudden illness at any time. Nowhere, neither in France nor the South of England, was he free from the likelihood of haemorrhage, fever and debilitation.' (Jenni Calder, *RLS: A Life Study*, p. 183.)

February: Returns to Hyères.

June–July: Royat.

Late summer: Bournemouth.

1885 Spring: Thomas Stevenson gives a house in Bournemouth, 'Skerryvore', to Fanny. The Stevensons settle there.

March: *A Child's Garden of Verses* published.

May: *More New Arabian Nights*, with Fanny, published.

November: *Prince Otto* published.

1886 January: *Dr Jekyll and Mr Hyde* published.

July: *Kidnapped* published.

November: With Colvin in London.

1887 May: In Edinburgh, for death of Thomas Stevenson. RLS depressed for several months.

August: 'My spirits are rising again . . . I almost begin to feel as if I should care to live . . .' (*Letters*, V; to Henley). *Underwoods* published. Sails for America with Fanny, Lloyd and widowed mother on 22 August.

September: Newport, RI, then settles at Saranac, NY.

December: *Memories and Portraits* published.

1888 April: New York City.

May: Manasquan, NJ.

June: San Francisco. 28 June, sets out on first Pacific voyage, on the *Casco*.

July–August: Marquesan Islands.

September: Paumotu Islands.

October: Society Islands (Tahiti). Stays with sub-chief Ori.

December: Sandwich Islands, then, till June 1889, Honolulu.

1889 June: *The Wrong Box* (with Lloyd Osbourne) published. Sets out on second cruise, aboard the *Equator*, to the Gilbert Islands.

September: *The Master of Ballantrae* published.

December: In Samoa, purchases estate, Vailima.

1890 February: Sydney.

April–August: Third cruise, on *Janet Nicoll*, to Gilberts, Marshalls, etc.

August–September: Sydney.

October: Settles in Samoa.

December: *Ballads* published.

1891 January: To Sydney, to meet mother returning from Scotland.

1892 April: *Across the Plains* published.

August: *A Footnote to History* published.

1893 February: Sydney.

April: *Island Nights' Entertainments* published.

August: Outbreak of war on Samoa.

September–October: Honolulu. *Catriona* published.

November: Returns to Vailima.

1894 3 December: Dies suddenly, not of longstanding tuberculosis, but of a stroke.

1895 Edinburgh Edition of RLS's works begins to appear, edited by Colvin, including *Songs of Travel*.

1896 *Weir of Hermiston* published.

1918 Just after the Great War Armistice, *New Poems and Variant Readings* published in London.

Introduction

Kidnapped is on the surface a very simple tale, indeed it could hardly be simpler. Several times in the text its hero, David Balfour, himself likens his story to that of an old ballad: a boy sets out in the world to seek his fortune, undergoes hardship and danger in his travels but returns as a man to claim his rightful inheritance. Yet why has it endured for so long and been admired by so many critics and such conscious artists as, among others, Henry James and Jorge Luis Borges? The notion that it is merely a supreme example of the well-told 'rattling good yarn' does not really suffice to answer this point. Twists of plot are largely confined to the start and end of the story and, in any case, it tends to be the relatively straightforward (in a narrative sense) 'Flight in the Heather' chapters which are so admired – especially by James.

Apart from its assurance in narrative pace and mood, its more complex qualities lie in its authenticity; of historical and topographical background, of individual characters and as a study of the complex series of dualities which make up the Scottish national psyche. *Kidnapped* is rooted in realism in a way that, for example, *Treasure Island* or the novels of Sir Walter Scott frequently are not. Some episodes, such as the account of being washed ashore on Earraid – 'I could see in the moonlight the dots of heather and the sparkling of the mica in the rocks' – and the description of the inn at Kinlochaline, have a documentary immediacy that is hard to find in Scott. While Scott's Highlands are romanticized and his characters tend to be 'types', Stevenson's knowledge of his country and its people is based on a close observation which he practised from an early age. As Walter Allen describes him in *The English Novel*, Stevenson is 'the born interpreter of the national [meaning Scottish] character'.

Writing of the final defeat of the Jacobite cause at Culloden in 1746 the latter-day 'Whig' historian, G. M. Trevelyan, was of the opinion that:

> Modern Scotland, – the Scotland of Burns and Sir Walter Scott, – emerged as a result of these changes, and of the great economic progress that accompanied them. There was evolved a united people, proud of itself and of its whole history; proud alike of Celt and Saxon, of Covenanter and Jacobite; with a national hagiology extending from Wallace and Bruce, through John Knox to Flora Macdonald, representing that singular blend in the national psychology of the dour and rational with the adventurous and romantic, of the passion for freedom with loyal devotion to a chief.
>
> (*History of England*, 1926)

Although one might not altogether accept this somewhat Panglossian sentiment, it is truly extraordinary the extent to which Scots can assimilate quite contradictory and conflicting strands in their own history – the enthusiastic Orangeman who can still regard the Massacre of Glencoe as a cause for sentimentality; the canny Lowland banker who dreams of Highland mists over his dram; the Highlander who waxes lyrical about the benefits of universal education and John Calvin. The cultural muddle over the two traditions finds its most bizarre expression in the Burns Supper, when Scots worldwide, from Hong Kong to Alberta, don a conventionalized Highland garb in order to celebrate the works of a Lowland poet. The placing in time of this cultural integration (some might say confusion) is hard to establish – Scott may have had something to do with it – but it certainly took place sometime between the events related in *Kidnapped* and its writing.

The fundamental duality in *Kidnapped* is not far to seek. On the one hand is the first-person narrator, David Balfour (Balfour was Stevenson's mother's name and his third given name),

representing Lowland Scotland – prudential, canny, Hanoverian and Whiggish, law-abiding and Presbyterian. In contrast is
the character of Alan Breck – feudal, romantic, proud to a fault,
a lover of lost causes, Jacobite. David's age is dawning; with the
political stability after the '45, Scotland – or at least Lowland
Scotland – will become prosperous with its banks and trading-
houses. Alan's age is on the way out. He is lost between a feudal
system where the masters have deserted, or are about to betray,
their people and a bourgeois society for which he is unequipped
and has, in any case, little taste. As with many historical novels,
this is part of the emotional powerhouse of the work – the idea
of characters caught up in forces which transcend their daily
lives; history as a series of culture wars. This is a necessary but
not a sufficient understanding of the novel. There are subtler
undercurrents to disrupt the clear-cut picture.

In a letter to J. M. Barrie in February 1892, Stevenson said
of *Kidnapped*:

> I was pleased to see how the Anglo-Saxon theory fell into the
> trap: I gave my Lowlander a Gaelic name, and even commented
> on the fact in the text; yet almost all critics recognized in David
> and Alan a Saxon and a Celt. I know not about England; in
> Scotland at least, where Gaelic was spoken in Fife little over the
> century ago, and in Galloway not much earlier, I deny that there
> exists such a thing as a pure Saxon, and I think it more than
> questionable if there be such a thing as a pure Celt.

There are other warning shots against accepting an over-
simplistic duality as well. The Highlander, Alan Breck, had
been on the Hanoverian side at Prestonpans; the seemingly
archetypical Whig, Uncle Ebenezer, had espoused the Jacobite
cause in his more dashing youth; the Lowland minister has a
Highland name – albeit that of Campbell.

Stevenson wrote *Kidnapped* at a time when he was physically
very ill, and feeling bitterly homesick and trapped. ('I am weary
of England; like Alan, "I weary for the heather," if not for the
deer' – 28 July 1886.) Life at 'Skerryvore' in genteel Bournemouth, where the thirty-five-year-old Stevenson was surrounded

by identical villas and called on by the vicar, must have seemed a far cry from his earlier bohemian wanderings or indeed from the Edinburgh of his youth where he had contrived to live on both sides of polite society. Like many a Scot he always appeared to be far happier when indisputably in exile or travelling overseas rather than merely slightly out of place in the intellectual and emotional suburbia which England seemed.

It is fair to say that, throughout his life, Stevenson was obsessed with his Scottishness and what it meant. In spite of being an exile for most of his adult life, it was an itch which he simply could not stop scratching. Time and again in his letters it is used as an only half-humorous stick with which to beat his English correspondents, or it comes to represent a fellow-feeling with his Scottish friends such as Charles Baxter. In the same letter to Barrie of February 1892, Stevenson wrote:

> We are both Scots besides, and I suspect both rather Scotty Scots; my own Scotchness tends to intermittency but is at times erisypelitous – if that be rightly spelt.[1] Lastly, I have gathered we had both made our stages in the metropolis of the winds [Edinburgh]: our Virgil's 'grey metropolis', and I count that a lasting bond. No place so brands a man.

This awareness had begun fairly early in life. In a letter from Suffolk to his mother in 1873, Stevenson writes:

> Melford scattered all round a big green, with an Elizabethan Hall and Park, great screens of trees that seem twice as high as trees should seem, and everything else what ought to be in a novel, and what one never expects to see in reality, made me cry out how good we were to live in Scotland, for the many hundredth time. I cannot get over my astonishment – indeed, it increases every day – at the hopeless gulf that there is between England and Scotland, and English and Scotch. Nothing is the same; and I feel as strange and outlandish here as I do in France or Germany.

This theme was to be developed in 'The Foreigner at Home', the first essay in *Memories and Portraits* (1887). It is worth quoting at length as it is the most candidly autobiographical piece of writing that Stevenson ever committed himself to. England was different:

> A Scotchman may tramp the better part of Europe and the United States, and never again receive so vivid an impression of foreign travel and strange lands and manners as on his first excursion into England.
>
> But it is not alone in scenery and architecture that we count England foreign. The constitution of society, the very pillars of the empire, surprise and even pain us. The dull, neglected peasant, sunk in matter, insolent, gross and servile, makes a startling contrast with our own long-legged, long-headed ploughman. A week or two in such a place as Suffolk leaves the Scotchman gasping. It seems incredible that within the boundaries of his own island a class should have been thus forgotten. Even the educated and intelligent, who hold our own opinions and speak in our own words, yet seem to hold them with a difference or from another reason, and to speak on all things with less interest and conviction. The first shock of English society is like a cold plunge.

But in the last two paragraphs of the piece, Stevenson lays bare a bafflement about Scotland itself – and asks many more questions than he is prepared to answer:

> The division of races is more sharply marked within the borders of Scotland itself than between the countries [i.e. Scotland and England]. Galloway and Buchan, Lothian and Lochaber, are like foreign parts; yet you may choose a man from any of them, and, ten to one, he shall prove to have the headmark of a Scot. A century and a half ago the Highlander wore a different costume, spoke a different language, worshipped in a different church, held different morals, and obeyed a different social constitution from his fellow-countrymen either of the south or north. Even the English, it is recorded, did not loathe the Highlander and the Highland costume as they were loathed by the remainder of the Scotch. Yet the Highlander felt himself a Scot. He would willingly raid into the Scotch lowlands; but his courage failed him at the

border, and he regarded England as a perilous, unhomely land. When the Black Watch, after years of foreign service, returned to Scotland, veterans leaped out and kissed the earth at Port Patrick. They had been in Ireland, stationed among men of their own race and language, where they were well liked and treated with affection; but it was the soil of Galloway that they kissed at the extreme end of the hostile lowlands, among a people who did not understand their speech, and who had hated, harried, and hanged them since the dawn of history. Last, and perhaps most curious, the sons of chieftains were often educated on the continent of Europe. They went abroad speaking Gaelic; they returned speaking, not English, but the broad dialect of Scotland. Now, what idea had they in their minds when they thus, in thought, identified themselves with their ancestral enemies? What was the sense in which they were Scotch and not English, or Scotch and not Irish? Can a bare name be thus influential on the minds and affections of men, and a political aggregation blind them to the nature of facts? The story of the Austrian Empire would seem to answer, No; the far more galling business of Ireland clenches the negative from nearer home. Is it common education, common morals, a common language or a common faith, that join men into nations? There were practically none of these in the case we are considering.

The fact remains: in spite of the difference of blood and language, the Lowlander feels himself the sentimental countryman of the Highlander. When they meet abroad, they fall upon each other's necks in spirit; even at home there is a kind of clannish intimacy in their talk. But from his compatriot in the south the Lowlander stands consciously apart. He has had a different training; he obeys different laws; he makes his will in other terms, is otherwise divorced and married; his eyes are not at home in an English landscape or with English houses; his ear continues to remark the English speech; and even though his tongue acquire the Southern knack, he will still have a strong Scotch accent of the mind.

Is it too fanciful to suggest that in the writing of *Kidnapped* Stevenson is trying to resolve some of these dilemmas – trying his hand at a sort of 'birth of a nation' portrait? In the same essay he certainly stresses the importance of the conflicting and contradictory strands of history, the 'wild clans, and hunted Covenanters', which form the Scottish sense of nation 'which alone the Scottish boy adopts in his imagination'.

If *Kidnapped* is in some ways a national epic of the conflicting forces of 'the dour and rational' against 'the adventurous and romantic' in post-Union Scotland, it is also about these forces being acted out within Stevenson himself – this 'Scot of Scots' as Henry James called him. In an almost throwaway comment in his radiantly insightful life of Stevenson, *Dreams of Exile*, Ian Bell writes:

> *Kidnapped* says as much about Stevenson as any autobiography. In David Balfour and Alan Breck he gave substance to two sides of his own character, adventurer and rationalist, man of duty and man of passion

... and also restless traveller with a mountain of Calvinist baggage to shoulder. If Alan Breck and David Balfour are two sides of Stevenson's character, what is the author's own attitude to his two creations who inhabit two different worlds but who try to look at the same one?

It is easy and obvious to draw attention to the flaws in Alan's character – vainglorious to an extreme, sentimental, cussedly out of touch with historical reality. There is no need to go on. When we come to David, however, it becomes more complex. In some senses he is the conventionalized first-person narrator, 'the universal representative, the person for whom every reader could substitute himself', as Coleridge described Robinson Crusoe. The character of David is also in the tradition of Scott's somewhat passive heroes, best exemplified by Edward Waverley who is also struggling with the same post-Union ambivalences. To the readers of today (and of Stevenson's day) it would seem obvious that they should feel closer to the rationality of David Balfour than to the emotional romanticism of Alan Breck, but yet again Stevenson fires some warning shots against this too simplistic picture.

While David is an endurer and survivor, Stevenson is at great pains to point out that he never initiates action or ever consciously makes a decision. When having to choose whether to throw in his lot with Alan Breck or with Hoseason (whom one would have thought he wouldn't trust an inch and to whom he certainly owed no favours), David deliberates at length but Stevenson makes it quite plain how the action actually moves on:

> I was still arguing it back and forth, and getting no great clearness, when I came into the round-house and saw the Jacobite eating his supper under the lamp; and at that my mind was made up all in a moment. I have no credit by it; it was by no choice of mine, but as if by compulsion, that I walked right up to the table and put my hand on his shoulder.

After the assassination of Glenure, David moralizes about why he should part with Alan but is easily talked round and, in truth, really has no choice to speak of. Although he would be unable openly to admit it to himself, his best hope of getting out of the Highlands is to stick with his expert guide.

> '. . . Either take to the heather with me, or else hang.'
> 'And that's a choice very easily made,' said I; and we shook hands upon it.

Again, during 'the flight in the heather' David weighs up his chances if he were to part with Alan and try to escape on his own. In reality they would be slim, but in any case, David does nothing about it and merely lets his feelings fester.

The episode of the playing cards in Cluny's Cage also points up the fact (if one hadn't begun to suspect this already) that David is something of a tendentious prig rather than Coleridge's 'universal representative':

> To be sure, I might have pleaded my fatigue, which was excuse enough; but I thought it behoved that I should bear a testimony.

In the finely paced chapter of 'The Quarrel', David shows himself to be as petty as Alan is not – but equally self-deluded. Nowhere else in the novel is the examination of the conflict between the (seemingly) rational with the emotional brought closer to the surface. As they come closer to the Lowlands, the strain of putting his law-abiding instincts to one side for so long, in order to accommodate his loyalty to Alan, becomes too much for David and he breaks down.

In the end, then, what are we to make of Stevenson's attitude to the character of David Balfour and the society he represents; his slightly unreliable and more than a little unattractive first-person narrator? Does one begin to suspect that Stevenson is examining a nagging worry about the dead hand of Calvinist materialism and Lowland respectability leading to some kind of paralysing moral passiveness – a paradoxical mix of repression of the spirit and complacency along with a misplaced respect for authority, which he certainly was aware of in himself? There is something deeply unpleasant about the David who chides Alan with the notion that because he has been beaten by the Campbells and the Whigs, 'It behoves you to speak of them as of your betters.'

Elsewhere David shows a touchingly naive faith in the rule of law – and an untouching belief in his own rectitude. Immediately after making his peace with Alan in the wood of Lettermore, he self-importantly proclaims,

> 'Oh!' says I, willing to give him a little lesson, 'I have no fear of the justice of my country.'
> 'As if this was your country!' said he. 'Or as if ye would be tried here, in a country of Stewarts!'
> 'It's all Scotland,' said I.

Not yet, it isn't, David, not yet. This is surprisingly blinkered in one who has undergone David's recent experience. The Lowland society which David regards as civilized leaves more than a little to be desired. Apart from trying to murder him, his uncle has conspired, possibly with the knowledge of a respectable

Edinburgh lawyer, to deprive him of his inheritance and sell him into slavery – a trade they presumably condone. This is not to mention the complicity of that stout pillar of the Kirk, Hoseason.

Yet elsewhere, in his more spontaneous moments, David can see the virtue in the Highland ways. When told of the Stewarts paying the second rent to maintain their chief, he bursts out,

> 'I call it noble,' I cried. 'I'm a Whig, or little better; but I call it noble.'

When crossing Mull, having been looked after by an elderly Highland couple, he is forced to admit, 'If these are the wild Highlanders, I could wish my own folk wilder.' Even the propagator of Lowland values, Henderland, admits of Alan, 'There's many a lying sneck-draw sits close in kirk in our own part of the country, and stands well in the world's eye, and maybe is a far worse man . . . Ay, ay, we might take a lesson by them.'

Here Stevenson is rehearsing the well-trodden tradition of pointing up Lowland Presbyterian hypocrisy, but where in the end do his real sympathies lie? Probably they are completely unresolved. Perhaps the main point to remember is that Stevenson is not in the end writing about two conflicting cultures within Scottish history, but about two deeply battling sets of sympathies within himself – and perhaps making an attempt to explain Scottishness to himself. This takes us back to the perceptive comments of Ian Bell about the autobiographical nature of *Kidnapped* and to Stevenson's own bafflement expressed in 'The Foreigner at Home'. Unlike Scott, whose sentimental Toryism always seems to point to an optimistic middle way between the two traditions, roughly equivalent to the early nineteenth-century *status quo*, Stevenson remains, in the words of Chesterton, 'intellectually on the side of the Whigs and morally on the side of the Jacobites'.

From the mouth of the highly ambivalent character of the lawyer, Rankeillor, we get a hint of the Edinburgh of the Scottish Enlightenment which is just about to dawn:

... they talk a great deal of charity and generosity; but in this disputable state of life, I often think the happiest consequences seem to flow when a gentleman consults his lawyer and takes all the law allows him.

David Hume or Adam Smith could scarcely have put it better. It is a pragmatic morality around which to organize a developing and newly complex mercantile society, but one can't help but feel that to Stevenson it is a little bit wanting in inspiration as a blueprint for the early days of a better nation.

The American historian Arthur Herman (see Selected Further Reading) has pointed out that, perhaps as a result of the laughably ignominious failure of Edinburgh to defend itself against the Highland army in 1745, there was a nagging worry about a lack of sinew in progressive society. No less a beacon of the Edinburgh Enlightenment than Adam Ferguson wrote in *An Essay on the History of Civil Society* (1767), '[today] the individual considers his community only so far as it can be rendered subservient to his personal advancement and profit.' Elsewhere Ferguson regretted the barriers between 'barbarous' and 'polite' peoples and found many virtues in the former. His reasons may have been particular. Although a Lowlander he was a Gaelic speaker and had acquired a great admiration for the Highland soldier while serving as a chaplain in the Black Watch. Whatever the reason, there was more than a hint of self-doubt underlying the Athens of the North which has a resonance even with the modern reader in a mistrust of the purely practical virtues. To quote Herman, 'The lesson Scott taught the modern world was that the past does not have to die or vanish: it can live on, in a nation's memory, and help to nourish its posterity.' This is something rather more fundamental than the romanticism of the '*Gone with the Wind* syndrome' alluded to by the Scottish historian Tom Devine in a similar context.

Consider the thoughts of David in the very last paragraphs as the 'hand of Providence' brings him in his drifting to the very doors of the British Linen Company's bank, after he has said goodbye to Alan. He is back in his own country, he has righted the injustice done against him and has secured his inheritance, but 'there was a cold gnawing in my inside like a remorse for something wrong'.

Historical Note

After the Jacobite defeat at Culloden in 1746 Charles Stewart of Ardshiel (*Tearlach Mor Aird Seile*) was forced to flee to France, leaving his estates in Appin forfeit to the Crown. His wife and children were evicted from Appin and his house burnt. His illegitimate half-brother James Stewart ('James of the Glen' or *Sheumais a' Ghlinne*), who had been pardoned after Culloden, looked after the Stewart interests in Appin. The factor appointed by the government in 1749 to collect the official rents in the Appin area was Colin Campbell of Glenure, nicknamed the 'Red Fox' on account of his auburn hair.

Contrary to the picture painted by Alan Breck in *Kidnapped*, it seems that Colin Campbell was by nature a reasonable man and indeed that he at first worked amicably with James Stewart, who had been a boyhood friend. However, in 1751 he received an official reprimand for his leniency – in particular towards the Camerons of Mamore and Lochaber to whom he was related through his mother's line.

One of the specific criticisms made of Campbell was that he continued to allow James Stewart to live on his farm at Achindarroch in Glen Duror. Possibly in an attempt to take the pressure off his clan, James agreed to vacate Achindarroch and move to a smaller property at nearby Acharn ('The House of Fear' in *Kidnapped*), leaving Achindarroch free for a new tenant of Campbell's choosing. However, James's acquiescence in this affair did not have the calming effect for which he hoped and only led to a wave of resentment among the Stewart tenantry and a cooling of the relationship between himself and Colin Campbell.

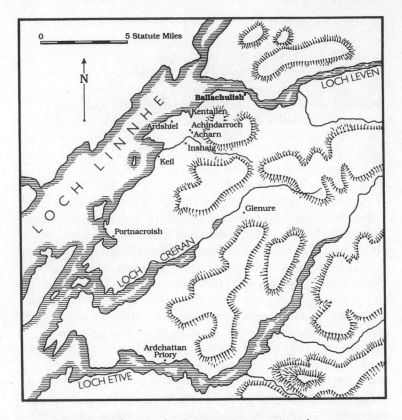

In the spring of 1752 the Appin area was riven by resentment
and rumour when Alan 'Breck' Stewart appeared on the scene
on one of his periodic visits from France (*breck* means 'spotted'
in Gaelic, referring to Alan's pock-marked skin). Alan was a
distant relation of James, who had brought him up after the
death of Alan's father. Alan had spent a wild youth accumu-
lating debt by drinking and gambling. True to the story of
Kidnapped, he enlisted in the government army and fought at
Prestonpans in the Essex Regiment under Cope. There he was
taken prisoner and deserted to the briefly victorious Jacobite
side. After Culloden he fled to France and served in one of David
Ogilvy's Scottish regiments in the French army. He would still

slip over to Scotland, recruiting for the French army or collecting the second rents which supported the Jacobite chiefs in exile. Whatever Alan's mission in Appin in the spring of 1752, his wildly unguarded tongue was to do his kinsmen no favours when he was overheard in the inn at Portnacroish loudly demanding, 'Who will bring me the skin of the red fox?'

Colin Campbell had ordered a series of evictions of suspected Jacobite sympathizers which was due to take place on 15 May. James, meanwhile, was desperately seeking legal advice (with some signs of success) as to how the eviction orders could be postponed and an appeal considered.

On the morning of 14 May Colin Campbell crossed Loch Leven from the Mamore side to Ballachulish. With him were his nephew, Mungo Campbell, who was a lawyer, his personal gillie, John MacKenzie, and a Sheriff's Officer, Donald Kennedy, who had come to witness the following day's evictions. At around five-thirty that afternoon they were passing through the thick woods of Lettermore on their way to Kentallen on the shores of Loch Linnhe where they planned to spend the night when a single shot rang out, fatally wounding Colin Campbell. By the standards of the weaponry of the day – it is almost inconceivable that a rifle barrel was used – it must have been a remarkably skilful (or lucky) engagement.

Local tradition has it that James of the Glen was working in the fields of Acharn when he saw a horseman approaching at the gallop and commented, 'Whoever that rider may be, the horse is not his own.' It was indeed John MacKenzie on Glenure's horse, having failed to find anyone at Kentallen, desperately seeking help for his master. On hearing the news, James is said to have exclaimed, 'Whoever is the culprit, I shall be the victim!' ('*Co 'sam bith an ciontach is mise an creineach!*')

The obvious suspect was Alan Breck, although in fact there was never anything other than circumstantial evidence against him. An immediate warrant was issued for his arrest but all attempts to apprehend him failed. While it was patently obvious that James was not guilty of the murder itself (too many witnesses had seen him at Acharn at the time), the authorities needed a scapegoat and he was consequently arrested without warrant at the inn at Inshaig in Duror on 16 May and taken under close escort to the garrison town of Fort William.

Appin was overrun by Redcoats while the prosecution gathered evidence for the trial, which was due to start in the Old Kirk at Inveraray, the seat of the Dukes of Argyll, on 21 September. It was only through the intervention of John Stewart of Ballachulish, who had some influence with the Campbells, that James was given access to a defence lawyer – and then only on 2 September at the roadside at Tyndrum when James was being transferred from Fort William to Inveraray under armed guard. The trial was heard before three judges including the Duke of Argyll himself. Of the fifteen 'good men and true' in the jury, eleven were Campbells. After a show trial involving a mountain of perjured evidence, the jury returned a unanimous 'guilty' verdict; unsurprisingly, James was sentenced to be hanged on 8 November for the sake of 'the future well-governing of these distant parts of Scotland'.

The sentence was duly executed at Ballachulish at noon on the appointed day. On the morning of the execution James took the Sacrament and protested his innocence. At the scaffold he recited the thirty-fifth psalm, which to this day is known throughout the Highlands as 'James of the Glen's Psalm' (*Salm Sheumus a' Ghlinne*): 'Plead my cause, O Lord, with them that strive with me: fight against them that fight against me.' After his death his body was chained to the gibbet and, under military guard, allowed to rot as an example of Hanoverian justice. When the flesh fell from the bone, the skeleton was wired together and continued to sway in the wind for a matter of three years. Finally, the body was recovered and is buried in the chapel at Keil overlooking Cuil Bay on Loch Linnhe, just south of Duror.

The body of Colin Campbell of Glenure, 'The Red Fox', was taken after a postmortem to Ardchattan Priory on the shores of Loch Etive, where it still lies buried.

As for Alan Breck, he is believed to have died quietly in France sometime after the onset of the French Revolution. In the Introduction to *Rob Roy*, Sir Walter Scott writes:

About 1789, a friend of mine, then residing at Paris, was invited
to see some procession which was supposed likely to interest
him, from the windows of an apartment occupied by a Scottish
Benedictine priest. He found, sitting by the fire, a tall, thin,
raw-boned, grim-looking old man, with the petit croix of
St Louis. His visage was strongly marked by the irregular projec-
tions of the cheek-bones and chin. His eyes were grey. His grizzled
hair exhibited marks of having been red, and his complexion
was weather-beaten, and remarkably freckled. Some civilities in
French passed between the old man and my friend, in the course
of which they talked of the streets and squares of Paris, till at
length the old soldier, for such he seemed, and such he was, said
with a sigh, in a sharp Highland accent, 'Deil ane o' them a' is
worth the Hie Street of Edinburgh!' On inquiry, this admirer of
Auld Reekie, which he was never to see again, proved to be Allan
[sic] Breck Stewart. He lived decently on his little pension, and
had, in no subsequent period of his life, shown anything of the
savage mood, in which he is generally believed to have assassin-
ated the enemy and oppressor, as he supposed him, of his family
and clan.

A further note has to be added here – although he is un-
doubtedly an historical figure, there is no mention of an Alan
Stewart in either the records of the Scottish regiments serving
France in the eighteenth century or in the annals of the Order
of St Louis.

The wife of Charles Stewart of Ardshiel, having fled Appin
in 1746, died in 1782 in poverty at Northampton, where she is
buried in the graveyard of the church of All Saints.

As to who fired the shot, it is believed to be a secret handed
down over the generations and known only to a few senior
members of the Stewart family of Appin. However, several
traditions persist. One is that a Cameron from Mamore was
the culprit (see note 30). Another is that a certain family of
MacColls, from the head of Loch Leven, who possessed a
particularly accurate firearm, were the guilty party. Evidence
from the trial and some words of James at the scaffold would
seem to implicate the latter (but see Selected Further Reading).

The site of James's execution (Cnap a' Chaolais) is marked by a monument erected by the Stewart Society in 1911. It can be seen just to the left of the road at the very beginning of the Ballachulish bridge as one crosses it heading north. It consists of a grey granite plinth headed by a white quartzite boulder from Acharn, said to have been James's favourite resting place when working in the fields. It bears the words, 'In memory of James Stewart of Acharn, who was executed on this spot on 8th November 1752 for a crime of which he was not guilty.'

The place of the murder itself is marked by a cairn. It can be reached by a track which heads into the hills about two kilometres west of the Ballachulish bridge.

Ardshiel (now Ardsheal) House, having been razed to the ground in 1746, was later rebuilt and is once again a private house, having been a hotel.

James's farm of Acharn lies in Glen Duror, about two kilometres from Achindarroch. The cottage is now in use as a barn.

Colin Campbell's house of Glenure stands, largely unchanged, beyond Fasnacloich, at the head of Loch Creran.

All of the other Appin locations mentioned in *Kidnapped* can be precisely traced with the book in one hand and a good map in the other.

Selected Further Reading

BIOGRAPHY

(There are over two hundred biographical works on the subject of Robert Louis Stevenson. An extensive list can be found at *http://dinamico.unibg.it/rls/biogs.htm*.)

Bell, Ian, *Dreams of Exile*, 1992. (This is a work of great psychological penetration and sensitivity.)

Calder, Jenni, *R. L. S. – A Life Study*, 1980. (Still in many ways the standard modern life.)

Daiches, David, *Robert Louis Stevenson and His World*, 1973. (A popular – and none the worse for that – general life of Stevenson, illustrated with contemporary photographs, documents, etc.)

GENERAL HISTORICAL CONTEXT

Dodgshon, Robert A., *From Chiefs to Landlords – Social and Economic Change in the Western Highlands and Islands, c.1493–1820*, 1998. (A fairly specialized work which attempts to quantify the phenomenon alluded to in note 24 and the shift to a cash economy.)

Herman, Arthur, *How the Scots Invented the Modern World – The True Story of How Western Europe's Poorest Nation Created Our World & Everything in It* (US edition), 2001. (When this was published in the UK it was entitled *The Scottish Enlightenment – The Scots' Invention of the Modern World*, 2002, with a title and preface designed perhaps to be less challenging to South Britons. The chapter on Sir Walter Scott and the Highland Revival is particularly insightful on the roots of Scottish cultural duality.)

Prebble, John, *Culloden*, 1961. (A detailed but remarkably readable account of the '45 Jacobite rebellion and its consequences for the clan system.)

Smout, T. C., *A History of the Scottish People – 1560–1830*, 1969. (*The Times Literary Supplement* said, 'No one who professes an interest in Scotland can afford to miss reading it.' It is particularly good on the economic forces which shaped the society.)

LETTERS

Booth, Bradford A. and Mehew, Ernest (eds.), *The Letters of Robert Louis Stevenson* (8 vols.), 1994–5. (Supplants the inadequate and highly selective 1899 edition by Sidney Colvin.)

Mehew, Ernest (ed.), *Selected Letters of Robert Louis Stevenson*, 1997. (Selection from the above.)

APPIN MURDER

This is probably not the place to explore the many traditions and theories surrounding 'Appin's old sorrow', but the following works may be of interest.

Carney, Seamus, *The Killing of the Red Fox – An Investigation into the Appin Murder*, 1989.

Holcombe, Lee, *Ancient Animosity – The Appin Murder and the End of Scottish Rebellion*, 2004. (This is a huge labour of love and exhaustive research which claims, fairly persuasively, to identify the assassin.)

McGrigor, Mary, *Grass Will Not Grow on My Grave – The Story of the Appin Murder*, 2002. (Contains an Appendix of James of the Glens' speech from the scaffold in full.)

Stuart, James Gibb, *West Highland Tales from the Dewar Manuscripts: Book I – The Appin Murder*, 1986. (The Dewar manuscripts are a mid nineteenth-century collection of oral tradition commissioned, ironically enough, by the Eighth Duke of Argyll and transcribed in Gaelic by John Dewar. This is a retelling in English of the traditions surrounding the Appin murder as collected only three or four generations after the event.)

MAPS

OS 'Explorer' Sheet 384, Glen Coe & Glen Etive – for Balachulish crossing and area of the murder.

OS 'Explorer' Sheet 376, Oban & North Lorn – for Appin and its environs.

LANGUAGE

The glossary in this edition of *Kidnapped* is of necessity extremely simplistic. Those who have an interest in the language of the novel will find *The Concise Scots Dictionary*, ed. Mairi Robinson, 1985, an invaluable guide to shades of meaning and regional variations.

Note on the Text

Kidnapped was first published in serial form in the magazine *Young Folks* (May to July 1886). The text reproduced here is substantively that of the first book edition published by Cassell and Company in July of the same year but it incorporates some minor revisions later made by Stevenson (see notes 13 and 28).

Footnote glosses which appear in the text are Stevenson's own. The glossary which is at the end of the book was prepared for this edition.

Note to Map

To David A. Stevenson, C. E.

The cousin to whom this letter is addressed had undertaken to prepare a map illustrating the course of the brig *Covenant* in the tale of *Kidnapped*.

[Skerryvore, Bournemouth, 1886]

Dear Davie,

On the small map please mark the course of a ship, in red, leaving Queensferry, going North about midway between the Orkneys and Shetlands, passing in near Cape Wrath, through the Minch, near in by Canna, round Coll and Tiree, close round their S. end and the S.W. end of Mull, where, close in by the S. side of Earraid, it is supposed to strike.

On the large map, a red line is to show the wanderings of my hero after his shipwreck. It must be sometimes dotted to show uncertainty; sometimes full. As thus, it begins on Earraid, he crosses at Low Water, and passes along the Ross and across Mull to Torosay: line dotted across Mull. He then goes by water to Kinlochaline and by road to the shore of the Linnhe Loch, just above Gairloch: line full. He passes the Linnhe to the S. corner of Loch Leven: wood of Lettermore on the advance beyond Rudha Bod Buith – *not* at Rudha Mor: line still full. Thence along the hilltops to Duror: full. Thence up the S. side of the river Duror, and the N. side of the river Creran, and over Ben Maol Chalicum and across the Coe below Meannerclach: dotted. Thence round the *outside of the hilltops* above the Coe and then above Loch Leven to a place above Coalisnacoan:

full. Thence along the hills on the S. bank of the river Leven: full till you get near its fountain. Wherefrom the line becomes dotted, and staggers up to Ben Alder. From Ben Alder full again, across Loch Ericht, and down its East side, and across the head of Loch Rannoch. My hero then takes the hills and turns the head waters of Glen Lyon, Glen Lochay and Glen Dochart; at such obvious points of his itinerary the lines might be full, and between dotted. The line (full again) descends Balquhidder from the top, turns down Strathire, strikes over Uam Var, hits Alan Water above Kippendaire, descends Alan Water to the Forth, along the N. bank of Forth to Stirling Bridge, and *by road* by Alloa, Clackmannan and Culross, till it issues from the map; for I fear we don't reach Limekilns; which we really should have done, for from that point my hero crosses the Forth to Cawiden, and thence to Queensferry. Terminus Malorum.

If room can be found all the places I have named might be named upon the map, except Glen Lyon, Glen Lochay, Glen Dochart, and the Duror and Creran Rivers and Rudha Bod Buithe, and Ben Maol Chalicum and Meannarclach. The improbability of the itinerary is not so great as it appears, for my hero was trying to escape – like all heroes . . .

It should be lettered 'Sketch of the cruise of the Brig *Covenant*, and the probable course of David Balfour's Wanderings'.

SKETCH of the CRUISE

And the probable course of DA

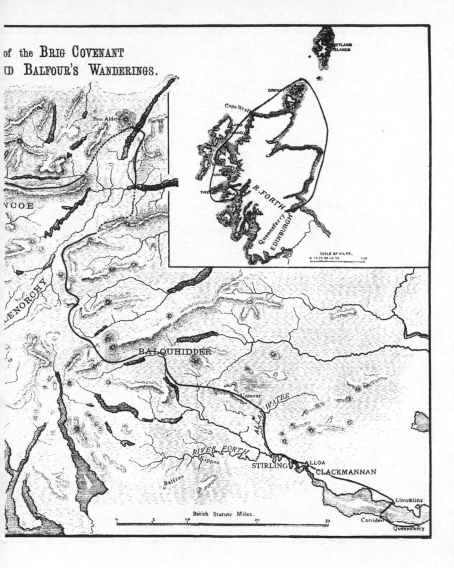

of the BRIG COVENANT
ᴅ BALFOUR'S WANDERINGS.

KIDNAPPED

DEDICATION

Mʸ ᴅᴇᴀʀ Cʜᴀʀʟᴇᴅ Bᴀxᴛᴇʀ,[2]

If you ever read this tale, you will likely ask yourself more questions than I should care to answer: as for instance how the Appin murder[3] has come to fall in the year 1751, how the Torran rocks have crept so near to Earraid, or why the printed trial is silent as to all that touches David Balfour. These are nuts beyond my ability to crack. But if you tried me on the point of Alan's guilt or innocence, I think I could defend the reading of the text. To this day you will find the tradition of Appin clear in Alan's favour. If you inquire, you may even hear that the descendants of 'the other man' who fired the shot are in the country to this day. But that other man's name, inquire as you please, you shall not hear; for the Highlander values a secret for itself and for the congenial exercise of keeping it. I might go on for long to justify one point and own another indefensible; it is more honest to confess at once how little I am touched by the desire of accuracy. This is no furniture for the scholar's library, but a book for the winter evening school-room when the tasks are over and the hour for bed draws near; and honest Alan, who was a grim old fire-eater in his day, has in this new avatar no more desperate purpose than to steal some young gentleman's attention from his Ovid, carry him awhile into the Highlands and the last century, and pack him to bed with some engaging images to mingle with his dreams.

As for you, my dear Charles, I do not even ask you to like the tale. But perhaps when he is older, your son will; he may then be pleased to find his father's name on the fly-leaf; and in the meanwhile it pleases me to set it there, in memory of many days that were happy and some (now perhaps as pleasant to remember) that were sad. If it is strange for me to look back from a distance both in time and space on these bygone adventures of our youth, it must be stranger for you who tread the same streets – who may to-morrow open the door of the old Speculative,[4] where we begin to rank with Scott and Robert Emmet and the beloved and inglorious Macbean – or may pass the corner of the close where that great society, the L.J.R.,[5] held its meetings and drank its beer, sitting in the seats of Burns and his companions. I think I see you, moving there by plain daylight, beholding with your natural eyes those places that have now become for your companion a part of the scenery of dreams. How, in the intervals of present business, the past must echo in your memory! Let it not echo often without some kind thoughts of your friend.

R.L.S.

SKERRYVORE,[6]
BOURNEMOUTH.

CONTENTS

KIDNAPPED:

MEMOIRS OF THE ADVENTURES OF

DAVID BALFOUR IN THE YEAR 1751

CHAPTER I

I set off upon my journey to the house of Shaws

I will begin the story of my adventures with a certain morning early in the month of June, the year of grace 1751, when I took the key for the last time out of the door of my father's house. The sun began to shine upon the summit of the hills as I went down the road; and by the time I had come as far as the manse, the blackbirds were whistling in the garden lilacs, and the mist that hung around the valley in the time of the dawn was beginning to arise and die away.

Mr Campbell, the minister of Essendean, was waiting for me by the garden gate, good man! He asked me if I had breakfasted; and hearing that I lacked for nothing, he took my hand in both of his and clapped it kindly under his arm.

'Well, Davie, lad,' said he, 'I will go with you as far as the ford, to set you on the way.'

And we began to walk forward in silence.

'Are ye sorry to leave Essendean?' said he, after a while.

'Why, sir,' said I, 'if I knew where I was going, or what was likely to become of me, I would tell you candidly. Essendean is a good place indeed, and I have been very happy there; but then I have never been anywhere else. My father and mother, since

they are both dead, I shall be no nearer to in Essendean than in
the Kingdom of Hungary; and to speak truth, if I thought I had
a chance to better myself where I was going, I would go with a
good will.'

'Ay?' said Mr Campbell. 'Very well, Davie. Then it behoves
me to tell your fortune; or so far as I may. When your mother
was gone, and your father (the worthy, Christian man) began
to sicken for his end, he gave me in charge a certain letter,
which he said was your inheritance. "So soon," says he, "as I
am gone, and the house is redd up and the gear disposed of"
(all which, Davie, hath been done) "give my boy this letter into
his hand, and start him off to the house of Shaws, not far from
Cramond. That is the place I came from," he said, "and it's
where it befits that my boy should return. He is a steady lad,"
your father said, "and a canny goer; and I doubt not he will
come safe, and be well liked where he goes."'

'The house of Shaws!' I cried. 'What had my poor father to
do with the house of Shaws?'

'Nay,' said Mr Campbell, 'who can tell that for a surety? But
the name of that family, Davie boy, is the name you bear –
Balfours[7] of Shaws: an ancient, honest, reputable house, per-
adventure in these latter days decayed. Your father, too, was a
man of learning as befitted his position; no man more plausibly
conducted school; nor had he the manner or the speech of
a common dominie; but (as ye will yourself remember) I took
aye a pleasure to have him to the manse to meet the gentry;
and those of my own house, Campbell of Kilrennet, Campbell
of Dunswire, Campbell of Minch, and others, all well-kenned
gentlemen, had pleasure in his society. Lastly, to put all the
elements of this affair before you, here is the testamentary letter
itself, superscrived by the own hand of our departed brother.'

He gave me the letter, which was addressed in these words:
'To the hands of Ebenezer Balfour, Esquire, of Shaws, in his
house of Shaws, these will be delivered by my son, David
Balfour.' My heart was beating hard at this great prospect now
suddenly opening before a lad of sixteen years of age, the son
of a poor country dominie in the Forest of Ettrick.

'Mr Campbell,' I stammered, 'and if you were in my shoes, would you go?'

'Of a surety,' said the minister, 'that would I, and without pause. A pretty lad like you should get to Cramond (which is near in by Edinburgh) in two days of walk. If the worst came to the worst, and your high relations (as I cannot but suppose them to be somewhat of your blood) should put you to the door, ye can but walk the two days back again and risp at the manse door. But I would rather hope that ye shall be well received, as your poor father forecast for you, and for anything that I ken, come to be a great man in time. And here, Davie, laddie,' he resumed, 'it lies near upon my conscience to improve this parting, and set you on the right guard against the dangers of the world.'

Here he cast about for a comfortable seat, lighted on a big boulder under a birch by the trackside, sate down upon it with a very long, serious upper lip, and the sun now shining in upon us between two peaks, put his pocket-handkerchief over his cocked hat to shelter him. There, then, with uplifted forefinger, he first put me on my guard against a considerable number of heresies, to which I had no temptation, and urged upon me to be instant in my prayers and reading of the Bible. That done, he drew a picture of the great house that I was bound to, and how I should conduct myself with its inhabitants.

'Be soople, Davie, in things immaterial,' said he. 'Bear ye this in mind, that, though gentle born, ye have had a country rearing. Dinnae shame us, Davie, dinnae shame us! In yon great, muckle house, with all these domestics, upper and under, show yourself as nice, as circumspect, as quick at the conception, and as slow of speech as any. As for the laird – remember he's the laird; I say no more: honour to whom honour. It's a pleasure to obey a laird; or should be, to the young.'

'Well, sir,' said I, 'it may be; and I'll promise you I'll try to make it so.'

'Why, very well said,' replied Mr Campbell, heartily. 'And now to come to the material, or (to make a quibble) to the immaterial. I have here a little packet which contains four things.' He tugged it, as he spoke, and with some difficulty, from the skirt pocket of his coat. 'Of these four things, the first is your legal due: the little pickle money for your father's books and plenishing, which I have bought (as I have explained from the first) in the design of re-selling at a profit to the incoming dominie. The other three are gifties that Mrs Campbell and myself would be blithe of your acceptance. The first, which is round, will likely please ye best at the first off-go; but, O Davie, laddie, it's but a drop of water in the sea; it'll help you but a step, and vanish like the morning. The second, which is flat and square and written upon, will stand by you through life, like a good staff for the road, and a good pillow to your head in sickness. And as for the last, which is cubical, that'll see you, it's my prayerful wish, into a better land.'

With that he got upon his feet, took off his hat, and prayed a little while aloud, and in affecting terms, for a young man setting out into the world; then suddenly took me in his arms and embraced me very hard; then held me at arm's length, looking at me with his face all working with sorrow; and then whipped about, and crying good-bye to me, set off backward by the way that we had come at a sort of jogging run. It might have been laughable to another, but I was in no mind to laugh. I watched him as long as he was in sight; and he never stopped hurrying, nor once looked back. Then it came in upon my mind that this was all his sorrow at my departure; and my conscience smote me hard and fast, because I, for my part, was overjoyed to get away out of that quiet country-side, and go to a great, busy house, among rich and respected gentlefolk of my own name and blood.

'Davie, Davie,' I thought, 'was ever seen such black ingratitude? Can you forget old favours and old friends at the mere whistle of a name? Fie, fie; think shame!'

And I sat down on the boulder the good man had just left, and opened the parcel to see the nature of my gifts. That which he had called cubical, I had never had much doubt of; sure enough it was a little Bible, to carry in a plaid-neuk. That which he had called round, I found to be a shilling piece; and the third, which was to help me so wonderfully both in health and sickness all the days of my life, was a little piece of coarse yellow paper, written upon thus in red ink:

> TO MAKE LILLY OF THE VALLEY WATER. – Take the flowers of lilly of the valley and distil them in sack, and drink a spooneful or two as there is occasion. It restores speech to those that have the dumb palsey. It is good against the Gout; it comforts the heart and strengthens the memory; and the flowers, put into a Glasse, close stopt, and set into ane hill of ants for a month, then take it out, and you will find a liquor which comes from the flowers, which keep in a vial; it is good, ill or well, and whether man or woman.

And then, in the minister's own hand, was added:

> Likewise for sprains, rub it in; and for the cholic, a great spooneful in the hour.

To be sure, I laughed over this; but it was rather tremulous laughter; and I was glad to get my bundle on my staff's end and set out over the ford and up the hill upon the farther side; till, just as I came on the green drove-road running wide through the heather, I took my last look of Kirk Essendean, the trees about the manse, and the big rowans in the kirkyard where my father and my mother lay.

CHAPTER II

I come to my journey's end

On the forenoon of the second day, coming to the top of a hill, I saw all the country fall away before me down to the sea; and in the midst of this descent, on a long ridge, the city of Edinburgh smoking like a kiln. There was a flag upon the castle, and ships moving or lying anchored in the firth; both of which, for as far away as they were, I could distinguish clearly; and both brought my country heart into my mouth.

Presently after, I came by a house where a shepherd lived, and got a rough direction for the neighbourhood of Cramond; and so, from one to another, worked my way to the westward of the capital by Colinton, till I came out upon the Glasgow road. And there, to my great pleasure and wonder, I beheld a regiment marching to the fifes, every foot in time; an old red-faced general on a grey horse at the one end, and at the other the company of Grenadiers, with their Pope's-hats. The pride of life seemed to mount into my brain at the sight of the redcoats and the hearing of that merry music.

A little farther on, and I was told I was in Cramond parish, and began to substitute in my inquiries the name of the house of Shaws. It was a word that seemed to surprise those of whom I sought my way. At first I thought the plainness of my appearance, in my country habit, and that all dusty from the road, consorted ill with the greatness of the place to which I was bound. But after two, or maybe three, had given me the same look and the same answer, I began to take it in my head there was something strange about the Shaws itself.

The better to set this fear at rest, I changed the form of my inquiries; and spying an honest fellow coming along a lane on the shaft of his cart, I asked him if he had ever heard tell of a house they called the house of Shaws.

He stopped his cart and looked at me, like the others.

'Ay,' said he. 'What for?'

'It's a great house?' I asked.

'Doubtless,' says he. 'The house is a big, muckle house.'

'Ay,' said I, 'but the folk that are in it?'

'Folk?' cried he. 'Are ye daft? There's nae folk there – to call folk.'

'What?' says I; 'not Mr Ebenezer?'

'Oh, ay,' says the man, 'there's the laird, to be sure, if it's him you're wanting. What'll like be your business, mannie?'

'I was led to think that I would get a situation,' I said, looking as modest as I could.

'What?' cries the carter, in so sharp a note that his very horse started; and then, 'Well, mannie,' he added, 'it's nane of my affairs; but ye seem a decent-spoken lad; and if ye'll take a word from me, ye'll keep clear of the Shaws.'

The next person I came across was a dapper little man in a beautiful white wig, whom I saw to be a barber on his rounds; and knowing well that barbers were great gossips, I asked him plainly what sort of a man was Mr Balfour of the Shaws.

'Hoot, hoot, hoot,' said the barber, 'nae kind of a man, nae kind of a man at all'; and began to ask me very shrewdly what my business was; but I was more than a match for him at that, and he went on to his next customer no wiser than he came.

I cannot well describe the blow this dealt to my illusions. The more indistinct the accusations were, the less I liked them, for they left the wider field to fancy. What kind of a great house was this, that all the parish should start and stare to be asked the way to it? or what sort of a gentleman, that his ill-fame should be thus current on the wayside? If an hour's walking would have brought me back to Essendean, I had left my adventure then and there, and returned to Mr Campbell's. But when I had come so far a way already, mere shame would not suffer me to desist till I had put the matter to the touch of proof; I was bound, out of mere self-respect, to carry it through; and little as I liked the sound of what I heard, and slow as I began to travel, I still kept asking my way and still kept advancing.

It was drawing on to sundown when I met a stout, dark, sour-looking woman coming trudging down a hill; and she, when I had put my usual question, turned sharp about, accompanied me back to the summit she had just left, and pointed to a great bulk of building standing very bare upon a green in the bottom of the next valley. The country was pleasant round about, running in low hills, pleasantly watered and wooded, and the crops, to my eyes, wonderfully good; but the house itself appeared to be a kind of ruin; no road led up to it; no smoke arose from any of the chimneys; nor was there any semblance of a garden. My heart sank. 'That!' I cried.

The woman's face lit up with a malignant anger. 'That is the house of Shaws!' she cried. 'Blood built it; blood stopped the building of it; blood shall bring it down. See here!' she cried again – 'I spit upon the ground, and crack my thumb at it! Black be its fall! If ye see the laird, tell him what ye hear; tell him this makes the twelve hunner and nineteen time that Jennet Clouston has called down the curse on him and his house, byre and stable, man, guest, and master, wife, miss, or bairn – black, black be their fall!'

And the woman, whose voice had risen to a kind of eldritch sing-song, turned with a skip, and was gone. I stood where she left me, with my hair on end. In these days folk still believed in witches and trembled at a curse; and this one, falling so pat, like a wayside omen, to arrest me ere I carried out my purpose, took the pith out of my legs.

I sat me down and stared at the house of Shaws. The more I looked, the pleasanter that country-side appeared; being all set with hawthorn bushes full of flowers; the fields dotted with sheep; a fine flight of rooks in the sky; and every sign of a kind soil and climate; and yet the barrack in the midst of it went sore against my fancy.

Country folk went by from the fields as I sat there on the side of the ditch, but I lacked the spirit to give them a good-e'en. At last the sun went down, and then, right up against the yellow sky, I saw a scroll of smoke go mounting, not much thicker, as it seemed to me, than the smoke of a candle; but still there it was, and meant a fire, and warmth, and cookery, and some living inhabitant that must have lit it; and this comforted my heart wonderfully – more, I feel sure, than a whole flask of the lily of the valley water that Mrs Campbell set so great a store by.

So I set forward by a little faint track in the grass that led in my direction. It was very faint indeed to be the only way to a place of habitation; yet I saw no other. Presently it brought me to stone uprights, with an unroofed lodge beside them, and coats of arms upon the top. A main entrance, it was plainly meant to be, but never finished; instead of gates of wrought iron, a pair of hurdles were tied across with a straw rope; and as there were no park walls, nor any sign of avenue, the track that I was following passed on the right hand of the pillars, and went wandering on toward the house.

The nearer I got to that, the drearier it appeared. It seemed like the one wing of a house that had never been finished. What should have been the inner end stood open on the upper floors, and showed against the sky with steps and stairs of uncompleted masonry. Many of the windows were unglazed, and bats flew in and out like doves out of a dove-cote.

The night had begun to fall as I got close; and in three of the lower windows, which were very high up, and narrow, and well barred, the changing light of a little fire began to glimmer.

Was this the palace I had been coming to? Was it within these walls that I was to seek new friends and begin great fortunes? Why, in my father's house on Essen-Waterside, the fire and the bright lights would show a mile away, and the door open to a beggar's knock.

I came forward cautiously, and giving ear as I came, heard some one rattling with dishes, and a little dry, eager cough that came in fits; but there was no sound of speech, and not a dog barked.

The door, as well as I could see it in the dim light, was a great piece of wood all studded with nails; and I lifted my hand with a faint heart under my jacket, and knocked once. Then I stood and waited. The house had fallen into a dead silence; a whole minute passed away, and nothing stirred but the bats overhead. I knocked again, and hearkened again. By this time my ears had grown so accustomed to the quiet, that I could hear the ticking of the clock inside as it slowly counted out the seconds; but whoever was in that house kept deadly still, and must have held his breath.

I was in two minds whether to run away; but anger got the upper hand, and I began instead to rain kicks and buffets on the door, and to shout out aloud for Mr Balfour. I was in full career, when I heard the cough right overhead, and jumping back and looking up, beheld a man's head in a tall nightcap, and the bell mouth of a blunderbuss, at one of the first storey windows.

'It's loaded,' said a voice.

'I have come here with a letter,' I said, 'to Mr Ebenezer Balfour of Shaws. Is he here?'

'From whom is it?' asked the man with the blunderbuss.

'That is neither here nor there,' said I, for I was growing very wroth.

'Well,' was the reply, 'ye can put it down upon the doorstep, and be off with ye.'

'I will do no such thing,' I cried. 'I will deliver it into Mr Balfour's hands, as it was meant I should. It is a letter of introduction.'

'A what?' cried the voice, sharply.

I repeated what I had said.

'Who are ye, yourself?' was the next question, after a considerable pause.

'I am not ashamed of my name,' said I. 'They call me David Balfour.'

At that, I made sure the man started, for I heard the blunder-buss rattle on the window-sill; and it was after quite a long pause, and with a curious change of voice, that the next question followed:

'Is your father dead?'

I was so much surprised at this, that I could find no voice to answer, but stood staring.

'Ay,' the man resumed, 'he'll be dead, no doubt; and that'll be what brings ye chapping to my door.' Another pause, and then, defiantly, 'Well, man,' he said, 'I'll let ye in'; and he disappeared from the window.

CHAPTER III

I make acquaintance of my uncle

Presently there came a great rattling of chains and bolts, and the door was cautiously opened, and shut to again behind me as soon as I had passed.

'Go into the kitchen and touch naething,' said the voice; and while the person of the house set himself to replacing the defences of the door, I groped my way forward and entered the kitchen.

The fire had burned up fairly bright, and showed me the barest room I think I ever put my eyes on. Half-a-dozen dishes stood upon the shelves; the table was laid for supper with a bowl of porridge, a horn spoon, and a cup of small beer. Besides what I have named, there was not another thing in that great, stone-vaulted, empty chamber, but lockfast chests arranged along the wall and a corner cupboard with a padlock.

As soon as the last chain was up, the man rejoined me. He was a mean, stooping, narrow-shouldered, clay-faced creature; and his age might have been anything between fifty and seventy. His nightcap was of flannel, and so was the nightgown that he wore, instead of coat and waistcoat, over his ragged shirt. He was long unshaved; but what most distressed and even daunted me, he would neither take his eyes away from me nor look me fairly in the face. What he was, whether by trade or birth, was more than I could fathom; but he seemed most like an old, unprofitable serving-man, who should have been left in charge of that big house upon board wages.

'Are ye sharp-set?' he asked, glancing at about the level of my knee. 'Ye can eat that drop parritch.'

I said I feared it was his own supper.

'Oh,' said he, 'I can do fine wanting it. I'll take the ale, though, for it slockens* my cough.' He drank the cup about half out, still keeping an eye upon me as he drank; and then suddenly held out his hand. 'Let's see the letter,' said he.

I told him the letter was for Mr Balfour; not for him.

'And who do ye think I am?' says he. 'Give me Alexander's letter!'

'You know my father's name?'

'It would be strange if I didnae,' he returned, 'for he was my born brother; and little as ye seem to like either me or my house, or my good parritch, I'm your born uncle, Davie, my man, and you my born nephew. So give us the letter, and sit down and fill your kyte.'

If I had been some years younger, what with shame, weariness, and disappointment, I believe I had burst into tears. As it was, I could find no words, neither black nor white, but handed him the letter, and sat down to the porridge with as little appetite for meat as ever a young man had.

Meanwhile, my uncle, stooping over the fire, turned the letter over and over in his hands.

'Do ye ken what's in it?' he asked, suddenly.

'You see for yourself, sir,' said I, 'that the seal has not been broken.'

'Ay,' said he, 'but what brought you here?'

'To give the letter,' said I.

'No,' says he, cunningly, 'but ye'll have had some hopes, nae doubt?'

'I confess, sir,' said I, 'when I was told that I had kinsfolk well-to-do, I did indeed indulge the hope that they might help me in my life. But I am no beggar; I look for no favours at your hands, and I want none that are not freely given. For as poor as I appear, I have friends of my own that will be blithe to help me.'

'Hoot-toot!' said Uncle Ebenezer, 'dinnae fly up in the snuff at me. We'll agree fine yet. And, Davie, my man, if you're done with that bit parritch, I could just take a sup of it myself. Ay,' he continued, as soon as he had ousted me from the stool

---

* Moistens.

and spoon, 'they're fine, halesome food – they're grand food, parritch.' He murmured a little grace to himself and fell to. 'Your father was very fond of his meat, I mind; he was a hearty, if not a great eater; but as for me, I could never do mair than pyke at food.' He took a pull at the small beer, which probably reminded him of hospitable duties; for his next speech ran thus: 'If ye're dry, ye'll find water behind the door.'

To this I returned no answer, standing stiffly on my two feet, and looking down upon my uncle with a mighty angry heart. He, on his part, continued to eat like a man under some pressure of time, and to throw out little darting glances now at my shoes and now at my home-spun stockings. Once only, when he had ventured to look a little higher, our eyes met; and no thief taken with a hand in a man's pocket could have shown more lively signals of distress. This set me in a muse, whether his timidity arose from too long a disuse of any human company; and whether perhaps, upon a little trial, it might pass off, and my uncle change into an altogether different man. From this I was awakened by his sharp voice.

'Your father's been long dead?' he asked.

'Three weeks, sir,' said I.

'He was a secret man, Alexander – a secret, silent man,' he continued. 'He never said muckle when he was young. He'll never have spoken muckle of me?'

'I never knew, sir, till you told it me yourself, that he had any brother.'

'Dear me, dear me!' said Ebenezer. 'Nor yet of Shaws, I daresay?'

'Not so much as the name, sir,' said I.

'To think o' that!' said he. 'A strange nature of a man!' For all that, he seemed singularly satisfied, but whether with himself, or me, or with this conduct of my father's, was more than I could read. Certainly, however, he seemed to be outgrowing that distaste, or ill-will, that he had conceived at first against my person; for presently he jumped up, came across the room behind me, and hit me a smack upon the shoulder. 'We'll agree fine yet!' he cried. 'I'm just as glad I let you in. And now come awa' to your bed.'

To my surprise, he lit no lamp or candle, but set forth into the dark passage, groped his way, breathing deeply, up a flight of steps, and paused before a door, which he unlocked. I was close upon his heels, having stumbled after him as best I might; and he bade me go in, for that was my chamber. I did as he bid, but paused after a few steps, and begged a light to go to bed with.

'Hoot-toot!' said Uncle Ebenezer, 'there's a fine moon.'

'Neither moon nor star, sir, and pit-mirk,'* said I. 'I cannae see the bed.'

'Hoot-toot, hoot-toot!' said he. 'Lights in a house is a thing I dinnae agree with. I'm unco feared of fires. Good night to ye, Davie, my man.' And before I had time to add a further protest, he pulled the door to, and I heard him lock me in from the outside.

I did not know whether to laugh or cry. The room was as cold as a well, and the bed, when I had found my way to it, as damp as a peat-hag; but by good fortune I had caught up my bundle and my plaid, and rolling myself in the latter, I lay down upon the floor under lee of the big bedstead, and fell speedily asleep.

With the first peep of day I opened my eyes, to find myself in a great chamber, hung with stamped leather, furnished with fine embroidered furniture, and lit by three fair windows. Ten years ago, or perhaps twenty, it must have been as pleasant a room to lie down or to awake in, as a man could wish; but damp, dirt, disuse, and the mice and spiders had done their worst since then. Many of the window-panes, besides, were broken; and indeed this was so common a feature in that house, that I believe my uncle must at some time have stood a siege from his indignant neighbours – perhaps with Jennet Clouston at their head.

Meanwhile the sun was shining outside; and being very cold in that miserable room, I knocked and shouted till my gaoler came and let me out. He carried me to the back of the house, where was a draw-well, and told me to 'wash my face there, if

* Dark as the pit.

I wanted', and when that was done, I made the best of my own way back to the kitchen, where he had lit the fire and was making the porridge. The table was laid with two bowls and two horn spoons, but the same single measure of small beer. Perhaps my eye rested on this particular with some surprise, and perhaps my uncle observed it; for he spoke up as if in answer to my thought, asking me if I would like to drink ale – for so he called it.

I told him such was my habit, but not to put himself about.

'Na, na,' said he; 'I'll deny you nothing in reason.'

He fetched another cup from the shelf; and then, to my great surprise, instead of drawing more beer, he poured an accurate half from one cup to the other. There was a kind of nobleness in this that took my breath away; if my uncle was certainly a miser, he was one of that thorough breed that goes near to make the vice respectable.

When we had made an end of our meal, my uncle Ebenezer unlocked a drawer, and drew out of it a clay pipe and a lump of tobacco, from which he cut one fill before he locked it up again. Then he sat down in the sun at one of the windows and silently smoked. From time to time his eyes came coasting round to me, and he shot out one of his questions. Once it was, 'And your mother?' and when I had told him that she, too, was dead, 'Ay, she was a bonnie lassie!' Then, after another long pause, 'Whae were these friends o' yours?'

I told him they were different gentlemen of the name of Campbell; though, indeed, there was only one, and that the minister, that had ever taken the least note of me; but I began to think my uncle made too light of my position, and finding myself all alone with him, I did not wish him to suppose me helpless.

He seemed to turn this over in his mind; and then, 'Davie, my man,' said he, 'ye've come to the right bit when ye came to your Uncle Ebenezer. I've a great notion of the family, and I mean to do the right by you; but while I'm taking a bit think to mysel' of what's the best thing to put you to – whether the law, or the meenistry, or maybe the army, whilk is what boys are fondest of – I wouldnae like the Balfours to be humbled before a wheen Hieland Campbells, and I'll ask you to keep your tongue within your teeth. Nae letters; nae messages; no kind of word to onybody; or else – there's my door.'

'Uncle Ebenezer,' said I, 'I've no manner of reason to suppose you mean anything but well by me. For all that, I would have you to know that I have a pride of my own. It was by no will of mine that I came seeking you; and if you show me your door again, I'll take you at the word.'

He seemed grievously put out. 'Hoots-toots,' said he, 'ca' cannie, man – ca' cannie! Bide a day or two. I'm nae warlock, to find a fortune for you in the bottom of a parritch bowl; but just you give me a day or two, and say naething to naebody, and as sure as sure, I'll do the right by you.'

'Very well,' said I, 'enough said. If you want to help me, there's no doubt but I'll be glad of it, and none but I'll be grateful.'

It seemed to me (too soon, I daresay) that I was getting the upper hand of my uncle; and I began next to say that I must have the bed and bedclothes aired and put to sun-dry; for nothing would make me sleep in such a pickle.

'Is this my house or yours?' said he, in his keen voice, and then all of a sudden broke off. 'Na, na,' said he, 'I didnae mean that. What's mine is yours, Davie, my man, and what's yours is mine. Blood's thicker than water; and there's naebody but you and me that ought the name.' And then on he rambled about the family, and its ancient greatness, and his father that began to enlarge the house, and himself that stopped the building as a sinful waste; and this put it in my head to give him Jennet Clouston's message.

'The limmer!' he cried. 'Twelve hunner and fifteen – that's every day since I had the limmer rowpit!* Dod, David, I'll have her roasted on red peats before I'm by with it! A witch – a proclaimed witch! I'll aff and see the session clerk.'

And with that he opened a chest, and got out a very old and well-preserved blue coat and waistcoat, and a good enough beaver hat, both without lace. These he threw on anyway, and

* Sold up.

taking a staff from the cupboard, locked all up again, and was for setting out, when a thought arrested him.

'I cannae leave you by yoursel' in the house,' said he. 'I'll have to lock you out.'

The blood came into my face. 'If you lock me out,' I said, 'it'll be the last you see of me in friendship.'

He turned very pale, and sucked his mouth in. 'This is no the way,' he said, looking wickedly at a corner of the floor – 'this is no the way to win my favour, David.'

'Sir,' says I, 'with a proper reverence for your age and our common blood, I do not value your favour at a boddle's purchase. I was brought up to have a good conceit of myself; and if you were all the uncle, and all the family, I had in the world ten times over, I wouldn't buy your liking at such prices.'

Uncle Ebenezer went and looked out of the window for a while. I could see him all trembling and twitching, like a man with palsy. But when he turned round, he had a smile upon his face.

'Well, well,' said he, 'we must bear and forbear. I'll no go; that's all that's to be said of it.'

'Uncle Ebenezer,' I said, 'I can make nothing out of this. You use me like a thief; you hate to have me in this house; you let me see it, every word and every minute; it's not possible that you can like me; and as for me, I've spoken to you as I never thought to speak to any man. Why do you seek to keep me, then? Let me gang back – let me gang back to the friends I have, and that like me!'

'Na, na; na, na,' he said, very earnestly. 'I like you fine; we'll agree fine yet; and for the honour of the house I couldnae let you leave the way ye came. Bide here quiet, there's a good lad; just you bide here quiet a bittie, and ye'll find that we agree.'

'Well, sir,' said I, after I had thought the matter out in silence, 'I'll stay a while. It's more just I should be helped by my own blood than strangers; and if we don't agree, I'll do my best it shall be through no fault of mine.'

CHAPTER IV

I run a great danger in the house of Shaws

For a day that was begun so ill, the day passed fairly well. We had the porridge cold again at noon, and hot porridge at night: porridge and small beer was my uncle's diet. He spoke but little, and that in the same way as before, shooting a question at me after a long silence; and when I sought to lead him in talk about my future, slipped out of it again. In a room next door to the kitchen, where he suffered me to go, I found a great number of books, both Latin and English, in which I took great pleasure all the afternoon. Indeed the time passed so lightly in this good company, that I began to be almost reconciled to my residence at Shaws; and nothing but the sight of my uncle, and his eyes playing hide and seek with mine, revived the force of my distrust.

One thing I discovered, which put me in some doubt. This was an entry on the fly-leaf of a chapbook (one of Patrick Walker's)[8] plainly written by my father's hand and thus conceived: 'To my brother Ebenezer on his fifth birthday.' Now, what puzzled me was this: That as my father was of course the younger brother, he must either have made some strange error, or he must have written, before he was yet five, an excellent, clear, manly hand of writing.

I tried to get this out of my head; but though I took down many interesting authors, old and new, history, poetry, and story-book, this notion of my father's hand of writing stuck to me; and when at length I went back into the kitchen, and sat down once more to porridge and small beer, the first thing I said to Uncle Ebenezer was to ask him if my father had not been very quick at his book.

'Alexander? No him!' was the reply. 'I was far quicker myself'; I was a clever chappie when I was young. Why, I could read as soon as he could.'

This puzzled me yet more; and a thought coming into my head, I asked if he and my father had been twins.

He jumped upon his stool, and the horn spoon fell out of his hand upon the floor. 'What gars ye ask that?' he said, and caught me by the breast of the jacket, and looked this time straight into my eyes: his own, which were little and light, and bright like a bird's, blinking and winking strangely.

'What do you mean?' I asked, very calmly, for I was far stronger than he, and not easily frightened. 'Take your hand from my jacket. This is no way to behave.'

My uncle seemed to make a great effort upon himself. 'Dod, man David,' he said, 'ye shouldnae speak to me about your father. That's where the mistake is.' He sat a while and shook, blinking in his plate: 'He was all the brother that ever I had,' he added, but with no heart in his voice; and then he caught up his spoon and fell to supper again, but still shaking.

Now this last passage, this laying of hands upon my person and sudden profession of love for my dead father, went so clean beyond my comprehension that it put me into both fear and hope. On the one hand, I began to think my uncle was perhaps insane and might be dangerous; on the other, there came up into my mind (quite unbidden by me and even discouraged) a story like some ballad I had heard folk singing, of a poor lad that was a rightful heir and a wicked kinsman that tried to keep him from his own. For why should my uncle play a part with a relative that came, almost a beggar, to his door, unless in his heart he had some cause to fear him?

With this notion, all unacknowledged, but nevertheless getting firmly settled in my head, I now began to imitate his covert looks; so that we sat at table like a cat and a mouse, each stealthily observing the other. Not another word had he to say to me, black or white, but was busy turning something secretly over in his mind; and the longer we sat and the more I looked at him, the more certain I became that the something was unfriendly to myself.

When he had cleared the platter, he got out a single pipeful of tobacco, just as in the morning, turned round a stool into the chimney corner, and sat a while smoking, with his back to me.

'Davie,' he said, at length, 'I've been thinking'; then he paused, and said it again. 'There's a wee bit siller that I half promised ye before ye were born,' he continued; 'promised it to your father. Oh, naething legal, ye understand; just gentlemen daffing at their wine. Well, I keepit that bit money separate – it was a great expense, but a promise is a promise – and it has grown by now to be a maitter of just precisely – just exactly' – and here he paused and stumbled – 'of just exactly forty pounds!' This last he rapped out with a sidelong glance over his shoulder; and the next moment added, almost with a scream, 'Scots!'

The pound Scots being the same thing as an English shilling, the difference made by this second thought was considerable; I could see, besides, that the whole story was a lie, invented with some end which it puzzled me to guess; and I made no attempt to conceal the tone of raillery in which I answered –

'Oh, think again, sir! Pounds sterling, I believe!'

'That's what I said,' returned my uncle: 'pounds sterling! And if you'll step out-by to the door a minute, just to see what kind of a night it is, I'll get it out to ye and call ye in again.'

I did his will, smiling to myself in my contempt that he should think I was so easily to be deceived. It was a dark night, with a few stars low down; and as I stood just outside the door, I heard a hollow moaning of wind far off among the hills. I said to myself there was something thundery and changeful in the weather, and little knew of what a vast importance that should prove to me before the evening passed.

When I was called in again, my uncle counted out into my hand seven and thirty golden guinea pieces; the rest was in his hand, in small gold and silver; but his heart failed him there, and he crammed the change into his pocket.

'There,' said he, 'that'll show you! I'm a queer man, and strange wi' strangers; but my word is my bond, and there's the proof of it.'

Now, my uncle seemed so miserly that I was struck dumb by this sudden generosity, and could find no words in which to thank him.

'No a word!' said he. 'Nae thanks; I want nae thanks. I do my duty; I'm no saying that everybody would have done it; but for my part (though I'm a careful body, too) it's a pleasure to me to do the right by my brother's son; and it's a pleasure to me to think that now we'll agree as such near friends should.'

I spoke him in return as handsomely as I was able; but all the while I was wondering what would come next, and why he had parted with his precious guineas; for as to the reason he had given, a baby would have refused it.

Presently, he looked towards me sideways.

'And see here,' says he, 'tit for tat.'

I told him I was ready to prove my gratitude in any reasonable degree, and then waited, looking for some monstrous demand. And yet, when at last he plucked up courage to speak, it was only to tell me (very properly, as I thought) that he was growing old and a little broken, and that he would expect me to help him with the house and the bit garden.

I answered, and expressed my readiness to serve.

'Well,' he said, 'let's begin.' He pulled out of his pocket a rusty key. 'There,' says he, 'there's the key of the stair-tower at the far end of the house. Ye can only win into it from the outside, for that part of the house is no finished. Gang ye in there, and up the stairs, and bring me down the chest that's at the top. There's papers in't,' he added.

'Can I have a light, sir?' said I.

'Na,' said he, very cunningly. 'Nae lights in my house.'

'Very well, sir,' said I. 'Are the stairs good?'

'They're grand,' said he; and then as I was going, 'Keep to the wall,' he added; 'there's nae bannisters. But the stairs are grand under foot.'

Out I went into the night. The wind was still moaning in the distance, though never a breath of it came near the house of Shaws. It had fallen blacker than ever; and I was glad to feel along the wall, till I came the length of the stair-tower door at the far end of the unfinished wing. I had got the key into the keyhole and had just turned it, when all upon a sudden, without sound of wind or thunder, the whole sky lighted up with wild fire and went black again. I had to put my hand over my eyes to get back to the colour of the darkness; and indeed I was already half blinded when I stepped into the tower.

It was so dark inside, it seemed a body could scarce breathe; but I pushed out with foot and hand, and presently struck the wall with the one, and the lowermost round of the stair with the other. The wall, by the touch, was of fine hewn stone; the steps too, though somewhat steep and narrow, were of polished mason-work, and regular and solid under foot. Minding my uncle's word about the bannisters, I kept close to the tower side, and felt my way in the pitch darkness with a beating heart.

The house of Shaws stood some five full storeys high, not counting lofts. Well, as I advanced, it seemed to me the stair grew airier and a thought more lightsome; and I was wondering what might be the cause of this change, when a second blink of the summer lightning came and went. If I did not cry out, it was because fear had me by the throat; and if I did not fall, it was more by Heaven's mercy than my own strength. It was not only that the flash shone in on every side through breaches in the wall, so that I seemed to be clambering aloft upon an open scaffold, but the same passing brightness showed me the steps were of unequal length, and that one of my feet rested that moment within two inches of the well.

This was the grand stair! I thought; and with the thought, a gust of a kind of angry courage came into my heart. My uncle had sent me here, certainly to run great risks, perhaps to die. I swore I would settle that 'perhaps', if I should break my neck for it; got me down upon my hands and knees; and as slowly as a snail, feeling before me every inch, and testing the solidity of every stone, I continued to ascend the stair. The darkness, by contrast with the flash, appeared to have redoubled; nor was that all, for my ears were now troubled and my mind confounded by a great stir of bats in the top part of the tower, and the foul beasts, flying downwards, sometimes beat about my face and body.

The tower, I should have said, was square; and in every

corner the step was made of a great stone of a different shape, to join the flights. Well, I had come close to one of these turns, when, feeling forward as usual, my hand slipped upon an edge and found nothing but emptiness beyond it. The stair had been carried no higher: to set a stranger mounting it in the darkness was to send him straight to his death; and (although, thanks to the lightning and my own precautions, I was safe enough) the mere thought of the peril in which I might have stood, and the dreadful height I might have fallen from, brought out the sweat upon my body and relaxed my joints.

But I knew what I wanted now, and turned and groped my way down again, with a wonderful anger in my heart. About half-way down, the wind sprang up in a clap and shook the tower, and died again; the rain followed; and before I had reached the ground level it fell in buckets. I put out my head into the storm, and looked along towards the kitchen. The door, which I had shut behind me when I left, now stood open, and shed a little glimmer of light; and I thought I could see a figure standing in the rain, quite still, like a mad hearkening. And then there came a blinding flash, which showed me my uncle plainly, just where I had fancied him to stand; and hard upon the heels of it, a great tow-row of thunder.

Now, whether my uncle thought the crash to be the sound of my fall, or whether he heard in it God's voice denouncing murder, I will leave you to guess. Certain it is, at least, that he was seized on by a kind of panic fear, and that he ran into the house and left the door open behind him. I followed as softly as I could, and, coming unheard into the kitchen, stood and watched him.

He had found time to open the corner cupboard and bring out a great case bottle of aqua vitæ, and now sat with his back towards me at the table. Ever and again he would be seized with a fit of deadly shuddering and groan aloud, and carrying the bottle to his lips, drink down the raw spirits by the mouthful.

I stepped forward, came close behind him where he sat, and suddenly clapping my two hands down upon his shoulders – 'Ah!' cried I.

My uncle gave a kind of broken cry like a sheep's bleat, flung up his arms, and tumbled to the floor like a dead man. I was somewhat shocked at this; but I had myself to look to first of all, and did not hesitate to let him lie as he had fallen. The keys were hanging in the cupboard; and it was my design to furnish myself with arms before my uncle should come again to his senses and the power of devising evil. In the cupboard were a few bottles, some apparently of medicine; a great many bills and other papers, which I should willingly enough have rummaged, had I had the time; and a few necessaries, that were nothing to my purpose. Thence I turned to the chests. The first was full of meal; the second of money-bags and papers tied into sheaves; in the third, with many other things (and these for the most part clothes) I found a rusty, ugly-looking Highland dirk without the scabbard. This, then, I concealed inside my waistcoat, and turned to my uncle.

He lay as he had fallen, all huddled, with one knee up and one arm sprawling abroad; his face had a strange colour of blue, and he seemed to have ceased breathing. Fear came on me that he was dead; then I got water and dashed it in his face; and with that he seemed to come a little to himself, working his mouth and fluttering his eyelids. At last he looked up and saw me, and there came into his eyes a terror that was not of this world.

'Come, come,' said I, 'sit up.'

'Are ye alive?' he sobbed. 'O man, are ye alive?'

'That am I,' said I. 'Small thanks to you!'

He had begun to seek for his breath with deep sighs. 'The blue phial,' said he – 'in the aumry – the blue phial.' His breath came slower still.

I ran to the cupboard, and, sure enough, found there a blue phial of medicine, with the dose written on it on a paper, and this I administered to him with what speed I might.

'It's the trouble,' said he, reviving a little; 'I have a trouble, Davie. It's the heart.'

I set him on a chair and looked at him. It is true I felt some pity for a man that looked so sick, but I was full besides of righteous anger; and I numbered over before him the points on which I wanted explanation: why he lied to me at every word; why he feared that I should leave him; why he disliked it to be hinted that he and my father were twins – 'Is that because it is true?' I asked; why he had given me money to which I was convinced I had no claim; and, last of all, why he had tried to kill me. He heard me all through in silence; and then, in a broken voice, begged me to let him go to bed.

'I'll tell ye the morn,' he said; 'as sure as death I will.'

And so weak was he that I could do nothing but consent. I locked him into his room, however, and pocketed the key; and then returning to the kitchen, made up such a blaze as had not shone there for many a long year, and wrapping myself in my plaid, lay down upon the chests and fell asleep.

CHAPTER V

I go to the Queen's Ferry

Much rain fell in the night; and the next morning there blew a bitter wintry wind out of the north-west, driving scattered clouds. For all that, and before the sun began to peep or the last of the stars had vanished, I made my way to the side of the burn, and had a plunge in a deep whirling pool. All aglow from my bath, I sat down once more beside the fire, which I replenished, and began gravely to consider my position.

There was now no doubt about my uncle's enmity; there was no doubt I carried my life in my hand, and he would leave no stone unturned that he might compass my destruction. But I was young and spirited, and like most lads that have been country-bred, I had a great opinion of my shrewdness. I had come to his door no better than a beggar and little more than a child; he had met me with treachery and violence; it would be a fine consummation to take the upper hand, and drive him like a herd of sheep.

I sat there nursing my knee and smiling at the fire; and I saw myself in fancy smell out his secrets one after another, and grow to be that man's king and ruler. The warlock of Essendean, they say, had made a mirror in which men could read the future; it must have been of other stuff than burning coal; for in all the shapes and pictures that I sat and gazed at, there was never a ship, never a seaman with a hairy cap, never a big bludgeon for my silly head, or the least sign of all those tribulations that were ripe to fall on me.

Presently, all swollen with conceit, I went up stairs and gave my prisoner his liberty. He gave me good morning civilly; and

I gave the same to him, smiling down upon him from the heights
of my sufficiency. Soon we were set to breakfast, as it might
have been the day before.

'Well, sir,' said I, with a jeering tone, 'have you nothing more
to say to me?' And then, as he made no articulate reply, 'It will
be time, I think, to understand each other,' I continued. 'You
took me for a country Johnnie Raw, with no more mother-wit
or courage than a porridge-stick. I took you for a good man,
or no worse than others at the least. It seems we were both
wrong. What cause you have to fear me, to cheat me, and to
attempt my life –'

He murmured something about a jest, and that he liked a bit
of fun; and then, seeing me smile, changed his tone, and assured
me he would make all clear as soon as we had breakfasted. I
saw by his face that he had no lie ready for me, though he was
hard at work preparing one; and I think I was about to tell him
so, when we were interrupted by a knocking at the door.

Bidding my uncle sit where he was, I went to open it, and
found on the doorstep a half-grown boy in sea-clothes. He had
no sooner seen me than he began to dance some steps of the
sea-hornpipe (which I had never before heard of, far less seen)
snapping his fingers in the air and footing it right cleverly. For
all that, he was blue with the cold; and there was something in
his face, a look between tears and laughter, that was highly
pathetic and consisted ill with this gaiety of manner.

'What cheer, mate?' says he, with a cracked voice.

I asked him soberly to name his pleasure.

'Oh, pleasure!' says he; and then began to sing:

> 'For it's my delight, of a shiny night,
>   In the season of the year.'⁹

'Well,' said I, 'if you have no business at all, I will even be so
unmannerly as to shut you out.'

'Stay, brother!' he cried. 'Have you no fun about you? or do
you want to get me thrashed? I've brought a letter from old
Heasy-oasy to Mr Belflower.' He showed me a letter as he
spoke. 'And I say, mate,' he added, 'I'm mortal hungry.'

'Well,' said I, 'come into the house, and you shall have a bite if I go empty for it.'

With that I brought him in and set him down to my own place, where he fell-to greedily on the remains of breakfast, winking to me between whiles, and making many faces, which I think the poor soul considered manly. Meanwhile, my uncle had read the letter and sat thinking;[10] then, suddenly, he got to his feet with a great air of liveliness, and pulled me apart into the farthest corner of the room.

'Read that,' said he, and put the letter in my hand.

Here it is, lying before me as I write:

> *The Hawes Inn*[11] at the Queen's Ferry.
>
> SIR, – I lie here with my hawser up and down, and send my cabin-boy to informe. If you have any further commands for overseas, to-day will be the last occasion, as the wind will serve us well out of the firth. I will not seek to deny that I have had crosses with your doer,* Mr Rankeillor; of which, if not speedily redd up, you may looke to see some losses follow. I have drawn a bill upon you, as per margin, and am, sir, your most obedt. humble servant,
>
> ELIAS HOSEASON.

'You see, Davie,' resumed my uncle, as soon as he saw that I had done, 'I have a venture with this man Hoseason, the captain of a trading brig, the *Covenant*,[12] of Dysart. Now, if you and me was to walk over with yon lad, I could see the captain at the Hawes, or maybe on board the *Covenant*, if there was papers to be signed; and so far from a loss of time, we can jog on to the lawyer, Mr Rankeillor's. After a' that's come and gone, ye would be swier† to believe me upon my naked word; but ye'll believe Rankeillor. He's factor to half the gentry in these parts; an auld man, forby: highly respeckit; and he kenned your father.'

I stood awhile and thought. I was going to some place of

* Agent.
† Unwilling.

shipping, which was doubtless populous, and where my uncle durst attempt no violence, and, indeed, even the society of the cabin-boy so far protected me. Once there, I believed I could force on the visit to the lawyer, even if my uncle were now insincere in proposing it; and perhaps, in the bottom of my heart, I wished a nearer view of the sea and ships. You are to remember I had lived all my life in the inland hills, and just two days before had my first sight of the firth lying like a blue floor, and the sailed ships moving on the face of it, no bigger than toys. One thing with another, I made up my mind.

'Very well,' says I, 'let us go to the Ferry.'

My uncle got into his hat and coat, and buckled an old rusty cutlass on; and then we trod the fire out, locked the door, and set forth upon our walk.

The wind, being in that cold quarter, the north-west, blew nearly in our faces as we went. It was the month of June; the grass was all white with daisies and the trees with blossom; but, to judge by our blue nails and aching wrists, the time might have been winter and the whiteness a December frost.

Uncle Ebenezer trudged in the ditch, jogging from side to side like an old ploughman coming home from work. He never said a word the whole way; and I was thrown for talk on the cabin-boy. He told me his name was Ransome, and that he had followed the sea since he was nine, but could not say how old he was, as he had lost his reckoning. He showed me tattoo marks, baring his breast in the teeth of the wind and in spite of my remonstrances, for I thought it was enough to kill him; he swore horribly whenever he remembered, but more like a silly schoolboy than a man; and boasted of many wild and bad things that he had done: stealthy thefts, false accusations, ay, and even murder; but all with such a dearth of likelihood in the details, and such a weak and crazy swagger in the delivery, as disposed me rather to pity than to believe him.

I asked him of the brig (which he declared was the finest ship that sailed) and of Captain Hoseason, in whose praise he was equally loud. Heasy-oasy (for so he still named the skipper) was a man, by his account, that minded for nothing either in heaven or earth; one that, as people said, would 'crack on all sail into the day of judgment'; rough, fierce, unscrupulous, and brutal; and all this my poor cabin-boy had taught himself to admire as something seamanlike and manly. He would only admit one flaw in his idol. 'He ain't no seaman,' he admitted. 'That's Mr Shuan that navigates the brig; he's the finest seaman in the trade, only for drink; and I tell you I believe it! Why, look 'ere'; and turning down his stocking, he showed me a great, raw, red wound that made my blood run cold. 'He done that – Mr Shuan done it,' he said, with an air of pride.

'What!' I cried, 'do you take such savage usage at his hands? Why, you are no slave, to be so handled!'

'No,' said the poor moon-calf, changing his tune at once, 'and so he'll find! See 'ere'; and he showed me a great case-knife, which he told me was stolen. 'Oh,' says he, 'let me see him try; I dare him to; I'll do for him! Oh, he ain't the first!' And he confirmed it with a poor, silly, ugly oath.

I have never felt such pity for any one in this wide world as I felt for that half-witted creature; and it began to come over me that the brig *Covenant* (for all her pious name) was little better than a hell upon the seas.

'Have you no friends?' said I.

He said he had a father in some English seaport, I forget which. 'He was a fine man, too,' he said; 'but he's dead.'

'In Heaven's name,' cried I, 'can you find no reputable life on shore?'

'Oh, no!' says he, winking and looking very sly; 'they would put me to a trade. I know a trick worth two of that, I do!'

I asked him what trade could be so dreadful as the one he followed, where he ran the continual peril of his life, not alone from wind and sea, but by the horrid cruelty of those who were his masters. He said it was very true; and then began to praise the life, and tell what a pleasure it was to get on shore with money in his pocket, and spend it like a man, and buy apples, and swagger, and surprise what he called stick-in-the-mud boys. 'And then it's not all as bad as that,' says he; 'there's worse off than me: there's the twenty-pounders. Oh, laws! you should see them taking on. Why, I've seen a man as old as you, I dessay' – (to him I seemed old) – 'ah, and he had a beard, too

– well, and as soon as we cleared out of the river, and he had
the drug out of his head – my! how he cried and carried on! I
made a fine fool of him, I tell you! And then there's little uns,
too: oh, little by me! I tell you, I keep them in order. When we
carry little uns, I have a rope's end of my own to wollop 'em.'
And so he ran on, until it came in on me that what he meant
by twenty-pounders were those unhappy criminals who were
sent over-seas to slavery in North America, or the still more
unhappy innocents who were kidnapped or trepanned (as the
word went) for private interest or vengeance.

Just then we came to the top of the hill, and looked down on
the Ferry and the Hope. The Firth of Forth (as is very well
known) narrows at this point to the width of a good-sized river,
which makes a convenient ferry going north, and turns the
upper reach into a land-locked haven for all manner of ships.
Right in the midst of the narrows lies an islet with some ruins;
on the south shore they have built a pier for the service of
the Ferry; and at the end of the pier, on the other side of the
road, and backed against a pretty garden of holly-trees and
hawthorns, I could see the building which they call the Hawes
Inn.

The town of Queensferry lies farther west, and the neighbourhood of the inn looked pretty lonely at that time of day, for the
boat had just gone north with passengers. A skiff, however, lay
beside the pier, with some seamen sleeping on the thwarts; this,
as Ransome told me, was the brig's boat waiting for the captain;
and about half a mile off, and all alone in the anchorage, he
showed me the *Covenant* herself. There was a sea-going bustle
on board; yards were swinging into place; and as the wind blew
from that quarter, I could hear the song of the sailors as they
pulled upon the ropes. After all I had listened to upon the way,
I looked at that ship with an extreme abhorrence; and from the
bottom of my heart I pitied all poor souls that were condemned
to sail in her.

We had all three pulled up on the brow of the hill; and now
I marched across the road and addressed my uncle. 'I think it
right to tell you, sir,' says I, 'there's nothing that will bring me
on board that *Covenant*.'

He seemed to waken from a dream. 'Eh?' he said. 'What's that?'

I told him over again.

'Well, well,' he said, 'we'll have to please ye, I suppose. But what are we standing here for? It's perishing cold; and if I'm no mistaken, they're busking the *Covenant* for sea.'

CHAPTER VI

What befell at the Queen's Ferry

As soon as we came to the inn, Ransome led us up the stair to a small room, with a bed in it, and heated like an oven by a great fire of coal. At a table hard by the chimney, a tall, dark, sober-looking man sat writing. In spite of the heat of the room, he wore a thick sea-jacket, buttoned to the neck, and a tall hairy cap drawn down over his ears; yet I never saw any man, not even a judge upon the bench, look cooler, or more studious and self-possessed, than this ship-captain.

He got to his feet at once, and coming forward, offered his large hand to Ebenezer. 'I am proud to see you, Mr Balfour,' said he, in a fine deep voice, 'and glad that ye are here in time. The wind's fair, and the tide upon the turn: we'll see the old coal-bucket burning on the Isle of May before to-night.'

'Captain Hoseason,' returned my uncle, 'you keep your room unco hot.'

'It's a habit I have, Mr Balfour,' said the skipper. 'I'm a cold-rife man by my nature; I have a cold blood, sir. There's neither fur, nor flannel – no, sir, nor hot rum, will warm up what they call the temperature. Sir, it's the same with most men that have been carbonadoed, as they call it, in the tropic seas.'

'Well, well, captain,' replied my uncle, 'we must all be the way we're made.'

But it chanced that this fancy of the captain's had a great share in my misfortunes. For though I had promised myself not to let my kinsman out of sight, I was both so impatient for a nearer look of the sea, and so sickened by the closeness of the room, that when he told me to 'run down-stairs and play myself awhile', I was fool enough to take him at his word.

Away I went, therefore, leaving the two men sitting down to a bottle and a great mass of papers; and crossing the road in front of the inn, walked down upon the beach. With the wind in that quarter, only little wavelets, not much bigger than I had seen upon a lake, beat upon the shore. But the weeds were new to me – some green, some brown and long, and some with little bladders that crackled between my fingers. Even so far up the firth, the smell of the sea water was exceedingly salt and stirring; the *Covenant*, besides, was beginning to shake out her sails, which hung upon the yards in clusters; and the spirit of all that I beheld put me in thoughts of far voyages and foreign places.

I looked, too, at the seamen with the skiff – big brown fellows, some in shirts, some with jackets, some with coloured handkerchiefs about their throats, one with a brace of pistols stuck into his pockets, two or three with knotty bludgeons, and all with their case-knives. I passed the time of day with one that looked less desperate than his fellows, and asked him of the sailing of the brig. He said they would get under way as soon as the ebb set, and expressed his gladness to be out of a port where there were no taverns and fiddlers; but all with such horrifying oaths, that I made haste to get away from him.

This threw me back on Ransome, who seemed the least wicked of that gang, and who soon came out of the inn and ran to me, crying for a bowl of punch. I told him I would give him no such thing, for neither he nor I was of an age for such indulgences. 'But a glass of ale you may have, and welcome,' said I. He mopped and mowed at me, and called me names; but he was glad to get the ale, for all that; and presently we were set down at a table in the front room of the inn, and both eating and drinking with a good appetite.

Here it occurred to me that, as the landlord was a man of that county, I might do well to make a friend of him. I offered him a share, as was much the custom in these days; but he was far too great a man to sit with such poor customers as Ransome and myself, and he was leaving the room, when I called him back to ask if he knew Mr Rankeillor.

'Hoot, ay,' says he, 'and a very honest man. And, oh, by-the-bye,' says he, 'was it you that came in with Ebenezer?' And when I had told him yes, 'Ye'll be no friend of his?' he asked, meaning, in the Scottish way, that I would be no relative.

I told him no, none.

'I thought not,' said he; 'and yet ye have a kind of gliff* of Mr Alexander.'

I said it seemed that Ebenezer was ill-seen in the country.

'Nae doubt,' said the landlord. 'He's a wicked auld man, and there's many would like to see him girnning in a tow:† Jennet Clouston and mony mair that he has harried out of house and hame. And yet he was ance a fine young fellow, too. But that was before the sough‡ gaed abroad about Mr Alexander; that was like the death of him.'

'And what was it?' I asked.

'Ou, just that he had killed him,' said the landlord. 'Did ye never hear that?'

'And what would he kill him for?' said I.

'And what for, but just to get the place,' said he.

'The place?' said I. 'The Shaws?'

'Nae other place that I ken,' said he.

'Ay, man?' said I. 'Is that so? Was my – was Alexander the eldest son?'

' 'Deed was he,' said the landlord. 'What else would he have killed him for?'

And with that he went away, as he had been impatient to do from the beginning.

Of course, I had guessed it a long while ago; but it is one thing to guess, another to know; and I sat stunned with my good fortune, and could scarce grow to believe that the same poor lad who had trudged in the dust from Ettrick Forest not two days ago, was now one of the rich of the earth, and had a house and broad lands, and if he but knew how to ride, might mount his horse to-morrow. All these pleasant things, and a thousand others, crowded into my mind, as I sat staring before me out of the inn window, and paying no heed to what I saw; only I remember that my eye lighted on Captain Hoseason

* Look.
† Rope.
‡ Report.

down on the pier among his seamen, and speaking with some authority. And presently he came marching back towards the house, with no mark of a sailor's clumsiness, but carrying his fine, tall figure with a manly bearing, and still with the same sober, grave expression on his face. I wondered if it was possible that Ransome's stories could be true, and half disbelieved them; they fitted so ill with the man's looks. But indeed, he was neither so good as I supposed him, nor quite so bad as Ransome did; for, in fact, he was two men, and left the better one behind as soon as he set foot on board his vessel.

The next thing, I heard my uncle calling me, and found the pair in the road together. It was the captain who addressed me, and that with an air (very flattering to a young lad) of grave equality.

'Sir,' said he, 'Mr Balfour tells me great things of you; and for my own part, I like your looks. I wish I was for longer here, that we might make the better friends; but we'll make the most of what we have. Ye shall come on board my brig for half-an-hour, till the ebb sets, and drink a bowl with me.'

Now, I longed to see the inside of a ship more than words can tell; but I was not going to put myself in jeopardy, and I told him my uncle and I had an appointment with a lawyer.

'Ay, ay,' said he, 'he passed me word of that. But, ye see, the boat'll set ye ashore at the town pier, and that's but a penny stonecast from Rankeillor's house.' And here he suddenly leaned down and whispered in my ear: 'Take care of the old tod;* he means mischief. Come aboard till I can get a word with ye.' And then, passing his arm through mine, he continued aloud, as he set off towards his boat: 'But come, what can I bring ye from the Carolinas? Any friend of Mr Balfour's can command. A roll of tobacco? Indian featherwork? A skin of a wild beast? a stone pipe? the mocking-bird that mews for all the world like a cat? the cardinal bird that is as red as blood? – take your pick and say your pleasure.'

By this time we were at the boat-side, and he was handing me in. I did not dream of hanging back; I thought (the poor

* Fox.

fool!) that I had found a good friend and helper, and I was rejoiced to see the ship. As soon as we were all set in our places, the boat was thrust off from the pier and began to move over the waters; and what with my pleasure in this new movement and my surprise at our low position, and the appearance of the shores, and the growing bigness of the brig as we drew near to it, I could hardly understand what the captain said, and must have answered him at random.

As soon as we were alongside (where I sat fairly gaping at the ship's height, the strong humming of the tide against its sides, and the pleasant cries of the seamen at their work) Hoseason, declaring that he and I must be the first aboard, ordered a tackle to be sent down from the main-yard. In this I was whipped into the air and set down again on the deck, where the captain stood ready waiting for me, and instantly slipped back his arm under mine. There I stood some while, a little dizzy with the unsteadiness of all around me, perhaps a little afraid, and yet vastly pleased with these strange sights; the captain meanwhile pointing out the strangest, and telling me their names and uses.

'But where is my uncle?' said I, suddenly.

'Ay,' said Hoseason, with a sudden grimness, 'that's the point.'

I felt I was lost. With all my strength, I plucked myself clear of him and ran to the bulwarks. Sure enough, there was the boat pulling for the town, with my uncle sitting in the stern. I gave a piercing cry – 'Help, help! Murder!' – so that both sides of the anchorage rang with it, and my uncle turned round where he was sitting, and showed me a face full of cruelty and terror.

It was the last I saw. Already strong hands had been plucking me back from the ship's side; and now a thunderbolt seemed to strike me; I saw a great flash of fire, and fell senseless.

CHAPTER VII

I go to sea in the brig Covenant *of Dysart*

I came to myself in darkness, in great pain, bound hand and foot, and deafened by many unfamiliar noises. There sounded in my ears a roaring of water as of a huge mill-dam; the thrashing of heavy sprays, the thundering of the sails, and the shrill cries of seamen. The whole world now heaved giddily up, and now rushed giddily downward; and so sick and hurt was I in body, and my mind so much confounded, that it took me a long while, chasing my thoughts up and down and ever stunned again by a fresh stab of pain, to realize that I must be lying somewhere bound in the belly of that unlucky ship, and that the wind must have strengthened to a gale. With the clear perception of my plight, there fell upon me a blackness of despair, a horror of remorse at my own folly, and a passion of anger at my uncle, that once more bereft me of my senses.

When I returned again to life, the same uproar, the same confused and violent movements, shook and deafened me; and presently, to my other pains and distresses, there was added the sickness of an unused landsman on the sea. In that time of my adventurous youth, I suffered many hardships; but none that was so crushing to my mind and body, or lit by so few hopes, as these first hours on board the brig.

I heard a gun fire, and supposed the storm had proved too strong for us, and we were firing signals of distress. The thought of deliverance, even by death in the deep sea, was welcome to me. Yet it was no such matter; but (as I was afterwards told) a common habit of the captain's, which I here set down to show that even the worst man may have his kindlier sides. We were then passing, it appeared, within some miles of Dysart, where

the brig was built, and where old Mrs Hoseason, the captain's
mother, had come some years before to live; and whether out-
ward or inward bound, the *Covenant* was never suffered to go
by that place by day, without a gun fired and colours shown.

I had no measure of time; day and night were alike in that
ill-smelling cavern of the ship's bowels where I lay; and the
misery of my situation drew out the hours to double. How
long, therefore, I lay waiting to hear the ship split upon some
rock, or to feel her reel head foremost into the depths of the
sea, I have not the means of computation. But sleep at length
stole from me the consciousness of sorrow.

I was wakened by the light of a hand-lantern shining in my
face. A small man of about thirty, with green eyes and a tangle
of fair hair, stood looking down at me.

'Well,' said he, 'how goes it?'

I answered by a sob; and my visitor then felt my pulse and
temples, and set himself to wash and dress the wound upon my
scalp.

'Ay,' said he, 'a sore dunt.* What, man? Cheer up! The
world's no done; you've made a bad start of it, but you'll make
a better. Have you had any meat?'

I said I could not look at it; and thereupon he gave me some
brandy and water in a tin pannikin, and left me once more to
myself.

The next time he came to see me, I was lying betwixt sleep
and waking, my eyes wide open in the darkness, the sickness
quite departed, but succeeded by a horrid giddiness and swimming that was almost worse to bear. I ached, besides, in every
limb, and the cords that bound me seemed to be of fire. The
smell of the hole in which I lay seemed to have become a part
of me; and during the long interval since his last visit I had
suffered tortures of fear, now from the scurrying of the ship's
rats, that sometimes pattered on my very face, and now from
the dismal imaginings that haunt the bed of fever.

The glimmer of the lantern, as a trap opened, shone in like
the heaven's sunlight; and though it only showed me the strong,

* Stroke.

dark beams of the ship that was my prison, I could have cried aloud for gladness. The man with the green eyes was the first to descend the ladder, and I noticed that he came somewhat unsteadily. He was followed by the captain. Neither said a word; but the first set to and examined me, and dressed my wound as before, while Hoseason looked me in my face with an odd, black look.

'Now, sir, you see for yourself,' said the first: 'a high fever, no appetite, no light, no meat: you see for yourself what that means.'

'I am no conjurer, Mr Riach,' said the captain.

'Give me leave, sir,' said Riach; 'you've a good head upon your shoulders, and a good Scotch tongue to ask with; but I will leave you no manner of excuse: I want that boy taken out of this hole and put in the forecastle.'

'What ye may want, sir, is a matter of concern to nobody but yoursel',' returned the captain; 'but I can tell ye that which is to be. Here he is; here he shall bide.'

'Admitting that you have been paid in a proportion,' said the other, 'I will crave leave humbly to say that I have not. Paid I am, and none too much, to be the second officer of this old tub; and you ken very well if I do my best to earn it. But I was paid for nothing more.'

'If ye could hold back your hand from the tin-pan, Mr Riach, I would have no complaint to make of ye,' returned the skipper; 'and instead of asking riddles, I make bold to say that ye would keep your breath to cool your porridge. We'll be required on deck,' he added, in a sharper note, and set one foot upon the ladder.

But Mr Riach caught him by the sleeve.

'Admitting that you have been paid to do a murder –' he began.

Hoseason turned upon him with a flash.

'What's that?' he cried. 'What kind of talk is that?'

'It seems it is the talk that you can understand,' said Mr Riach, looking him steadily in the face.

'Mr Riach, I have sailed with ye three cruises,' replied the captain. 'In all that time, sir, ye should have learned to know

me: I'm a stiff man, and a dour man; but for what ye say the now
– fie, fie! – it comes from a bad heart and a black conscience. If
ye say the lad will die –'

'Ay, will he!' said Mr Riach.

'Well, sir, is not that enough?' said Hoseason. 'Flit him where
ye please!'

Thereupon the captain ascended the ladder; and I, who had
lain silent throughout this strange conversation, beheld Mr
Riach turn after him and bow as low as to his knees in what
was plainly a spirit of derision. Even in my then state of sickness,
I perceived two things: that the mate was touched with liquor,
as the captain hinted, and that (drunk or sober) he was like to
prove a valuable friend.

Five minutes afterwards my bonds were cut, I was hoisted on
a man's back, carried up to the forecastle, and laid in a bunk
on some sea-blankets; where the first thing that I did was to
lose my senses.

It was a blessed thing indeed to open my eyes again upon the
daylight, and to find myself in the society of men. The forecastle
was a roomy place enough, set all about with berths, in which
the men of the watch below were seated smoking, or lying
down asleep. The day being calm and the wind fair, the scuttle
was open, and not only the good daylight, but from time to
time (as the ship rolled) a dusty beam of sunlight shone in, and
dazzled and delighted me. I had no sooner moved, moreover,
than one of the men brought me a drink of something healing
which Mr Riach had prepared, and bade me lie still and I should
soon be well again. There were no bones broken, he explained:
'A clour* on the head was naething. Man,' said he, 'it was me
that gave it ye!'

Here I lay for the space of many days a close prisoner, and
not only got my health again, but came to know my companions. They were a rough lot indeed, as sailors mostly are;
being men rooted out of all the kindly parts of life, and condemned to toss together on the rough seas, with masters no less
cruel. There were some among them that had sailed with the

* Blow.

pirates and seen things it would be a shame even to speak of; some were men that had run from the king's ships, and went with a halter round their necks, of which they made no secret; and all, as the saying goes, were 'at a word and a blow' with their best friends. Yet I had not been many days shut up with them before I began to be ashamed of my first judgment, when I had drawn away from them at the Ferry pier, as though they had been unclean beasts. No class of man is altogether bad; but each has its own faults and virtues; and these shipmates of mine were no exception to the rule. Rough they were, sure enough; and bad, I suppose; but they had many virtues. They were kind when it occurred to them, simple even beyond the simplicity of a country lad like me, and had some glimmerings of honesty.

There was one man of maybe forty, that would sit on my berthside for hours, and tell me of his wife and child. He was a fisher that had lost his boat, and thus been driven to the deep-sea voyaging. Well, it is years ago now; but I have never forgotten him. His wife (who was 'young by him', as he often told me) waited in vain to see her man return; he would never again make the fire for her in the morning, nor yet keep the bairn when she was sick. Indeed, many of these poor fellows (as the event proved) were upon their last cruise; the deep seas and cannibal fish received them; and it is a thankless business to speak ill of the dead.

Among other good deeds that they did, they returned my money, which had been shared among them; and though it was about a third short, I was very glad to get it, and hoped great good from it in the land I was going to. The ship was bound for the Carolinas; and you must not suppose that I was going to that place merely as an exile. The trade was even then much depressed; since that, and with the rebellion of the colonies and the formation of the United States, it has, of course, come to an end; but in these days of my youth, white men were still sold into slavery on the plantations, and that was the destiny to which my wicked uncle had condemned me.

The cabin-boy Ransome (from whom I had first heard of these atrocities) came in at times from the round-house, where he berthed and served, now nursing a bruised limb in silent agony, now raving against the cruelty of Mr Shuan. It made my heart bleed; but the men had a great respect for the chief mate, who was, as they said, 'the only seaman of the whole jing-bang, and none such a bad man when he was sober'. Indeed, I found there was a strange peculiarity about our two mates: that Mr Riach was sullen, unkind, and harsh when he was sober, and Mr Shuan would not hurt a fly except when he was drinking. I asked about the captain; but I was told drink made no difference upon that man of iron.

I did my best in the small time allowed me to make something like a man, or rather I should say something like a boy, of the poor creature, Ransome. But his mind was scarce truly human. He could remember nothing of the time before he came to sea; only that his father had made clocks, and had a starling in the parlour, which could whistle 'The North Countrie'; all else had been blotted out in these years of hardship and cruelties. He had a strange notion of the dry land, picked up from sailors' stories: that it was a place where lads were put to some kind of slavery called a trade, and where apprentices were continually lashed and clapped into foul prisons. In a town, he thought every second person a decoy, and every third house a place in which seamen would be drugged and murdered. To be sure, I could tell him how kindly I had myself been used upon that dry land he was so much afraid of, and how well fed and carefully taught both by my friends and my parents: and if he had been recently hurt, he would weep bitterly and swear to run away; but if he was in his usual crackbrain humour or (still more) if he had had a glass of spirits in the round-house, he would deride the notion.

It was Mr Riach (Heaven forgive him!) who gave the boy drink; and it was, doubtless, kindly meant; but besides that it was ruin to his health, it was the pitifullest thing in life to see this unhappy, unfriended creature staggering, and dancing, and talking he knew not what. Some of the men laughed, but not all; others would grow as black as thunder (thinking, perhaps, of their own childhood or their own children) and bid him stop that nonsense, and think what he was doing. As for me, I felt ashamed to look at him, and the poor child still comes about me in my dreams.

All this time, you should know, the *Covenant* was meeting continual head-winds and tumbling up and down against head-seas, so that the scuttle was almost constantly shut, and the forecastle lighted only by a swinging lantern on a beam. There was constant labour for all hands; the sails had to be made and shortened every hour; the strain told on the men's temper; there was a growl of quarrelling all day long from berth to berth; and as I was never allowed to set my foot on deck, you can picture to yourselves how weary of my life I grew to be, and how impatient for a change.

And a change I was to get, as you shall hear; but I must first tell of a conversation I had with Mr Riach, which put a little heart in me to bear my troubles. Getting him in a favourable stage of drink (for indeed he never looked near me when he was sober) I pledged him to secrecy, and told him my whole story.

He declared it was like a ballad; that he would do his best to help me; that I should have paper, pen, and ink, and write one line to Mr Campbell and another to Mr Rankeillor; and that if I had told the truth, ten to one he would be able (with their help) to pull me through and set me in my rights.

'And in the meantime,' says he, 'keep your heart up. You're not the only one, I'll tell you that. There's many a man hoeing tobacco over-seas that should be mounting his horse at his own door at home; many and many! And life is all a variorum, at the best. Look at me: I'm a laird's son and more than half a doctor, and here I am, man-Jack to Hoseason!'

I thought it would be civil to ask him for his story.

He whistled loud.

'Never had one,' said he. 'I liked fun, that's all.' And he skipped out of the forecastle.

CHAPTER VIII

The round-house

One night, about twelve o'clock,[13] a man of Mr Riach's watch
(which was on deck) came down for his jacket; and instantly
there began to go a whisper about the forecastle that 'Shuan
had done for him at last'. There was no need of a name; we all
knew who was meant; but we had scarce time to get the idea
rightly in our heads, far less to speak of it, when the scuttle was
again flung open, and Captain Hoseason came down the ladder.
He looked sharply round the bunks in the tossing light of the
lantern; and then, walking straight up to me, he addressed me,
to my surprise, in tones of kindness.

'My man,' said he, 'we want ye to serve in the round-house.
You and Ransome are to change berths. Run away aft with ye.'

Even as he spoke, two seamen appeared in the scuttle, carrying Ransome in their arms; and the ship at that moment giving
a great sheer into the sea, and the lantern swinging, the light
fell direct on the boy's face. It was as white as wax, and had a
look upon it like a dreadful smile. The blood in me ran cold,
and I drew in my breath as if I had been struck.

'Run away aft; run away aft with ye!' cried Hoseason.

And at that I brushed by the sailors and the boy (who neither
spoke nor moved), and ran up the ladder on deck.

The brig was sheering swiftly and giddily through a long,
cresting swell. She was on the starboard tack, and on the left
hand, under the arched foot of the foresail, I could see the
sunset still quite bright. This, at such an hour of the night,
surprised me greatly; but I was too ignorant to draw the true
conclusion – that we were going north-about round Scotland,
and were now on the high sea between the Orkney and the

Shetland Islands, having avoided the dangerous currents of the Pentland Firth. For my part, who had been so long shut in the dark and knew nothing of head-winds, I thought we might be half-way or more across the Atlantic. And indeed (beyond that I wondered a little at the lateness of the sunset light) I gave no heed to it, and pushed on across the decks, running between the seas, catching at ropes, and only saved from going overboard by one of the hands on deck, who had been always kind to me.

The round-house, for which I was bound, and where I was now to sleep and serve, stood some six feet above the decks, and considering the size of the brig, was of good dimensions. Inside were a fixed table and bench, and two berths, one for the captain and the other for the two mates, turn and turn about. It was all fitted with lockers from top to bottom, so as to stow away the officers' belongings and a part of the ship's stores; there was a second store-room underneath, which you entered by a hatchway in the middle of the deck; indeed, all the best of the meat and drink and the whole of the powder were collected in this place; and all the firearms, except the two pieces of brass ordnance, were set in a rack in the aftermost wall of the round-house. The most of the cutlasses were in another place.

A small window with a shutter on each side, and a skylight in the roof, gave it light by day; and after dark, there was a lamp always burning. It was burning when I entered, not brightly, but enough to show Mr Shuan sitting at the table, with the brandy bottle and a tin pannikin in front of him. He was a tall man, strongly made and very black; and he stared before him on the table like one stupid.

He took no notice of my coming in; nor did he move when the captain followed and leant on the berth beside me, looking darkly at the mate. I stood in great fear of Hoseason, and had my reasons for it; but something told me I need not be afraid of him just then; and I whispered in his ear, 'How is he?' He shook his head like one that does not know and does not wish to think, and his face was very stern.

Presently Mr Riach came in. He gave the captain a glance that meant the boy was dead as plain as speaking, and took his place like the rest of us; so that we all three stood without a word, staring down at Mr Shuan, and Mr Shuan (on his side) sat without a word, looking hard upon the table.

All of a sudden he put out his hand to take the bottle; and at that Mr Riach started forward and caught it away from him, rather by surprise than violence, crying out, with an oath, that there had been too much of this work altogether, and that a judgment would fall upon the ship. And as he spoke (the weather sliding-doors standing open) he tossed the bottle into the sea.

Mr Shuan was on his feet in a trice; he still looked dazed, but he meant murder, ay, and would have done it, for the second time that night, had not the captain stepped in between him and his victim.

'Sit down!' roars the captain. 'Ye sot and swine, do ye know what ye've done? Ye've murdered the boy!'

Mr Shuan seemed to understand; for he sat down again and put up his hand to his brow.

'Well,' he said, 'he brought me a dirty pannikin!'

At that word, the captain and I and Mr Riach all looked at each other for a second with a kind of frightened look; and then Hoseason walked up to his chief officer, took him by the shoulder, led him across to his bunk, and bade him lie down and go to sleep, as you might speak to a bad child. The murderer cried a little, but he took off his sea-boots and obeyed.

'Ah!' cried Mr Riach, with a dreadful voice, 'ye should have interfered long syne. It's too late now.'

'Mr Riach,' said the captain, 'this night's work must never be kennt in Dysart. The boy went overboard, sir; that's what the story is; and I would give five pounds out of my pocket it was true!' He turned to the table. 'What made ye throw the good bottle away?' he added. 'There was nae sense in that, sir. Here, David, draw me another. They're in the bottom locker;' and he tossed me a key. 'Ye'll need a glass yourself, sir,' he added, to Riach. 'Yon was an ugly thing to see.'

So the pair sat down and hob-a-nobbed; and while they did so, the murderer, who had been lying and whimpering in his berth, raised himself upon his elbow and looked at them and at me.

That was the first night of my new duties; and in the course of the next day I had got well into the run of them. I had to serve at the meals, which the captain took at regular hours, sitting down with the officer who was off duty; all the day through I would be running with a dram to one or other of my three masters; and at night I slept on a blanket thrown on the deck boards at the aftermost end of the round-house, and right in the draught of the two doors. It was a hard and a cold bed; nor was I suffered to sleep without interruption; for some one would be always coming in from deck to get a dram, and when a fresh watch was to be set, two and sometimes all three would sit down and brew a bowl together. How they kept their health, I know not, any more than how I kept my own.

And yet in other ways it was an easy service. There was no cloth to lay; the meals were either of oatmeal porridge or salt junk, except twice a week, when there was duff: and though I was clumsy enough and (not being firm on my sea-legs) sometimes fell with what I was bringing them, both Mr Riach and the captain were singularly patient. I could not but fancy they were making up lee-way with their consciences, and that they would scarce have been so good with me if they had not been worse with Ransome.

As for Mr Shuan, the drink, or his crime, or the two together, had certainly troubled his mind. I cannot say I ever saw him in his proper wits. He never grew used to my being there, stared at me continually (sometimes, I could have thought, with terror) and more than once drew back from my hand when I was serving him. I was pretty sure from the first that he had no clear mind of what he had done; and on my second day in the round-house I had the proof of it. We were alone, and he had been staring at me a long time, when, all at once, up he got, as pale as death, and came close up to me, to my great terror. But I had no cause to be afraid of him.

'You were not here before?' he asked.

'No, sir,' said I.

'There was another boy?' he asked again; and when I had answered him, 'Ah!' says he, 'I thought that,' and went and sat down, without another word, except to call for brandy.

You may think it strange, but for all the horror I had, I was still sorry for him. He was a married man, with a wife in Leith; but whether or no he had a family, I have now forgotten; I hope not.

Altogether it was no very hard life for the time it lasted, which (as you are to hear) was not long. I was as well fed as the best of them; even their pickles, which were the great dainty, I was allowed my share of; and had I liked, I might have been drunk from morning to night, like Mr Shuan. I had company, too, and good company of its sort. Mr Riach, who had been to the college, spoke to me like a friend when he was not sulking, and told me many curious things, and some that were informing; and even the captain, though he kept me at the stick's end the most part of the time, would sometimes unbuckle a bit, and tell me of the fine countries he had visited.

The shadow of poor Ransome, to be sure, lay on all four of us, and on me and Mr Shuan, in particular, most heavily. And then I had another trouble of my own. Here I was, doing dirty work for three men that I looked down upon, and one of whom, at least, should have hung upon a gallows; that was for the present; and as for the future, I could only see myself slaving alongside of negroes in the tobacco fields. Mr Riach, perhaps from caution, would never suffer me to say another word about my story; the captain, whom I tried to approach, rebuffed me like a dog and would not hear a word; and as the days came and went, my heart sank lower and lower, till I was even glad of the work which kept me from thinking.

CHAPTER IX

The man with the belt of gold

More than a week went by, in which the ill-luck that had hitherto pursued the *Covenant* upon this voyage grew yet more strongly marked. Some days she made a little way; others, she was driven actually back. At last we were beaten so far to the south that we tossed and tacked to and fro the whole of the ninth day, within sight of Cape Wrath and the wild, rocky coast on either hand of it. There followed on that a council of the officers, and some decision which I did not rightly understand, seeing only the result: that we had made a fair wind of a foul one and were running south.

The tenth afternoon, there was a falling swell and a thick, wet, white fog that hid one end of the brig from the other. All afternoon, when I went on deck, I saw men and officers listening hard over the bulwarks – 'for breakers', they said; and though I did not so much as understand the word, I felt danger in the air, and was excited.

May-be about ten at night, I was serving Mr Riach and the captain at their supper, when the ship struck something with a great sound, and we heard voices singing out. My two masters leaped to their feet.

'She's struck,' said Mr Riach.

'No, sir,' said the captain. 'We've only run a boat down.'

And they hurried out.

The captain was in the right of it. We had run down a boat in the fog, and she had parted in the midst and gone to the bottom with all her crew, but one. This man (as I heard afterwards) had been sitting in the stern as a passenger, while the rest were on the benches rowing. At the moment of the blow, the stern had been thrown into the air, and the man (having his hands free, and for all he was encumbered with a frieze overcoat that came below his knees) had leaped up and caught hold of the brig's bowsprit. It showed he had luck and much agility and unusual strength, that he should have thus saved himself from such a pass. And yet, when the captain brought him into the round-house, and I set eyes on him for the first time, he looked as cool as I did.

He was smallish in stature,[14] but well set and as nimble as a goat; his face was of a good open expression, but sunburnt very dark, and heavily freckled and pitted with the small-pox; his eyes were unusually light and had a kind of dancing madness in them, that was both engaging and alarming; and when he took off his great-coat, he laid a pair of fine, silver-mounted pistols on the table, and I saw that he was belted with a great sword. His manners, besides, were elegant, and he pledged the captain handsomely. Altogether I thought of him, at the first sight, that here was a man I would rather call my friend than my enemy.

The captain, too, was taking his observations, but rather of the man's clothes than his person. And to be sure, as soon as he had taken off the great-coat, he showed forth mighty fine for the round-house of a merchant brig: having a hat with feathers, a red waistcoat, breeches of black plush, and a blue coat with silver buttons and handsome silver lace: costly clothes, though somewhat spoiled with the fog and being slept in.

'I'm vexed, sir, about the boat,' says the captain.

'There are some pretty men gone to the bottom,' said the stranger, 'that I would rather see on the dry land again than half a score of boats.'

'Friends of yours?' said Hoseason.

'You have none such friends in your country,' was the reply. 'They would have died for me like dogs.'

'Well, sir,' said the captain, still watching him, 'there are more men in the world than boats to put them in.'

'And that's true too,' cried the other, 'and ye seem to be a gentleman of great penetration.'

'I have been in France, sir,' says the captain, so that it was plain he meant more by the words than showed upon the face of them.

'Well, sir,' says the other, 'and so has many a pretty man, for the matter of that.'

'No doubt, sir,' says the captain; 'and fine coats.'

'Oho!' says the stranger, 'is that how the wind sets?' And he laid his hand quickly on his pistols.

'Don't be hasty,' said the captain. 'Don't do a mischief, before ye see the need for it. Ye've a French soldier's coat upon your back and a Scotch tongue in your head, to be sure; but so has many an honest fellow in these days, and I dare say none the worse of it.'

'So?' said the gentleman in the fine coat: 'are ye of the honest party?' (meaning, Was he a Jacobite? for each side, in these sort of civil broils, takes the name of honesty for its own).

'Why, sir,' replied the captain, 'I am a true-blue Protestant, and I thank God for it.' (It was the first word of any religion I had ever heard from him, but I learnt afterwards he was a great church-goer while on shore.) 'But, for all that,' says he, 'I can be sorry to see another man with his back to the wall.'

'Can ye so, indeed?' asks the Jacobite. 'Well, sir, to be quite plain with ye, I am one of those honest gentlemen that were in trouble about the years forty-five and six; and (to be still quite plain with ye) if I got into the hands of any of the red-coated gentry, it's like it would go hard with me. Now, sir, I was for France; and there was a French ship cruising here to pick me up; but she gave us the go-by in the fog – as I wish from the heart that ye had done yoursel'! And the best that I can say is this: If ye can set me ashore where I was going, I have that upon me will reward you highly for your trouble.'

'In France?' says the captain. 'No, sir; that I cannot do. But where ye come from – we might talk of that.'

And then, unhappily, he observed me standing in my corner, and packed me off to the galley to get supper for the gentleman. I lost no time, I promise you; and when I came back into the round-house, I found the gentleman had taken a money-belt from about his waist, and poured out a guinea or two upon the

table. The captain was looking at the guineas, and then at the
belt, and then at the gentleman's face; and I thought he seemed
excited.

'Half of it,' he cried, 'and I'm your man!'

The other swept back the guineas into the belt, and put it
on again under his waistcoat. 'I have told ye, sir,' said he, 'that
not one doit of it belongs to me. It belongs to my chieftain' –
and here he touched his hat – 'and while I would be but a silly
messenger to grudge some of it that the rest might come safe, I
should show myself a hound indeed if I bought my own carcase
any too dear. Thirty guineas on the sea-side, or sixty if ye set
me on the Linnhe loch. Take it, if ye will; if not, ye can do your
worst.'

'Ay,' said Hoseason. 'And if I give ye over to the soldiers?'

'Ye would make a fool's bargain,' said the other. 'My chief,
let me tell you, sir, is forfeited, like every honest man in Scotland. His estate is in the hands of the man they call King George;
and it is his officers that collect the rents, or try to collect them.
But for the honour of Scotland, the poor tenant bodies take a
thought upon their chief lying in exile; and this money is a part
of that very rent for which King George is looking. Now, sir,
ye seem to me to be a man that understands things: bring this
money within the reach of Government, and how much of it'll
come to you?'

'Little enough, to be sure,' said Hoseason; and then, 'If they
knew,' he added, dryly. 'But I think, if I was to try, that I could
hold my tongue about it.'

'Ah, but I'll begowk* ye there!' cried the gentleman. 'Play
me false, and I'll play you cunning. If a hand's laid upon me,
they shall ken what money it is.'

'Well,' returned the captain, 'what must be must. Sixty
guineas, and done. Here's my hand upon it.'

'And here's mine,' said the other.

And thereupon the captain went out (rather hurriedly, I
thought), and left me alone in the round-house with the stranger.

At that period (so soon after the forty-five) there were many

* Befool.

exiled gentlemen coming back at the peril of their lives, either
to see their friends or to collect a little money; and as for the
Highland chiefs that had been forfeited, it was a common matter of talk how their tenants would stint themselves to send
them money, and their clansmen outface the soldiery to get it
in, and run the gauntlet of our great navy to carry it across. All
this I had, of course, heard tell of; and now I had a man under
my eyes whose life was forfeit on all these counts and upon one
more; for he was not only a rebel and a smuggler of rents, but
had taken service with King Louis of France. And as if all this
were not enough, he had a belt full of golden guineas round his
loins. Whatever my opinions, I could not look on such a man
without a lively interest.

'And so you're a Jacobite?' said I, as I set meat before him.

'Ay,' said he, beginning to eat. 'And you, by your long face,
should be a Whig?'*

'Betwixt and between,' said I, not to annoy him; for indeed
I was as good a Whig as Mr Campbell could make me.

'And that's naething,' said he. 'But I'm saying, Mr Betwixt-
and-Between,' he added, 'this bottle of yours is dry; and it's
hard if I'm to pay sixty guineas and be grudged a dram upon
the back of it.'

'I'll go and ask for the key,' said I, and stepped on deck.

The fog was as close as ever, but the swell almost down. They
had laid the brig to, not knowing precisely where they were,
and the wind (what little there was of it) not serving well for
their true course. Some of the hands were still hearkening for
breakers; but the captain and the two officers were in the waist
with their heads together. It struck me, I don't know why, that
they were after no good; and the first word I heard, as I drew
softly near, more than confirmed me.

It was Mr Riach, crying out as if upon a sudden thought:

'Couldn't we wile him out of the round-house?'

'He's better where he is,' returned Hoseason; 'he hasn't room
to use his sword.'

* Whig or Whigamore was the cant name for those who were loyal to King
George.

'Well, that's true,' said Riach; 'but he's hard to come at.'

'Hut!' said Hoseason. 'We can get the man in talk, one upon each side, and pin him by the two arms; or if that'll not hold, sir, we can make a run by both the doors and get him under hand before he has the time to draw.'

At this hearing, I was seized with both fear and anger at these treacherous, greedy, bloody men that I sailed with. My first mind was to run away; my second was bolder.

'Captain,' said I, 'the gentleman is seeking a dram, and the bottle's out. Will you give me the key?'

They all started and turned about.

'Why, here's our chance to get the firearms!' Riach cried; and then to me: 'Hark ye, David,' he said, 'do ye ken where the pistols are?'

'Ay, ay,' put in Hoseason. 'David kens; David's a good lad. Ye see, David my man, yon wild Hielandman is a danger to the ship, besides being a rank foe to King George, God bless him!'

I had never been so be-Davided since I came on board; but I said yes, as if all I heard were quite natural.

'The trouble is,' resumed the captain, 'that all our firelocks, great and little, are in the round-house under this man's nose; likewise the powder. Now, if I, or one of the officers, was to go in and take them, he would fall to thinking. But a lad like you, David, might snap up a horn and a pistol or two without remark. And if ye can do it cleverly, I'll bear it in mind when it'll be good for you to have friends; and that's when we come to Carolina.'

Here Mr Riach whispered him a little.

'Very right, sir,' said the captain; and then to myself: 'And see here, David, yon man has a beltful of gold, and I give you my word that you shall have your fingers in it.'

I told him I would do as he wished, though indeed I had scarce breath to speak with; and upon that he gave me the key of the spirit locker, and I began to go slowly back to the round-house. What was I to do? They were dogs and thieves; they had stolen me from my own country; they had killed poor Ransome; and was I to hold the candle to another murder? But then, upon the other hand, there was the fear of death very plain before me; for what could a boy and a man, if they were as brave as lions, against a whole ship's company?

I was still arguing it back and forth, and getting no great clearness, when I came into the round-house and saw the Jacobite eating his supper under the lamp; and at that my mind was made up all in a moment. I have no credit by it; it was by no choice of mine, but as if by compulsion, that I walked right up to the table and put my hand on his shoulder.

'Do ye want to be killed?' said I.

He sprang to his feet, and looked a question at me as clear as if he had spoken.

'Oh!' cried I, 'they're all murderers here; it's a ship full of them! They've murdered a boy already. Now it's you.'

'Ay, ay,' said he; 'but they haven't got me yet.' And then looking at me curiously, 'Will ye stand with me?'

'That will I!' said I. 'I am no thief, nor yet murderer. I'll stand by you.'

'Why, then,' said he, 'what's your name?'

'David Balfour,' said I; and then thinking that a man with so fine a coat must like fine people, I added for the first time 'of Shaws'.

It never occurred to him to doubt me, for a Highlander is used to see great gentlefolk in great poverty; but as he had no estate of his own, my words nettled a very childish vanity he had.

'My name is Stewart,' he said, drawing himself up. 'Alan Breck, they call me. A king's name is good enough for me,[15] though I bear it plain and have the name of no farm-midden to clap to the hind-end of it.'

And having administered this rebuke, as though it were something of a chief importance, he turned to examine our defences.

The round-house was built very strong, to support the breaching of the seas. Of its five apertures, only the skylight and the two doors were large enough for the passage of a man. The doors, besides, could be drawn close: they were of stout oak, and ran in grooves, and were fitted with hooks to keep them either shut or open, as the need arose. The one that was already shut, I secured in this fashion; but when I was proceeding to slide to the other, Alan stopped me.

'David,' said he – 'for I cannae bring to mind the name of your landed estate, and so will make so bold as call you David – that door, being open, is the best part of my defences.'

'It would be yet better shut,' says I.

'Not so, David,' says he. 'Ye see, I have but one face; but so long as that door is open and my face to it, the best part of my enemies will be in front of me, where I would aye wish to find them.'

Then he gave me from the rack a cutlass (of which there were a few besides the firearms), choosing it with great care, shaking his head and saying he had never in all his life seen poorer weapons; and next he set me down to the table with a powder-horn, a bag of bullets, and all the pistols, which he bade me charge.

'And that will be better work, let me tell you,' said he, 'for a gentleman of decent birth, than scraping plates and raxing* drams to a wheen tarry sailors.'

Thereupon he stood up in the midst with his face to the door, and drawing his great sword, made trial of the room he had to wield it in.

'I must stick to the point,' he said, shaking his head; 'and that's a pity, too. It doesn't set my genius, which is all for the upper guard. And now,' said he, 'do you keep on charging the pistols, and give heed to me.'

I told him I would listen closely. My chest was tight, my mouth dry, the light dark to my eyes; the thought of the numbers that were soon to leap in upon us kept my heart in a flutter; and the sea, which I heard washing round the brig, and where I thought my dead body would be cast ere morning, ran in my mind strangely.

'First of all,' said he, 'how many are against us?'

I reckoned them up; and such was the hurry of my mind, I had to cast the numbers twice. 'Fifteen,' said I.

* Reaching.

Alan whistled. 'Well,' said he, 'that can't be cured. And now follow me. It is my part to keep this door, where I look for the main battle. In that, ye have no hand. And mind and dinnae fire to this side unless they get me down; for I would rather have ten foes in front of me than one friend like you cracking pistols at my back.'

I told him, indeed I was no great shot.

'And that's very bravely said,' he cried, in a great admiration of my candour. 'There's many a pretty gentleman that wouldnae dare to say it.'

'But then, sir,' said I, 'there is the door behind you, which they may perhaps break in.'

'Ay,' said he, 'and that is a part of your work. No sooner the pistols charged, than ye must climb up into yon bed where ye're handy at the window; and if they lift hand against the door, ye're to shoot. But that's not all. Let's make a bit of a soldier of ye, David. What else have ye to guard?'

'There's the skylight,' said I. 'But indeed, Mr Stewart, I would need to have eyes upon both sides to keep the two of them; for when my face is at the one, my back is to the other.'

'And that's very true,' said Alan. 'But have ye no ears to your head?'

'To be sure!' cried I. 'I must hear the bursting of the glass!'

'Ye have some rudiments of sense,' said Alan, grimly.

CHAPTER X

The siege of the round-house

But now our time of truce was come to an end. Those on deck had waited for my coming till they grew impatient; and scarce had Alan spoken, when the captain showed face in the open door.

'Stand!' cried Alan, and pointed his sword at him.

The captain stood, indeed; but he neither winced nor drew back a foot.

'A naked sword?' says he. 'This is a strange return for hospitality.'

'Do ye see me?' said Alan. 'I am come of kings; I bear a king's name. My badge is the oak. Do ye see my sword? It has slashed the heads off mair Whigamores than you have toes upon your feet. Call up your vermin to your back, sir, and fall on! The sooner the clash begins, the sooner ye'll taste this steel throughout your vitals.'

The captain said nothing to Alan, but he looked over at me with an ugly look. 'David,' said he, 'I'll mind this'; and the sound of his voice went through me with a jar.

Next moment he was gone.

'And now,' said Alan, 'let your hand keep your head, for the grip is coming.'

Alan drew a dirk, which he held in his left hand in case they should run in under his sword. I, on my part, clambered up into the berth with an armful of pistols and something of a heavy heart, and set open the window where I was to watch. It was a small part of the deck that I could overlook, but enough for our purpose. The sea had gone down, and the wind was steady and kept the sails quiet; so that there was a great stillness in the ship, in which I made sure I heard the sound of muttering voices. A little after, and there came a clash of steel upon the deck, by which I knew they were dealing out the cutlasses and one had been let fall; and after that, silence again.

I do not know if I was what you call afraid; but my heart beat like a bird's, both quick and little; and there was a dimness came before my eyes which I continually rubbed away, and which continually returned. As for hope, I had none; but only a darkness of despair and a sort of anger against all the world that made me long to sell my life as dear as I was able. I tried to pray, I remember, but that same hurry of my mind, like a man running, would not suffer me to think upon the words; and my chief wish was to have the thing begin and be done with it.

It came all of a sudden when it did, with a rush of feet and a roar, and then a shout from Alan, and a sound of blows and some one crying out as if hurt. I looked back over my shoulder, and saw Mr Shuan in the doorway, crossing blades with Alan.

'That's him that killed the boy!' I cried.

'Look to your window!' said Alan; and as I turned back to my place, I saw him pass his sword through the mate's body.

It was none too soon for me to look to my own part; for my head was scarce back at the window, before five men carrying a spare yard for a battering-ram, ran past me and took post to drive the door in. I had never fired with a pistol in my life, and not often with a gun; far less against a fellow-creature. But it was now or never; and just as they swang the yard, I cried out, 'Take that!' and shot into their midst.

I must have hit one of them, for he sang out and gave back a step, and the rest stopped as if a little disconcerted. Before they had time to recover, I sent another ball over their heads; and at my third shot (which went as wide as the second) the whole party threw down the yard and ran for it.

Then I looked round again into the deck-house. The whole place was full of the smoke of my own firing, just as my ears seemed to be burst with the noise of the shots. But there was Alan, standing as before; only now his sword was running blood to the hilt, and himself so swelled with triumph and fallen into so fine an attitude, that he looked to be invincible. Right before him on the floor was Mr Shuan, on his hands and knees; the blood was pouring from his mouth, and he was sinking slowly lower, with a terrible, white face; and just as I looked, some of those from behind caught hold of him by the heels and dragged him bodily out of the round-house. I believe he died as they were doing it.

'There's one of your Whigs for ye!' cried Alan; and then turning to me, he asked if I had done much execution.

I told him I had winged one, and thought it was the captain.

'And I've settled two,' says he. 'No, there's not enough blood let; they'll be back again. To your watch, David. This was but a dram before meat.'

I settled back to my place, re-charging the three pistols I had fired, and keeping watch with both eye and ear.

Our enemies were disputing not far off upon the deck, and that so loudly that I could hear a word or two above the washing of the seas.

'It was Shuan bauchled* it,' I heard one say.

And another answered him with a 'Wheesht, man! He's paid the piper.'

After that the voices fell again into the same muttering as before. Only now, one person spoke most of the time, as though laying down a plan, and first one and then another answered him briefly, like men taking orders. By this, I made sure they were coming on again, and told Alan.

'It's what we have to pray for,' said he. 'Unless we can give them a good distaste of us, and done with it, there'll be nae sleep for either you or me. But this time, mind, they'll be in earnest.'

By this, my pistols were ready, and there was nothing to do but listen and wait. While the brush lasted, I had not the time to think if I was frighted; but now, when all was still again, my mind ran upon nothing else. The thought of the sharp swords and the cold steel was strong in me; and presently, when I began to hear stealthy steps and a brushing of men's clothes

* Bungled.

against the round-house wall, and knew they were taking their places in the dark, I could have found it in my mind to cry out aloud.

All this was upon Alan's side; and I had begun to think my share of the fight was at an end, when I heard some one drop softly on the roof above me.

Then there came a single call on the sea-pipe, and that was the signal. A knot of them made one rush of it, cutlass in hand, against the door; and at the same moment, the glass of the skylight was dashed in a thousand pieces, and a man leaped through and landed on the floor. Before he got his feet, I had clapped a pistol to his back, and might have shot him, too; only at the touch of him (and him alive) my whole flesh misgave me, and I could no more pull the trigger than I could have flown.

He had dropped his cutlass as he jumped, and when he felt the pistol, whipped straight round and laid hold of me, roaring out an oath; and at that either my courage came again, or I grew so much afraid as came to the same thing; for I gave a shriek and shot him in the midst of the body. He gave the most horrible, ugly groan and fell to the floor. The foot of a second fellow, whose legs were dangling through the skylight, struck me at the same time upon the head; and at that I snatched another pistol and shot this one through the thigh, so that he slipped through and tumbled in a lump on his companion's body. There was no talk of missing, any more than there was time to aim; I clapped the muzzle to the very place and fired.

I might have stood and stared at them for long, but I heard Alan shout as if for help, and that brought me to my senses.

He had kept the door so long; but one of the seamen, while he was engaged with others, had run in under his guard and caught him about the body. Alan was dirking him with his left hand, but the fellow clung like a leech. Another had broken in and had his cutlass raised. The door was thronged with their faces. I thought we were lost, and catching up my cutlass, fell on them in flank.

But I had not time to be of help. The wrestler dropped at last; and Alan, leaping back to get his distance, ran upon the others like a bull, roaring as he went. They broke before him

like water, turning, and running, and falling one against another
in their haste. The sword in his hands flashed like quicksilver
into the huddle of our fleeing enemies; and at every flash there
came the scream of a man hurt. I was still thinking we were
lost, when lo! they were all gone, and Alan was driving them
along the deck as a sheepdog chases sheep.

Yet he was no sooner out than he was back again, being as
cautious as he was brave; and meanwhile the seamen continued
running and crying out as if he was still behind them; and we
heard them tumble one upon another into the forecastle, and
clap-to the hatch upon the top.

The round-house was like a shambles; three were dead inside,
another lay in his death agony across the threshold; and there
were Alan and I victorious and unhurt.

He came up to me with open arms. 'Come to my arms!' he
cried, and embraced and kissed me hard upon both cheeks.
'David,' said he, 'I love you like a brother. And oh, man,' he
cried in a kind of ecstasy, 'am I no a bonny fighter?'

Thereupon he turned to the four enemies, passed his sword
clean through each of them, and tumbled them out of doors
one after the other. As he did so, he kept humming and singing
and whistling to himself, like a man trying to recall an air; only
what *he* was trying, was to make one. All the while, the flush
was in his face, and his eyes were as bright as a five-year-old
child's with a new toy. And presently he sat down upon the
table, sword in hand; the air that he was making all the time
began to run a little clearer, and then clearer still; and then out
he burst with a great voice into a Gaelic song.

I have translated it here, not in verse (of which I have no
skill) but at least in the king's English. He sang it often afterwards, and the thing became popular; so that I have heard it,
and had it explained to me, many's the time.

> This is the song of the sword of Alan:
> The smith made it,
> The fire set it;
> Now it shines in the hand of Alan Breck.

Their eyes were many and bright,
Swift were they to behold,
Many the hands they guided:
The sword was alone.

The dun deer troop over the hill,
They are many, the hill is one;
The dun deer vanish,
The hill remains.

Come to me from the hills of heather,
Come from the isles of the sea.
O far-beholding eagles,
Here is your meat.

Now this song which he made (both words and music) in the hour of our victory, is something less than just to me, who stood beside him in the tussle. Mr Shuan and five more were either killed outright or thoroughly disabled; but of these, two fell by my hand, the two that came by the skylight. Four more were hurt, and of that number, one (and he not the least important) got his hurt from me. So that, altogether, I did my fair share both of the killing and the wounding, and might have claimed a place in Alan's verses. But poets (as a very wise man once told me) have to think upon their rhymes; and in good prose talk, Alan always did me more than justice.

In the meanwhile, I was innocent of any wrong being done me. For not only I knew no word of the Gaelic; but what with the long suspense of the waiting, and the scurry and strain of our two spirts of fighting, and, more than all, the horror I had of some of my own share in it, the thing was no sooner over than I was glad to stagger to a seat. There was that tightness on my chest that I could hardly breathe; the thought of the two men I had shot sat upon me like a nightmare; and all upon a sudden, and before I had a guess of what was coming, I began to sob and cry like any child.

Alan clapped my shoulder, and said I was a brave lad and wanted nothing but a sleep.

'I'll take the first watch,' said he. 'Ye've done well by me, David, first and last; and I wouldn't lose you for all Appin – no, nor for Breadalbane.'

So he made up my bed on the floor, and took the first spell, pistol in hand and sword on knee; three hours by the captain's watch upon the wall. Then he roused me up, and I took my turn of three hours; before the end of which it was broad day, and a very quiet morning, with a smooth, rolling sea that tossed the ship and made the blood run to and fro on the round-house floor, and a heavy rain that drummed upon the roof. All my watch there was nothing stirring; and by the banging of the helm, I knew they had even no one at the tiller. Indeed (as I learned afterwards) they were so many of them hurt or dead, and the rest in so ill a temper, that Mr Riach and the captain had to take turn and turn like Alan and me, or the brig might have gone ashore and nobody the wiser. It was a mercy the night had fallen so still, for the wind had gone down as soon as the rain began. Even as it was, I judged by the wailing of a great number of gulls that went crying and fishing round the ship, that she must have drifted pretty near the coast or one of the islands of the Hebrides; and at last, looking out of the door of the round-house, I saw the great stone hills of Skye on the right hand, and, a little more astern, the strange isle of Rum.

CHAPTER XI

The captain knuckles under

Alan and I sat down to breakfast about six of the clock. The floor was covered with broken glass and in a horrid mess of blood, which took away my hunger. In all other ways we were in a situation not only agreeable but merry; having ousted the officers from their own cabin, and having at command all the drink in the ship – both wine and spirits – and all the dainty part of what was eatable, such as the pickles and the fine sort of biscuit. This, of itself, was enough to set us in good humour; but the richest part of it was this, that the two thirstiest men that ever came out of Scotland (Mr Shuan being dead) were now shut in the fore-part of the ship and condemned to what they hated most – cold water.

'And depend upon it,' Alan said, 'we shall hear more of them ere long. Ye may keep a man from the fighting but never from his bottle.'

We made good company for each other. Alan, indeed, expressed himself most lovingly; and taking a knife from the table, cut me off one of the silver buttons from his coat.

'I had them,' says he, 'from my father, Duncan Stewart; and now give ye one of them to be a keepsake for last night's work. And wherever ye go and show that button, the friends of Alan Breck will come around you.'

He said this as if he had been Charlemagne, and commanded armies; and indeed, much as I admired his courage, I was always in danger of smiling at his vanity: in danger, I say, for had I not kept my countenance, I would be afraid to think what a quarrel might have followed.

As soon as we were through with our meal, he rummaged in the captain's locker till he found a clothes-brush; and then taking off his coat, began to visit his suit and brush away the stains, with such care and labour as I supposed to have been only usual with women. To be sure, he had no other; and besides (as he said) it belonged to a King and so behoved to be royally looked after.

For all that, when I saw what care he took to pluck out the threads where the button had been cut away, I put a higher value on his gift.

He was still so engaged, when we were hailed by Mr Riach from the deck, asking for a parley; and I, climbing through the skylight and sitting on the edge of it, pistol in hand and with a bold front, though inwardly in fear of broken glass, hailed him back again and bade him speak out. He came to the edge of the round-house, and stood on a coil of rope, so that his chin was on a level with the roof; and we looked at each other a while in silence. Mr Riach, as I do not think he had been very forward in the battle, so he had got off with nothing worse than a blow upon the cheek: but he looked out of heart and very weary, having been all night afoot, either standing watch or doctoring the wounded.

'This is a bad job,' said he at last, shaking his head.

'It was none of our choosing,' said I.

'The captain,' says he, 'would like to speak with your friend. They might speak at the window.'

'And how do we know what treachery he means?' cried I.

'He means none, David,' returned Mr Riach; 'and if he did, I'll tell ye the honest truth, we couldnae get the men to follow.'

'Is that so?' said I.

'I'll tell ye more than that,' said he. 'It's not only the men; it's me. I'm frich'ened, Davie.' And he smiled across at me. 'No,' he continued, 'what we want is to be shut of him.'

Thereupon I consulted with Alan, and the parley was agreed to and parole given upon either side; but this was not the whole of Mr Riach's business, and he now begged me for a dram with such instancy and such reminders of his former kindness, that at last I handed him a pannikin with about a gill of brandy. He drank a part, and then carried the rest down upon the deck, to share it (I suppose) with his superior.

A little after, the captain came (as was agreed) to one of the windows, and stood there in the rain, with his arm in a sling, and looking stern and pale, and so old that my heart smote me for having fired upon him.

Alan at once held a pistol in his face.

'Put that thing up!' said the captain. 'Have I not passed my word, sir? or do ye seek to affront me?'

'Captain,' says Alan, 'I doubt your word is a breakable. Last night ye haggled and argle-bargled like an apple-wife; and then passed me your word, gave me your hand to back it; and ye ken very well what was the upshot. Be damned to your word!' says he.

'Well, well, sir,' said the captain, 'ye'll get little good by swearing.' (And truly that was a fault of which the captain was quite free.) 'But we have other things to speak,' he continued, bitterly. 'Ye've made a sore hash of my brig; I haven't hands enough left to work her; and my first officer (whom I could ill spare) has got your sword throughout his vitals, and passed without speech. There is nothing left me, sir, but to put back into the port of Glasgow after hands; and there (by your leave) ye will find them that are better able to talk to you.'

'Ay?' said Alan; 'and faith, I'll have a talk with them mysel'! Unless there's naebody speaks English in that town. I have a bonny tale for them. Fifteen tarry sailors upon the one side, and a man and a halfling boy upon the other! Oh, man, it's peetiful!'

Hoseason flushed red.

'No,' continued Alan, 'that'll no do. Ye'll just have to set me ashore as we agreed.'

'Ay,' said Hoseason, 'but my first officer is dead – ye ken best how. There's none of the rest of us acquaint with this coast, sir; and it's one very dangerous to ships.'

'I give ye your choice,' says Alan. 'Set me on dry ground in Appin, or Ardgour, or in Morven, or Arisaig, or Morar; or, in brief where ye please, within thirty miles of my own country; except in a country of the Campbells'. That's a broad target. If ye miss that, ye must be as feckless at the sailoring as I have found ye at the fighting. Why, my poor country people in their bit cobles* pass from island to island in all weathers, ay, and by night too, for the matter of that.'

'A coble's not a ship, sir,' said the captain. 'It has nae draught of water.'

'Well, then, to Glasgow if ye list!' says Alan. 'We'll have the laugh of ye at the least.'

'My mind runs little upon laughing,' said the captain. 'But all this will cost money, sir.'

'Well, sir,' says Alan, 'I am nae weathercock. Thirty guineas, if ye land me on the sea-side; and sixty, if ye put me in the Linnhe Loch.'

'But see, sir, where we lie, we are but a few hours' sail from Ardnamurchan,' said Hoseason. 'Give me sixty, and I'll set ye there.'

'And I'm to wear my brogues and run jeopardy of the red coats to please you?' cries Alan. 'No, sir, if ye want sixty guineas, earn them, and set me in my own country.'

'It's to risk the brig, sir,' said the captain, 'and your own lives along with her.'

'Take it or want it,' says Alan.

'Could ye pilot us at all?' asked the captain, who was frowning to himself.

'Well, it's doubtful,' said Alan. 'I'm more of a fighting man (as ye have seen for yoursel') than a sailor-man. But I have been often enough picked up and set down upon this coast, and should ken something of the lie of it.'

The captain shook his head, still frowning.

'If I had lost less money on this unchancy cruise,' says he, 'I would see you in a rope's-end before I risked my brig, sir. But be it as ye will. As soon as I get a slant of wind (and there's some coming, or I'm the more mistaken) I'll put it in hand. But there's one thing more. We may meet in with a king's ship and she may lay us aboard, sir, with no blame of mine: they keep

* Coble: a small boat used in fishing.

the cruisers thick upon this coast, ye ken who for. Now, sir, if that was to befall, ye might leave the money.'

'Captain,' says Alan, 'if ye see a pennant, it shall be your part to run away. And now, as I hear you're a little short of brandy in the forepart, I'll offer ye a change: a bottle of brandy against two buckets of water.'

That was the last clause of the treaty, and was duly executed on both sides; so that Alan and I could at last wash out the round-house and be quit of the memorials of those whom we had slain, and the captain and Mr Riach could be happy again in their own way, the name of which was drink.

CHAPTER XII

I hear of the Red Fox

Before we had done cleaning out the round-house, a breeze
sprang up from a little to the east of north. This blew off the
rain and brought out the sun.

And here I must explain; and the reader would do well to
look at a map.[16] On the day when the fog fell and we ran down
Alan's boat, we had been running through the Little Minch. At
dawn after the battle, we lay becalmed to the east of the Isle of
Canna or between that and Isle Eriska in the chain of the Long
Island. Now to get from there to the Linnhe Loch, the straight
course was through the narrows of the Sound of Mull. But the
captain had no chart; he was afraid to trust his brig so deep
among the islands; and the wind serving well, he preferred to
go by west of Tiree and come up under the southern coast of
the great Isle of Mull.

All day the breeze held in the same point, and rather fresh-
ened than died down; and towards afternoon, a swell began to
set in from round the outer Hebrides. Our course, to go round
about the inner isles, was to the west of south, so that at first
we had this swell upon our beam, and were much rolled about.
But after nightfall, when we had turned the end of Tiree and
began to head more to the east, the sea came right astern.

Meanwhile, the early part of the day, before the swell came
up, was very pleasant; sailing, as we were, in a bright sunshine
and with many mountainous islands upon different sides. Alan
and I sat in the round-house with the doors open on each side
(the wind being straight astern) and smoked a pipe or two of
the captain's fine tobacco. It was at this time we heard each
other's stories, which was the more important to me, as I gained

some knowledge of that wild Highland country, on which I was
so soon to land. In those days, so close on the back of the great
rebellion, it was needful a man should know what he was doing
when he went upon the heather.

It was I that showed the example, telling him all my misfortune; which he heard with great good nature. Only, when I
came to mention that good friend of mine, Mr Campbell the
minister, Alan fired up and cried out that he hated all that were
of that name.

'Why,' said I, 'he is a man you should be proud to give your
hand to.'

'I know nothing I would help a Campbell to,' says he, 'unless
it was a leaden bullet. I would hunt all of that name like
blackcocks. If I lay dying, I would crawl upon my knees to my
chamber window for a shot at one.'

'Why, Alan,' I cried, 'what ails ye at the Campbells?'

'Well,' says he, 'ye ken very well that I am an Appin Stewart,[17]
and the Campbells have long harried and wasted those of my
name; ay, and got lands of us by treachery – but never with the
sword,' he cried loudly, and with the word brought down his
fist upon the table. But I paid the less attention to this, for I
knew it was usually said by those who have the underhand.
'There's more than that,' he continued, 'and all in the same
story: lying words, lying papers, tricks fit for a pedlar, and
the show of what's legal over all, to make a man the more
angry.'

'You that are so wasteful of your buttons,' said I, 'I can
hardly think you would be a good judge of business.'

'Ah,' says he, falling again to smiling, 'I got my wastefulness
from the same man I got the buttons from; and that was my
poor father, Duncan Stewart, grace be to him! He was the
prettiest man of his kindred; and the best swordsman in the
Hielands, David, and that is the same as to say, in all the world,
I should ken, for it was him that taught me. He was in the Black
Watch, when first it was mustered; and like other gentleman
privates, had a gillie at his back to carry his firelock for him on
the march. Well, the king, it appears, was wishful to see Hieland
swordsmanship; and my father and three more were chosen out

and sent to London town, to let him see it at the best. So they were had into the palace and showed the whole art of the sword for two hours at a stretch, before King George and Queen Carline, and the Butcher Cumberland, and many more of whom I havenae mind. And when they were through, the King (for all he was a rank usurper) spoke them fair and gave each man three guineas in his hand. Now, as they were going out of the palace, they had a porter's lodge to go by; and it came in on my father, as he was perhaps the first private Hieland gentleman that had ever gone by that door, it was right he should give the poor porter a proper notion of their quality. So he gives the King's three guineas into the man's hand, as if it was his common custom; the three others that came behind him did the same; and there they were on the street, never a penny the better for their pains. Some say it was one, that was the first to fee the King's porter; and some say it was another; but the truth of it is, that it was Duncan Stewart, as I am willing to prove with either sword or pistol. And that was the father that I had, God rest him!'

'I think he was not the man to leave you rich,' said I.

'And that's true,' said Alan. 'He left me my breeks to cover me, and little besides. And that was how I came to enlist, which was a black spot upon my character at the best of times, and would still be a sore job for me if I fell among the red-coats.'

'What,' cried I, 'were you in the English army?'

'That was I,' said Alan. 'But I deserted to the right side at Preston Pans – and that's some comfort.'

I could scarcely share this view: holding desertion under arms for an unpardonable fault in honour. But for all I was so young, I was wiser than say my thought. 'Dear, dear,' says I, 'the punishment is death.'

'Ay,' said he, 'if they got hands on me, it would be a short shrift and a lang tow for Alan! But I have the King of France's commission in my pocket, which would aye be some protection.'

'I misdoubt it much,' said I.

'I have doubts mysel',' said Alan, drily.

'And, good heaven, man,' cried I, 'you that are a condemned

rebel, and a deserter, and a man of the French King's – what tempts ye back into this country? It's a braving of Providence.'

'Tut,' says Alan, 'I have been back every year since forty-six!'

'And what brings ye, man?' cried I.

'Well, ye see, I weary for my friends and country,' said he. 'France is a braw place, nae doubt; but I weary for the heather and the deer. And then I have bit things that I attend to. Whiles I pick up a few lads to serve the King of France: recruits, ye see; and that's aye a little money. But the heart of the matter is the business of my chief, Ardshiel.'

'I thought they called your chief Appin,' said I.

'Ay, but Ardshiel is the captain of the clan,' said he, which scarcely cleared my mind. 'Ye see, David, he that was all his life so great a man, and come of the blood and bearing the name of kings, is now brought down to live in a French town like a poor and private person. He that had four hundred swords at his whistle, I have seen, with these eyes of mine, buying butter in the market-place, and taking it home in a kale-leaf. This is not only a pain but a disgrace to us of his family and clan. There are the bairns forby, the children and the hope of Appin, that must be learned their letters and how to hold a sword, in that far country. Now, the tenants of Appin have to pay a rent to King George; but their hearts are staunch, they are true to their chief; and what with love and a bit of pressure, and maybe a threat or two, the poor folk scrape up a second rent for Ardshiel. Well, David, I'm the hand that carries it.' And he struck the belt about his body, so that the guineas rang.

'Do they pay both?' cried I.

'Ay, David, both,' says he.

'What? two rents?' I repeated.

'Ay, David,' said he. 'I told a different tale to yon captain man; but this is the truth of it. And it's wonderful to me how little pressure is needed. But that's the handiwork of my good kinsman and my father's friend, James of the Glens; James Stewart, that is: Ardshiel's half-brother. He it is that gets the money in, and does the management.'

This was the first time I heard the name of that James Stewart, who was afterwards so famous at the time of his hanging. But

I took little heed at the moment, for all my mind was occupied with the generosity of these poor Highlanders.

'I call it noble,' I cried. 'I'm a Whig, or little better; but I call it noble.'

'Ay,' said he, 'ye're a Whig, but ye're a gentleman; and that's what does it. Now, if ye were one of the cursed race of Campbell, ye would gnash your teeth to hear tell of it. If ye were the Red Fox . . .' And at that name, his teeth shut together, and he ceased speaking. I have seen many a grim face, but never a grimmer than Alan's when he had named the Red Fox.

'And who is the Red Fox?' I asked, daunted, but still curious.

'Who is he?' cried Alan. 'Well, and I'll tell you that. When the men of the clans were broken at Culloden, and the good cause went down, and the horses rode over the fetlocks in the best blood of the north, Ardshiel had to flee like a poor deer upon the mountains – he and his lady and his bairns. A sair job we had of it before we got him shipped; and while he still lay in the heather, the English rogues, that couldnae come at his life, were striking at his rights. They stripped him of his powers; they stripped him of his lands; they plucked the weapons from the hands of his clansmen, that had borne arms for thirty centuries; ay, and the very clothes off their backs – so that it's now a sin to wear a tartan plaid, and a man may be cast into a gaol if he has but a kilt about his legs. One thing they couldnae kill. That was the love the clansmen bore their chief. These guineas are the proof of it. And now, in there steps a man, a Campbell, red-headed Colin of Glenure –'

'Is that him you call the Red Fox?' said I.

'Will ye bring me his brush?'[18] cries Alan, fiercely. 'Ay, that's the man. In he steps, and gets papers from King George, to be so-called King's factor on the lands of Appin. And at first he sings small, and is hail-fellow-well-met with Sheamus – that's James of the Glens, my chieftain's agent. But by-and-bye, that came to his ears that I have just told you; how the poor commons of Appin, the farmers and the crofters and the boumen, were wringing their very plaids to get a second rent, and send it over-seas for Ardshiel and his poor bairns. What was it ye called it, when I told ye?'

'I called it noble, Alan,' said I.

'And you little better than a common Whig!' cries Alan. 'But when it came to Colin Roy, the black Campbell blood in him ran wild. He sat gnashing his teeth at the wine table. What! should a Stewart get a bite of bread, and him not be able to prevent it? Ah! Red Fox, if ever I hold you at a gun's end, the Lord have pity upon ye!' (Alan stopped to swallow down his anger.) 'Well, David, what does he do? He declares all the farms to let. And thinks he, in his black heart, I'll soon get other tenants that'll overbid these Stewarts, and Maccolls, and Macrobs (for these are all names in my clan, David) "and then," thinks he, "Ardshiel will have to hold his bonnet on a French roadside."'

'Well,' said I, 'what followed?'

Alan laid down his pipe, which he had long since suffered to go out, and set his two hands upon his knees.

'Ay,' said he, 'ye'll never guess that! For these same Stewarts, and Maccolls, and Macrobs (that had two rents to pay, one to King George by stark force, and one to Ardshiel by natural kindness), offered him a better price than any Campbell in all broad Scotland; and far he sent seeking them – as far as to the sides of Clyde and the cross of Edinburgh – seeking, and fleeching, and begging them to come, where there was a Stewart to be starved and a red-headed hound of a Campbell to be pleasured!'

'Well, Alan,' said I, 'that is a strange story, and a fine one too. And Whig as I may be, I am glad the man was beaten.'

'Him beaten?' echoed Alan. 'It's little ye ken of Campbells and less of the Red Fox. Him beaten? No: nor will be, till his blood's on the hillside! But if the day comes, David man, that I can find time and leisure for a bit of hunting, there grows not enough heather in all Scotland to hide him from my vengeance!'

'Man Alan,' said I, 'ye are neither very wise nor very Christian to blow off so many words of anger. They will do the man ye call the Fox no harm, and yourself no good. Tell me your tale plainly out. What did he next?'

'And that's a good observe, David,' said Alan. 'Troth and indeed, they will do him no harm; the more's the pity! And barring that about Christianity (of which my opinion is quite otherwise, or I would be nae Christian) I am much of your mind.'

'Opinion here or opinion there,' said I, 'it's a kent thing that Christianity forbids revenge.'

'Ay,' said he, 'it's well seen it was a Campbell taught ye! It would be a convenient world for them and their sort, if there was no such a thing as a lad and a gun behind a heather bush! But that's nothing to the point. This is what he did.'

'Ay,' said I, 'come to that.'

'Well, David,' said he, 'since he couldnae be rid of the loyal commons by fair means, he swore he would be rid of them by foul. Ardshiel was to starve: that was the thing he aimed at. And since them that fed him in his exile wouldnae be bought out – right or wrong, he would drive them out. Therefore he sent for lawyers, and papers, and red-coats to stand at his back. And the kindly folk of that country must all pack and tramp, every father's son out of his father's house, and out of the place where he was bred and fed, and played when he was a callant. And who are to succeed them? Bare-leggit beggars! King George is to whistle for his rents; he maun dow with less; he can spread his butter thinner: what cares Red Colin? If he can hurt Ardshiel, he has his wish; if he can pluck the meat from my chieftain's table, and the bit toys out of his children's hands, he will gang hame singing to Glenure!'

'Let me have a word,' said I. 'Be sure, if they take less rents, be sure Government has a finger in the pie. It's not this Campbell's fault, man – it's his orders. And if ye killed this Colin to-morrow, what better would ye be? There would be another factor in his shoes, as fast as spur can drive.'

'Ye're a good lad in a fight,' said Alan; 'but man! ye have Whig blood in ye!'

He spoke kindly enough, but there was so much anger under his contempt that I thought it was wise to change the conversation. I expressed my wonder how, with the Highlands covered with troops and guarded like a city in a siege, a man in his situation could come and go without arrest.

'It's easier than ye would think,' said Alan. 'A bare hillside (ye see) is like all one road; if there's a sentry at one place, ye just go by another. And then heather's a great help. And everywhere there are friends' houses and friends' byres and haystacks. And besides, when folk talk of a country covered with troops, it's but a kind of a byword at the best. A soldier covers nae mair of it than his boot-soles. I have fished a water with a sentry on the other side of the brae, and killed a fine trout; and I have sat in a heather bush within six feet of another, and learned a real bonny tune from his whistling. This was it,' said he, and whistled me the air.

'And then, besides,' he continued, 'it's no sae bad now as it was in forty-six. The Hielands are what they call pacified. Small wonder, with never a gun or a sword left from Cantyre[19] to Cape Wrath, but what tenty* folk have hidden in their thatch! But what I would like to ken, David, is just how long? Not long, ye would think, with men like Ardshiel in exile and men like the Red Fox sitting birling the wine and oppressing the poor at home. But it's a kittle thing to decide what folk 'll bear, and what they will not. Or why would Red Colin be riding his horse all over my poor country of Appin, and never a pretty lad to put a bullet in him?'

And with this Alan fell into a muse, and for a long time sate very sad and silent.

I will add the rest of what I have to say about my friend, that he was skilled in all kinds of music, but principally pipe-music; was a well-considered poet in his own tongue; had read several books both in French and English; was a dead shot, a good angler, and an excellent fencer with the small sword as well as with his own particular weapon. For his faults, they were on his face, and I now knew them all. But the worst of them, his childish propensity to take offence and to pick quarrels, he greatly laid aside in my case, out of regard for the battle of the round-house. But whether it was because I had done well myself, or because I had been a witness of his own much greater prowess, is more than I can tell. For though he had a great taste for courage in other men, yet he admired it most in Alan Breck.

* Careful.

CHAPTER XIII

The loss of the brig

It was already late at night, and as dark as it ever would be at that season of the year (and that is to say, it was still pretty bright), when Hoseason clapped his head into the round-house door.

'Here,' said he, 'come out and see if ye can pilot.'

'Is this one of your tricks?' asked Alan.

'Do I look like tricks?' cries the captain. 'I have other things to think of – my brig's in danger!'

By the concerned look of his face, and, above all, by the sharp tones in which he spoke of his brig, it was plain to both of us he was in deadly earnest; and so Alan and I, with no great fear of treachery, stepped on deck.

The sky was clear; it blew hard, and was bitter cold; a great deal of daylight lingered; and the moon, which was nearly full, shone brightly. The brig was close hauled, so as to round the south-west corner of the Island of Mull; the hills of which (and Ben More above them all, with a wisp of mist upon the top of it) lay full upon the larboard[20] bow. Though it was no good point of sailing for the *Covenant*, she tore through the seas at a great rate, pitching and straining, and pursued by the westerly swell.

Altogether it was no such ill night to keep the seas in; and I had begun to wonder what it was that sat so heavily upon the captain, when the brig rising suddenly on the top of a high swell, he pointed and cried to us to look. Away on the lee bow, a thing like a fountain rose out of the moonlit sea, and immediately after we heard a low sound of roaring.

'What do ye call that?' asked the captain, gloomily.

'The sea breaking on a reef,' said Alan. 'And now ye ken where it is; and what better would ye have?'

'Ay,' said Hoseason, 'if it was the only one.'

And sure enough just as he spoke there came a second fountain further to the south.

'There!' said Hoseason. 'Ye see for yourself. If I had kent of these reefs, if I had had a chart, or if Shuan had been spared, it's not sixty guineas, no, nor six hundred, would have made me risk my brig in sic a stoneyard! But you, sir, that was to pilot us, have ye never a word?'

'I'm thinking,' said Alan, 'there'll be what they call the Torran Rocks.'[21]

'Are there many of them?' says the captain.

'Truly, sir, I am nae pilot,' said Alan; 'but it sticks in my mind there are ten miles of them.'

Mr Riach and the captain looked at each other.

'There's a way through them, I suppose?' said the captain.

'Doubtless,' said Alan; 'but where? But it somehow runs in my mind once more, that it is clearer under the land.'

'So?' said Hoseason. 'We'll have to haul our wind then, Mr Riach; we'll have to come as near in about the end of Mull as we can take her, sir; and even then we'll have the land to kep the wind off us, and that stoneyard on our lee. Well, we're in for it now, and may as well crack on.'

With that he gave an order to the steersman, and sent Riach to the foretop. There were only five men on deck, counting the officers; these were all that were fit (or, at least, both fit and willing) for their work; and two of these were hurt. So, as I say, it fell to Mr Riach to go aloft, and he sat there looking out and hailing the deck with news of all he saw.

'The sea to the south is thick,' he cried; and then, after a while, 'It does seem clearer in by the land.'

'Well, sir,' said Hoseason to Alan, 'we'll try your way of it. But I think I might as well trust to a blind fiddler. Pray God you're right.'

'Pray God I am!' says Alan to me. 'But where did I hear it? Well, well, it will be as it must.'

As we got nearer to the turn of the land the reefs began to be sown here and there on our very path; and Mr Riach sometimes cried down to us to change the course. Sometimes, indeed, none too soon; for one reef was so close on the brig's weather board that when a sea burst upon it the lighter sprays fell upon her deck and wetted us like rain.

The brightness of the night showed us these perils as clearly as by day, which was, perhaps, the more alarming. It showed me, too, the face of the captain as he stood by the steersman, now on one foot, now on the other, and sometimes blowing in his hands, but still listening and looking and as steady as steel. Neither he nor Mr Riach had shown well in the fighting; but I saw they were brave in their own trade, and admired them all the more because I found Alan very white.

'Ochone, David,' says he, 'this is no the kind of death I fancy.'

'What, Alan!' I cried, 'you're not afraid?'

'No,' said he, wetting his lips, 'but you'll allow yourself, it's a cold ending.'

By this time, now and then sheering to one side or the other to avoid a reef, but still hugging the wind and the land, we had got round Iona and begun to come alongside Mull. The tide at the tail of the land ran very strong, and threw the brig about. Two hands were put to the helm, and Hoseason himself would sometimes lend a help; and it was strange to see three strong men throw their weight upon the tiller, and it (like a living thing) struggle against and drive them back. This would have been the greater danger, had not the sea been for some while free of obstacles. Mr Riach, besides, announced from the top that he saw clear water ahead.

'Ye were right,' said Hoseason to Alan. 'Ye have saved the brig, sir; I'll mind that when we come to clear accounts.' And I believe he not only meant what he said, but would have done it; so high a place did the *Covenant* hold in his affections.

But this is matter only for conjecture, things having gone otherwise than he forecast.

'Keep her away a point,' sings out Mr Riach. 'Reef to windward!'

And just at the same time the tide caught the brig, and threw the wind out of her sails. She came round into the wind like a

top, and the next moment struck the reef with such a dunch as
threw us all flat upon the deck, and came near to shake Mr
Riach from his place upon the mast.

I was on my feet in a minute. The reef on which we had
struck was close in under the south-west end of Mull, off a
little isle they call Earraid, which lay low and black upon the
larboard. Sometimes the swell broke clean over us; sometimes
it only ground the poor brig upon the reef, so that we could
hear her beat herself to pieces; and what with the great noise
of the sails, and the singing of the wind, and the flying of the
spray in the moonlight, and the sense of danger, I think my
head must have been partly turned, for I could scarcely understand the things I saw.

Presently I observed Mr Riach and the seamen busy round
the skiff; and still in the same blank, ran over to assist them;
and as soon as I set my hand to work, my mind came clear
again. It was no very easy task, for the skiff lay amidships
and was full of hamper, and the breaking of the heavier seas
continually forced us to give over and hold on; but we all
wrought like horses while we could.

Meanwhile such of the wounded as could move came clambering out of the fore-scuttle and began to help; while the rest
that lay helpless in their bunks harrowed me with screaming
and begging to be saved.

The captain took no part. It seemed he was struck stupid. He
stood holding by the shrouds, talking to himself and groaning
out aloud whenever the ship hammered on the rock. His brig
was like wife and child to him; he had looked on, day by day,
at the mishandling of poor Ransome; but when it came to the
brig, he seemed to suffer along with her.

All the time of our working at the boat, I remember only one
other thing: that I asked Alan, looking across at the shore, what
country it was; and he answered, it was the worst possible for
him, for it was a land of the Campbells.

We had one of the wounded men told off to keep a watch
upon the seas and cry us warning. Well, we had the boat about
ready to be launched, when this man sang out pretty shrill: 'For
God's sake, hold on!' We knew by his tone that it was something

more than ordinary; and sure enough, there followed a sea so huge that it lifted the brig right up and canted her over on her beam. Whether the cry came too late or my hold was too weak, I know not; but at the sudden tilting of the ship I was cast clean over the bulwarks into the sea.

I went down, and drank my fill; and then came up, and got a blink of the moon; and then down again. They say a man sinks the third time for good. I cannot be made like other folk, then; for I would not like to write how often I went down or how often I came up again. All the while, I was being hurled along, and beaten upon and choked, and then swallowed whole; and the thing was so distracting to my wits, that I was neither sorry nor afraid.

Presently, I found I was holding to a spar, which helped me somewhat. And then all of a sudden I was in quiet water, and began to come to myself.

It was the spare yard I had got hold of, and I was amazed to see how far I had travelled from the brig. I hailed her, indeed; but it was plain she was already out of cry. She was still holding together; but whether or not they had yet launched the boat, I was too far off and too low down to see.

While I was hailing the brig, I spied a tract of water lying between us, where no great waves came, but which yet boiled white all over and bristled in the moon with rings and bubbles. Sometimes the whole tract swung to one side, like the tail of a live serpent; sometimes, for a glimpse, it all would disappear and then boil up again. What it was I had no guess, which for the time increased my fear of it; but I now know it must have been the roost or tide race, which had carried me away so fast and tumbled me about so cruelly, and at last, as if tired of that play, had flung out me and the spare yard upon its landward margin.

I now lay quite becalmed, and began to feel that a man can die of cold as well as of drowning. The shores of Earraid were close in; I could see in the moonlight the dots of heather and the sparkling of the mica in the rocks.

'Well,' thought I to myself, 'if I cannot get as far as that, it's strange!'

I had no skill of swimming, Essen water being small in our neighbourhood; but when I laid hold upon the yard with both arms, and kicked out with both feet, I soon begun to find that I was moving. Hard work it was, and mortally slow; but in about an hour of kicking and splashing, I had got well in between the points of a sandy bay surrounded by low hills.

The sea was here quite quiet; there was no sound of any surf; the moon shone clear; and I thought in my heart I had never seen a place so desert and desolate. But it was dry land; and when at last it grew so shallow that I could leave the yard and wade ashore upon my feet, I cannot tell if I was more tired or more grateful. Both at least, I was: tired as I never was before that night; and grateful to God as I trust I have been often, though never with more cause.

CHAPTER XIV

The islet

With my stepping ashore I began the most unhappy part of my adventures. It was half-past twelve in the morning, and though the wind was broken by the land, it was a cold night. I dared not sit down (for I thought I should have frozen), but took off my shoes and walked to and fro upon the sand, barefoot, and beating my breast, with infinite weariness. There was no sound of man or cattle; not a cock crew, though it was about the hour of their first waking; only the surf broke outside in the distance, which put me in mind of my perils and those of my friend. To walk by the sea at that hour of the morning, and in a place so desert-like and lonesome, struck me with a kind of fear.

As soon as the day began to break I put on my shoes and climbed a hill – the ruggedest scramble I ever undertook – falling, the whole way, between big blocks of granite or leaping from one to another. When I got to the top the dawn was come. There was no sign of the brig, which must have lifted from the reef and sunk. The boat, too, was nowhere to be seen. There was never a sail upon the ocean; and in what I could see of the land, was neither house nor man.

I was afraid to think what had befallen my shipmates, and afraid to look longer at so empty a scene. What with my wet clothes and weariness, and my belly that now began to ache with hunger, I had enough to trouble me without that. So I set off eastward along the south coast, hoping to find a house where I might warm myself, and perhaps get news of those I had lost. And at the worst, I considered the sun would soon rise and dry my clothes.

After a little, my way was stopped by a creek or inlet of the sea, which seemed to run pretty deep into the land; and as I had no means to get across, I must needs change my direction to go about the end of it. It was still the roughest kind of walking; indeed the whole, not only of Earraid, but of the neighbouring part of Mull (which they call the Ross) is nothing but a jumble of granite rocks with heather in among. At first the creek kept narrowing as I had looked to see; but presently to my surprise it began to widen out again. At this I scratched my head, but had still no notion of the truth; until at last I came to a rising ground, and it burst upon me all in a moment that I was cast upon a little, barren isle, and cut off on every side by the salt seas.

Instead of the sun rising to dry me, it came on to rain, with a thick mist; so that my case was lamentable.

I stood in the rain, and shivered, and wondered what to do, till it occurred to me that perhaps the creek was fordable. Back I went to the narrowest point and waded in. But not three yards from shore, I plumped in head over ears; and if ever I was heard of more it was rather by God's grace than my own prudence. I was no wetter (for that could hardly be) but I was all the colder for this mishap; and having lost another hope, was the more unhappy.

And now, all at once, the yard came in my head. What had carried me through the roost, would surely serve me to cross this little quiet creek in safety. With that I set off, undaunted, across the top of the isle, to fetch and carry it back. It was a weary tramp in all ways, and if hope had not buoyed me up, I must have cast myself down and given up. Whether with the sea salt, or because I was growing fevered, I was distressed with thirst, and had to stop, as I went, and drink the peaty water out of the hags.

I came to the bay at last, more dead than alive; and at the first glance, I thought the yard was something further out than when I left it. In I went, for the third time, into the sea. The sand was smooth and firm and shelved gradually down; so that I could wade out till the water was almost to my neck and the little waves splashed into my face. But at that depth my feet began to leave me and I durst venture in no further. As for the yard, I saw it bobbing very quietly some twenty feet in front of me.

I had borne up well until this last disappointment; but at that I came ashore, and flung myself down upon the sands and wept.

The time I spent upon the island is still so horrible a thought to me, that I must pass it lightly over. In all the books I have read of people cast away,[22] they had either their pockets full of tools, or a chest of things would be thrown upon the beach along with them, as if on purpose. My case was very different. I had nothing in my pockets but money and Alan's silver button; and being inland bred, I was as much short of knowledge as of means.

I knew indeed that shell-fish were counted good to eat; and among the rocks of the isle I found a great plenty of limpets, which at first I could scarcely strike from their places, not knowing quickness to be needful. There were, besides, some of the little shells that we call buckies; I think periwinkle is the English name. Of these two I made my whole diet, devouring them cold and raw as I found them; and so hungry was I, that at first they seemed to me delicious.

Perhaps they were out of season, or perhaps there was something wrong in the sea about my island. But at least I had no sooner eaten my first meal than I was seized with giddiness and retching, and lay for a long time no better than dead. A second trial of the same food (indeed I had no other) did better with me and revived my strength. But as long as I was on the island, I never knew what to expect when I had eaten; sometimes all was well, and sometimes I was thrown into a miserable sickness; nor could I ever distinguish what particular fish it was that hurt me.

All day it streamed rain; the island ran like a sop; there was no dry spot to be found; and when I lay down that night, between two boulders that made a kind of roof, my feet were in a bog.

The second day I crossed the island to all sides. There was no one part of it better than another; it was all desolate and rocky; nothing living on it but game birds which I lacked the means to kill, and the gulls which haunted the outlying rocks in a prodigious number. But the creek, or straits, that cut off the isle from the main land of the Ross, opened out on the north into a bay, and the bay again opened into the sound of Iona; and it was the neighbourhood of this place that I chose to be my home; though if I had thought upon the very name of home in such a spot, I must have burst out weeping.

I had good reasons for my choice. There was in this part of the isle a little hut of a house like a pig's hut, where fishers used to sleep when they came there upon their business; but the turf roof of it had fallen entirely in; so that the hut was of no use to me, and gave me less shelter than my rocks. What was more important, the shell-fish on which I lived grew there in great plenty; when the tide was out I could gather a peck at a time: and this was doubtless a convenience. But the other reason went deeper. I had become in no way used to the horrid solitude of the isle, but still looked round me on all sides (like a man that was hunted) between fear and hope that I might see some human creature coming. Now, from a little up the hillside over the bay, I could catch a sight of the great, ancient church and the roofs of the people's houses in Iona. And on the other hand, over the low country of the Ross, I saw smoke go up, morning and evening, as if from a homestead in a hollow of the land.

I used to watch this smoke, when I was wet and cold, and had my head half turned with loneliness; and think of the fireside and the company, till my heart burned. It was the same with the roofs of Iona. Altogether, this sight I had of men's homes and comfortable lives, although it put a point on my own sufferings, yet it kept hope alive, and helped me to eat my raw shell-fish (which had soon grown to be a disgust) and saved me from the sense of horror I had whenever I was quite alone with dead rocks, and fowls, and the rain, and the cold sea.

I say it kept hope alive; and indeed it seemed impossible that I should be left to die on the shores of my own country, and within view of a church tower and the smoke of men's houses. But the second day passed; and though as long as the light lasted I kept a bright look-out for boats on the Sound or men passing on the Ross, no help came near me. It still rained; and

I turned in to sleep, as wet as ever and with a cruel sore throat, but a little comforted, perhaps, by having said good night to my next neighbours, the people of Iona.

Charles the Second declared a man could stay outdoors more days in the year in the climate of England than in any other. This was very like a king with a palace at his back and changes of dry clothes. But he must have had better luck on his flight from Worcester than I had on that miserable isle. It was the height of the summer; yet it rained for more than twenty-four hours, and did not clear until the afternoon of the third day.

This was the day of incidents. In the morning I saw a red deer, a buck with a fine spread of antlers, standing in the rain on the top of the island; but he had scarce seen me rise from under my rock, before he trotted off upon the other side. I supposed he must have swum the straits; though what should bring any creature to Earraid, was more than I could fancy.

A little after, as I was jumping about after my limpets, I was startled by a guinea-piece, which fell upon a rock in front of me and glanced off into the sea. When the sailors gave me my money again, they kept back not only about a third of the whole sum, but my father's leather purse; so that from that day out, I carried my gold loose in a pocket with a button. I now saw there must be a hole, and clapped my hand to the place in a great hurry. But this was to lock the stable door after the steed was stolen. I had left the shore at Queensferry with near on fifty pounds; now I found no more than two guinea-pieces and a silver shilling.

It is true I picked up a third guinea a little after, where it lay shining on a piece of turf. That made a fortune of three pounds and four shillings, English money, for a lad, the rightful heir of an estate, and now starving on an isle at the extreme end of the wild Highlands.

This state of my affairs dashed me still further; and indeed my plight on that third morning was truly pitiful. My clothes were beginning to rot; my stockings in particular were quite worn through, so that my shanks went naked; my hands had grown quite soft with the continual soaking; my throat was very sore, my strength had much abated, and my heart so turned against the horrid stuff I was condemned to eat, that the very sight of it came near to sicken me.

And yet the worst was not yet come.

There is a pretty high rock on the north-west of Earraid, which (because it had a flat top and overlooked the Sound) I was much in the habit of frequenting; not that ever I stayed in one place, save when asleep, my misery giving me no rest. Indeed I wore myself down with continual and aimless goings and comings in the rain.

As soon, however, as the sun came out, I lay down on the top of that rock to dry myself. The comfort of the sunshine is a thing I cannot tell. It set me thinking hopefully of my deliverance, of which I had begun to despair; and I scanned the sea and the Ross with a fresh interest. On the south of my rock, a part of the island jutted out and hid the open ocean, so that a boat could thus come quite near me upon that side, and I be none the wiser.

Well, all of a sudden, a coble with a brown sail and a pair of fishers aboard of it, came flying round that corner of the isle, bound for Iona. I shouted out, and then fell on my knees on the rock and reached up my hands and prayed to them. They were near enough to hear – I could even see the colour of their hair; and there was no doubt but they observed me, for they cried out in the Gaelic tongue, and laughed. But the boat never turned aside, and flew on, right before my eyes, for Iona.

I could not believe such wickedness, and ran along the shore from rock to rock, crying on them piteously; even after they were out of reach of my voice, I still cried and waved to them; and when they were quite gone, I thought my heart would have burst. All the time of my troubles I wept only twice. Once, when I could not reach the yard; and now, the second time, when these fishers turned a deaf ear to my cries. But this time I wept and roared like a wicked child, tearing up the turf with my nails and grinding my face in the earth. If a wish would kill men, those two fishers would never have seen morning, and I should likely have died upon my island.

When I was a little over my anger, I must eat again, but with such loathing of the mess as I could now scarce control. Sure enough, I should have done as well to fast, for my fishes poisoned me again. I had all my first pains; my throat was so sore I could scarce swallow; I had a fit of strong shuddering, which clucked my teeth together; and there came on me that dreadful sense of illness, which we have no name for either in Scotch or English. I thought I should have died, and made my peace with God, forgiving all men, even my uncle and the fishers; and as soon as I had thus made up my mind to the worst, clearness came upon me: I observed the night was falling dry; my clothes were dried a good deal; truly, I was in a better case than ever before, since I had landed on the isle; and so I got to sleep at last, with a thought of gratitude.

The next day (which was the fourth of this horrible life of mine) I found my bodily strength run very low. But the sun shone, the air was sweet, and what I managed to eat of the shell-fish agreed well with me and revived my courage.

I was scarce back on my rock (where I went always the first thing after I had eaten) before I observed a boat coming down the Sound, and with her head, as I thought, in my direction.

I began at once to hope and fear exceedingly; for I thought these men might have thought better of their cruelty and be coming back to my assistance. But another disappointment, such as yesterday's, was more than I could bear. I turned my back, accordingly, upon the sea, and did not look again till I had counted many hundreds. The boat was still heading for the island. The next time I counted the full thousand, as slowly as I could, my heart beating so as to hurt me. And then it was out of all question. She was coming straight to Earraid!

I could no longer hold myself back, but ran to the sea side and out, from one rock to another, as far as I could go. It is a marvel I was not drowned; for when I was brought to a stand at last, my legs shook under me, and my mouth was so dry, I must wet it with the sea-water before I was able to shout.

All this time the boat was coming on; and now I was able to perceive it was the same boat and the same two men as yesterday. This I knew by their hair, which the one had of a bright yellow and the other black. But now there was a third man along with them, who looked to be of a better class.

As soon as they were come within easy speech, they let down their sail and lay quiet. In spite of my supplications, they drew no nearer in, and what frightened me most of all, the new man tee-hee'd with laughter as he talked and looked at me.

Then he stood up in the boat and addressed me a long while, speaking fast and with many wavings of his hand. I told him I had no Gaelic; and at this he became very angry, and I began to suspect he thought he was talking English. Listening very close, I caught the word 'whateffer' several times; but all the rest was Gaelic, and might have been Greek and Hebrew for me.

'Whatever,' said I, to show him I had caught a word.

'Yes, yes – yes, yes,' says he, and then he looked at the other men, as much as to say, 'I told you I spoke English,' and began again as hard as ever in the Gaelic.

This time I picked out another word, 'tide'. Then I had a flash of hope. I remembered he was always waving his hand towards the mainland of the Ross.

'Do you mean when the tide is out – ?' I cried, and could not finish.

'Yes, yes,' said he. 'Tide.'

At that I turned tail upon their boat (where my adviser had once more begun to tee-hee with laughter) leaped back the way I had come, from one stone to another, and set off running across the isle as I had never run before. In about half an hour I came out upon the shores of the creek; and, sure enough, it was shrunk into a little trickle of water, through which I dashed, not above my knees, and landed with a shout on the main island.

A sea-bred boy would not have stayed a day on Earraid; which is only what they call a tidal islet, and except in the bottom of the neaps, can be entered and left twice in every twenty-four hours, either dry-shod, or at the most by wading. Even I, who had the tide going out and in before me in the bay, and even watched for the ebbs, the better to get my shell-fish – even I (I say) if I had sat down to think, instead of raging at my fate, must have soon guessed the secret, and got free. It was no wonder the fishers had not understood me. The wonder was rather that they had ever guessed my pitiful illusion, and taken the trouble to come back. I had starved with cold and hunger on that island for close upon one hundred hours. But for the fishers, I might have left my bones there, in pure folly. And even as it was, I had paid for it pretty dear, not only in past sufferings, but in my present case; being clothed like a beggar-man, scarce able to walk, and in great pain of my sore throat.

I have seen wicked men and fools, a great many of both; and I believe they both get paid in the end; but the fools first.

CHAPTER XV

The lad with the silver button:
through the Isle of Mull

The Ross of Mull, which I had now got upon, was rugged and trackless, like the isle I had just left; being all bog, and briar, and big stone. There may be roads for them that know that country well; but for my part I had no better guide than my own nose, and no other landmark than Ben More.

I aimed as well as I could for the smoke I had seen so often from the island; and with all my great weariness and the difficulty of the way, came upon the house in the bottom of a little hollow, about five or six at night. It was low and longish, roofed with turf and built of unmortared stones; and on a mound in front of it, an old gentleman sat smoking his pipe in the sun.

With what little English he had, he gave me to understand that my shipmates had got safe ashore, and had broken bread in that very house on the day after.

'Was there one,' I asked, 'dressed like a gentleman?'

He said they all wore rough great coats; but to be sure, the first of them, the one that came alone, wore breeches and stockings, while the rest had sailors' trousers.

'Ah,' said I, 'and he would have a feathered hat?'

He told me, no, that he was bare-headed like myself.

At first I thought Alan might have lost his hat; and then the rain came in my mind, and I judged it more likely he had it out of harm's way under his great coat. This set me smiling, partly because my friend was safe, partly to think of his vanity in dress.

And then the old gentleman clapped his hand to his brow, and cried out that I must be the lad with the silver button.

'Why, yes!' said I, in some wonder.

'Well, then,' said the old gentleman, 'I have a word for you that you are to follow your friend to his country, by Torosay.'

He then asked me how I had fared, and I told him my tale. A south-country man would certainly have laughed; but this old gentleman (I call him so because of his manners, for his clothes were dropping off his back) heard me all through with nothing but gravity and pity. When I had done, he took me by the hand, led me into his hut (it was no better) and presented me before his wife, as if she had been the Queen and I a duke.

The good woman set oat-bread before me and a cold grouse, patting my shoulder and smiling to me all the time, for she had no English; and the old gentleman (not to be behind) brewed me a strong punch out of their country spirit. All the while I was eating, and after that when I was drinking the punch, I could scarce come to believe in my good fortune; and the house, though it was thick with the peat-smoke and as full of holes as a colander, seemed like a palace.

The punch threw me in a strong sweat and a deep slumber; the good people let me lie; and it was near noon of the next day before I took the road, my throat already easier and my spirits quite restored by good fare and good news. The old gentleman, although I pressed him hard, would take no money, and gave me an old bonnet for my head; though I am free to own I was no sooner out of view of the house, than I very jealously washed this gift of his in a wayside fountain.

Thought I to myself: 'If these are the wild Highlanders, I could wish my own folk wilder.'

I not only started late, but I must have wandered nearly half the time. True, I met plenty of people, grubbing in little miserable fields that would not keep a cat, or herding little kine about the bigness of asses. The Highland dress being forbidden by law since the rebellion,[23] and the people condemned to the lowland habit, which they much disliked, it was strange to see the variety of their array. Some went bare, only for a hanging cloak or great coat, and carried their trousers on their backs like a useless burthen; some had made an imitation of the tartan with little parti-coloured stripes patched together like an old wife's quilt; others, again, still wore the highland philabeg, but by putting a few stitches between the legs, transformed it into a pair of trousers like a Dutchman's. All those makeshifts were condemned and punished, for the law was harshly applied, in hopes to break up the clan spirit; but in that out-of-the-way, sea-bound isle, there were few to make remarks and fewer to tell tales.

They seemed in great poverty; which was no doubt natural, now that rapine was put down, and the chiefs kept no longer an open house;[24] and the roads (even such a wandering, country by-track as the one I followed) were infested with beggars. And here again I marked a difference from my own part of the country. For our lowland beggars – even the gownsmen themselves, who beg by patent – had a louting, flattering way with them and if you gave them a plack and asked change, would very civilly return you a boddle. But these Highland beggars stood on their dignity, asked alms only to buy snuff (by their account) and would give no change.

To be sure, this was no concern of mine, except in so far as it entertained me by the way. What was much more to the purpose, few had any English, and these few (unless they were of the brotherhood of beggars) not very anxious to place it at my service. I knew Torosay to be my destination, and repeated the name to them and pointed; but instead of simply pointing in reply, they would give me a screed of the Gaelic that set me foolish; so it was small wonder if I went out of my road as often as I stayed in it.

At last, about eight at night, and already very weary, I came to a lone house, where I asked admittance, and was refused, until I bethought me of the power of money in so poor a country, and held up one of my guineas in my finger and thumb. Thereupon, the man of the house, who had hitherto pretended to have no English, and driven me from his door by signals, suddenly began to speak as clearly as was needful, and agreed for five shillings to give me a night's lodging and guide me the next day to Torosay.

I slept uneasily that night, fearing I should be robbed; but I might have spared myself the pain; for my host was no robber, only miserably poor and a great cheat. He was not alone in his poverty; for the next morning, we must go five miles about to the house of what he called a rich man to have one of my guineas changed. This was perhaps a rich man for Mull; he would have scarce been thought so in the south; for it took all he had, the whole house was turned upside down, and a neighbour brought under contribution, before he could scrape together twenty shillings in silver. The odd shilling he kept for himself, protesting he could ill afford to have so great a sum of money lying 'locked up'. For all that he was very courteous and well spoken, made us both sit down with his family to dinner, and brewed punch in a fine china bowl, over which my rascal guide grew so merry that he refused to start.

I was for getting angry, and appealed to the rich man (Hector Maclean was his name) who had been a witness to our bargain and to my payment of the five shillings. But Maclean had taken his share of the punch, and vowed that no gentleman should leave his table after the bowl was brewed; so there was nothing for it but to sit and hear Jacobite toasts and Gaelic songs, till all were tipsy and staggered off to the bed or the barn for their night's rest.

Next day (the fourth of my travels) we were up before five upon the clock; but my rascal guide got to the bottle at once, and it was three hours before I had him clear of the house, and then (as you shall hear) only for a worse disappointment.

As long as we went down a heathery valley that lay before Mr Maclean's house, all went well; only my guide looked constantly over his shoulder, and when I asked him the cause, only grinned at me. No sooner, however, had we crossed the back of a hill, and got out of sight of the house windows, than he told me Torosay lay right in front, and that a hill-top (which he pointed out) was my best landmark.

'I care very little for that,' said I, 'since you are going with me.'

The impudent cheat answered me in the Gaelic that he had no English.

'My fine fellow,' I said, 'I know very well your English comes and goes. Tell me what will bring it back? Is it more money you wish?'

'Five shillings mair,' said he, 'and hersel' will bring ye there.'

I reflected a while and then offered him two, which he accepted greedily, and insisted on having in his hands at once – 'for luck', as he said, but I think it was rather for my misfortune.

The two shillings carried him not quite as many miles; at the end of which distance, he sat down upon the wayside and took off his brogues from his feet, like a man about to rest.

I was now red-hot. 'Ha!' said I, 'have you no more English?' He said impudently, 'no'.

At that I boiled over and lifted my hand to strike him; and he, drawing a knife from his rags, squatted back and grinned at me like a wild-cat. At that, forgetting everything but my anger, I ran in upon him, put aside his knife with my left and struck him in the mouth with the right. I was a strong lad and very angry, and he but a little man; and he went down before me heavily. By good luck, his knife flew out of his hand as he fell.

I picked up both that and his brogues, wished him a good morning and set off upon my way, leaving him bare-foot and disarmed. I chuckled to myself as I went, being sure I was done with that rogue, for a variety of reasons. First, he knew he could have no more of my money; next, the brogues were worth in that country only a few pence; and lastly the knife, which was really a dagger, it was against the law for him to carry.

In about half-an-hour of walk, I overtook a great, ragged man, moving pretty fast but feeling before him with a staff. He was quite blind, and told me he was a catechist, which should have put me at my ease. But his face went against me; it seemed dark and dangerous and secret; and presently, as we began to go on alongside, I saw the steel butt of a pistol sticking from under the flap of his coat-pocket. To carry such a thing meant a fine of fifteen pounds sterling upon a first offence, and trans-portation to the colonies upon a second. Nor could I quite see why a religious teacher should go armed, or what a blind man could be doing with a pistol.

I told him about my guide, for I was proud of what I had done, and my vanity for once got the heels of my prudence. At the mention of the five shillings he cried out so loud that I made up my mind I should say nothing of the other two, and was glad he could not see my blushes.

'Was it too much?' I asked, a little faltering.

'Too much!' cries he. 'Why, I will guide you to Torosay myself for a dram of brandy. And give you the great pleasure of my company (me that is a man of some learning) in the bargain.'

I said I did not see how a blind man could be a guide; but at that he laughed aloud, and said his stick was eyes enough for an eagle.

'In the Isle of Mull, at least,' says he, 'where I knew every stone and heather-bush by mark of head. See, now,' he said, striking right and left, as if to make sure, 'down there a burn is running; and at the head of it there stands a bit of a small hill with a stone cocked upon the top of that; and it's hard at the foot of the hill, that the way runs by to Torosay; and the way here, being for droves, is plainly trodden, and will show grassy through the heather.'

I had to own he was right in every feature, and told my wonder.

'Ha!' says he, 'that's nothing. Would ye believe me now, that before the Act came out, and when there were weepons in this country, I could shoot? Ay, could I!' cries he, and then with a leer: 'If ye had such a thing as a pistol here to try with, I would show ye how it's done.'

I told him I had nothing of the sort, and gave him a wider berth. If he had known, his pistol stuck at that time quite plainly out of his pocket, and I could see the sun twinkle on the steel of the butt. But by the better luck for me, he knew nothing, thought all was covered, and lied on in the dark.

He then began to question me cunningly, where I came from, whether I was rich, whether I could change a five-shilling piece for him (which he declared he had that moment in his sporran) and all the time he kept edging up to me, and I avoiding him. We were now upon a sort of green cattle-track which crossed the hills towards Torosay, and we kept changing sides upon that like dancers in a reel. I had so plainly the upper-hand that my spirits rose, and indeed I took a pleasure in this game of blind-man's buff; but the catechist grew angrier and angrier, and at last began to swear in Gaelic and to strike for my legs with his staff.

Then I told him that, sure enough, I had a pistol in my pocket as well as he, and if he did not strike across the hill due south I would even blow his brains out.

He became at once very polite; and after trying to soften me for some time, but quite in vain, he cursed me once more in the Gaelic and took himself off. I watched him striding along, through bog and brier, tapping with his stick, until he turned the end of a hill and disappeared in the next hollow. Then I struck on again for Torosay, much better pleased to be alone than to travel with that man of learning. This was an unlucky day; and these two, of whom I had just rid myself one after the other, were the two worst men I met with in the Highlands.

At Torosay, on the sound of Mull and looking over to the mainland of Morven, there was an inn with an innkeeper, who was a Maclean, it appeared, of a very high family; for to keep an inn is thought even more genteel in the Highlands than it is with us, perhaps as partaking of hospitality, or perhaps because the trade is idle and drunken. He spoke good English, and finding me to be something of a scholar, tried me first in French, where he easily beat me, and then in the Latin, in which I don't know which of us did best. This pleasant rivalry put us at once upon friendly terms; and I sat up and drank punch with him (or to be more correct, sat up and watched him drink it) until he was so tipsy that he wept upon my shoulder.

I tried him, as if by accident, with a sight of Alan's button; but it was plain he had never seen or heard of it. Indeed, he bore some grudge against the family and friends of Ardshiel, and before he was drunk he read me a lampoon, in very good Latin, but with a very ill meaning, which he had made in elegiac verses upon a person of that house.

When I told him of my catechist, he shook his head, and said I was lucky to have got clear off. 'That is a very dangerous man,' he said; 'Duncan Mackiegh is his name; he can shoot by the ear at several yards, and has been often accused of highway robberies, and once of murder.'

'The cream of it is,' says I, 'that he called himself a catechist.'

'And why should he not?' says he, 'when that is what he is? It was Maclean of Duart gave it to him because he was blind. But, perhaps, it was a peety,' says my host, 'for he is always on the road, going from one place to another to hear the young folk say their religion; and doubtless, that is a great temptation to the poor man.'

At last, when my landlord could drink no more, he showed me to a bed, and I lay down in very good spirits; having travelled the greater part of that big and crooked Island of Mull, from Earraid to Torosay, fifty miles as the crow flies and (with my wanderings) much nearer a hundred, in four days and with little fatigue. Indeed I was by far in better heart and health of body at the end of that long tramp than I had been at the beginning.

CHAPTER XVI

The lad with the silver button:
across Morven

There is a regular ferry from Torosay to Kinlochaline on the mainland. Both shores of the Sound are in the country of the strong clan of the Macleans, and the people that passed the ferry with me were almost all of that clan. The skipper of the boat, on the other hand, was called Neil Roy Macrob; and since Macrob was one of the names of Alan's clansmen, and Alan himself had sent me to that ferry, I was eager to come to private speech of Neil Roy.

In the crowded boat this was of course impossible, and the passage was a very slow affair. There was no wind, and as the boat was wretchedly equipped, we could pull but two oars on one side, and one on the other. The men gave way, however, with a good will, the passengers taking spells to help them, and the whole company giving the time in Gaelic boat-songs. And what with the songs, and the sea air, and the good nature and spirit of all concerned, and the bright weather, the passage was a pretty thing to have seen.

But there was one melancholy part. In the mouth of Loch Aline we found a great sea-going ship at anchor; and this I supposed at first to be one of the King's cruisers which were kept along that coast, both summer and winter, to prevent communication with the French. As we got a little nearer, it became plain she was a ship of merchandise; and what still more puzzled me, not only her decks, but the sea-beach also, were quite black with people, and skiffs were continually plying to and fro between them. Yet nearer, and there began to come to our ears a great sound of mourning, the people on board and those on the shore crying and lamenting one to another so as to pierce the heart.

Then I understood this was an emigrant ship bound for the American colonies.[25]

We put the ferry-boat alongside, and the exiles leaned over the bulwarks, weeping and reaching out their hands to my fellow-passengers, among whom they counted some near friends. How long this might have gone on I do not know, for they seemed to have no sense of time: but at last the captain of the ship, who seemed near beside himself (and no great wonder) in the midst of this crying and confusion, came to the side and begged us to depart.

Thereupon Neil sheered off; and the chief singer in our boat struck into a melancholy air, which was presently taken up both by the emigrants and their friends upon the beach, so that it sounded from all sides like a lament for the dying. I saw the tears run down the cheeks of the men and women in the boat, even as they bent at the oars; and the circumstances, and the music of the song (which is one called 'Lochaber no more')[26] were highly affecting even to myself.

At Kinlochaline I got Neil Roy upon one side on the beach, and said I made sure he was one of Appin's men.

'And what for no?' said he.

'I am seeking somebody,' said I; 'and it comes in my mind that you will have news of him. Alan Breck Stewart is his name.' And very foolishly, instead of showing him the button, I sought to pass a shilling in his hand.

At this he drew back. 'I am very much affronted,' he said; 'and this is not the way that one shentleman should behave to another at all. The man you ask for is in France; but if he was in my sporran,' says he, 'and your belly full of shillings, I would not hurt a hair upon his body.'

I saw I had gone the wrong way to work, and without wasting time upon apologies, showed him the button lying in the hollow of my palm.

'Aweel, aweel,' said Neil; 'and I think ye might have begun with that end of the stick, whatever! But if ye are the lad with the silver button, all is well, and I have the word to see that ye come safe. But if ye will pardon me to speak plainly,' says he, 'there is a name that you should never take into your mouth, and that is the name of Alan Breck; and there is a thing that ye would never do, and that is to offer your dirty money to a Hieland shentleman.'

It was not very easy to apologize; for I could scarce tell him (what was the truth) that I had never dreamed he would set up to be a gentleman until he told me so. Neil on his part had no wish to prolong his dealings with me, only to fulfil his orders and be done with it; and he made haste to give me my route. This was to lie the night in Kinlochaline in the public inn; to cross Morven the next day to Ardgour, and lie the night in the house of one John of the Claymore, who was warned that I might come; the third day, to be set across one loch at Corran and another at Balachulish, and then ask my way to the house of James of the Glens, at Aucharn in Duror of Appin. There was a good deal of ferrying, as you hear; the sea in all this part running deep into the mountains and winding about their roots. It makes the country strong to hold and difficult to travel, but full of prodigious wild and dreadful prospects.

I had some other advice from Neil; to speak with no one by the way, to avoid Whigs, Campbells, and the 'red-soldiers'; to leave the road and lie in a bush, if I saw any of the latter coming 'for it was never chancy to meet in with them', and in brief, to conduct myself like a robber or a Jacobite agent, as perhaps Neil thought me.

The inn at Kinlochaline was the most beggarly vile place that ever pigs were styed in, full of smoke, vermin, and silent Highlanders. I was not only discontented with my lodging, but with myself for my mismanagement of Neil, and thought I could hardly be worse off. But very wrongly, as I was soon to see; for I had not been half an hour at the inn (standing in the door most of the time, to ease my eyes from the peat smoke) when a thunderstorm came close by, the springs broke in a little hill on which the inn stood, and one end of the house became a running water. Places of public entertainment were bad enough all over Scotland in those days; yet it was a wonder to myself, when I had to go from the fireside to the bed in which I slept, wading over the shoes.

Early in my next day's journey I overtook a little, stout, solemn man, walking very slowly with his toes turned out, sometimes reading in a book and sometimes marking the place with his finger, and dressed decently and plainly in something of a clerical style.

This I found to be another catechist, but of a different order from the blind man of Mull: being indeed one of those sent out by the Edinburgh Society for Propagating Christian Knowledge,[27] to evangelize the more savage places of the Highlands. His name was Henderland; he spoke with the broad south-country tongue, which I was beginning to weary for the sound of; and besides common countryship, we soon found we had a more particular bond of interest. For my good friend, the minister of Essendean, had translated into the Gaelic in his by-time a number of hymns and pious books, which Henderland used in his work, and held in great esteem. Indeed it was one of these he was carrying and reading when we met.

We fell in company at once, our ways lying together as far as to Kingairloch. As we went, he stopped and spoke with all the wayfarers and workers that we met or passed; and though of course I could not tell what they discoursed about, yet I judged Mr Henderland must be well liked in the countryside, for I observed many of them to bring out their mulls and share a pinch of snuff with him.

I told him as far in my affairs as I judged wise: as far, that is, as they were none of Alan's; and gave Balachulish as the place I was travelling to, to meet a friend; for I thought Aucharn, or even Duror, would be too particular and might put him on the scent.

On his part, he told me much of his work and the people he worked among, the hiding priests and Jacobites, the Disarming Act, the dress, and many other curiosities of the time and place. He seemed moderate: blaming Parliament in several points, and especially because they had framed the Act more severely against those who wore the dress than against those who carried weapons.

This moderation put it in my mind to question him of the Red Fox and the Appin tenants: questions which, I thought, would seem natural enough in the mouth of one travelling to that country.

He said it was a bad business. 'It's wonderful,' said he, 'where the tenants find the money, for their life is mere starvation. (Ye don't carry such a thing as snuff, do ye, Mr Balfour? No. Well, I'm better wanting it.) But these tenants (as I was saying) are doubtless partly driven to it. James Stewart in Duror (that's him they call James of the Glens) is half-brother to Ardshiel, the captain of the clan; and he is a man much looked up to, and drives very hard. And then there's one they call Alan Breck –'

'Ah!' cried I, 'what of him?'

'What of the wind that bloweth where it listeth?' said Henderland. 'He's here and awa; here to-day and gone to-morrow: a fair heather-cat. He might be glowering at the two of us out of yon whin-bush, and I wouldnae wonder! Ye'll no carry such a thing as snuff, will ye?'

I told him no, and that he had asked the same thing more than once.

'It's highly possible,' said he, sighing. 'But it seems strange ye shouldnae carry it. However, as I was saying, this Alan Breck is a bold, desperate customer, and well kent to be James's right hand. His life is forfeit already; he would boggle at naething; and maybe, if a tenant-body was to hang back, he would get a dirk in his wame.'

'You make a poor story of it all, Mr Henderland,' said I. 'If it is all fear upon both sides, I care to hear no more of it.'

'Na,' said Mr Henderland, 'but there's love too, and self-denial that should put the like of you and me to shame. There's something fine about it; no perhaps Christian, but humanly fine. Even Alan Breck, by all that I hear, is a child to be respected. There's many a lying sneck-draw sits close in kirk in our own part of the country, and stands well in the world's eye, and maybe is a far worse man, Mr Balfour, than yon misguided shedder of man's blood. Ay, ay, we might take a lesson by them. – Ye'll perhaps think I've been too long in the Hielands?' he added, smiling to me.

I told him not at all; that I had seen much to admire among the Highlanders; and if he came to that, Mr Campbell himself was a Highlander.

'Ay,' said he, 'that's true. It's a fine blood.'

'And what is the King's agent about?' I asked.

'Colin Campbell?' says Henderland. 'Putting his head in a bees' byke!'

'He is to turn the tenants out by force, I hear?' said I.

'Yes,' says he, 'but the business has gone back and forth, as folk say. First, James of the Glens rode to Edinburgh and got some lawyer (a Stewart, nae doubt – they all hing together like bats in a steeple) and had the proceedings stayed. And then Colin Campbell cam' in again, and had the upper-hand before the Barons of Exchequer. And now they tell me the first of the tenants are to flit to-morrow. It's to begin at Duror under James's very windows, which doesnae seem wise by my humble way of it.'

'Do you think they'll fight?' I asked.

'Well,' says Henderland, 'they're disarmed – or supposed to be – for there's still a good deal of cold iron lying by in quiet places. And then Colin Campbell has the sogers coming. But for all that, if I was his lady wife, I wouldnae be well pleased till I got him home again. They're queer customers, the Appin Stewarts.'

I asked if they were worse than their neighbours.

'No they,' said he. 'And that's the worst part of it. For if Colin Roy can get his business done in Appin, he has it all to begin again in the next country, which they call Mamore, and which is one of the countries of the Camerons. He's King's factor upon both, and from both he has to drive out the tenants; and indeed, Mr Balfour (to be open with ye) it's my belief that if he escapes the one lot, he'll get his death by the other.'

So we continued talking and walking the great part of the day; until at last, Mr Henderland, after expressing his delight in my company, and satisfaction at meeting with a friend of Mr Campbell's ('whom,' says he, 'I will make bold to call that sweet singer of our covenanted Zion') proposed that I should make a short stage, and lie the night in his house a little beyond

Kingairloch. To say truth, I was overjoyed; for I had no great
desire for John of the Claymore, and since my double misadven-
ture, first with the guide and next with the gentleman skipper,
I stood in some fear of any Highland stranger. Accordingly we
shook hands upon the bargain, and came in the afternoon to a
small house, standing alone by the shore of the Linnhe Loch.
The sun was already gone from the desert mountains of
Ardgour upon the hither side, but shone on those of Appin on
the farther; the loch lay as still as a lake, only the gulls were
crying round the sides of it; and the whole place seemed solemn
and uncouth.

We had no sooner come to the door of Mr Henderland's
dwelling, than to my great surprise (for I was now used to the
politeness of Highlanders) he burst rudely past me, dashed into
the room, caught up a jar and a small horn spoon, and began
ladling snuff into his nose in most excessive quantities. Then
he had a hearty fit of sneezing, and looked round upon me with
a rather silly smile.

'It's a vow I took,' says he. 'I took a vow upon me that I
wouldnae carry it. Doubtless it's a great privation; but when
I think upon the martyrs, not only to the Scottish Covenant but
to other points of Christianity, I think shame to mind it.'

As soon as we had eaten (and porridge and whey was the
best of the good man's diet) he took a grave face and said he
had a duty to perform by Mr Campbell, and that was to inquire
into my state of mind towards God. I was inclined to smile at
him, since the business of the snuff; but he had not spoken long
before he brought the tears into my eyes. There are two things
that men should never weary of, goodness and humility; we get
none too much of them in this rough world and among cold,
proud people; but Mr Henderland had their very speech upon
his tongue. And though I was a good deal puffed up with my
adventures and with having come off, as the saying is, with
flying colours; yet he soon had me on my knees beside a simple,
poor old man, and both proud and glad to be there.

Before we went to bed he offered me sixpence to help me on
my way, out of a scanty store he kept in the turf wall of his
house; at which excess of goodness I knew not what to do. But

at last he was so earnest with me, that I thought it the more mannerly part to let him have his way, and so left him poorer than myself.

CHAPTER XVII

The death of the Red Fox

The next day Mr Henderland found for me a man who had a boat of his own and was to cross the Linnhe Loch that afternoon into Appin, fishing. Him he prevailed on to take me, for he was one of his flock; and in this way I saved a long day's travel and the price of the two public ferries I must otherwise have passed.

It was near noon before we set out; a dark day, with clouds, and the sun shining upon little patches. The sea was here very deep and still, and had scarce a wave upon it; so that I must put the water to my lips before I could believe it to be truly salt. The mountains on either side were high, rough and barren, very black and gloomy in the shadow of the clouds, but all silver-laced with little watercourses where the sun shone upon them. It seemed a hard country, this of Appin, for people to care as much about as Alan did.

There was but one thing to mention. A little after we had started, the sun shone upon a little moving clump of scarlet close in along the waterside to the north. It was much of the same red as soldiers' coats; every now and then, too, there came little sparks and lightning, as though the sun had struck upon bright steel.

I asked my boatman what it should be; and he answered he supposed it was some of the red soldiers coming from Fort William into Appin, against the poor tenantry of the country. Well, it was a sad sight to me; and whether it was because of my thoughts of Alan, or from something prophetic in my bosom, although this was but the second time I had seen King George's troops, I had no good will to them.

At last we came so near the point of land at the entering in of Loch Leven that I begged to be set on shore. My boatman (who was an honest fellow and mindful of his promise to the catechist) would fain have carried me on to Balachulish; but as this was to take me farther from my secret destination, I insisted, and was set on shore at last under the wood of Lettermore (or Lettervore, for I have heard it both ways) in Alan's country of Appin.

This was a wood of birches, growing on a steep, craggy side of a mountain that overhung the loch. It had many openings and ferny howes;[28] and a road or bridle track ran north and south through the midst of it, by the edge of which, where was a spring, I sat down to eat some oat-bread of Mr Henderland's, and think upon my situation.

Here I was not only troubled by a cloud of stinging midges, but far more by the doubts of my mind. What I ought to do, why I was going to join myself with an outlaw and a would-be murderer like Alan, whether I should not be acting more like a man of sense to tramp back to the south country direct, by my own guidance and at my own charges, and what Mr Campbell or even Mr Henderland would think of me if they should ever learn my folly and presumption: these were the doubts that now began to come in on me stronger than ever.

As I was so sitting and thinking, a sound of men and horses came to me through the wood; and presently after, at a turning of the road, I saw four travellers come into view. The way was in this part so rough and narrow that they came single and led their horses by the reins. The first was a great, red-headed gentleman, of an imperious and flushed face, who carried his hat in his hand and fanned himself, for he was in a breathing heat. The second, by his decent black garb and white wig, I correctly took to be a lawyer. The third was a servant, and wore some part of his clothes in tartan, which showed that his master was of a Highland family, and either an outlaw or else in singular good odour with the Government, since the wearing of tartan was against the Act. If I had been better versed in these things, I would have known the tartan to be of the Argyle (or Campbell) colours. This servant had a good-sized port-manteau strapped on his horse, and a net of lemons (to brew punch with) hanging at the saddle-bow; as was often enough the custom with luxurious travellers in that part of the country.

As for the fourth, who brought up the tail, I had seen his like before, and knew him at once to be a sheriff's officer.

I had no sooner seen these people coming than I made up my mind (for no reason that I can tell) to go through with my adventure; and when the first came alongside of me, I rose up from the bracken and asked him the way to Aucharn.

He stopped and looked at me, as I thought, a little oddly; and then, turning to the lawyer, 'Mungo,' said he, 'there's many a man would think this more of a warning than two pyats. Here am I on my road to Duror on the job ye ken; and here is a young lad starts up out of the bracken, and speers if I am on the way to Aucharn.'

'Glenure,' said the other, 'this is an ill subject for jesting.'

These two had now drawn close up and were gazing at me, while the two followers had halted about a stone-cast in the rear.

'And what seek ye in Aucharn?' said Colin Roy Campbell of Glenure; him they called the Red Fox; for he it was that I had stopped.

'The man that lives there,' said I.

'James of the Glens,' says Glenure, musingly; and then to the lawyer: 'Is he gathering his people, think ye?'

'Anyway,' says the lawyer, 'we shall do better to bide where we are, and let the soldiers rally us.'

'If you are concerned for me,' said I, 'I am neither of his people nor yours, but an honest subject of King George, owing no man and fearing no man.'

'Why, very well said,' replies the Factor. 'But if I may make so bold as ask, what does this honest man so far from his country? and why does he come seeking the brother of Ardshiel? I have power here, I must tell you. I am King's Factor upon several of these estates, and have twelve files of soldiers at my back.'

'I have heard a waif word in the country,' said I, a little nettled, 'that you were a hard man to drive.'

He still kept looking at me, as if in doubt.

'Well,' said he, at last, 'your tongue is bold; but I am no unfriend to plainness. If ye had asked me the way to the door of James Stewart on any other day but this, I would have set ye right and bidden ye God speed. But to-day – eh, Mungo?' And he turned again to look at the lawyer.

But just as he turned there came the shot of a firelock from higher up the hill; and with the very sound of it Glenure fell upon the road.

'Oh, I am dead!' he cried, several times over.

The lawyer had caught him up and held him in his arms, the servant standing over and clasping his hands. And now the wounded man looked from one to another with scared eyes, and there was a change in his voice that went to the heart.

'Take care of yourselves,' says he. 'I am dead.'

He tried to open his clothes as if to look for the wound, but his fingers slipped on the buttons. With that he gave a great sigh, his head rolled on his shoulder, and he passed away.

The lawyer said never a word, but his face was as sharp as a pen and as white as the dead man's; the servant broke out into a great noise of crying and weeping, like a child; and I, on my side, stood staring at them in a kind of horror. The sheriff's officer had run back at the first sound of the shot, to hasten the coming of the soldiers.

At last the lawyer laid down the dead man in his blood upon the road, and got to his own feet with a kind of stagger.

I believe it was his movement that brought me to my senses; for he had no sooner done so than I began to scramble up the hill, crying out, 'The murderer! the murderer!'

So little a time had elapsed, that when I got to the top of the first steepness, and could see some part of the open mountain, the murderer was still moving away at no great distance. He was a big man, in a black coat, with metal buttons, and carried a long fowling-piece.

'Here!' I cried. 'I see him!'

At that the murderer gave a little, quick look over his shoulder, and began to run. The next moment he was lost in a fringe of birches; then he came out again on the upper side, where I could see him climbing like a jackanapes, for that part was again very steep; and then he dipped behind a shoulder, and I saw him no more.

All this time I had been running on my side, and had got a good way up, when a voice cried upon me to stand.

I was at the edge of the upper wood, and so now, when I halted and looked back, I saw all the open part of the hill below me.

The lawyer and the sheriff's officer were standing just above the road, crying and waving on me to come back; and on their left, the red-coats, musket in hand, were beginning to struggle singly out of the lower wood.

'Why should I come back?' I cried. 'Come you on!'

'Ten pounds if ye take that lad!' cried the lawyer. 'He's an accomplice. He was posted here to hold us in talk.'

At that word (which I could hear quite plainly, though it was to the soldiers and not to me that he was crying it) my heart came in my mouth with quite a new kind of terror. Indeed, it is one thing to stand the danger of your life, and quite another to run the peril of both life and character. The thing, besides, had come so suddenly, like thunder out of a clear sky, that I was all amazed and helpless.

The soldiers began to spread, some of them to run, and others to put up their pieces and cover me; and still I stood.

'Jouk* in here among the trees,' said a voice, close by.

Indeed, I scarce knew what I was doing, but I obeyed; and as I did so, I heard the firelocks bang and the balls whistle in the birches.

Just inside the shelter of the trees I found Alan Breck standing, with a fishing-rod. He gave me no salutation; indeed it was no time for civilities; only 'Come!' says he, and set off running along the side of the mountain towards Balachulish; and I, like a sheep, to follow him.

Now we ran among the birches; now stooping behind low humps upon the mountain side; now crawling on all fours among the heather. The pace was deadly; my heart seemed bursting against my ribs; and I had neither time to think nor

* Duck.

breath to speak with. Only I remember seeing with wonder, that Alan every now and then would straighten himself to his full height and look back; and every time he did so, there came a great faraway cheering and crying of the soldiers.

Quarter of an hour later, Alan stopped, clapped down flat in the heather, and turned to me.

'Now,' said he, 'it's earnest. Do as I do for your life.'

And at the same speed, but now with infinitely more precaution, we traced back again across the mountain side by the same way that we had come, only perhaps higher; till at last Alan threw himself down in the upper wood of Lettermore, where I found him at the first, and lay, with his face in the bracken, panting like a dog.

My own sides so ached, my head so swam, my tongue so hung out of my mouth with heat and dryness that I lay beside him like one dead.

CHAPTER XVIII

I talk with Alan in the wood of Lettermore

Alan was the first to come round. He rose, went to the border of the wood, peered out a little, and then returned and sat down.

'Well,' said he, 'yon was a hot burst, David.'

I said nothing, nor so much as lifted my face. I had seen murder done, and a great, ruddy, jovial gentleman struck out of life in a moment; the pity of that sight was still sore within me, and yet that was but a part of my concern. Here was murder done upon the man Alan hated; here was Alan skulking in the trees and running from the troops; and whether his was the hand that fired or only the head that ordered, signified but little. By my way of it, my only friend in that wild country was blood-guilty in the first degree; I held him in horror; I could not look upon his face; I would have rather lain alone in the rain on my cold isle, than in that warm wood beside a murderer.

'Are ye still wearied?' he asked again.

'No,' said I, still with my face in the bracken; 'no, I am not wearied now, and I can speak. You and me must twine,'* I said. 'I liked you very well, Alan; but your ways are not mine, and they're not God's; and the short and the long of it is just that we must twine.'

'I will hardly twine from ye, David, without some kind of reason for the same,' said Alan, mighty gravely. 'If ye ken anything against my reputation, it's the least thing that ye should do, for old acquaintance sake, to let me hear the name of it; and if ye have only taken a distaste to my society, it will be proper for me to judge if I'm insulted.'

* Part.

'Alan,' said I, 'what is the sense of this? Ye ken very well yon Campbell-man lies in his blood upon the road.'

He was silent for a little; then says he, 'Did ever ye hear tell of the story of the Man and the Good People?' – by which he meant the fairies.

'No,' said I, 'nor do I want to hear it.'

'With your permission, Mr Balfour, I will tell it you, whatever,' says Alan. 'The man, ye should ken, was cast upon a rock in the sea, where it appears the Good People were in use to come and rest as they went through to Ireland. The name of this rock is called the Skerryvore,[29] and it's not far from where we suffered shipwreck. Well, it seems the man cried so sore, if he could just see his little bairn before he died! that at last the king of the Good People took peety upon him, and sent one flying that brought back the bairn in a poke* and laid it down beside the man where he lay sleeping. So when the man woke, there was a poke beside him and something into the inside of it that moved. Well, it seems he was one of these gentry that think aye the worst of things; and for greater security, he stuck his dirk throughout that poke before he opened it, and there was his bairn dead. I am thinking to myself, Mr Balfour, that you and the man are very much alike.'

'Do you mean you had no hand in it?' cried I, sitting up.

'I will tell you first of all, Mr Balfour of Shaws, as one friend to another,' said Alan, 'that if I were going to kill a gentleman, it would not be in my own country, to bring trouble on my clan; and I would not go wanting sword and gun, and with a long fishing-rod upon my back.'

'Well,' said I, 'that's true!'

'And now,' continued Alan, taking out his dirk and laying his hand upon it in a certain manner, 'I swear upon the Holy Iron I had neither art nor part, act nor thought in it.'

'I thank God for that!' cried I, and offered him my hand.

He did not appear to see it.

'And here is a great deal of work about a Campbell!' said he. 'They are not so scarce, that I ken!'

* Bag.

'At least,' said I, 'you cannot justly blame me, for you know very well what you told me in the brig. But the temptation and the act are different, I thank God again for that. We may all be tempted; but to take a life in cold blood, Alan!' And I could say no more for the moment. 'And do you know who did it?' I added. 'Do you know that man in the black coat?'

'I have nae clear mind about his coat,' said Alan, cunningly; 'but it sticks in my head that it was blue.'

'Blue or black, did ye know him?' said I.

'I couldnae just conscientiously swear to him,' says Alan. 'He gaed very close by me, to be sure, but it's a strange thing that I should just have been tying my brogues.'

'Can you swear that you don't know him, Alan?' I cried, half angered, half in a mind to laugh at his evasions.

'Not yet,' says he; 'but I've a grand memory for forgetting, David.'

'And yet there was one thing I saw clearly,' said I; 'and that was, that you exposed yourself and me to draw the soldiers.'

'It's very likely,' said Alan; 'and so would any gentleman. You and me were innocent of that transaction.'

'The better reason, since we were falsely suspected, that we should get clear,' I cried. 'The innocent should surely come before the guilty.'

'Why, David,' said he, 'the innocent have aye a chance to get assoiled in court; but for the lad that shot the bullet, I think the best place for him will be the heather. Them that havenae dipped their hands in any little difficulty, should be very mindful of the case of them that have. And that is the good Christianity. For if it was the other way round about, and the lad whom I couldnae just clearly see had been in our shoes, and we in his (as might very well have been) I think we would be a good deal obliged to him oursel's if he would draw the soldiers.'

When it came to this, I gave Alan up. But he looked so innocent all the time, and was in such clear good faith in what he said, and so ready to sacrifice himself for what he deemed his duty, that my mouth was closed. Mr Henderland's words came back to me: that we ourselves might take a lesson by these wild Highlanders. Well, here I had taken mine. Alan's morals were all tail-first; but he was ready to give his life for them, such as they were.

'Alan,' said I, 'I'll not say it's the good Christianity as I understand it, but it's good enough. And here I offer ye my hand for the second time.'

Whereupon he gave me both of his, saying surely I had cast a spell upon him, for he could forgive me anything. Then he grew very grave, and said we had not much time to throw away, but must both flee that country: he, because he was a deserter, and the whole of Appin would now be searched like a chamber, and every one obliged to give a good account of himself; and I, because I was certainly involved in the murder.

'Oh!' says I, willing to give him a little lesson, 'I have no fear of the justice of my country.'

'As if this was your country!' said he. 'Or as if ye would be tried here, in a country of Stewarts!'

'It's all Scotland,' said I.

'Man, I whiles wonder at ye,' said Alan. 'This is a Campbell that's been killed. Well, it'll be tried in Inverara, the Campbell's head place; with fifteen Campbells in the jury-box, and the biggest Campbell of all (and that's the Duke) sitting cocking on the bench. Justice, David? The same justice, by all the world, as Glenure found a while ago at the road-side.'

This frighted me a little, I confess, and would have frighted me more if I had known how nearly exact were Alan's predictions; indeed it was but in one point that he exaggerated, there being but eleven Campbells on the jury; though as the other four were equally in the Duke's dependance, it mattered less than might appear. Still, I cried out that he was unjust to the Duke of Argyle who (for all he was a Whig), was yet a wise and honest nobleman.

'Hoot!' said Alan, 'the man's a Whig, nae doubt; but I would never deny he was a good chieftain to his clan. And what would the clan think if there was a Campbell shot, and naebody hanged, and their own chief the Justice General? But I have often observed,' says Alan, 'that you Low-country bodies have no clear idea of what's right and wrong.'

At this I did at last laugh out aloud; when to my surprise, Alan joined in and laughed as merrily as myself.

'Na, na,' said he, 'we're in the Hielands, David; and when I tell ye to run, take my word and run. Nae doubt it's a hard thing to skulk and starve in the heather, but it's harder yet to lie shackled in a red-coat prison.'

I asked him whither we should flee; and as he told me 'to the Lowlands', I was a little better inclined to go with him; for indeed I was growing impatient to get back and have the upper-hand of my uncle. Besides, Alan made so sure there would be no question of justice in the matter, that I began to be afraid he might be right. Of all deaths, I would truly like least to die by the gallows; and the picture of that uncanny instrument came into my head with extraordinary clearness (as I had once seen it engraved at the top of a pedlar's ballad) and took away my appetite for courts of justice.

'I'll chance it, Alan,' said I. 'I'll go with you.'

'But mind you,' said Alan, 'it's no small thing. Ye maun lie bare and hard, and brook many an empty belly. Your bed shall be the moorcock's, and your life shall be like the hunted deer's, and ye shall sleep with your hand upon your weapons. Ay, man, ye shall taigle many a weary foot, or we get clear! I tell ye this at the start, for it's a life that I ken well. But if ye ask what other chance ye have, I answer: Nane. Either take to the heather with me, or else hang.'

'And that's a choice very easily made,' said I; and we shook hands upon it.

'And now let's take another keek at the red-coats,' says Alan, and he led me to the north-eastern fringe of the wood.

Looking out between the trees, we could see a great side of mountain, running down exceeding steep into the waters of the loch. It was a rough part, all hanging stone, and heather, and bit scrags of birchwood; and away at the far end towards Balachulish, little wee red soldiers were dipping up and down over hill and howe, and growing smaller every minute. There was no cheering now, for I think they had other uses for what breath was left them; but they still stuck to the trail, and doubtless thought that we were close in front of them.

Alan watched them, smiling to himself.

'Ay,' said he, 'they'll be gey weary before they've got to the end of that employ! And so you and me, David, can sit down and eat a bite, and breathe a bit longer, and take a dram from my bottle. Then we'll strike for Aucharn, the house of my kinsman, James of the Glens, where I must get my clothes, and my arms, and money to carry us along; and then David, we'll cry "Forth, Fortune!" and take a cast among the heather.'

So we sat again and ate and drank, in a place whence we could see the sun going down into a field of great, wild and houseless mountains, such as I was now condemned to wander in with my companion. Partly as we so sat, and partly afterwards, on the way to Aucharn, each of us narrated his adventures; and I shall here set down so much of Alan's as seems either curious or needful.

It appears he ran to the bulwarks as soon as the wave was passed; saw me, and lost me, and saw me again, as I tumbled in the roost; and at last had one glimpse of me clinging on the yard. It was this that put him in some hope I would maybe get to land after all, and made him leave those clues and messages which had brought me (for my sins) to that unlucky country of Appin.

In the meanwhile, those still on the brig had got the skiff launched, and one or two were on board of her already, when there came a second wave greater than the first, and heaved the brig out of her place, and would certainly have sent her to the bottom, had she not struck and caught on some projection of the reef. When she had struck first, it had been bows-on, so that the stern had hitherto been lowest. But now her stern was thrown in the air, and the bows plunged under the sea; and with that, the water began to pour into the fore-scuttle like the pouring of a mill-dam.

It took the colour out of Alan's face, even to tell what followed. For there were still two men lying impotent in their bunks; and these, seeing the water pour in and thinking the ship had foundered, begun to cry out aloud, and that with such harrowing cries that all who were on deck tumbled one after another into the skiff and fell to their oars. They were not two hundred yards away, when there came a third great sea; and at that the brig lifted clean over the reef; her canvas filled for a moment, and she seemed to sail in chase of them, but settling all the while; and presently she drew down and down, as if a hand was drawing her; and the sea closed over the *Covenant* of Dysart.

Never a word they spoke as they pulled ashore, being stunned with the horror of that screaming; but they had scarce set foot upon the beach when Hoseason woke up, as if out of a muse, and bade them lay hands upon Alan. They hung back indeed, having little taste for the employment; but Hoseason was like a fiend; crying that Alan was alone, that he had a great sum about him, that he had been the means of losing the brig and drowning all their comrades, and that here was both revenge and wealth upon a single cast. It was seven against one; in that part of the shore there was no rock that Alan could set his back to; and the sailors began to spread out and come behind him.

'And then,' said Alan, 'the little man with the red head – I havenae mind of the name that he is called.'

'Riach,' said I.

'Ay,' said Alan, 'Riach! Well, it was him that took up the clubs for me, asked the men if they werenae feared of a judgment, and says he, "Dod, I'll put my back to the Hielandman's mysel'." That's none such an entirely bad little man, yon little man with the red head,' said Alan. 'He has some spunks of decency.'

'Well,' said I, 'he was kind to me in his way.'

'And so he was to Alan,' said he; 'and by my troth, I found his way a very good one! But ye see, David, the loss of the ship and the cries of these poor lads sat very ill upon the man; and I'm thinking that would be the cause of it.'

'Well, I would think so,' says I; 'for he was as keen as any of the rest at the beginning. But how did Hoseason take it?'

'It sticks in my mind that he would take it very ill,' says Alan. 'But the little man cried to me to run, and indeed I thought it was a good observe, and ran. The last that I saw they were all in a knot upon the beach, like folk that were not agreeing very well together.'

'What do you mean by that?' said I.

'Well, the fists were going,' said Alan; 'and I saw one man go down like a pair of breeks. But I thought it would be better no to wait. Ye see there's a strip of Campbells in that end of Mull, which is no good company for a gentleman like me. If it hadnae been for that I would have waited and looked for ye mysel', let alone giving a hand to the little man.' (It was droll how Alan dwelt on Mr Riach's stature, for, to say the truth, the one was not much smaller than the other.) 'So,' says he, continuing, 'I set my best foot forward, and whenever I met in with any one I cried out there was a wreck ashore. Man, they didnae stop to fash with me! Ye should have seen them linking for the beach! And when they got there they found they had had the pleasure of a run, which is aye good for a Campbell. I'm thinking it was a judgment on the clan that the brig went down in the lump and didnae break. But it was a very unlucky thing for you, that same; for if any wreck had come ashore they would have hunted high and low, and would soon have found ye.'

CHAPTER XIX

The house of fear

Night fell as we were walking, and the clouds, which had broken up in the afternoon, settled in and thickened, so that it fell, for the season of the year, extremely dark. The way we went was over rough mountain sides; and though Alan pushed on with an assured manner, I could by no means see how he directed himself.

At last, about half-past ten of the clock, we came to the top of a brae, and saw lights below us. It seemed a house door stood open and let out a beam of fire and candle-light; and all round the house and steading five or six persons were moving hurriedly about, each carrying a lighted brand.

'James must have tint his wits,' said Alan. 'If this was the soldiers instead of you and me, he would be in a bonny mess. But I dare say he'll have a sentry on the road, and he would ken well enough no soldiers would find the way that we came.'

Hereupon he whistled three times, in a particular manner. It was strange to see how, at the first sound of it, all the moving torches came to a stand, as if the bearers were affrighted; and how, at the third, the bustle began again as before.

Having thus set folks' minds at rest, we came down the brae, and were met at the yard gate (for this place was like a well-doing farm) by a tall, handsome man of more than fifty, who cried out to Alan in the Gaelic.

'James Stewart,' said Alan, 'I will ask ye to speak in Scotch, for here is a young gentleman with me that has nane of the other. This is him,' he added, putting his arm through mine, 'a young gentleman of the lowlands, and a laird in his country too, but I am thinking it will be the better for his health if we give his name the go-by.'

James of the Glens turned to me for a moment, and greeted me courteously enough; the next he had turned to Alan.

'This has been a dreadful accident,' he cried. 'It will bring trouble on the country.' And he wrung his hands.

'Hoots!' said Alan, 'ye must take the sour with the sweet, man. Colin Roy is dead, and be thankful for that!'

'Ay,' said James, 'and by my troth, I wish he was alive again! It's all very fine to blow and boast beforehand; but now it's done, Alan; and who's to bear the wyte* of it? The accident fell out in Appin – mind ye that, Alan; it's Appin that must pay; and I am a man that has a family.'

While this was going on I looked about me at the servants. Some were on ladders, digging in the thatch of the house or the farm buildings, from which they brought out guns, swords, and different weapons of war; others carried them away; and by the sound of mattock blows from somewhere further down the brae, I suppose they buried them. Though they were all so busy, there prevailed no kind of order in their efforts; men struggled together for the same gun and ran into each other with their burning torches; and James was continually turning about from his talk with Alan, to cry out orders which were apparently never understood. The faces in the torchlight were like those of people overborne with hurry and panic; and though none spoke above his breath, their speech sounded both anxious and angry.

It was about this time that a lassie came out of the house carrying a pack or bundle; and it has often made me smile to think how Alan's instinct awoke at the mere sight of it.

'What's that the lassie has?' he asked.

'We're just setting the house in order, Alan,' said James, in his frightened and somewhat fawning way. 'They'll search Appin with candles, and we must have all things straight. We're digging the bit guns and swords into the moss, ye see; and these, I am thinking, will be your ain French clothes.'

'Bury my French clothes!' cried Alan. 'Troth, no!' And he

* Blame.

laid hold upon the packet and retired into the barn to shift himself, recommending me in the meanwhile to his kinsman.

James carried me accordingly into the kitchen, and sat down with me at table, smiling and talking at first in a very hospitable manner. But presently the gloom returned upon him; he sat frowning, and biting his fingers; only remembered me from time to time; and then gave me but a word or two and a poor smile, and back into his private terrors. His wife sat by the fire and wept, with her face in her hands; his eldest son was crouched upon the floor, running over a great mass of papers and now and again setting one alight and burning it to the bitter end; all the while a servant lass with a red face was rummaging about the room, in a blind hurry of fear, and whimpering as she went; and every now and again one of the men would thrust in his face from the yard, and cry for orders.

At last James could keep his seat no longer, and begged my permission to be so unmannerly as walk about. 'I am but poor company altogether, sir,' says he, 'but I can think of nothing but this dreadful accident, and the trouble it is like to bring upon quite innocent persons.'

A little after he observed his son burning a paper, which he thought should have been kept; and at that his excitement burst out so that it was painful to witness. He struck the lad repeatedly.

'Are you gone gyte?'* he cried. 'Do you wish to hang your father?' and forgetful of my presence, carried on at him a long time together in the Gaelic, the young man answering nothing; only the wife, at the name of hanging, throwing her apron over her face and sobbing out louder than before.

This was all wretched for a stranger like myself to hear and see; and I was right glad when Alan returned, looking like himself in his fine French clothes, though (to be sure) they were now grown almost too battered and withered to deserve the name of fine. I was then taken out in my turn by another of the sons, and given that change of clothing of which I had stood so long in need, and a pair of Highland brogues made of

* Mad.

deer-leather, rather strange at first, but after a little practice very easy to the feet.

By the time I came back Alan must have told his story; for it seemed understood that I was to fly with him, and they were all busy upon our equipment. They gave us each a sword and pistols, though I professed my inability to use the former; and with these, and some ammunition, a bag of oatmeal, an iron pan, and a bottle of right French brandy, we were ready for the heather. Money, indeed, was lacking. I had about two guineas left; Alan's belt having been despatched by another hand, that trusty messenger had no more than seventeen-pence to his whole fortune; and as for James, it appears he had brought himself so low with journeys to Edinburgh and legal expenses on behalf of the tenants, that he could only scrape together three-and-fivepence-halfpenny, the most of it in coppers.

'This'll no do,' said Alan.

'Ye must find a safe bit somewhere near by,' said James, 'and get word sent to me. Ye see, ye'll have to get this business prettily off, Alan. This is no time to be stayed for a guinea or two. They're sure to get wind of ye, sure to seek ye, and by my way of it, sure to lay on ye the wyte of this day's accident. If it falls on you, it falls on me that am your near kinsman and harboured ye while ye were in the country. And if it comes on me –' he paused, and bit his fingers, with a white face. 'It would be a painful thing for our friends if I was to hang,' said he.

'It would be an ill day for Appin,' says Alan.

'It's a day that sticks in my throat,' said James. 'Oh man, man, man – man Alan! you and me have spoken like two fools!' he cried, striking his hand upon the wall so that the house rang again.

'Well, and that's true, too,' said Alan; 'and my friend from the lowlands here' (nodding at me) 'gave me a good word upon that head, if I would only have listened to him.'

'But see here,' said James, returning to his former manner, 'if they lay me by the heels, Alan, it's then that you'll be needing the money. For with all that I have said and that you have said, it will look very black against the two of us; do ye mark that? Well, follow me out, and ye'll see that I'll have to get a paper out against ye mysel'; I'll have to offer a reward for ye; ay, will I! It's a sore thing to do between such near friends; but if I get the dirdum* of this dreadful accident, I'll have to fend for myself, man. Do ye see that?'

He spoke with a pleading earnestness, taking Alan by the breast of the coat.

'Ay,' said Alan, 'I see that.'

'And ye'll have to be clear of the country, Alan – ay, and clear of Scotland – you and your friend from the lowlands, too. For I'll have to paper your friend from the lowlands. Ye see that, Alan – say that ye see that!'

I thought Alan flushed a bit. 'This is unco hard on me that brought him here, James,' said he, throwing his head back. 'It's like making me a traitor!'

'Now, Alan, man!' cried James. 'Look things in the face! He'll be papered anyway; Mungo Campbell 'll be sure to paper him; what matters if I paper him too? And then, Alan, I am a man that has a family.' And then, after a little pause on both sides: 'And, Alan, it'll be a jury of Campbells,' said he.

'There's one thing,' said Alan, musingly, 'that naebody kens his name.'

'Nor yet they shallnae, Alan! There's my hand on that,' cried James, for all the world as if he had really known my name and was foregoing some advantage. 'But just the habit he was in, and what he looked like, and his age, and the like? I couldnae well do less.'

'I wonder at your father's son,' cried Alan, sternly. 'Would ye sell the lad with a gift? would ye change his clothes and then betray him?'

'No, no, Alan,' said James. 'No, no: the habit he took off – the habit Mungo saw him in.' But I thought he seemed crestfallen; indeed, he was clutching at every straw, and all the time, I dare say, saw the faces of his hereditary foes on the bench and in the jury-box, and the gallows in the background.

'Well, sir,' says Alan, turning to me, 'what say ye to that? Ye

* Blame.

are here under the safeguard of my honour; and it's my part to
see nothing done but what shall please you.'

'I have but one word to say,' said I; 'for to all this dispute I
am a perfect stranger. But the plain common sense is to set the
blame where it belongs, and that is on the man that fired the
shot. Paper him, as ye call it, set the hunt on him; and let honest,
innocent folk show their faces in safety.'

But at this both Alan and James cried out in horror; bidding
me hold my tongue, for that was not to be thought of; and
asking me 'What the Camerons would think?'[30] (which confirmed me, it must have been a Cameron from Mamore that
did the act) and if I did not see that the lad might be caught? 'Ye
havenae surely thought of that?' said they, with such innocent
earnestness, that my hands dropped at my side and I despaired
of argument.

'Very well, then,' said I, 'paper me, if you please, paper Alan,
paper King George! We're all three innocent, and that seems to
be what's wanted! But at least, sir,' said I to James, recovering
from my little fit of annoyance, 'I am Alan's friend, and if I can
be helpful to friends of his, I will not stumble at the risk.'

I thought it best to put a fair face on my consent, for I saw
Alan troubled; and besides (thinks I to myself) as soon as my
back is turned, they will paper me, as they call it, whether I
consent or not. But in this I saw I was wrong; for I had no
sooner said the words, than Mrs Stewart leaped out of her
chair, came running over to us, and wept first upon my neck
and then on Alan's, blessing God for our goodness to her family.

'As for you, Alan, it was no more than your bounden duty,'
she said. 'But for this lad that has come here and seen us at our
worst, and seen the goodman fleeching like a suitor, him that
by rights should give his commands like any king – as for you,
my lad,' she says, 'my heart is wae not to have your name, but
I have your face; and as long as my heart beats under my
bosom, I will keep it, and think of it, and bless it.' And with
that she kissed me, and burst once more into such sobbing, that
I stood abashed.

'Hoot, hoot,' said Alan, looking mighty silly. 'The day comes
unco soon in this month of July; and to-morrow there'll be a

fine to-do in Appin, a fine riding of dragoons, and crying of "Cruachan!"*[31] and running of red coats; and it behoves you and me to be the sooner gone.'

Thereupon we said farewell, and set out again, bending somewhat eastward, in a fine mild dark night, and over much the same broken country as before.

* The rallying word of the Campbells.

CHAPTER XX

The flight in the heather: the rocks

Sometimes we walked, sometimes ran; and as it drew on to morning, walked ever the less and ran the more. Though, upon its face, that country appeared to be a desert, yet there were huts and houses of the people, of which we must have passed more than twenty, hidden in quiet places of the hills. When we came to one of these, Alan would leave me in the way, and go himself and rap upon the side of the house and speak a while at the window with some sleeper awakened. This was to pass the news; which, in that country, was so much of a duty that Alan must pause to attend to it even while fleeing for his life; and so well attended to by others, that in more than half of the houses where we called they had heard already of the murder. In the others, as well as I could make out (standing back at a distance and hearing a strange tongue) the news was received with more of consternation than surprise.

For all our hurry, day began to come in while we were still far from any shelter. It found us in a prodigious valley, strewn with rocks and where ran a foaming river. Wild mountains stood around it; there grew there neither grass nor trees; and I have sometimes thought since then, that it may have been the valley called Glencoe, where the massacre was in the time of King William.[32] But for the details of our itinerary, I am all to seek; our way lying now by short cuts, now by great detours; our pace being so hurried; our time of journeying usually by night; and the names of such places as I asked and heard, being in the Gaelic tongue and the more easily forgotten.

The first peep of morning, then, showed us this horrible place, and I could see Alan knit his brow.

'This is no fit place for you and me,' he said. 'This is a place they're bound to watch.'

And with that he ran harder than ever down to the water side, in a part where the river was split in two among three rocks. It went through with a horrid thundering that made my belly quake; and there hung over the lynn a little mist of spray. Alan looked neither to the right nor to the left, but jumped clean upon the middle rock and fell there on his hands and knees to check himself, for that rock was small and he might have pitched over on the far side. I had scarce time to measure the distance or to understand the peril, before I had followed him, and he had caught and stopped me.

So there we stood, side by side upon a small rock slippery with spray, a far broader leap in front of us, and the river dinning upon all sides. When I saw where I was, there came on me a deadly sickness of fear, and I put my hand over my eyes. Alan took me and shook me; I saw he was speaking, but the roaring of the falls and the trouble of my mind prevented me from hearing; only I saw his face was red with anger, and that he stamped upon the rock. The same look showed me the water raging by, and the mist hanging in the air; and with that, I covered my eyes again and shuddered.

The next minute Alan had set the brandy bottle to my lips, and forced me to drink about a gill, which sent the blood into my head again. Then, putting his hands to his mouth and his mouth to my ear, he shouted 'Hang or drown!' and turning his back upon me, leaped over the farther branch of the stream, and landed safe.

I was now alone upon the rock, which gave me the more room; the brandy was singing in my ears; I had this good example fresh before me, and just wit enough to see that if I did not leap at once, I should never leap at all. I bent low on my knees and flung myself forth, with that kind of anger of despair that has sometimes stood me in stead of courage. Sure enough, it was but my hands that reached the full length; these slipped, caught again, slipped again; and I was sliddering back into the lynn, when Alan seized me, first by the hair, then by the collar, and with a great strain dragged me into safety.

Never a word he said, but set off running again for his life, and I must stagger to my feet and run after him. I had been weary before, but now I was sick and bruised, and partly drunken with the brandy; I kept stumbling as I ran, I had a stitch that came near to overmaster me; and when at last Alan paused under a great rock that stood there among a number of others, it was none too soon for David Balfour.

A great rock, I have said; but by rights it was two rocks leaning together at the top, both some twenty feet high, and at the first sight inaccessible. Even Alan (though you may say he had as good as four hands) failed twice in an attempt to climb them; and it was only at the third trial, and then by standing on my shoulders and leaping up with such force as I thought must have broken my collar-bone, that he secured a lodgment. Once there, he let down his leathern girdle; and with the aid of that and a pair of shallow footholds in the rock, I scrambled up beside him.

Then I saw why we had come there; for the two rocks, being both somewhat hollow on the top and sloping one to the other, made a kind of dish or saucer, where as many as three or four men might have lain hidden.

All this while Alan had not said a word, and had run and climbed with such a savage, silent frenzy of hurry, that I knew he was in mortal fear of some miscarriage. Even now we were on the rock he said nothing, nor so much as relaxed the frowning look upon his face; but clapped flat down, and keeping only one eye above the edge of our place of shelter, scouted all round the compass. The dawn had come quite clear; we could see the stony sides of the valley, and its bottom, which was bestrewed with rocks, and the river, which went from one side to another, and made white falls; but nowhere the smoke of a house, nor any living creature but some eagles screaming round a cliff.

Then at last Alan smiled.

'Ay,' said he, 'now we have a chance'; and then looking at me with some amusement, 'Ye're no very gleg* at the jumping,' said he.

* Brisk.

At this I suppose I coloured with mortification, for he added at once, 'Hoots! small blame to ye! To be feared of a thing and yet to do it, is what makes the prettiest kind of a man. And then there was water there, and water's a thing that dauntons even me. No, no,' said Alan, 'it's no you that's to blame, it's me.'

I asked him why.

'Why,' said he, 'I have proved myself a gomeral this night. For first of all I take a wrong road, and that in my own country of Appin; so that the day has caught us where we should never have been; and thanks to that, we lie here in some danger and mair discomfort. And next (which is the worst of the two, for a man that has been so much among the heather as myself) I have come wanting a water-bottle, and here we lie for a long summer's day with naething but neat spirit. Ye may think that a small matter; but before it comes night, David, ye'll give me news of it.'

I was anxious to redeem my character, and offered, if he would pour out the brandy, to run down and fill the bottle at the river.

'I wouldnae waste the good spirit either,' says he. 'It's been a good friend to you this night; or in my poor opinion, ye would still be cocking on yon stone. And what's mair,' says he, 'ye may have observed (you that's a man of so much penetration) that Alan Breck Stewart was perhaps walking quicker than his ordinar'.'

'You!' I cried, 'you were running fit to burst.'

'Was I so?' said he. 'Well, then, ye may depend upon it, there was nae time to be lost. And now here is enough said; gang you to your sleep, lad, and I'll watch.'

Accordingly, I lay down to sleep; a little peaty earth had drifted in between the top of the two rocks, and some bracken grew there, to be a bed to me; the last thing I heard was still the crying of the eagles.

I dare say it would be nine in the morning when I was roughly awakened, and found Alan's hand pressed upon my mouth.

'Wheesht!' he whispered. 'Ye were snoring.'

'Well,' said I, surprised at his anxious and dark face, 'and why not?'

He peered over the edge of the rock, and signed to me to do the like.

It was now high day, cloudless, and very hot. The valley was as clear as in a picture. About half a mile up the water was a camp of red-coats; a big fire blazed in their midst, at which some were cooking; and near by, on the top of a rock about as high as ours, there stood a sentry, with the sun sparkling on his arms. All the way down along the river-side were posted other sentries; here near together, there widelier scattered; some planted like the first, on places of command, some on the ground level and marching and counter-marching, so as to meet half way. Higher up the glen, where the ground was more open, the chain of posts was continued by horse-soldiers, whom we could see in the distance riding to and fro. Lower down, the infantry continued; but as the stream was suddenly swelled by the confluence of a considerable burn, they were more widely set, and only watched the fords and stepping-stones.

I took but one look at them, and ducked again into my place. It was strange indeed to see this valley, which had lain so solitary in the hour of dawn, bristling with arms and dotted with the red coats and breeches.

'Ye see,' said Alan, 'this was what I was afraid of, Davie: that they would watch the burn-side. They began to come in about two hours ago, and, man! but ye're a grand hand at the sleeping! We're in a narrow place. If they get up the sides of the hill, they could easy spy us with a glass; but if they'll only keep in the foot of the valley, we'll do yet. The posts are thinner down the water; and, come night, we'll try our hand at getting by them.'

'And what are we to do till night?' I asked.

'Lie here,' says he, 'and birstle.'

That one good Scotch word, 'birstle', was indeed the most of the story of the day that we had now to pass. You are to remember that we lay on the bare top of a rock, like scones upon a girdle; the sun beat upon us cruelly; the rock grew so heated, a man could scarce endure the touch of it; and the little patch of earth and fern, which kept cooler, was only large enough for one at a time. We took turn about to lie on the naked rock, which was indeed like the position of that saint that was martyred on a gridiron; and it ran in my mind how strange it was, that in the same climate and at only a few days' distance, I should have suffered so cruelly, first from cold upon my island, and now from heat upon this rock.

All the while we had no water, only raw brandy for a drink, which was worse than nothing; but we kept the bottle as cool as we could, burying it in the earth, and got some relief by bathing our breasts and temples.

The soldiers kept stirring all day in the bottom of the valley, now changing guard, now in patrolling parties hunting among the rocks. These lay round in so great a number, that to look for men among them was like looking for a needle in a bottle of hay; and being so hopeless a task, it was gone about with the less care. Yet we could see the soldiers pike their bayonets among the heather, which sent a cold thrill into my vitals; and they would sometimes hang about our rock, so that we scarce dared to breathe.

It was in this way that I first heard the right English speech; one fellow as he went by actually clapping his hand upon the sunny face of the rock on which we lay, and plucking it off again with an oath.

'I tell you it's 'ot,' says he; and I was amazed at the clipping tones and the odd sing-song in which he spoke, and no less at that strange trick of dropping out the letter h. To be sure, I had heard Ransome; but he had taken his ways from all sorts of people, and spoke so imperfectly at the best, that I set down the most of it to childishness. My surprise was all the greater to hear that manner of speaking in the mouth of a grown man; and indeed I have never grown used to it; nor yet altogether with the English grammar, as perhaps a very critical eye might here and there spy out even in these memoirs.

The tediousness and pain of these hours upon the rock grew only the greater as the day went on; the rock getting still the hotter and the sun fiercer. There were giddiness, and sickness, and sharp pangs like rheumatism, to be supported. I minded then, and have often minded since, on the lines in our Scotch psalm:

The moon by night thee shall not smite,
Nor yet the sun by day:[33]

and indeed it was only by God's blessing that we were neither
of us sun-smitten.

At last, about two, it was beyond men's bearing, and there
was now temptation to resist, as well as pain to thole. For the
sun being now got a little into the west, there came a patch of
shade on the east side of our rock, which was the side sheltered
from the soldiers.

'As well one death as another,' said Alan, and slipped over
the edge and dropped on the ground on the shadowy side.

I followed him at once, and instantly fell all my length, so
weak was I and so giddy with that long exposure. Here, then,
we lay for an hour or two, aching from head to foot, as weak
as water, and lying quite naked to the eye of any soldier who
should have strolled that way. None came, however, all passing
by on the other side; so that our rock continued to be our shield
even in this new position.

Presently we began again to get a little strength, and as the
soldiers were now lying closer along the riverside, Alan proposed that we should try a start. I was by this time afraid of
but one thing in the world; and that was to be set back upon
the rock; anything else was welcome to me; so we got ourselves
at once in marching order, and began to slip from rock to rock
one after the other, now crawling flat on our bellies in the
shade, now making a run for it, heart in mouth.

The soldiers, having searched this side of the valley after a
fashion, and being perhaps somewhat sleepy with the sultriness
of the afternoon, had now laid by much of their vigilance, and
stood dozing at their posts or only kept a look-out along the
banks of the river; so that in this way, keeping down the valley
and at the same time towards the mountains, we drew steadily
away from their neighbourhood. But the business was the most
wearing I had ever taken part in. A man had need of a hundred
eyes in every part of him, to keep concealed in that uneven
country and within cry of so many and scattered sentries. When
we must pass an open place, quickness was not all, but a swift

judgment not only of the lie of the whole country, but of the solidity of every stone on which we must set foot; for the afternoon was now fallen so breathless that the rolling of a pebble sounded abroad like a pistol shot, and would start the echo calling among the hills and cliffs.

By sundown we had made some distance, even by our slow rate of progress, though to be sure the sentry on the rock was still plainly in our view. But now we came on something that put all fears out of season; and that was a deep rushing burn, that tore down, in that part, to join the glen river. At the sight of this we cast ourselves on the ground and plunged head and shoulders in the water; and I cannot tell which was the more pleasant, the great shock as the cool stream went over us, or the greed with which we drank of it.

We lay there (for the banks hid us), drank again and again, bathed our chests, let our wrists trail in the running water till they ached with the chill; and at last, being wonderfully renewed, we got out the meal-bag and made drammach in the iron pan. This, though it is but cold water mingled with oatmeal, yet makes a good enough dish for a hungry man; and where there are no means of making fire, or (as in our case) good reason for not making one, it is the chief stand-by of those who have taken to the heather.

As soon as the shadow of the night had fallen, we set forth again, at first with the same caution, but presently with more boldness, standing our full height and stepping out at a good pace of walking. The way was very intricate, lying up the steep sides of mountains and along the brows of cliffs; clouds had come in with the sunset, and the night was dark and cool; so that I walked without much fatigue, but in continual fear of falling and rolling down the mountains, and with no guess at our direction.

The moon rose at last and found us still on the road; it was in its last quarter and was long beset with clouds; but after a while shone out, and showed me many dark heads of mountains, and was reflected far underneath us on the narrow arm of a sea-loch.

At this sight we both paused: I struck with wonder to find

myself so high and walking (as it seemed to me) upon clouds:
Alan to make sure of his direction.

Seemingly he was well pleased, and he must certainly have
judged us out of ear-shot of all our enemies; for throughout the
rest of our night-march he beguiled the way with whistling of
many tunes, warlike, merry, plaintive; reel tunes that made the
foot go faster; tunes of my own south country that made me
fain to be home from my adventures; and all these, on the great,
dark, desert mountains, making company upon the way.

CHAPTER XXI

The flight in the heather: the Heugh of Corrynakiegh

Early as day comes in the beginning of July, it was still dark when we reached our destination, a cleft in the head of a great mountain, with a water running through the midst, and upon the one hand a shallow cave in a rock. Birches grew there in a thin, pretty wood, which a little further on was changed into a wood of pines. The burn was full of trout; the wood of cushat-doves; on the open side of the mountain beyond whaups would be always whistling, and cuckoos were plentiful. From the mouth of the cleft we looked down upon a part of Mamore, and on the sea-loch that divides that country from Appin; and this from so great a height, as made it my continual wonder and pleasure to sit and behold them.

The name of the cleft was the Heugh of Corrynakiegh; and although from its height and being so near upon the sea, it was often beset with clouds, yet it was on the whole a pleasant place, and the five days we lived in it went happily.

We slept in the cave, making our bed of heather bushes which we cut for that purpose, and covering ourselves with Alan's great coat. There was a low concealed place, in a turning of the glen, where we were so bold as to make fire: so that we could warm ourselves when the clouds set in, and cook hot porridge, and grill the little trouts that we caught with our hands under the stones and overhanging banks of the burn. This was indeed our chief pleasure and business; and not only to save our meal against worse times, but with a rivalry that much amused us, we spent a great part of our days at the water side, stripped to the waist and groping about or (as they say) guddling for these fish. The largest we got might have been a quarter of a pound;

but they were of good flesh and flavour, and when broiled upon the coals, lacked only a little salt to be delicious.

In any by-time Alan must teach me to use my sword, for my ignorance had much distressed him; and I think besides, as I had sometimes the upper-hand of him in the fishing, he was not sorry to turn to an exercise where he had so much the upper-hand of me. He made it somewhat more of a pain than need have been, for he stormed at me all through the lessons in a very violent manner of scolding, and would push me so close that I made sure he must run me through the body. I was often tempted to turn tail, but held my ground for all that, and got some profit of my lessons; if it was but to stand on guard with an assured countenance, which is often all that is required. So, though I could never in the least please my master, I was not altogether displeased with myself.

In the meanwhile, you are not to suppose that we neglected our chief business, which was to get away.

'It will be many a long day,' Alan said to me on our first morning, 'before the red-coats think upon seeking Corryna-kiegh; so now we must get word sent to James, and he must find the siller for us.'

'And how shall we send that word?' says I. 'We are here in a desert place, which yet we dare not leave; and unless ye get the fowls of the air to be your messengers, I see not what we shall be able to do.'

'Ay?' said Alan. 'Ye're a man of small contrivance, David.'

Thereupon he fell in a muse, looking in the embers of the fire; and presently, getting a piece of wood, he fashioned it in a cross, the four ends of which he blackened on the coals. Then he looked at me a little shyly.

'Could ye lend me my button?' says he. 'It seems a strange thing to ask a gift again, but I own I am laith to cut another.'

I gave him the button; whereupon he strung it on a strip of his great coat which he had used to bind the cross; and tying in a little sprig of birch and another of fir, he looked upon his work with satisfaction.

'Now,' said he, 'there is a little clachan' (what is called a hamlet in the English) 'not very far from Corrynakiegh, and it has the name of Koalisnacoan. There, there are living many friends of mine whom I could trust with my life, and some that I am no just so sure of. Ye see, David, there will be money set upon our heads; James himsel' is to set money on them; and as for the Campbells, they would never spare siller where there was a Stewart to be hurt. If it was otherwise, I would go down to Koalisnacoan whatever, and trust my life into these people's hands as lightly as I would trust another with my glove.'

'But being so?' said I.

'Being so,' said he, 'I would as lief they didnae see me. There's bad folk everywhere, and what's far worse, weak ones. So when it comes dark again, I will steal down into that clachan, and set this that I have been making in the window of a good friend of mine, John Breck Maccoll,[34] a bouman* of Appin's.'

'With all my heart,' says I; 'and if he finds it, what is he to think?'

'Well,' says Alan, 'I wish he was a man of more penetration, for by my troth I am afraid he will make little enough of it! But this is what I have in my mind. This cross is something in the nature of the cross-tarrie, or fiery cross, which is the signal of gathering in our clans; yet he will know well enough the clan is not to rise, for there it is standing in his window, and no word with it. So he will say to himsel', *The clan is not to rise, but there is something*. Then he will see my button, and that was Duncan Stewart's. And then he will say to himsel', *The son of Duncan is in the heather, and has need of me*.'

'Well,' said I, 'it may be. But even supposing so, there is a good deal of heather between here and the Forth.'

'And that is a very true word,' says Alan. 'But then John Breck will see the sprig of birch and the sprig of pine; and he will say to himsel' (if he is a man of any penetration at all, which I misdoubt) *Alan will be lying in a wood which is both of pines and birches*. Then he will think to himsel', *That is not so very rife hereabout*; and then he will come and give us a look up in Corrynakiegh. And if he does not, David, the devil may

* A bouman is a tenant who takes stock from the landlord and shares with him the increase.

fly away with him, for what I care; for he will no be worth the salt to his porridge.'

'Eh, man,' said I, drolling with him a little, 'you're very ingenious! But would it not be simpler for you to write him a few words in black and white?'

'And that is an excellent observe, Mr Balfour of Shaws,' says Alan, drolling with me; 'and it would certainly be much simpler for me to write to him, but it would be a sore job for John Breck to read it. He would have to go to the school for two-three years; and it's possible we might be wearied waiting on him.'

So that night Alan carried down his fiery cross and set it in the bouman's window. He was troubled when he came back; for the dogs had barked and the folk run out from their houses; and he thought he had heard a clatter of arms and seen a red-coat come to one of the doors. On all accounts, we lay the next day in the borders of the wood and kept a close look-out; so that if it was John Breck that came, we might be ready to guide him, and if it was the red-coats, we should have time to get away.

About noon a man was to be spied, straggling up the open side of the mountain in the sun, and looking round him as he came, from under his hand. No sooner had Alan seen him than he whistled; the man turned and came a little towards us: then Alan would give another 'peep!' and the man would come still nearer; and so by the sound of whistling, he was guided to the spot where we lay.

He was a ragged, wild, bearded man, about forty, grossly disfigured with the smallpox, and looked both dull and savage. Although his English was very bad and broken, yet Alan (according to his very handsome use, whenever I was by) would suffer him to speak no Gaelic. Perhaps the strange language made him appear more backward than he really was; but I thought he had little good-will to serve us, and what he had was the child of terror.

Alan would have had him carry a message to James; but the bouman would hear of no message. 'She was forget it,' he said in his screaming voice; and would either have a letter or wash his hands of us.

I thought Alan would be gravelled at that, for we lacked the means of writing in that desert. But he was a man of more resources than I knew; searched the wood until he found a quill of a cushat-dove, which he shaped into a pen; made himself a kind of ink with gunpowder from his horn and water from the running stream; and tearing a corner from his French military commission (which he carried in his pocket, like a talisman to keep him from the gallows) he sat down and wrote as follows:

DEAR KINSMAN, – Please send the money by the bearer to the place he kens of.

Your affectionate cousin,

A. S.

This he entrusted to the bouman, who promised to make what manner of speed he best could, and carried it off with him down the hill.

He was three full days gone, but about five in the evening of the third, we heard a whistling in the wood, which Alan answered; and presently the bouman came up the water-side, looking for us, right and left. He seemed less sulky than before, and indeed he was no doubt well pleased to have got to the end of such a dangerous commission.

He gave us the news of the country; that it was alive with red-coats; that arms were being found, and poor folk brought in trouble daily; and that James and some of his servants were already clapped in prison at Fort William, under strong suspicion of complicity. It seemed, it was noised on all sides that Alan Breck had fired the shot; and there was a bill issued for both him and me, with one hundred pounds reward.

This was all as bad as could be; and the little note the bouman had carried us from Mrs Stewart was of a miserable sadness. In it she besought Alan not to let himself be captured, assuring him, if he fell in the hands of the troops, both he and James were no better than dead men. The money she had sent was all that she could beg or borrow, and she prayed heaven we could be doing with it. Lastly, she said she enclosed us one of the bills in which we were described.

This we looked upon with great curiosity and not a little fear, partly as a man may look in a mirror, partly as he might look into the barrel of an enemy's gun to judge if it be truly aimed. Alan was advertised as 'a small, pock-marked, active man of thirty-five or thereby, dressed in a feathered hat, a French side-coat of blue with silver buttons and lace a great deal tarnished, a red waistcoat and breeches of black shag'; and I as 'a tall strong lad of about eighteen, wearing an old blue coat, very ragged, an old Highland bonnet, a long homespun waistcoat, blue breeches; his legs bare; low-country shoes, wanting the toes; speaks like a lowlander, and has no beard'.

Alan was well enough pleased to see his finery so fully remembered and set down; only when he came to the word tarnish, he looked upon his lace like one a little mortified. As for myself, I thought I cut a miserable figure in the bill; and yet was well enough pleased too, for since I had changed these rags, the description had ceased to be a danger and become a source of safety.

'Alan,' said I, 'you should change your clothes.'

'Na, troth!' said Alan, 'I have nae others. A fine sight I would be, if I went back to France in a bonnet!'

This put a second reflection in my mind: that if I were to separate from Alan and his tell-tale clothes I should be safe against arrest, and might go openly about my business. Nor was this all; for suppose I was arrested when I was alone, there was little against me; but suppose I was taken in company with the reputed murderer, my case would begin to be grave. For generosity's sake, I dare not speak my mind upon this head; but I thought of it none the less.

I thought of it all the more, too, when the bouman brought out a green purse with four guineas in gold, and the best part of another in small change. True, it was more than I had. But then Alan, with less than five guineas, had to get as far as France; I, with my less than two, not beyond Queensferry; so that, taking things in their proportion, Alan's society was not only a peril to my life but a burden on my purse.

But there was no thought of the sort in the honest head of my companion. He believed he was serving, helping, and protecting me. And what could I do but hold my peace, and chafe, and take my chance of it?

'It's little enough,' said Alan, putting the purse in his pocket, 'but it'll do my business. And now John Breck, if ye will hand me over my button, this gentleman and me will be for taking the road.'

But the bouman, after feeling about in a hairy purse that hung in front of him in the Highland manner (though he wore otherwise the lowland habit, with sea-trousers) began to roll his eyes strangely, and at last said, 'Her nainsel will loss it,' meaning he thought he had lost it.

'What!' cried Alan, 'you will lose my button, that was my father's before me? Now, I will tell you what is in my mind, John Breck: it is in my mind this is the worst day's work that ever ye did since ye were born.'

And as Alan spoke, he set his hands on his knees and looked at the bouman with a smiling mouth, and that dancing light in his eyes that meant mischief to his enemies.

Perhaps the bouman was honest enough; perhaps he had meant to cheat and then, finding himself alone with two of us in a desert place, cast back to honesty as being safer; at least, and all at once, he seemed to find that button and handed it to Alan.

'Well, and it is a good thing for the honour of the Maccolls,' said Alan, and then to me, 'Here is my button back again, and I thank you for parting with it, which is of a piece with all your friendships to me.' Then he took the warmest parting of the bouman. 'For,' says he, 'ye have done very well by me, and set your neck at a venture, and I will always give you the name of a good man.'

Lastly, the bouman took himself off by one way; and Alan and I (getting our chattels together) struck into another to resume our flight.

CHAPTER XXII

The flight in the heather: the moor

More than eleven hours of incessant, hard travelling brought
us early in the morning to the end of a range of mountains. In
front of us there lay a piece of low, broken, desert land, which
we must now cross. The sun was not long up, and shone straight
in our eyes; a little, thin mist went up from the face of the
moorland like a smoke; so that (as Alan said) there might have
been twenty squadron of dragoons there and we none the wiser.

We sat down, therefore, in a howe of the hill-side till the mist
should have risen, and made ourselves a dish of drammach,
and held a council of war.

'David,' said Alan, 'this is the kittle bit. Shall we lie here till
it comes night, or shall we risk it and stave on ahead?'

'Well,' said I, 'I am tired indeed, but I could walk as far again,
if that was all.'

'Ay, but it isnae,' said Alan, 'nor yet the half. This is how we
stand: Appin's fair death to us. To the south it's all Campbells,
and no to be thought of. To the north; well, there's no muckle
to be gained by going north; neither for you, that wants to get
at Queensferry, nor yet for me, that wants to get to France.
Well then, we'll can strike east.'

'East be it!' says I, quite cheerily; but I was thinking, in to
myself: 'Oh, man, if you would only take one point of the
compass and let me take any other, it would be the best for
both of us.'

'Well, then, east, ye see, we have the muirs,' said Alan. 'Once
there, David, it's mere pitch-and-toss. Out on yon bald, naked,
flat place, where can a body turn to? Let the red-coats come
over a hill, they can spy you miles away; and the sorrow's in

their horses' heels, they would soon ride you down. It's no good place, David; and I'm free to say, it's worse by daylight than by dark.'

'Alan,' said I, 'hear my way of it. Appin's death for us; we have none too much money, nor yet meal; the longer they seek, the nearer they may guess where we are; it's all a risk; and I give my word to go ahead until we drop.'

Alan was delighted. 'There are whiles,' said he, 'when ye are altogether too canny and Whiggish to be company for a gentleman like me; but there come other whiles when ye show yoursel' a mettle spark; and it's then, David, that I love ye like a brother.'

The mist rose and died away, and showed us that country lying as waste as the sea; only the moorfowl and the peewees crying upon it, and far over to the east, a herd of deer, moving like dots. Much of it was red with heather; much of the rest broken up with bogs and hags and peaty pools; some had been burnt black in a heath fire; and in another place there was quite a forest of dead firs, standing like skeletons. A wearier looking desert man never saw; but at least it was clear of troops, which was our point.

We went down accordingly into the waste, and began to make our toilsome and devious travel towards the eastern verge. There were the tops of mountains all round (you are to remember) from whence we might be spied at any moment; so it behoved us to keep in the hollow parts of the moor, and when these turned aside from our direction, to move upon its naked face with infinite care. Sometimes, for half an hour together, we must crawl from one heather bush to another, as hunters do when they are hard upon the deer. It was a clear day again, with a blazing sun; the water in the brandy bottle was soon gone; and altogether, if I had guessed what it would be to crawl half the time upon my belly and to walk much of the rest stooping nearly to the knees, I should certainly have held back from such a killing enterprise.

Toiling and resting and toiling again, we wore away the morning; and about noon lay down in a thick bush of heather to sleep. Alan took the first watch; and it seemed to me I had scarce closed my eyes before I was shaken up to take the second. We had no clock to go by; and Alan stuck a sprig of heath in the ground to serve instead; so that as soon as the shadow of the bush should fall so far to the east, I might know to rouse him. But I was by this time so weary that I could have slept twelve hours at a stretch; I had the taste of sleep in my throat; my joints slept even when my mind was waking; the hot smell of the heather, and the drone of the wild bees, were like possets to me; and every now and again I would give a jump and find I had been dozing.

The last time I woke I seemed to come back from further away, and thought the sun had taken a great start in the heavens. I looked at the sprig of heath, and at that I could have cried aloud; for I saw I had betrayed my trust. My head was nearly turned with fear and shame; and at what I saw, when I looked out around me on the moor, my heart was like dying in my body. For sure enough, a body of horse-soldiers had come down during my sleep, and were drawing near to us from the south-east, spread out in the shape of a fan and riding their horses to and fro in the deep parts of the heather.

When I waked Alan, he glanced first at the soldiers, then at the mark and the position of the sun, and knitted his brows with a sudden, quick look, both ugly and anxious, which was all the reproach I had of him.

'What are we to do now?' I asked.

'We'll have to play at being hares,' said he. 'Do ye see yon mountain?' pointing to one on the north-eastern sky.

'Ay,' said I.

'Well, then,' says he, 'let us strike for that. Its name is Ben Alder; it is a wild, desert mountain full of hills and hollows, and if we can win to it before the morn, we may do yet.'

'But, Alan,' cried I, 'that will take us across the very coming of the soldiers!'

'I ken that fine,' said he; 'but if we are driven back on Appin, we are two dead men. So now, David man, be brisk!'

With that he began to run forward on his hands and knees with an incredible quickness, as though it were his natural way of going. All the time, too, he kept winding in and out in the lower parts of the moorland where we were the best concealed. Some of these had been burned or at least scathed with fire; and there rose in our faces (which were close to the ground) a blinding, choking dust as fine as smoke. The water was long out; and this posture of running on the hands and knees brings an overmastering weakness and weariness, so that the joints ache and the wrists faint under your weight.

Now and then, indeed, where was a big bush of heather, we lay a while, and panted, and putting aside the leaves, looked back at the dragoons. They had not spied us, for they held straight on; a half-troop, I think, covering about two miles of ground, and beating it mighty thoroughly as they went. I had awakened just in time; a little later, and we must have fled in front of them, instead of escaping on one side. Even as it was, the least misfortune might betray us; and now and again, when a grouse rose out of the heather with a clap of wings, we lay as still as the dead and were afraid to breathe.

The aching and faintness of my body, the labouring of my heart, the soreness of my hands, and the smarting of my throat and eyes in the continual smoke of dust and ashes, had soon grown to be so unbearable that I would gladly have given up. Nothing but the fear of Alan lent me enough of a false kind of courage to continue. As for himself (and you are to bear in mind that he was cumbered with a greatcoat) he had first turned crimson, but as time went on, the redness began to be mingled with patches of white; his breath cried and whistled as it came; and his voice, when he whispered his observations in my ear during our halts, sounded like nothing human. Yet he seemed in no way dashed in spirits, nor did he at all abate in his activity; so that I was driven to marvel at the man's endurance.

At length, in the first gloaming of the night, we heard a trumpet sound, and looking back from among the heather, saw the troop beginning to collect. A little after, they had built a fire and camped for the night, about the middle of the waste.

At this I begged and besought that we might lie down and sleep.

'There shall be no sleep the night!' said Alan. 'From now on, these weary dragoons of yours will keep the crown of the muirland, and none will get out of Appin but winged fowls. We got through in the nick of time, and shall we jeopard what we've gained? Na, na, when the day comes, it shall find you and me in a fast place on Ben Alder.'

'Alan,' I said, 'it's not the want of will: it's the strength that I want. If I could, I would; but as sure as I'm alive I cannot.'

'Very well, then,' said Alan. 'I'll carry ye.'

I looked to see if he were jesting; but no, the little man was in dead earnest; and the sight of so much resolution shamed me.

'Lead away!' said I. 'I'll follow.'

He gave me one look, as much as to say 'Well done, David!' and off he set again at his top speed.

It grew cooler and even a little darker (but not much) with the coming of the night. The sky was cloudless; it was still early in July, and pretty far north; in the darkest part of that night, you would have needed pretty good eyes to read, but for all that, I have often seen it darker in a winter midday. Heavy dew fell and drenched the moor like rain; and this refreshed me for a while. When we stopped to breathe, and I had time to see all about me, the clearness and sweetness of the night, the shapes of the hills like things asleep, and the fire dwindling away behind us, like a bright spot in the midst of the moor, anger would come upon me in a clap that I must still drag myself in agony and eat the dust like a worm.

By what I have read in books, I think few that have held a pen were ever really wearied, or they would write of it more strongly. I had no care of my life, neither past nor future, and I scarce remembered there was such a lad as David Balfour. I did not think of myself, but just of each fresh step which I was sure would be my last, with despair – and of Alan, who was the cause of it, with hatred. Alan was in the right trade as a soldier; this is the officer's part to make men continue to do things, they know not wherefore, and when, if the choice was offered, they would lie down where they were and be killed. And I dare say I would have made a good enough private; for in these last hours, it never occurred to me that I had any choice, but just to obey as long as I was able, and die obeying.

Day began to come in, after years, I thought; and by that time we were past the greatest danger, and could walk upon our feet like men, instead of crawling like brutes. But, dear heart have mercy! what a pair we must have made, going double like old grandfathers, stumbling like babes, and as white as dead folk. Never a word passed between us; each set his mouth and kept his eyes in front of him, and lifted up his foot and set it down again, like people lifting weights at a country play;* all the while, with the moorfowl crying 'peep!' in the heather, and the light coming slowly clearer in the east.

I say Alan did as I did. Not that ever I looked at him, for I had enough ado to keep my feet; but because it is plain he must have been as stupid with weariness as myself, and looked as little where we were going, or we should not have walked into an ambush like blind men.

It fell in this way. We were going down a heathery brae, Alan leading and I following a pace or two behind, like a fiddler and his wife; when upon a sudden the heather gave a rustle, three or four ragged men leaped out, and the next moment we were lying on our backs, each with a dirk at his throat.

I don't think I cared: the pain of this rough handling was quite swallowed up by the pains of which I was already full; and I was too glad to have stopped walking to mind about a dirk. I lay looking up in the face of the man that held me; and I mind his face was black with the sun and his eyes very light, but I was not afraid of him. I heard Alan and another whispering in the Gaelic; and what they said was all one to me.

Then the dirks were put up, our weapons were taken away, and we were set face to face, sitting in the heather.

'They are Cluny's men,' said Alan. 'We couldnae have fallen better. We're just to bide here with these, which are his out-sentries, till they can get word to the chief of my arrival.'

Now Cluny Macpherson,[35] the chief of the clan Vourich, had been one of the leaders of the great rebellion six years before; there was a price on his life; and I had supposed him long ago in France, with the rest of the heads of that desperate party. Even

* Village fair.

tired as I was, the surprise of what I heard half wakened me.

'What?' I cried. 'Is Cluny still here?'

'Ay is he so!' said Alan. 'Still in his own country and kept by his own clan. King George can do no more.'

I think I would have asked farther, but Alan gave me the put-off. 'I am rather wearied,' he said, 'and I would like fine to get a sleep.' And without more words, he rolled on his face in a deep heather bush, and seemed to sleep at once.

There was no such thing possible for me. You have heard grasshoppers whirring in the grass in the summer time? Well, I had no sooner closed my eyes, than my body, and above all my head, belly, and wrists, seemed to be filled with whirring grasshoppers; and I must open my eyes again at once, and tumble and toss, and sit up and lie down; and look at the sky which dazzled me, or at Cluny's wild and dirty sentries, peering out over the top of the brae and chattering to each other in the Gaelic.

That was all the rest I had, until the messenger returned; when, as it appeared that Cluny would be glad to receive us, we must get once more upon our feet and set forward. Alan was in excellent good spirits, much refreshed by his sleep, very hungry, and looking pleasantly forward to a dram and a dish of hot collops, of which, it seems, the messenger had brought him word. For my part, it made me sick to hear of eating. I had been dead-heavy before, and now I felt a kind of dreadful lightness, which would not suffer me to walk. I drifted like a gossamer; the ground seemed to me a cloud, the hills a feather-weight, the air to have a current, like a running burn, which carried me to and fro. With all that, a sort of horror of despair sat on my mind, so that I could have wept at my own helplessness.

I saw Alan knitting his brows at me, and supposed it was in anger; and that gave me a pang of light-headed fear, like what a child may have. I remember, too, that I was smiling, and could not stop smiling, hard as I tried; for I thought it was out of place at such a time. But my good companion had nothing in his mind but kindness; and the next moment, two of the gillies had me by the arms, and I began to be carried forward with great swiftness (or so it appeared to me, although I dare say it was slowly enough in truth) through a labyrinth of dreary glens and hollows and into the heart of that dismal mountain of Ben Alder.

CHAPTER XXIII

Cluny's Cage

We came at last to the foot of an exceeding steep wood, which scrambled up a craggy hillside, and was crowned by a naked precipice.

'It's here,' said one of the guides, and we struck up hill.

The trees clung upon the slope, like sailors on the shrouds of a ship; and their trunks were like the rounds of a ladder, by which we mounted.

Quite at the top, and just before the rocky face of the cliff sprang above the foliage, we found that strange house which was known in the country as 'Cluny's Cage'. The trunks of several trees had been wattled across, the intervals strengthened with stakes, and the ground behind this barricade levelled up with earth to make the floor. A tree, which grew out from the hillside, was the living centre-beam of the roof. The walls were of wattle and covered with moss. The whole house had something of an egg shape; and it half hung, half stood in that steep, hillside thicket, like a wasp's nest in a green hawthorn.

Within, it was large enough to shelter five or six persons with some comfort. A projection of the cliff had been cunningly employed to be the fireplace; and the smoke rising against the face of the rock, and being not dissimilar in colour, readily escaped notice from below.

This was but one of Cluny's hiding places; he had caves, besides, and underground chambers in several parts of his country; and following the reports of his scouts, he moved from one to another as the soldiers drew near or moved away. By this manner of living, and thanks to the affection of his clan, he had not only stayed all this time in safety, while so many others had fled or been taken and slain; but stayed four or five years longer, and only went to France at last by the express command of his master. There he soon died; and it is strange to reflect that he may have regretted his Cage upon Ben Alder.

When we came to the door he was seated by his rock chimney, watching a gillie about some cookery. He was mighty plainly habited, with a knitted nightcap drawn over his ears, and smoked a foul cutty pipe. For all that he had the manners of a king, and it was quite a sight to see him rise out of his place to welcome us.

'Well, Mr Stewart, come awa' sir!' said he, 'and bring in your friend that as yet I dinna ken the name of.'

'And how is yourself, Cluny?' said Alan. 'I hope ye do brawly, sir. And I am proud to see ye, and to present to ye my friend the Laird of Shaws, Mr David Balfour.'

Alan never referred to my estate without a touch of a sneer, when we were alone; but with strangers, he rang the words out like a herald.

'Step in by, the both of ye, gentlemen,' says Cluny. 'I make ye welcome to my house, which is a queer, rude place for certain, but one where I have entertained a royal personage, Mr Stewart – ye doubtless ken the personage I have in my eye. We'll take a dram for luck, and as soon as this handless man of mine has the collops ready, we'll dine and take a hand at the cartes as gentlemen should. My life is a bit driegh,' says he, pouring out the brandy; 'I see little company, and sit and twirl my thumbs, and mind upon a great day that is gone by, and weary for another great day that we all hope will be upon the road. And so here's a toast to ye: The Restoration!'

Thereupon we all touched glasses and drank. I am sure I wished no ill to King George; and if he had been there himself in proper person, it's like he would have done as I did. No sooner had I taken out the dram than I felt hugely better, and could look on and listen, still a little mistily perhaps, but no longer with the same groundless horror and distress of mind.

It was certainly a strange place, and we had a strange host. In his long hiding, Cluny had grown to have all manner of precise habits, like those of an old maid. He had a particular place, where no one else must sit; the Cage was arranged in a particular way, which none must disturb; cookery was one of his chief fancies, and even while he was greeting us in, he kept an eye to the collops.

It appears, he sometimes visited or received visits from his wife and one or two of his nearest friends, under the cover of night; but for the more part lived quite alone, and communicated only with his sentinels and the gillies that waited on him in the Cage. The first thing in the morning, one of them, who was a barber, came and shaved him, and gave him the news of the country, of which he was immoderately greedy. There was no end to his questions; he put them as earnestly as a child; and at some of the answers, laughed out of all bounds of reason, and would break out again laughing at the mere memory, hours after the barber was gone.

To be sure, there might have been a purpose in his questions; for though he was thus sequestered, and like the other landed gentlemen of Scotland, stripped by the late Act of Parliament of legal powers, he still exercised a patriarchal justice in his clan. Disputes were brought to him in his hiding-hole to be decided; and the men of his country, who would have snapped their fingers at the Court of Session, laid aside revenge and paid down money at the bare word of this forfeited and hunted outlaw. When he was angered, which was often enough, he gave his commands and breathed threats of punishment like any king; and his gillies trembled and crouched away from him like children before a hasty father. With each of them, as he entered, he ceremoniously shook hands, both parties touching their bonnets at the same time in a military manner. Altogether, I had a fair chance to see some of the inner workings of a Highland clan; and this with a proscribed, fugitive chief; his country conquered; the troops riding upon all sides in quest of him, sometimes within a mile of where he lay; and when the least of the ragged fellows whom he rated and threatened, could have made a fortune by betraying him.

On that first day, as soon as the collops were ready, Cluny gave them with his own hand a squeeze of a lemon (for he was well supplied with luxuries) and bade us draw in to our meal.

'They,' said he, meaning the collops, 'are such as I gave His Royal Highness in this very house; bating the lemon juice, for at that time we were glad to get the meat and never fashed for kitchen. Indeed, there were mair dragoons than lemons in my country in the year forty-six.'

I do not know if the collops were truly very good, but my heart rose against the sight of them, and I could eat but little. All the while Cluny entertained us with stories of Prince Charlie's stay in the Cage, giving us the very words of the speakers, and rising from his place to show us where they stood. By these, I gathered the Prince was a gracious, spirited boy, like the son of a race of polite kings, but not so wise as Solomon. I gathered, too, that while he was in the Cage, he was often drunk; so the fault that has since, by all accounts, made such a wreck of him, had even then begun to show itself.

We were no sooner done eating than Cluny brought out an old, thumbed, greasy pack of cards, such as you may find in a mean inn; and his eyes brightened in his face as he proposed that we should fall to playing.

Now this was one of the things I had been brought up to eschew like disgrace; it being held by my father neither the part of a Christian nor yet of a gentleman, to set his own livelihood and fish for that of others, on the cast of painted pasteboard. To be sure, I might have pleaded my fatigue, which was excuse enough; but I thought it behoved that I should bear a testimony. I must have got very red in the face, but I spoke steadily, and told them I had no call to be a judge of others, but for my own part, it was a matter in which I had no clearness.

Cluny stopped mingling the cards. 'What in deil's name is this?' says he. 'What kind of Whiggish, canting talk is this, for the house of Cluny Macpherson?'

'I will put my hand in the fire for Mr Balfour,' says Alan. 'He is an honest and a mettle gentleman, and I would have ye bear in mind who says it. I bear a king's name,' says he, cocking his hat; 'and I and any that I call friend are company for the best. But the gentleman is tired, and should sleep; if he has no mind to the cartes, it will never hinder you and me. And I'm fit and willing, sir, to play ye any game that ye can name.'

'Sir,' says Cluny, 'in this poor house of mine I would have you to ken that any gentleman may follow his pleasure. If your friend would like to stand on his head, he is welcome. And if either he, or you, or any other man, is not preceesely satisfied, I will be proud to step outside with him.'

I had no will that these two friends should cut their throats for my sake.

'Sir,' said I, 'I am very wearied, as Alan says; and what's more, as you are a man that likely has sons of your own, I may tell you it was a promise to my father.'

'Say nae mair, say nae mair,' said Cluny, and pointed me to a bed of heather in a corner of the Cage. For all that he was displeased enough, looked at me askance, and grumbled when he looked. And indeed it must be owned that both my scruples and the words in which I declared them, smacked somewhat of the Covenanter, and were little in their place among wild Highland Jacobites.

What with the brandy and the venison, a strange heaviness had come over me; and I had scarce lain down upon the bed before I fell into a kind of trance, in which I continued almost the whole time of our stay in the Cage. Sometimes I was broad awake and understood what passed; sometimes I only heard voices or men snoring, like the voice of a silly river; and the plaids upon the wall dwindled down and swelled out again, like firelight shadows on the roof. I must sometimes have spoken or cried out, for I remember I was now and then amazed at being answered; yet I was conscious of no particular nightmare, only of a general, black, abiding horror – a horror of the place I was in, and the bed I lay in, and the plaids on the wall, and the voices, and the fire, and myself.

The barber-gillie, who was a doctor too, was called in to prescribe for me; but as he spoke in the Gaelic, I understood not a word of his opinion, and was too sick even to ask for a translation. I knew well enough I was ill, and that was all I cared about.

I paid little heed while I lay in this poor pass. But Alan and Cluny were most of the time at the cards, and I am clear that Alan must have begun by winning; for I remember sitting up, and seeing them hard at it, and a great glittering pile of as much as sixty or a hundred guineas on the table. It looked strange enough, to see all this wealth in a nest upon a cliff-side, wattled about growing trees. And even then, I thought it seemed deep water for Alan to be riding, who had no better battle-horse than a green purse and a matter of five pounds.

The luck, it seems, changed on the second day. About noon I was wakened as usual for dinner, and as usual refused to eat, and was given a dram with some bitter infusion which the barber had prescribed. The sun was shining in at the open door of the Cage, and this dazzled and offended me. Cluny sat at the table, biting the pack of cards. Alan had stooped over the bed, and had his face close to my eyes; to which, troubled as they were with the fever, it seemed of the most shocking bigness.

He asked me for a loan of my money.

'What for?' said I.

'Oh, just for a loan,' said he.

'But why?' I repeated. 'I don't see.'

'Hut, David!' said Alan, 'ye wouldnae grudge me a loan?'

I would though, if I had had my senses! But all I thought of then was to get his face away, and I handed him my money.

On the morning of the third day, when we had been forty-eight hours in the Cage, I awoke with a great relief of spirits, very weak and weary indeed, but seeing things of the right size and with their honest, everyday appearance. I had a mind to eat, moreover; rose from bed of my own movement; and as soon as we had breakfasted, stepped to the entry of the Cage and sat down outside in the top of the wood. It was a grey day with a cool, mild air: and I sat in a dream all morning, only disturbed by the passing by of Cluny's scouts and servants coming with provisions and reports; for as the coast was at that time clear, you might almost say he held court openly.

When I returned, he and Alan had laid the cards aside, and were questioning a gillie; and the chief turned about and spoke to me in the Gaelic.

'I have no Gaelic, sir,' said I.

Now since the card question, everything I said or did had the power of annoying Cluny. 'Your name has more sense than yourself, then,' said he, angrily; 'for it's good Gaelic. But the point is this. My scout reports all clear in the south, and the question is have ye the strength to go?'

I saw cards on the table, but no gold; only a heap of little written papers, and these all on Cluny's side. Alan, besides, had an odd look, like a man not very well content; and I began to have a strong misgiving.

'I do not know if I am as well as I should be,' said I, looking at Alan; 'but the little money we have has a long way to carry us.'

Alan took his under-lip into his mouth, and looked upon the ground.

'David,' says he, at last, 'I've lost it; there's the naked truth.'

'My money too?' said I.

'Your money too,' says Alan, with a groan. 'Ye shouldnae have given it me. I'm daft when I get to the cartes.'

'Hoot-toot, hoot-toot,' said Cluny. 'It was all daffing; it's all nonsense. Of course, ye'll have your money back again, and the double of it, if ye'll make so free with me. It would be a singular thing for me to keep it. It's not to be supposed that I would be any hindrance to gentlemen in your situation; that would be a singular thing!' cries he, and began to pull gold out of his pocket, with a mighty red face.

Alan said nothing, only looked on the ground.

'Will you step to the door with me, sir?' said I.

Cluny said he would be very glad, and followed me readily enough, but he looked flustered and put out.

'And now, sir,' says I, 'I must first acknowledge your generosity.'

'Nonsensical nonsense!' cries Cluny. 'Where's the generosity? This is just a most unfortunate affair; but what would ye have me do – boxed up in this bee-skep of a cage of mine – but just set my friends to the cartes, when I can get them? And if they lose, of course, it's not to be supposed –' And here he came to a pause.

'Yes,' said I, 'if they lose, you give them back their money; and if they win, they carry away yours in their pouches! I have said before that I grant your generosity; but to me, sir, it's a very painful thing to be placed in this position.'

There was a little silence, in which Cluny seemed always as if he was about to speak, but said nothing. All the time he grew redder and redder in the face.

'I am a young man,' said I, 'and I ask your advice. Advise me as you would your son. My friend fairly lost this money, after having fairly gained a far greater sum of yours; can I accept it back again? would that be the right part for me to play? Whatever I do, you can see for yourself it must be hard upon a man of any pride.'

'It's rather hard on me, too, Mr Balfour,' said Cluny, 'and ye give me very much the look of a man that has entrapped poor people to their hurt. I wouldnae have my friends come to any house of mine to accept affronts; no,' he cried, with a sudden heat of anger, 'nor yet to give them!'

'And so you see, sir,' said I, 'there is something to be said upon my side; and this gambling is a very poor employ for gentlefolks. But I am still waiting your opinion.'

I am sure if ever Cluny hated any man it was David Balfour. He looked me all over with a warlike eye, and I saw the challenge at his lips. But either my youth disarmed him, or perhaps his own sense of justice. Certainly it was a mortifying matter for all concerned, and not least for Cluny; the more credit that he took it as he did.

'Mr Balfour,' said he, 'I think you are too nice and covenanting, but for all that you have the spirit of a very pretty gentleman. Upon my honest word, ye may take this money – it's what I would tell my son – and here's my hand along with it!'

CHAPTER XXIV

The flight in the heather: the quarrel

Alan and I were put across Loch Errocht under cloud of night, and went down its eastern shore to another hiding place near the head of Loch Rannoch, whither we were led by one of the gillies from the Cage. This fellow carried all our luggage and Alan's great coat in the bargain, trotting along under the burthen, far less than the half of which used to weigh me to the ground, like a stout hill pony with a feather; yet he was a man that, in plain contest, I could have broken on my knee.

Doubtless it was a great relief to walk disencumbered; and perhaps without that relief, and the consequent sense of liberty and lightness, I could not have walked at all. I was but new risen from a bed of sickness; and there was nothing in the state of our affairs to hearten me for much exertion; travelling, as we did, over the most dismal deserts in Scotland, under a cloudy heaven, and with divided hearts among the travellers.

For long, we said nothing; marching alongside or one behind the other, each with a set countenance; I, angry and proud, and drawing what strength I had from these two violent and sinful feelings: Alan angry and ashamed, ashamed that he had lost my money, angry that I should take it so ill.

The thought of a separation ran always the stronger in my mind; and the more I approved of it, the more ashamed I grew of my approval. It would be a fine, handsome, generous thing, indeed, for Alan to turn round and say to me: 'Go, I am in the most danger, and my company only increases yours.' But for me to turn to the friend who certainly loved me, and say to him: 'You are in great danger, I am in but little; your friendship is a burden; go take your risks and bear your hardships alone –'

no, that was impossible; and even to think of it privily to myself, made my cheeks to burn.

And yet Alan had behaved like a child and (what is worse) a treacherous child. Wheedling my money from me while I lay half-conscious, was scarce better than theft; and yet here he was trudging by my side, without a penny to his name, and by what I could see, quite blithe to sponge upon the money he had driven me to beg. True, I was ready to share it with him; but it made me rage to see him count upon my readiness.

These were the two things uppermost in my mind; and I could open my mouth upon neither without black ungenerosity. So I did the next worst, and said nothing, nor so much as looked once at my companion, save with the tail of my eye.

At last, upon the other side of Loch Errocht, going over a smooth, rushy place, where the walking was easy, he could bear it no longer, and came close to me.

'David,' says he, 'this is no way for two friends to take a small accident. I have to say that I'm sorry; and so that's said. And now if you have anything, ye'd better say it.'

'Oh,' says I, 'I have nothing.'

He seemed disconcerted; at which I was meanly pleased.

'No,' said he, with rather a trembling voice, 'but when I say I was to blame?'

'Why, of course, ye were to blame,' said I, coolly; 'and you will bear me out that I have never reproached you.'

'Never,' says he; 'but ye ken very well that ye've done worse. Are we to part? Ye said so once before. Are ye to say it again? There's hills and heather enough between here and the two seas, David; and I will own I'm no very keen to stay where I'm no wanted.'

This pierced me like a sword, and seemed to lay bare my private disloyalty.

'Alan Breck!' I cried; and then: 'Do you think I am one to turn my back on you in your chief need? You dursn't say it to my face. My whole conduct's there to give the lie to it. It's true, I fell asleep upon the muir; but that was from weariness, and you do wrong to cast it up to me –'

'Which is what I never did,' said Alan.

'But aside from that,' I continued, 'what have I done that you should even me to dogs by such a supposition? I never yet failed a friend, and it's not likely I'll begin with you. There are things between us that I can never forget, even if you can.'

'I will only say this to ye, David,' said Alan, very quietly, 'that I have long been owing ye my life, and now I owe ye money. Ye should try to make that burden light for me.'

This ought to have touched me, and in a manner it did, but the wrong manner. I felt I was behaving badly; and was now not only angry with Alan, but angry with myself in the bargain; and it made me the more cruel.

'You asked me to speak,' said I. 'Well, then, I will. You own yourself that you have done me a disservice; I have had to swallow an affront; I have never reproached you, I never named the thing till you did. And now you blame me,' cried I, 'because I cannae laugh and sing as if I was glad to be affronted. The next thing will be that I'm to go down upon my knees and thank you for it! Ye should think more of others, Alan Breck. If ye thought more of others, ye would perhaps speak less about yourself; and when a friend that likes you very well, has passed over an offence without a word, you would be blithe to let it lie, instead of making it a stick to break his back with. By your own way of it, it was you that was to blame; then it shouldnae be you to seek the quarrel.'

'Aweel,' said Alan, 'say nae mair.'

And we fell back into our former silence; and came to our journey's end, and supped, and lay down to sleep, without another word.

The gillie put us across Loch Rannoch in the dusk of the next day, and gave us his opinion as to our best route. This was to get us up at once into the tops of the mountains: to go round by a circuit, turning the heads of Glen Lyon, Glen Lochay, and Glen Dochart, and come down upon the lowlands by Kippen and the upper waters of the Forth. Alan was little pleased with a route which led us through the country of his blood-foes, the Glenorchy Campbells. He objected that by turning to the east, we should come almost at once among the Athole Stewarts, a race of his own name and lineage although following a different chief, and come besides by a far easier and swifter way to the place whither we were bound. But the gillie, who was indeed the chief man of Cluny's scouts, had good reasons to give him on all hands, naming the force of troops in every district, and alleging finally (as well as I could understand) that we should nowhere be so little troubled as in a country of the Campbells.

Alan gave way at last, but with only half a heart. 'It's one of the dowiest countries in Scotland,' said he. 'There's naething there that I ken, but heath, and crows, and Campbells. But I see that ye're a man of some penetration; and be it as ye please!'

We set forth accordingly by this itinerary; and for the best part of three nights travelled on eerie mountains and among the well-heads of wild rivers; often buried in mist, almost continually blown and rained upon, and not once cheered by any glimpse of sunshine. By day, we lay and slept in the drenching heather; by night, incessantly clambered upon breakneck hills and among rude crags. We often wandered; we were often so involved in fog, that we must lie quiet till it lightened. A fire was never to be thought of. Our only food was drammach and a portion of cold meat that we had carried from the Cage; and as for drink, Heaven knows we had no want of water.

This was a dreadful time, rendered the more dreadful by the gloom of the weather and the country. I was never warm; my teeth chattered in my head; I was troubled with a very sore throat, such as I had on the isle; I had a painful stitch in my side, which never left me; and when I slept in my wet bed, with the rain beating above and the mud oozing below me, it was to live over again in fancy the worst part of my adventures – to see the tower of Shaws lit by lightning, Ransome carried below on the men's backs, Shuan dying on the round-house floor, or Colin Campbell grasping at the bosom of his coat. From such broken slumbers, I would be aroused in the gloaming, to sit up in the same puddle where I had slept, and sup cold drammach; the rain driving sharp in my face or running down my back in icy trickles; the mist enfolding us like as in a gloomy chamber – or perhaps, if the wind blew, falling suddenly apart and showing us the gulf of some dark valley where the streams were crying aloud.

The sound of an infinite number of rivers came up from all round. In this steady rain the springs of the mountain were broken up; every glen gushed water like a cistern; every stream was in high spate, and had filled and overflowed its channel. During our night tramps, it was solemn to hear the voice of them below in the valleys, now booming like thunder, now with an angry cry. I could well understand the story of the Water Kelpie, that demon of the streams, who is fabled to keep wailing and roaring at the ford until the coming of the doomed traveller. Alan I saw believed it, or half believed it; and when the cry of the river rose more than usually sharp, I was little surprised (though, of course, I would still be shocked) to see him cross himself in the manner of the Catholics.

During all these horrid wanderings we had no familiarity, scarcely even that of speech. The truth is that I was sickening for my grave, which is my best excuse. But besides that I was of an unforgiving disposition from my birth, slow to take offence, slower to forget it, and now incensed both against my companion and myself. For the best part of two days he was unweariedly kind; silent, indeed, but always ready to help, and always hoping (as I could very well see) that my displeasure would blow by. For the same length of time I stayed in myself, nursing my anger, roughly refusing his services, and passing him over with my eyes as if he had been a bush or a stone.

The second night, or rather the peep of the third day, found us upon a very open hill, so that we could not follow our usual plan and lie down immediately to eat and sleep. Before we had reached a place of shelter, the grey had come pretty clear, for though it still rained, the clouds ran higher; and Alan, looking in my face, showed some marks of concern.

'Ye had better let me take your pack,' said he, for perhaps the ninth time since we had parted from the scout beside Loch Rannoch.

'I do very well, I thank you,' said I, as cold as ice.

Alan flushed darkly. 'I'll not offer it again,' he said. 'I'm not a patient man, David.'

'I never said you were,' said I, which was exactly the rude, silly speech of a boy of ten.

Alan made no answer at the time, but his conduct answered for him. Henceforth, it is to be thought, he quite forgave himself for the affair at Cluny's; cocked his hat again, walked jauntily, whistled airs, and looked at me upon one side with a provoking smile.

The third night we were to pass through the western end of the country of Balquidder. It came clear and cold, with a touch in the air like frost, and a northerly wind that blew the clouds away and made the stars bright. The streams were full, of course, and still made a great noise among the hills; but I observed that Alan thought no more upon the Kelpie, and was in high good spirits. As for me, the change of weather came too late; I had lain in the mire so long that (as the Bible has it) my very clothes 'abhorred me'; I was dead weary, deadly sick and full of pains and shiverings; the chill of the wind went through me, and the sound of it confused my ears. In this poor state I had to bear from my companion something in the nature of a persecution. He spoke a good deal, and never without a taunt. 'Whig' was the best name he had to give me. 'Here,' he would say, 'here's a dub for ye to jump, my Whiggie! I ken you're a fine jumper!' And so on; all the time with a gibing voice and face.

I knew it was my own doing, and no one else's; but I was too miserable to repent. I felt I could drag myself but little farther; pretty soon, I must lie down and die on these wet mountains like a sheep or a fox, and my bones must whiten there like the bones of a beast. My head was light, perhaps; but I began to love the prospect, I began to glory in the thought of such a death, alone in the desert, with the wild eagles besieging my last moments. Alan would repent then, I thought; he would remember, when I was dead, how much he owed me, and the remembrance would be torture. So I went like a sick, silly, and bad-hearted schoolboy, feeding my anger against a fellow-man, when I would have been better on my knees, crying on God for mercy. And at each of Alan's taunts, I hugged myself. 'Ah!' thinks I to myself, 'I have a better taunt in readiness; when I lie down and die, you will feel it like a buffet in your face; ah, what a revenge! ah, how you will regret your ingratitude and cruelty!'

All the while, I was growing worse and worse. Once I had fallen, my legs simply doubling under me, and this had struck Alan for the moment; but I was afoot so briskly, and set off again with such a natural manner, that he soon forgot the incident. Flushes of heat went over me, and then spasms of shuddering. The stitch in my side was hardly bearable. At last I began to feel that I could trail myself no farther: and with that, there came on me all at once the wish to have it out with Alan, let my anger blaze, and be done with my life in a more sudden manner. He had just called me 'Whig'. I stopped.

'Mr Stewart,' said I, in a voice that quivered like a fiddle-string, 'you are older than I am, and should know your manners. Do you think it either very wise or very witty to cast my politics in my teeth? I thought, where folk differed, it was the part of gentlemen to differ civilly; and if I did not, I may tell you I could find a better taunt than some of yours.'

Alan had stopped opposite to me, his hat cocked, his hands in his breeches pockets, his head a little on one side. He listened, smiling evilly, as I could see by the starlight; and when I had done he began to whistle a Jacobite air. It was the air made in mockery of General Cope's defeat at Preston Pans:[36]

> Hey, Johnnie Cope, are ye waukin' yet?
> And are your drums a-beatin' yet?

And it came in my mind that Alan, on the day of that battle, had been engaged upon the royal side.

'Why do ye take that air, Mr Stewart?' said I. 'Is that to remind me you have been beaten on both sides?'

The air stopped on Alan's lips. 'David!' said he.

'But it's time these manners ceased,' I continued; 'and I mean you shall henceforth speak civilly of my King and my good friends the Campbells.'

'I am a Stewart –' began Alan.

'Oh!' says I, 'I ken ye bear a king's name. But you are to

remember, since I have been in the Highlands, I have seen a good many of those that bear it; and the best I can say of them is this, that they would be none the worse of washing.'

'Do you know that you insult me?' said Alan, very low.

'I am sorry for that,' said I, 'for I am not done; and if you distaste the sermon, I doubt the pirliecue* will please you as little. You have been chased in the field by the grown men of my party; it seems a poor kind of pleasure to outface a boy. Both the Campbells and the Whigs have beaten you; you have run before them like a hare. It behoves you to speak of them as of your betters.'

Alan stood quite still, the tails of his great coat clapping behind him in the wind.

'This is a pity,' he said at last. 'There are things said that cannot be passed over.'

'I never asked you to,' said I. 'I am as ready as yourself.'

'Ready?' said he.

'Ready,' I repeated. 'I am no blower and boaster like some that I could name. Come on!' And drawing my sword, I fell on guard as Alan himself had taught me.

'David!' he cried. 'Are ye daft? I cannae draw upon ye, David. It's fair murder.'

'That was your look-out when you insulted me,' said I.

'It's the truth!' cried Alan, and he stood for a moment, wringing his mouth in his hand like a man in sore perplexity. 'It's the bare truth,' he said, and drew his sword. But before I could touch his blade with mine, he had thrown it from him and fallen to the ground. 'Na, na,' he kept saying, 'na, na – I cannae, I cannae.'

At this the last of my anger oozed all out of me; and I found myself only sick, and sorry, and blank, and wondering at myself. I would have given the world to take back what I had said; but a word once spoken, who can recapture it? I minded me of all Alan's kindness and courage in the past, how he had helped and cheered and borne with me in our evil days; and then recalled my own insults, and saw that I had lost for

* A second sermon.

ever that doughty friend. At the same time, the sickness that
hung upon me seemed to redouble, and the pang in my side
was like a sword for sharpness. I thought I must have swooned
where I stood.

This it was that gave me a thought. No apology could blot
out what I had said; it was needless to think of one, none could
cover the offence; but where an apology was vain, a mere cry
for help might bring Alan back to my side. I put my pride away
from me. 'Alan!' I said; 'if you cannae help me, I must just die
here.'

He started up sitting, and looked at me.

'It's true,' said I. 'I'm by with it. Oh, let me get into the bield
of a house – I'll can die there easier.' I had no need to pretend;
whether I chose or not, I spoke in a weeping voice that would
have melted a heart of stone.

'Can ye walk?' asked Alan.

'No,' said I, 'not without help. This last hour, my legs have
been fainting under me; I've a stitch in my side like a red-hot
iron; I cannae breathe right. If I die, ye'll can forgive me, Alan?
In my heart, I liked ye fine – even when I was the angriest.'

'Wheesht, wheesht!' cried Alan. 'Dinnae say that! David man,
ye ken –' He shut his mouth upon a sob. 'Let me get my arm
about ye,' he continued; 'that's the way! Now lean upon me
hard. Gude kens where there's a house! We're in Balwhidder,
too; there should be no want of houses, no, nor friends' houses
here. Do ye gang easier so, Davie?'

'Ay,' said I, 'I can be doing this way'; and I pressed his arm
with my hand.

Again he came near sobbing. 'Davie,' said he, 'I'm no a
right man at all; I have neither sense nor kindness; I couldnae
remember ye were just a bairn, I couldnae see ye were dying on
your feet; Davie, ye'll have to try and forgive me.'

'Oh, man, let's say no more about it!' said I. 'We're neither
one of us to mend the other – that's the truth! We must just
bear and forbear, man Alan! Oh, but my stitch is sore! Is there
nae house?'

'I'll find a house to ye, David,' he said, stoutly. 'We'll follow down the burn, where there's bound to be houses. My poor man, will ye no be better on my back?'

'Oh, Alan,' says I, 'and me a good twelve inches taller?'

'Ye're no such a thing,' cried Alan, with a start. 'There may be a trifling matter of an inch or two; I'm no saying I'm just exactly what ye would call a tall man, whatever; and I dare say,' he added, his voice tailing off in a laughable manner, 'now when I come to think of it, I dare say ye'll be just about right. Ay, it'll be a foot, or near hand; or may be even mair!'

It was sweet and laughable to hear Alan eat his words up in the fear of some fresh quarrel. I could have laughed, had not my stitch caught me so hard; but if I had laughed, I think I must have wept too.

'Alan,' cried I, 'what makes ye so good to me? what makes ye care for such a thankless fellow?'

'Deed, and I don't know,' said Alan. 'For just precisely what I thought I liked about ye, was that ye never quarrelled; – and now I like ye better!'

CHAPTER XXV

In Balquidder

At the door of the first house we came to, Alan knocked, which was no very safe enterprise in such a part of the Highlands as the Braes of Balquidder. No great clan held rule there; it was filled and disputed by small septs, and broken remnants, and what they call 'chiefless folks', driven into the wild country about the springs of Forth and Teith by the advance of the Campbells. Here were Stewarts and Maclarens, which came to the same thing, for the Maclarens followed Alan's chief in war, and made but one clan with Appin. Here, too, were many of that old, proscribed, nameless, red-handed clan of the Macgregors.[37] They had always been ill considered, and now worse than ever, having credit with no side or party in the whole country of Scotland. Their chief, Macgregor of Macgregor, was in exile; the more immediate leader of that part of them about Balquidder, James More, Rob Roy's eldest son, lay waiting his trial in Edinburgh Castle; they were in ill-blood with Highlander and Lowlander, with the Grahames, the Maclarens and the Stewarts; and Alan, who took up the quarrel of any friend however distant, was extremely wishful to avoid them.

Chance served us very well; for it was a household of Maclarens that we found, where Alan was not only welcome for his name's sake but known by reputation. Here then I was got to bed without delay, and a doctor fetched, who found me in a sorry plight. But whether because he was a very good doctor, or I a very young, strong man, I lay bed-ridden for no more than a week, and before a month I was able to take the road again with a good heart.

All this time Alan would not leave me; though I often pressed him, and indeed his foolhardiness in staying was a common subject of outcry with the two or three friends that were let into the secret. He hid by day in a hole of the braes under a little wood; and at night when the coast was clear, would come into the house to visit me. I need not say if I was pleased to see him; Mrs Maclaren, our hostess, thought nothing good enough for such a guest; and as Duncan Dhu (which was the name of our host) had a pair of pipes in his house and was much of a lover of music, the time of my recovery was quite a festival, and we commonly turned night into day.

The soldiers let us be; although once a party of two companies and some dragoons went by in the bottom of the valley, where I could see them through the window as I lay in bed. What was much more astonishing, no magistrate came near me, and there was no question put of whence I came or whither I was going; and in that time of excitement, I was as free of all inquiry as though I had lain in a desert. Yet my presence was known before I left to all the people in Balquidder and the adjacent parts; many coming about the house on visits and these (after the custom of the country) spreading the news among their neighbours. The bills, too, had now been printed. There was one pinned near the foot of my bed, where I could read my own not very flattering portrait and, in larger characters, the amount of the blood money that had been set upon my life. Duncan Dhu and the rest that knew that I had come there in Alan's company, could have entertained no doubt of who I was; and many others must have had their guess. For though I had changed my clothes, I could not change my age or person; and lowland boys of eighteen were not so rife in these parts of the world, and above all about that time, that they could fail to put one thing with another and connect me with the bill. So it was, at least. Other folk keep a secret among two or three near friends, and somehow it leaks out; but among these clansmen, it is told to a whole countryside, and they will keep it for a century.

There was but one thing happened worth narrating; and that is the visit I had of Robin Oig,[38] one of the sons of the notorious Rob Roy. He was sought upon all sides on a charge of carrying a young woman from Balfron and marrying her (as was alleged) by force; yet he stepped about Balquidder like a gentleman in his own walled policy. It was he who had shot James Maclaren at the plough stilts, a quarrel never satisfied; yet he walked into the house of his blood enemies as a rider might into a public inn.

Duncan had time to pass me word of who it was; and we looked at one another in concern. You should understand, it was then close upon the time of Alan's coming; the two were little likely to agree; and yet if we sent word or sought to make a signal, it was sure to arouse suspicion in a man under so dark a cloud as the Macgregor.

He came in with a great show of civility, but like a man among inferiors; took off his bonnet to Mrs Maclaren, but clapped it on his head again to speak to Duncan; and having thus set himself (as he would have thought) in a proper light, came to my bedside and bowed.

'I am given to know, sir,' says he, 'that your name is Balfour.'

'They call me David Balfour,' said I, 'at your service.'

'I would give ye my name in return, sir,' he replied, 'but it's one somewhat blown upon of late days; and it'll perhaps suffice if I tell ye that I am own brother to James More Drummond or Macgregor, of whom ye will scarce have failed to hear.'

'No, sir,' said I, a little alarmed; 'nor yet of your father, Macgregor-Campbell.' And I sat up and bowed in bed; for I thought best to compliment him, in case he was proud of having had an outlaw to his father.

He bowed in return. 'But what I am come to say, sir,' he went on, 'is this. In the year '45, my brother raised a part of the "Gregara", and marched six companies to strike a stroke for the good side; and the surgeon that marched with our clan and cured my brother's leg when it was broken in the brush at Prestonpans, was a gentleman of the same name precisely as yourself. He was brother to Balfour of Baith; and if you are in any reasonable degree of nearness one of that gentleman's kin, I have come to put myself and my people at your command.'

You are to remember that I knew no more of my descent than any cadger's dog; my uncle, to be sure, had prated of some of our high connections, but nothing to the present purpose; and there was nothing left me but that bitter disgrace of owning that I could not tell.

Robin told me shortly he was sorry he had put himself about, turned his back upon me without a sign of salutation, and as he went towards the door, I could hear him telling Duncan that I was 'only some kinless loon that didn't know his own father'. Angry as I was at these words and ashamed of my own ignorance, I could scarce keep from smiling that a man who was under the lash of the law (and was indeed hanged some three years later) should be so nice as to the descent of his acquaintances.

Just in the door, he met Alan coming in; and the two drew back and looked at each other like strange dogs. They were neither of them big men, but they seemed fairly to swell out with pride. Each wore a sword, and by a movement of his haunch, thrust clear the hilt of it, so that it might be the more readily grasped and the blade drawn.

'Mr Stewart, I am thinking,' says Robin.

'Troth, Mr Macgregor, it's not a name to be ashamed of,' answered Alan.

'I did not know ye were in my country, sir,' says Robin.

'It sticks in my mind that I am in the country of my friends the Maclarens,' says Alan.

'That's a kittle point,' returned the other. 'There may be two words to say to that. But I think I will have heard that you are a man of your sword?'

'Unless ye were born deaf, Mr Macgregor, ye will have heard a good deal more than that,' says Alan. 'I am not the only man that can draw steel in Appin; and when my kinsman and captain, Ardshiel, had a talk with a gentleman of your name, not so many years back, I could never hear that the Macgregor had the best of it.'

'Do ye mean my father, sir?' says Robin.

'Well, I wouldnae wonder,' said Alan. 'The gentleman I have in my mind had the ill-taste to clap Campbell to his name.'

'My father was an old man,' returned Robin. 'The match was unequal. You and me would make a better pair, sir.'

'I was thinking that,' said Alan.

I was half out of bed, and Duncan had been hanging at the elbow of these fighting cocks, ready to intervene upon the least occasion. But when that word was uttered, it was a case of now or never; and Duncan, with something of a white face to be sure, thrust himself between.

'Gentlemen,' said he, 'I will have been thinking of a very different matter, whateffer. Here are my pipes, and here are you two gentlemen who are baith acclaimed pipers. It's an auld dispute which one of ye's the best. Here will be a braw chance to settle it.'

'Why, sir,' said Alan, still addressing Robin, from whom indeed he had not so much as shifted his eyes, nor yet Robin from him, 'why, sir,' says Alan, 'I think I will have heard some sough* of the sort. Have ye music, as folk say? Are ye a bit of a piper?'

'I can pipe like a Macrimmon!'[39] cries Robin.

'And that is a very bold word,' quoth Alan.

'I have made bolder words good before now,' returned Robin, 'and that against better adversaries.'

'It is easy to try that,' says Alan.

Duncan Dhu made haste to bring out the pair of pipes that was his principal possession, and to set before his guests a mutton-ham and a bottle of that drink which they call Athole brose, and which is made of old whiskey, strained honey and sweet cream, slowly beaten together in the right order and proportion. The two enemies were still on the very breach of a quarrel; but down they sat, one upon each side of the peat fire, with a mighty show of politeness. Maclaren pressed them to taste his mutton-ham and 'the wife's brose', reminding them the wife was out of Athole and had a name far and wide for her skill in that confection. But Robin put aside these hospitalities as bad for the breath.

'I would have ye to remark, sir,' said Alan, 'that I havenae broken bread for near upon ten hours, which will be worse for the breath than any brose in Scotland.'

* Rumour.

'I will take no advantages, Mr Stewart,' replied Robin. 'Eat and drink; I'll follow you.'

Each ate a small portion of the ham and drank a glass of the brose to Mrs Maclaren; and then after a great number of civilities, Robin took the pipes and played a little spring in a very ranting manner.

'Ay, ye can blow,' said Alan; and taking the instrument from his rival, he first played the same spring in a manner identical with Robin's; and then wandered into variations, which, as he went on, he decorated with a perfect flight of grace-notes, such as pipers love, and call the 'warblers'.

I had been pleased with Robin's playing, Alan's ravished me.

'That's no very bad, Mr Stewart,' said the rival, 'but ye show a poor device in your warblers.'

'Me!' cried Alan, the blood starting to his face. 'I give ye the lie.'

'Do ye own yourself beaten at the pipes, then,' said Robin, 'that ye seek to change them for the sword?'

'And that's very well said, Mr Macgregor,' returned Alan; 'and in the meantime' (laying a strong accent on the word) 'I take back the lie. I appeal to Duncan.'

'Indeed, ye need appeal to naebody,' said Robin. 'Ye're a far better judge than any Maclaren in Balquidder: for it's a God's truth that you're a very creditable piper for a Stewart. Hand me the pipes.'

Alan did as he asked; and Robin proceeded to imitate and correct some part of Alan's variations, which it seemed that he remembered perfectly.

'Ay, ye have music,' said Alan, gloomily.

'And now be the judge yourself, Mr Stewart,' said Robin; and taking up the variations from the beginning, he worked them throughout to so new a purpose, with such ingenuity and sentiment, and with so odd a fancy and so quick a knack in the grace-notes, that I was amazed to hear him.

As for Alan, his face grew dark and hot, and he sat and gnawed his fingers, like a man under some deep affront. 'Enough!' he cried. 'Ye can blow the pipes – make the most of that.' And he made as if to rise.

But Robin only held out his hand as if to ask for silence, and struck into the slow measure of a pibroch. It was a fine piece of music in itself, and nobly played; but it seems besides it was a piece peculiar to the Appin Stewarts and a chief favourite with Alan. The first notes were scarce out, before there came a change in his face; when the time quickened, he seemed to grow restless in his seat; and long before that piece was at an end, the last signs of his anger died from him, and he had no thought but for the music.

'Robin Oig,' he said, when it was done, 'ye are a great piper. I am not fit to blow in the same kingdom with ye. Body of me! ye have mair music in your sporran than I have in my head! And though it still sticks in my mind that I could maybe show ye another of it with the cold steel, I warn ye before hand – it'll no be fair! It would go against my heart to haggle a man that can blow the pipes as you can!'

Thereupon that quarrel was made up; all night long the brose was going and the pipes changing hands; and the day had come pretty bright, and the three men were none the better for what they had been taking, before Robin as much as thought upon the road.

It was the last I saw of him, for I was in the Low Countries at the University of Leyden, when he stood his trial, and was hanged in the Grassmarket. And I have told this at so great length, partly because it was the last incident of any note that befell me on the wrong side of the Highland Line,[40] and partly because (as the man came to be hanged) it's in a manner history.

CHAPTER XXVI

End of the flight: we pass the Forth

The month, as I have said, was not yet out, but it was already far through August, and beautiful warm weather, with every sign of an early and great harvest, when I was pronounced able for my journey. Our money was now run to so low an ebb that we must think first of all on speed; for if we came not soon to Mr Rankeillor's, or if when we came there he should fail to help me, we must surely starve. In Alan's view, besides, the hunt must have now greatly slackened; and the line of the Forth and even Stirling Bridge, which is the main pass over that river, would be watched with little interest.

'It's a chief principle in military affairs,' said he, 'to go where ye are least expected. Forth is our trouble; ye ken the saying, "Forth bridles the wild Hielandman." Well, if we seek to creep round about the head of that river and come down by Kippen or Balfron, it's just precisely there that they'll be looking to lay hands on us. But if we stave on straight to the auld Brig' of Stirling, I'll lay my sword they let us pass unchallenged.'

The first night, accordingly, we pushed to the house of a Maclaren in Strathire, a friend of Duncan's, where we slept the twenty-first of the month, and whence we set forth again about the fall of night to make another easy stage. The twenty-second we lay in a heather bush on a hillside in Uam Var, within view of a herd of deer, the happiest ten hours of sleep in a fine, breathing sunshine and on bone-dry ground, that I have ever tasted. That night we struck Allan Water, and followed it down; and coming to the edge of the hills saw the whole Carse of Stirling underfoot, as flat as a pancake, with the town and castle

on a hill in the midst of it, and the moon shining on the Links
of Forth.

'Now,' said Alan, 'I kenna if ye care, but ye're in your own
land again. We passed the Hieland Line in the first hour; and
now if we could but pass yon crooked water, we might cast our
bonnets in the air.'

In Allan Water, near by where it falls into the Forth, we
found a little sandy islet, overgrown with burdock, butterbur
and the like low plants, that would just cover us if we lay flat.
Here it was we made our camp, within plain view of Stirling
Castle, whence we could hear the drums beat as some part of
the garrison paraded. Shearers worked all day in a field on one
side of the river, and we could hear the stones going on the
hooks and the voices and even the words of the men talking. It
behoved to lie close and keep silent. But the sand of the little
isle was sun-warm, the green plants gave us shelter for our
heads, we had food and drink in plenty; and to crown all, we
were within sight of safety.

As soon as the shearers quit their work and the dusk began
to fall, we waded ashore and struck for the Bridge of Stirling,
keeping to the fields and under the field fences.

The bridge is close under the castle hill, an old, high, narrow
bridge with pinnacles along the parapet; and you may conceive
with how much interest I looked upon it, not only as a place
famous in history, but as the very doors of salvation to Alan
and myself. The moon was not yet up when we came there; a
few lights shone along the front of the fortress, and lower down
a few lighted windows in the town; but it was all mighty still,
and there seemed to be no guard upon the passage.

I was for pushing straight across; but Alan was more wary.

'It looks unco' quiet,' said he; 'but for all that we'll lie down
here cannily behind a dyke, and make sure.'

So we lay for about a quarter of an hour, whiles whispering,
whiles lying still and hearing nothing earthly but the washing
of the water on the piers. At last there came by an old, hobbling
woman with a crutch stick; who first stopped a little, close to
where we lay, and bemoaned herself and the long way she had
travelled; and then set forth again up the steep spring of the

bridge. The woman was so little, and the night still so dark, that we soon lost sight of her; only heard the sound of her steps, and her stick, and a cough that she had by fits, draw slowly farther away.

'She's bound to be across now,' I whispered.

'Na,' said Alan, 'her foot still sounds boss* upon the bridge.'

And just then – 'Who goes?' cried a voice, and we heard the butt of a musket rattle on the stones. I must suppose the sentry had been sleeping, so that had we tried, we might have passed unseen; but he was awake now, and the chance forfeited.

'This 'll never do,' said Alan. 'This 'll never, never do for us, David.'

And without another word, he began to crawl away through the fields; and a little after, being well out of eye-shot, got to his feet again, and struck along a road that led to the eastward. I could not conceive what he was doing; and indeed I was so sharply cut by the disappointment, that I was little likely to be pleased with anything. A moment back, and I had seen myself knocking at Mr Rankeillor's door to claim my inheritance, like a hero in a ballad; and here was I back again, a wandering, hunted blackguard, on the wrong side of Forth.

'Well?' said I.

'Well,' said Alan, 'what would ye have? They're none such fools as I took them for. We have still the Forth to pass, Davie – weary fall the rains that fed and the hillsides that guided it!'

'And why go east?' said I.

'Ou, just upon the chance!' said he. 'If we cannae pass the river, we'll have to see what we can do for the firth.'

'There are fords upon the river, and none upon the firth,' said I.

'To be sure there are fords, and a bridge forbye,' quoth Alan; 'and of what service, when they are watched?'

'Well,' said I, 'but a river can be swum.'

'By them that have the skill of it,' returned he; 'but I have yet to hear that either you or me is much of a hand at that exercise; and for my own part, I swim like a stone.'

---

* Hollow.

'I'm not up to you in talking back, Alan,' I said; 'but I can see we're making bad worse. If it's hard to pass a river, it stands to reason it must be worse to pass a sea.'

'But there's such a thing as a boat,' says Alan, 'or I'm the more deceived.'

'Ay, and such a thing as money,' says I. 'But for us that have neither one nor other, they might just as well not have been invented.'

'Ye think so?' said Alan.

'I do that,' said I.

'David,' says he, 'ye're a man of small invention and less faith. But let me set my wits upon the hone, and if I cannae beg, borrow, nor yet steal a boat, I'll make one!'

'I think I see ye!' said I. 'And what's more than all that: if ye pass a bridge, it can tell no tales; but if we pass the firth, there's the boat on the wrong side – somebody must have brought it – the countryside will all be in a bizz –'

'Man!' cried Alan, 'if I make a boat, I'll make a body to take it back again! So deave me with no more of your nonsense, but walk (for that's what you've got to do) – and let Alan think for ye.'

All night, then, we walked through the north side of the Carse under the high line of the Ochil mountains; and by Alloa and Clackmannan and Culross, all of which we avoided; and about ten in the morning, mighty hungry and tired, came to the little clachan of Limekilns. This is a place that sits near in by the waterside, and looks across the Hope to the town of the Queensferry. Smoke went up from both of these, and from other villages and farms upon all hands. The fields were being reaped; two ships lay anchored, and boats were coming and going on the Hope. It was altogether a right pleasant sight to me; and I could not take my fill of gazing at these comfortable, green, cultivated hills and the busy people both of the field and sea.

For all that, there was Mr Rankeillor's house on the south shore, where I had no doubt wealth awaited me; and here was I upon the north, clad in poor enough attire of an outlandish fashion, with three silver shillings left to me of all my fortune, a price set upon my head, and an outlawed man for my sole company.

'O, Alan!' said I, 'to think of it! Over there, there's all that heart could want waiting me; and the birds go over, and the boats go over – all that please can go, but just me only! O, man, but it's a heartbreak!'

In Limekilns we entered a small change-house, which we only knew to be a public by the wand over the door, and bought some bread and cheese from a good-looking lass that was the servant. This we carried with us in a bundle, meaning to sit and eat it in a bush of wood on the sea-shore, that we saw some third part of a mile in front. As we went, I kept looking across the water and sighing to myself; and though I took no heed of it, Alan had fallen into a muse. At last he stopped in the way.

'Did ye take heed of the lass we bought this of?' says he, tapping on the bread and cheese.

'To be sure,' said I, 'and a bonny lass she was.'

'Ye thought that?' cries he. 'Man David, that's good news.'

'In the name of all that's wonderful, why so?' says I. 'What good can that do?'

'Well,' said Alan, with one of his droll looks, 'I was rather in hopes it would maybe get us that boat.'

'If it were the other way about, it would be liker it,' said I.

'That's all that you ken, ye see,' said Alan. 'I don't want the lass to fall in love with ye, I want her to be sorry for ye, David; to which end, there is no manner of need that she should take you for a beauty. Let me see' (looking me curiously over). 'I wish ye were a wee thing paler; but apart from that ye'll do fine for my purpose – ye have a fine, hang-dog, rag-and-tatter, clappermaclaw kind of a look to ye, as if ye had stolen the coat from a potato-bogle. Come; right about, and back to the change-house for that boat of ours.'

I followed him laughing.

'David Balfour,' said he, 'ye're a very funny gentleman by your way of it, and this is a very funny employ for ye, no doubt. For all that, if ye have any affection for my neck (to say nothing of your own) ye will perhaps be kind enough to take this matter responsibly. I am going to do a bit of play-acting, the bottom ground of which is just exactly as serious as the gallows for the pair of us. So bear it, if ye please, in mind, and conduct yourself according.'

'Well, well,' said I, 'have it as you will.'

As we got near the clachan, he made me take his arm and hang upon it like one almost helpless with weariness; and by the time he pushed open the change-house door, he seemed to be half carrying me. The maid appeared surprised (as well she might be) at our speedy return; but Alan had no words to spare for her in explanation, helped me to a chair, called for a tass of brandy with which he fed me in little sips, and then breaking up the bread and cheese helped me to eat it like a nursery-lass; the whole with that grave, concerned, affectionate countenance, that might have imposed upon a judge. It was small wonder if the maid were taken with the picture we presented, of a poor, sick, overwrought lad and his most tender comrade. She drew quite near, and stood leaning with her back on the next table.

'What's like wrong with him?' said she at last.

Alan turned upon her, to my great wonder, with a kind of fury. 'Wrong?' cries he. 'He's walked more hundreds of miles than he has hairs upon his chin, and slept oftener in wet heather than dry sheets. Wrong, quo' she! Wrong enough, I would think! Wrong, indeed!' and he kept grumbling to himself, as he fed me, like a man ill-pleased.

'He's young for the like of that,' said the maid.

'Ower young,' said Alan, with his back to her.

'He would be better riding,' says she.

'And where could I get a horse to him?' cried Alan, turning on her with the same appearance of fury. 'Would ye have me steal?'

I thought this roughness would have sent her off in dudgeon, as indeed it closed her mouth for the time. But my companion knew very well what he was doing; and for as simple as he was in some things of life, had a great fund of roguishness in such affairs as these.

'Ye neednae tell me,' she said at last – 'ye're gentry.'

'Well,' said Alan, softened a little (I believe against his will) by this artless comment, 'and suppose we were? did ever you hear that gentrice put money in folk's pockets?'

She sighed at this, as if she were herself some disinherited great lady. 'No,' says she, 'that's true indeed.'

I was all this while chafing at the part I played, and sitting tongue-tied between shame and merriment; but somehow at this I could hold in no longer, and bade Alan let me be, for I was better already. My voice stuck in my throat, for I ever hated to take part in lies; but my very embarrassment helped on the plot, for the lass no doubt set down my husky voice to sickness and fatigue.

'Has he nae friends?' said she, in a tearful voice.

'That has he so!' cried Alan, 'if we could but win to them! – friends and rich friends, beds to lie in, food to eat, doctors to see to him – and here he must tramp in the dubs and sleep in the heather like a beggarman.'

'And why that?' says the lass.

'My dear,' says Alan, 'I cannae very safely say; but I'll tell ye what I'll do instead,' says he, 'I'll whistle ye a bit tune.' And with that he leaned pretty far over the table, and in a mere breath of a whistle, but with a wonderful pretty sentiment, gave her a few bars of 'Charlie is my darling'.[41]

'Wheesht,' says she, and looked over her shoulder to the door.

'That's it,' said Alan.

'And him so young!' cries the lass.

'He's old enough to –' and Alan struck his forefinger on the back part of his neck, meaning that I was old enough to lose my head.

'It would be a black shame,' she cried, flushing high.

'It's what will be, though,' said Alan, 'unless we manage the better.'

At this the lass turned and ran out of that part of the house, leaving us alone together, Alan in high good humour at the furthering of his schemes, and I in bitter dudgeon at being called a Jacobite and treated like a child.

'Alan,' I cried, 'I can stand no more of this.'

'Ye'll have to sit it then, Davie,' said he. 'For if ye upset the pot now, ye may scrape your own life out of the fire, but Alan Breck is a dead man.'

This was so true that I could only groan; and even my groan served Alan's purpose, for it was overheard by the lass as she came flying in again with a dish of white puddings and a bottle of strong ale.

'Poor lamb!' says she, and had no sooner set the meat before us, than she touched me on the shoulder with a little friendly touch, as much as to bid me cheer up. Then she told us to fall to, and there would be no more to pay; for the inn was her own, or at least her father's, and he was gone for the day to Pittencrieff. We waited for no second bidding, for bread and cheese is but cold comfort and the puddings smelt excellently well; and while we sat and ate, she took up that same place by the next table, looking on, and thinking, and frowning to herself, and drawing the string of her apron through her hand.

'I'm thinking ye have rather a long tongue,' she said at last to Alan.

'Ay,' said Alan; 'but ye see I ken the folk I speak to.'

'I would never betray ye,' said she, 'if ye mean that.'

'No,' said he, 'ye're not that kind. But I'll tell ye what ye would do, ye would help.'

'I couldnae,' said she, shaking her head. 'Na, I couldnae.'

'No,' said he, 'but if ye could?'

She answered him nothing.

'Look here, my lass,' said Alan, 'there are boats in the kingdom of Fife, for I saw two (no less) upon the beach, as I came in by your town's end. Now if we could have the use of a boat to pass under cloud of night into Lothian, and some secret, decent kind of a man to bring that boat back again and keep his counsel, there would be two souls saved – mine to all likelihood – his to a dead surety. If we lack that boat, we have but three shillings left in this wide world; and where to go, and how to do, and what other place there is for us except the chains of a gibbet – I give you my naked word, I kenna! Shall we go wanting, lassie? Are ye to lie in your warm bed and think upon us, when the wind gowls in the chimney and the rain tirls on the roof? Are ye to eat your meat by the cheeks of a red fire, and think upon this poor sick lad of mine, biting his finger ends on a blae muir for cauld and hunger? Sick or sound, he must aye be moving; with the death grapple at his throat he must aye be trailing in the rain on the lang roads; and when he gants his last on a rickle of cauld stanes, there will be nae friends near him but only me and God.'

At this appeal, I could see the lass was in great trouble of mind, being tempted to help us, and yet in some fear she might be helping malefactors; and so now I determined to step in myself and to allay her scruples with a portion of the truth.

'Did ever you hear,' said I, 'of Mr Rankeillor of the Ferry?'

'Rankeillor the writer?' said she. 'I daursay that!'

'Well,' said I, 'it's to his door that I am bound, so you may judge by that if I am an ill-doer; and I will tell you more, that though I am indeed, by a dreadful error, in some peril of my life, King George has no truer friend in all Scotland than myself.'

Her face cleared up mightily at this, although Alan's darkened.

'That's more than I would ask,' said she. 'Mr Rankeillor is a kennt man.' And she bade us finish our meat, get clear of the Clachan as soon as might be, and lie close in the bit wood on the sea beach. 'And ye can trust me,' says she, 'I'll find some means to put you over.'

At this we waited for no more, but shook hands with her upon the bargain, made short work of the puddings, and set forth again from Limekilns as far as to the wood. It was a small piece of perhaps a score of elders and hawthorns and a few young ashes, not thick enough to veil us from passers-by upon the road or beach. Here we must lie, however, making the best of the brave warm weather and the good hopes we now had of a deliverance, and planning more particularly what remained for us to do.

We had but one trouble all day: when a strolling piper came and sat in the same wood with us; a red-nosed, blear-eyed, drunken dog, with a great bottle of whiskey in his pocket, and a long story of wrongs that had been done him by all sorts of persons, from the Lord President of the Court of Session who had denied him justice, down to the Baillies of Inverkeithing who had given him more of it than he desired. It was impossible but he should conceive some suspicion of two men lying all day concealed in a thicket and having no business to allege. As long as he stayed there, he kept us in hot water with prying questions; and after he was gone, as he was a man not very likely to hold his tongue, we were in the greater impatience to be gone ourselves.

The day came to an end with the same brightness; the night fell quiet and clear; lights came out in houses and hamlets and then, one after another, began to be put out; but it was past eleven, and we were long since strangely tortured with anxieties, before we heard the grinding of oars upon the rowing pins. At that, we looked out and saw the lass herself coming rowing to us in a boat. She had trusted no one with our affairs, not even her sweetheart, if she had one; but as soon as her father was asleep, had left the house by a window, stolen a neighbour's boat, and come to our assistance single-handed.

I was abashed how to find expression for my thanks; but she was no less abashed at the thought of hearing them; begged us to lose no time and to hold our peace, saying (very properly) that the heart of our matter was in haste and silence; and so, what with one thing and another, she had set us on the Lothian shore not far from Carriden, had shaken hands with us, and was out again at sea and rowing for Limekilns, before there was one word said either of her service or our gratitude.

Even after she was gone, we had nothing to say, as indeed nothing was enough for such a kindness. Only Alan stood a great while upon the shore shaking his head.

'It is a very fine lass,' he said at last. 'David, it is a very fine lass.' And a matter of an hour later, as we were lying in a den on the seashore and I had been already dozing, he broke out again in commendations of her character. For my part, I could say nothing, she was so simple a creature that my heart smote me both with remorse and fear; remorse because we had traded upon her ignorance; and fear lest we should have anyway involved her in the dangers of our situation.

CHAPTER XXVII

I come to Mr Rankeillor

The next day it was agreed that Alan should fend for himself till sunset; but as soon as it began to grow dark, he should lie in the fields by the roadside near to Newhalls, and stir for naught until he heard me whistling. At first I proposed I should give him for a signal the 'Bonnie House of Airlie',[42] which was a favourite of mine; but he objected that as the piece was very commonly known, any ploughman might whistle it by accident; and taught me instead a little fragment of a Highland air, which has run in my head from that day to this, and will likely run in my head when I lie dying. Every time it comes to me, it takes me off to that last day of my uncertainty, with Alan sitting up in the bottom of the den, whistling and beating the measure with a finger, and the grey of the dawn coming on his face.

I was in the long street of Queensferry before the sun was up. It was a fairly built burgh, the houses of good stone, many slated; the town-hall not so fine, I thought, as that of Peebles, nor yet the street so noble; but take it altogether, it put me to shame for my foul tatters.

As the morning went on, and the fires began to be kindled, and the windows to open, and the people to appear out of the houses, my concern and despondency grew ever the blacker. I saw now that I had no grounds to stand upon; and no clear proof of my rights, nor so much as of my own identity. If it was all a bubble, I was indeed sorely cheated and left in a sore pass. Even if things were as I conceived, it would in all likelihood take time to establish my contentions; and what time had I to spare with less than three shillings in my pocket, and a condemned, hunted man upon my hands to ship out of the country?

Truly, if my hope broke with me, it might come to the gallows yet for both of us. And as I continued to walk up and down, and saw people looking askance at me upon the street or out of windows, and nudging or speaking one to another with smiles, I began to take a fresh apprehension: that it might be no easy matter even to come to speech of the lawyer, far less to convince him of my story.

For the life of me I could not muster up the courage to address any of these reputable burghers; I thought shame even to speak with them in such a pickle of rags and dirt; and if I had asked for the house of such a man as Mr Rankeillor, I supposed they would have burst out laughing in my face. So I went up and down, and through the street, and down to the harbour-side, like a dog that has lost its master, with a strange gnawing in my inwards, and every now and then a movement of despair. It grew to be high day at last, perhaps nine in the forenoon; and I was worn with these wanderings, and chanced to have stopped in front of a very good house on the landward side, a house with beautiful, clear glass windows, flowering knots upon the sills, the walls new-harled,* and a chase-dog sitting yawning on the step like one that was at home. Well, I was even envying this dumb brute, when the door fell open and there issued forth a shrewd, ruddy, kindly consequential man in a well-powdered wig and spectacles. I was in such a plight that no one set eyes on me once, but he looked at me again; and this gentleman, as it proved, was so much struck with my poor appearance that he came straight up to me and asked me what I did.

I told him I was come to the Queensferry on business, and taking heart of grace, asked him to direct me to the house of Mr Rankeillor.

'Why,' said he, 'that is his house that I have just come out of; and for a rather singular chance, I am that very man.'

'Then, sir,' said I, 'I have to beg the favour of an interview.'

'I do not know your name,' said he, 'nor yet your face.'

'My name is David Balfour,' said I.

---

* Newly rough-cast.

'David Balfour?' he repeated, in rather a high tone, like one surprised. 'And where have you come from, Mr David Balfour?' he asked, looking me pretty drily in the face.

'I have come from a great many strange places, sir,' said I; 'but I think it would be as well to tell you where and how in a more private manner.'

He seemed to muse awhile, holding his lip in his hand, and looking now at me and now upon the causeway of the street.

'Yes,' says he, 'that will be the best, no doubt.' And he led me back with him into his house, cried out to some one whom I could not see that he would be engaged all morning, and brought me into a little dusty chamber full of books and documents. Here he sate down, and bade me be seated; though I thought he looked a little ruefully from his clean chair to my muddy rags. 'And now,' says he, 'if you have any business, pray be brief and come swiftly to the point. *Nec gemino bellum Trojanum orditur ab ovo*[43] – do you understand that?' says he, with a keen look.

'I will even do as Horace says, sir,' I answered, smiling, 'and carry you *in medias res*.'[44] He nodded as if he was well pleased, and indeed his scrap of Latin had been set to test me. For all that, and though I was somewhat encouraged, the blood came in my face when I added: 'I have reason to believe myself some rights on the estate of Shaws.'

He got a paper book out of a drawer and set it before him open. 'Well?' said he.

But I had shot my bolt and sat speechless.

'Come, come, Mr Balfour,' said he, 'you must continue. Where were you born?'

'In Essendean, sir,' said I, 'the year 1734, the 12th of March.'

He seemed to follow this statement in his paper book; but what that meant I knew not. 'Your father and mother?' said he.

'My father was Alexander Balfour, schoolmaster of that place,' said I, 'and my mother Grace Pitarrow; I think her people were from Angus.'

'Have you any papers proving your identity?' asked Mr Rankeillor.

'No, sir,' said I, 'but they are in the hands of Mr Campbell, the minister, and could be readily produced. Mr Campbell, too, would give me his word; and for that matter, I do not think my uncle would deny me.'

'Meaning Mr Ebenezer Balfour?' says he.

'The same,' said I.

'Whom you have seen?' he asked.

'By whom I was received into his own house,' I answered.

'Did you ever meet a man of the name of Hoseason?' asked Mr Rankeillor.

'I did so, sir, for my sins,' said I; 'for it was by his means and the procurement of my uncle, that I was kidnapped within sight of this town, carried to sea, suffered shipwreck and a hundred other hardships, and stand before you to-day in this poor accoutrement.'

'You say you were shipwrecked,' said Rankeillor; 'where was that?'

'Off the south end of the Isle of Mull,' said I. 'The name of the isle on which I was cast up is the Island Earraid.'

'Ah!' says he, smiling, 'you are deeper than me in the geography. But so far, I may tell you, this agrees pretty exactly with other informations that I hold. But you say you were kidnapped; in what sense?'

'In the plain meaning of the word, sir,' said I. 'I was on my way to your house, when I was trepanned on board the brig, cruelly struck down, thrown below, and knew no more of anything till we were far at sea. I was destined for the plantations; a fate that, in God's providence, I have escaped.'

'The brig was lost on June the 27th,' says he, looking in his book, 'and we are now at August the 24th. Here is a considerable hiatus, Mr Balfour, of near upon two months. It has already caused a vast amount of trouble to your friends; and I own I shall not be very well contented until it is set right.'

'Indeed, sir,' said I, 'these months are very easily filled up; but yet before I told my story, I would be glad to know that I was talking to a friend.'

'This is to argue in a circle,' said the lawyer. 'I cannot be convinced till I have heard you. I cannot be your friend till I am properly informed. If you were more trustful, it would better befit your time of life. And you know, Mr Balfour, we have a proverb in the country that evil-doers are aye evil-dreaders.'

'You are not to forget, sir,' said I, 'that I have already suffered by my trustfulness; and was shipped off to be a slave by the very man that (if I rightly understand) is your employer.'

All this while, I had been gaining ground with Mr Rankeillor, and in proportion as I gained ground, gaining confidence. But at this sally, which I made with something of a smile myself, he fairly laughed aloud.

'No, no,' said he, 'it is not so bad as that. *Fui, non sum.*[45] I *was* indeed your uncle's man of business; but while you (*imberbis juvenis custode remoto*)[46] were gallivanting in the west, a good deal of water has run under the bridges; and if your ears did not sing, it was not for lack of being talked about. On the very day of your sea disaster, Mr Campbell stalked into my office, demanding you from all the winds. I had never heard of your existence; but I had known your father; and from matters in my competence (to be touched upon hereafter) I was disposed to fear the worst. Mr Ebenezer admitted having seen you; declared (what seemed improbable) that he had given you considerable sums; and that you had started for the continent of Europe, intending to fulfil your education, which was probable and praiseworthy. Interrogated how you had come to send no word to Mr Campbell, he deponed that you had expressed a great desire to break with your past life. Further interrogated where you now were, protested ignorance, but believed you were in Leyden. That is a close sum of his replies. I am not exactly sure that any one believed him,' continued Mr Rankeillor with a smile; 'and in particular he so much dis-relished some expressions of mine that (in a word) he showed me to the door. We were then at a full stand; for whatever shrewd suspicions we might entertain, we had no shadow of probation. In the very article, comes Captain Hoseason with the story of your drowning; whereupon all fell through; with no consequences but concern to Mr Campbell, injury to my pocket, and another blot upon your uncle's character, which

could very ill afford it. And now, Mr Balfour,' said he, 'you
understand the whole process of these matters, and can judge
for yourself to what extent I may be trusted.'

Indeed he was more pedantic than I can represent him, and
placed more scraps of Latin in his speech; but it was all uttered
with a fine geniality of eye and manner which went far to
conquer my distrust. Moreover, I could see he now treated me
as if I was myself beyond a doubt; so that first point of my
identity seemed fully granted.

'Sir,' said I, 'if I tell you my story, I must commit a friend's
life to your discretion. Pass me your word it shall be sacred;
and for what touches myself, I will ask no better guarantee than
just your face.'

He passed me his word very seriously. 'But,' said he, 'these
are rather alarming prolocutions; and if there are in your story
any little jostles to the law, I would beg you to bear in mind
that I am a lawyer, and pass lightly.'

Thereupon I told him my story from the first, he listening
with his spectacles thrust up and his eyes closed, so that I
sometimes feared he was asleep. But no such matter! he heard
every word (as I found afterward) with such quickness of hearing and precision of memory as often surprised me. Even
strange, outlandish Gaelic names, heard for that time only, he
remembered and would remind me of, years after. Yet when I
called Alan Breck in full, we had an odd scene. The name of
Alan had of course rung through Scotland, with the news of
the Appin murder and the offer of the reward; and it had no
sooner escaped me than the lawyer moved in his seat and
opened his eyes.

'I would name no unnecessary names, Mr Balfour,' said he;
'above all of Highlanders, many of whom are obnoxious to
the law.'

'Well, it might have been better not,' said I; 'but since I have
let it slip, I may as well continue.'

'Not at all,' said Mr Rankeillor. 'I am somewhat dull of
hearing, as you may have remarked; and I am far from sure I
caught the name exactly. We will call your friend, if you please,
Mr Thomson[47] – that there may be no reflections. And in future,

I would take some such way with any Highlander that you may
have to mention – dead or alive.'

By this, I saw he must have heard the name all too clearly
and had already guessed I might be coming to the murder. If
he chose to play this part of ignorance, it was no matter of
mine; so I smiled, said it was no very Highland sounding name,
and consented. Through all the rest of my story Alan was Mr
Thomson; which amused me the more, as it was a piece of
policy after his own heart. James Stewart, in like manner, was
mentioned under the style of Mr Thomson's kinsman; Colin
Campbell passed as a Mr Glen; and to Cluny, when I came to
that part of my tale, I gave the name of 'Mr Jameson, a Highland
chief'. It was truly the most open farce, and I wondered that
the lawyer should care to keep it up; but after all it was quite
in the taste of that age, when there were two parties in the state,
and quiet persons, with no very high opinions of their own,
sought out every cranny to avoid offence to either.

'Well, well,' said the lawyer, when I had quite done, 'this is
a great epic, a great Odyssey of yours. You must tell it, sir, in
a sound Latinity when your scholarship is riper; or in English
if you please, though for my part I prefer the stronger tongue.
You have rolled much; *quae regio in terris*[48] – what parish in
Scotland (to make a homely translation) has not been filled
with your wanderings? You have shown, besides, a singular
aptitude for getting into false positions; and, yes, upon the
whole, for behaving well in them. This Mr Thomson seems to
me a gentleman of some choice qualities, though perhaps a
trifle bloody-minded. It would please me none the worse, if
(with all his merits) he were soused in the North Sea, for the
man, Mr David, is a sore embarrassment. But you are doubtless
quite right to adhere to him; indubitably, he adhered to you. *It
comes* – we may say – he was your true companion; nor less,
paribus curis vestigia figit,[49] for I daresay you would both take
an orra thought upon the gallows. Well, well, these days are
fortunately by; and I think (speaking humanly) that you are
near the end of your troubles.'

As he thus moralized on my adventures, he looked upon me
with so much humour and benignity that I could scarce contain

my satisfaction. I had been so long wandering with lawless people, and making my bed upon the hills and under the bare sky, that to sit once more in a clean, covered house, and to talk amicably with a gentleman in broadcloth, seemed mighty elevations. Even as I thought so, my eye fell on my unseemly tatters, and I was once more plunged in confusion. But the lawyer saw and understood me. He rose, called over the stair to lay another plate, for Mr Balfour would stay to dinner, and led me into a bedroom in the upper part of the house. Here he set before me water and soap and a comb; and laid out some clothes that belonged to his son; and here, with another apposite tag, he left me to my toilet.

CHAPTER XXVIII

I go in quest of my inheritance

I made what change I could in my appearance; and blithe was I to look in the glass and find the beggar-man a thing of the past, and David Balfour come to life again. And yet I was ashamed of the change too, and above all, of the borrowed clothes. When I had done, Mr Rankeillor caught me on the stair, made me his compliments, and had me again into the cabinet.

'Sit ye down, Mr David,' said he, 'and now that you are looking a little more like yourself, let me see if I can find you any news. You will be wondering, no doubt, about your father and your uncle? To be sure it is a singular tale; and the explanation is one that I blush to have to offer you. For,' says he, really with embarrassment, 'the matter hinges on a love affair.'

'Truly,' said I, 'I cannot very well join that notion with my uncle.'

'But your uncle, Mr David, was not always old,' replied the lawyer, 'and what may perhaps surprise you more, not always ugly. He had a fine, gallant air; people stood in their doors to look after him, as he went by upon a mettle horse. I have seen it with these eyes, and I ingenuously confess, not altogether without envy; for I was a plain lad myself and a plain man's son; and in those days, it was a case of *Odi te, qui bellus es, Sabelle.*'[50]

'It sounds like a dream,' said I.

'Ay, ay,' said the lawyer, 'that is how it is with youth and age. Nor was that all, but he had a spirit of his own that seemed to promise great things in the future. In 1715, what must he do but run away to join the rebels? It was your father that pursued him, found him in a ditch, and brought him back *multum gementem*;[51] to the mirth of the whole county. However, *majora canamus*[52] – the two lads fell in love, and that with the same lady. Mr Ebenezer, who was the admired and the beloved, and the spoiled one, made, no doubt, mighty certain of the victory; and when he found he had deceived himself, screamed like a peacock. The whole country heard of it; now he lay sick at home, with his silly family standing round the bed in tears; now he rode from public house to public house and shouted his sorrows into the lug of Tom, Dick, and Harry. Your father, Mr David, was a kind gentleman; but he was weak, dolefully weak; took all this folly with a long countenance; and one day – by your leave! – resigned the lady. She was no such fool, however; it's from her you must inherit your excellent good sense; and she refused to be bandied from one to another. Both got upon their knees to her; and the upshot of the matter for that while, was that she showed both of them the door. That was in August; dear me! the same year I came from college. The scene must have been highly farcical.'

I thought myself it was a silly business, but I could not forget my father had a hand in it. 'Surely, sir, it had some note of tragedy,' said I.

'Why, no, sir, not at all,' returned the lawyer. 'For tragedy implies some ponderable matter in dispute, some *dignus vindice nodus*;[53] and this piece of work was all about the petulance of a young ass that had been spoiled, and wanted nothing so much as to be tied up and soundly belted. However, that was not your father's view; and the end of it was, that from concession to concession on your father's part, and from one height to another of squalling, sentimental selfishness upon your uncle's, they came at last to drive a sort of bargain, from whose ill-results you have recently been smarting. The one man took the lady, the other the estate. Now, Mr David, they talk a great deal of charity and generosity; but in this disputable state of life, I often think the happiest consequences seem to flow when a gentleman consults his lawyer and takes all the law allows him. Anyhow, this piece of Quixotry upon your father's part, as it was unjust in itself, has brought forth a monstrous family of injustices. Your father and mother lived and died poor folk; you were poorly reared; and in the meanwhile, what a time it has been for the tenants on the estate of Shaws! And I might add (if it was a matter I cared much about) what a time for Mr Ebenezer!'

'And yet that is certainly the strangest part of all,' said I, 'that a man's nature should thus change.'

'True,' said Mr Rankeillor. 'And yet I imagine it was natural enough. He could not think that he had played a handsome part. Those who knew the story gave him the cold shoulder; those who knew it not, seeing one brother disappear, and the other succeed in the estate, raised a cry of murder; so that upon all sides, he found himself evited. Money was all he got by his bargain; well, he came to think the more of money. He was selfish when he was young, he is selfish now that he is old; and the latter end of all these pretty manners and fine feelings, you have seen for yourself.'

'Well sir,' said I, 'and in all this, what is my position?'

'The estate is yours beyond a doubt,' replied the lawyer. 'It matters nothing what your father signed, you are the heir of entail. But your uncle is a man to fight the indefensible; and it would be likely your identity that he would call in question. A lawsuit is always expensive, and a family lawsuit always scandalous; besides which, if any of your doings with your friend Mr Thomson were to come out, we might find that we had burned our fingers. The kidnapping, to be sure, would be a court card upon our side, if we could only prove it. But it may be difficult to prove; and my advice (upon the whole) is to make a very easy bargain with your uncle, perhaps even leaving him at Shaws where he has taken root for a quarter of a century, and contenting yourself in the meanwhile with a fair provision.'

I told him I was very willing to be easy, and that to carry familiar concerns before the public was a step from which I was naturally much averse. In the meantime (thinking to myself) I began to see the outlines of that scheme on which we afterwards acted.

'The great affair,' I asked, 'is to bring home to him the kidnapping?'

'Surely,' said Mr Rankeillor, 'and if possible, out of court. For mark you here, Mr David: we could no doubt find some men of the *Covenant* who would swear to your reclusion; but once they were in the box, we could no longer check their testimony, and some word of your friend Mr Thomson must certainly crop out. Which (from what you have let fall) I cannot think to be desirable.'

'Well, sir,' said I, 'here is my way of it.' And I opened my plot to him.

'But this would seem to involve my meeting the man Thomson?' says he, when I had done.

'I think so, indeed, sir,' said I.

'Dear doctor!' cries he, rubbing his brow. 'Dear doctor! No, Mr David, I am afraid your scheme is inadmissible. I say nothing against your friend Mr Thomson; I know nothing against him; and if I did – mark this, Mr David! – it would be my duty to lay hands on him. Now I put it to you: is it wise to meet? He may have matters to his charge. He may not have told you all. His name may not be even Thomson!' cries the lawyer, twinkling; 'for some of these fellows will pick up names by the roadside as another would gather haws.'

'You must be the judge, sir,' said I.

But it was clear my plan had taken hold upon his fancy, for he kept musing to himself till we were called to dinner and the company of Mrs Rankeillor; and that lady had scarce left us again to ourselves and a bottle of wine, ere he was back harping on my proposal. When and where was I to meet my friend Mr Thomson; was I sure of Mr T.'s discretion; supposing we could catch the old fox tripping, would I consent to such and such a term of an agreement – these and the like questions he kept asking at long intervals, while he thoughtfully rolled his wine upon his tongue. When I had answered all of them, seemingly to his contentment, he fell into a still deeper muse, even the claret being now forgotten. Then he got a sheet of paper and a pencil, and set to work writing and weighing every word; and at last touched a bell and had his clerk into the chamber.

'Torrance,' said he, 'I must have this written out fair against to-night; and when it is done, you will be so kind as put on your hat and be ready to come along with this gentleman and me, for you will probably be wanted as a witness.'

'What, sir,' cried I, as soon as the clerk was gone, 'are you to venture it?'

'Why, so it would appear,' says he, filling his glass. 'But let us speak no more of business. The very sight of Torrance brings in my head a little, droll matter of some years ago, when I had made a tryst with the poor oaf at the cross of Edinburgh. Each had gone his proper errand; and when it came four o'clock, Torrance had been taking a glass and did not know his master, and I, who had forgot my spectacles, was so blind without them, that I give you my word I did not know my own clerk.' And thereupon he laughed heartily.

I said it was an odd chance, and smiled out of politeness; but what held me all the afternoon in wonder, he kept returning and dwelling on this story, and telling it again with fresh details and laughter; so that I began at last to be quite put out of countenance and feel ashamed for my friend's folly.

Towards the time I had appointed with Alan, we set out from the house, Mr Rankeillor and I arm in arm, and Torrance following behind with the deed in his pocket and a covered basket in his hand. All through the town, the lawyer was bowing right and left, and continually being button-holed by gentlemen on matters of burgh or private business; and I could see he was one greatly looked up to in the county. At last we were clear of the houses, and began to go along the side of the haven and towards the Hawes Inn and the ferry pier, the scene of my misfortune. I could not look upon the place without emotion, recalling how many that had been there with me that day were now no more: Ransome taken, I could hope, from the evil to come; Shuan passed where I dared not follow him; and the poor souls that had gone down with the brig in her last plunge. All these, and the brig herself, I had outlived; and come through these hardships and fearful perils without scathe. My only thought should have been of gratitude; and yet I could not behold the place without sorrow for others and a chill of recollected fear.

I was so thinking when, upon a sudden, Mr Rankeillor cried out, clapped his hand to his pockets, and began to laugh.

'Why,' he cries, 'if this be not a farcical adventure! After all that I said, I have forgot my glasses!'

At that, of course, I understood the purpose of his anecdote, and knew that if he had left his spectacles at home, it had been done on purpose, so that he might have the benefit of Alan's help without the awkwardness of recognizing him. And indeed it was well thought upon; for now (suppose things to go the very worst) how could Rankeillor swear to my friend's identity, or how be made to bear damaging evidence against myself? For all that, he had been a long while of finding out his want, and had spoken to and recognized a good few persons as we came through the town; and I had little doubt myself that he saw reasonably well.

As soon as we were past the Hawes (where I recognized the landlord smoking his pipe in the door, and was amazed to see him look no older) Mr Rankeillor changed the order of march, walking behind with Torrance and sending me forward in the manner of a scout. I went up the hill, whistling from time to time my Gaelic air; and at length I had the pleasure to hear it answered and to see Alan rise from behind a bush. He was somewhat dashed in spirits, having passed a long day alone skulking in the county, and made but a poor meal in an alehouse near Dundas. But at the mere sight of my clothes, he began to brighten up; and as soon as I had told him in what a forward state our matters were, and the part I looked to him to play in what remained, he sprang into a new man.

'And that is a very good notion of yours,' says he; 'and I dare to say that you could lay your hands upon no better man to put it through, than Alan Breck. It is not a thing (mark ye) that anyone could do, but takes a gentleman of penetration. But it sticks in my head your lawyer-man will be somewhat wearying to see me,' says Alan.

Accordingly I cried and waved on Mr Rankeillor, who came up alone and was presented to my friend, Mr Thomson.

'Mr Thomson, I am pleased to meet you,' said he. 'But I have forgotten my glasses; and our friend, Mr David here' (clapping me on the shoulder) 'will tell you that I am little better than blind, and that you must not be surprised if I pass you by tomorrow.'

This he said, thinking that Alan would be pleased; but the Highlandman's vanity was ready to startle at a less matter than that.

'Why, sir,' says he, stiffly, 'I would say it mattered the less as we are met here for a particular end, to see justice done to Mr Balfour; and by what I can see, not very likely to have much else in common. But I accept your apology, which was a very proper one to make.'

'And that is more than I could look for, Mr Thomson,' said Rankeillor, heartily. 'And now as you and I are the chief actors in this enterprise, I think we should come into a nice agreement; to which end, I propose that you should lend me your arm, for (what with the dusk and the want of my glasses) I am not very clear as to the path; and as for you, Mr David, you will find Torrance a pleasant kind of body to speak with. Only let me remind you, it's quite needless he should hear more of your adventures or those of – ahem – Mr Thomson.'

Accordingly these two went on ahead in very close talk, and Torrance and I brought up the rear.

Night was quite come when we came in view of the house of Shaws. Ten had been gone some time; it was dark and mild, with a pleasant, rustling wind in the south-west that covered the sound of our approach; and as we drew near we saw no glimmer of light in any portion of the building. It seemed my uncle was already in bed, which was indeed the best thing for our arrangements. We made our last whispered consultations some fifty yards away; and then the lawyer and Torrance and I crept quietly up and crouched down beside the corner of the house; and as soon as we were in our places, Alan strode to the door without concealment and began to knock.

CHAPTER XXIX

I come into my kingdom

For some time Alan volleyed upon the door, and his knocking only roused the echoes of the house and neighbourhood. At last, however, I could hear the noise of a window gently thrust up, and knew that my uncle had come to his observatory. By what light there was, he would see Alan standing, like a dark shadow, on the steps; the three witnesses were hidden quite out of his view; so that there was nothing to alarm an honest man in his own house. For all that, he studied his visitor awhile in silence, and when he spoke his voice had a quaver of misgiving.

'What's this?' says he. 'This is nae kind of time of night for decent folk; and I hae nae trokings* wi' night-hawks. What brings ye here? I have a blunderbush.'

'Is that yoursel', Mr Balfour?' returned Alan, stepping back and looking up into the darkness. 'Have a care of that blunder-buss; they're nasty things to burst.'

'What brings ye here? and whae are ye?' says my uncle, angrily.

'I have no manner of inclination to rowt out my name to the countryside,' said Alan; 'but what brings me here is another story, being more of your affairs than mine; and if ye're sure it's what ye would like, I'll set it to a tune and sing it to you.'

'And what is't?' asked my uncle.

'David,' says Alan.

'What was that?' cried my uncle, in a mighty changed voice.

'Shall I give ye the rest of the name, then?' said Alan.

---

* Dealings.

There was a pause; and then, 'I'm thinking I'll better let ye in,' says my uncle, doubtfully.

'I daresay that,' said Alan; 'but the point is, Would I go? Now I will tell you what I am thinking. I am thinking that it is here upon this doorstep that we must confer upon this business; and it shall be here or nowhere at all whatever; for I would have you to understand that I am as stiffnecked as yoursel', and a gentleman of better family.'

This change of note disconcerted Ebenezer; he was a little while digesting it; and then says he, 'Weel, weel, what must be must,' and shut the window. But it took him a long time to get down stairs, and a still longer to undo the fastenings, repenting (I daresay) and taken with fresh claps of fear at every second step and every bolt and bar. At last, however, we heard the creak of the hinges, and it seems my uncle slipped gingerly out and (seeing that Alan had stepped back a pace or two) sate him down on the top doorstep with the blunderbuss ready in his hands.

'And now,' says he, 'mind I have my blunderbush, and if ye take a step nearer ye're as good as deid.'

'And a very civil speech,' says Alan, 'to be sure.'

'Na,' says my uncle, 'but this is no a very chancy kind of a proceeding, and I'm bound to be prepared. And now that we understand each other, ye'll can name your business.'

'Why,' says Alan, 'you that are a man of so much understanding, will doubtless have perceived that I am a Hieland gentleman. My name has nae business in my story; but the county of my friends is no very far from the Isle of Mull, of which ye will have heard. It seems there was a ship lost in those parts; and the next day a gentleman of my family was seeking wreck-wood for his fire along the sands, when he came upon a lad that was half drowned. Well, he brought him to; and he and some other gentlemen took and clapped him in an auld, ruined castle, where from that day to this he has been a great expense to my friends. My friends are a wee wild-like, and not so particular about the law as some that I could name; and finding that the lad owned some decent folk, and was your born nephew, Mr Balfour, they asked me to give ye a bit call and to confer upon the matter. And I may tell ye at the off-go, unless we can agree upon some terms, ye are little likely to set eyes upon him. For my friends,' added Alan, simply, 'are no very well off.'

My uncle cleared his throat. 'I'm no very caring,' says he. 'He wasnae a good lad at the best of it, and I've nae call to interfere.'

'Ay, ay,' said Alan, 'I see what ye would be at: pretending ye don't care, to make the ransome smaller.'

'Na,' said my uncle, 'it's the mere truth. I take nae manner of interest in the lad, and I'll pay nae ransome, and ye can make a kirk and a mill of him for what I care.'

'Hoot, sir,' says Alan. 'Blood's thicker than water, in the deil's name! Ye cannae desert your brother's son for the fair shame of it; and if ye did, and it came to be kennt, ye wouldnae be very popular in your countryside, or I'm the more deceived.'

'I'm no just very popular the way it is,' returned Ebenezer; 'and I dinnae see how it would come to be kennt. No by me, onyway; nor yet by you or your friends. So that's idle talk, my buckie,' says he.

'Then it'll have to be David that tells it,' said Alan.

'How that?' says my uncle, sharply.

'Ou, just this way,' says Alan. 'My friends would doubtless keep your nephew as long as there was any likelihood of siller to be made of it, but if there was nane, I am clearly of opinion they would let him gang where he pleased, and be damned to him!'

'Ay, but I'm no very caring about that either,' said my uncle. 'I wouldnae be muckle made up with that.'

'I was thinking that,' said Alan.

'And what for why?' asked Ebenezer.

'Why, Mr Balfour,' replied Alan, 'by all that I could hear, there were two ways of it: either ye liked David and would pay to get him back; or else ye had very good reasons for not wanting him, and would pay for us to keep him. It seems it's not the first; well then, it's the second; and blythe am I to ken it, for it should be a pretty penny in my pocket and the pockets of my friends.'

'I dinnae follow ye there,' said my uncle.

'No?' said Alan. 'Well, see here: you dinnae want the lad back; well, what do ye want done with him, and how much will ye pay?'

My uncle made no answer, but shifted uneasily on his seat.

'Come, sir,' cried Alan. 'I would have ye to ken that I am a gentleman; I bear a king's name; I am nae rider to kick my shanks at your hall door. Either give me an answer in civility, and that out of hand; or by the top of Glencoe, I will ram three feet of iron through your vitals.'

'Eh, man,' cried my uncle, scrambling to his feet, 'give me a meenit! What's like wrong with ye? I'm just a plain man, and nae dancing master; and I'm trying to be as ceevil as it's morally possible. As for that wild talk, it's fair disrepitable. Vitals, says you! And where would I be with my blunderbush?' he snarled.

'Powder and your auld hands are but as the snail to the swallow against the bright steel in the hands of Alan,' said the other. 'Before your jottering finger could find the trigger, the hilt would dirl on your breast bane.'

'Eh, man, whae's denying it?' said my uncle. 'Pit it as ye please, hae't your ain way; I'll do naething to cross ye. Just tell me what like ye'll be wanting, and ye'll see that we'll can agree fine.'

'Troth, sir,' said Alan, 'I ask for nothing but plain dealing. In two words: do ye want the lad killed or kept?'

'O, sirs!' cried Ebenezer. 'O, sirs, me! that's no kind of language!'

'Killed or kept?' repeated Alan.

'O keepit, keepit!' wailed my uncle. 'We'll have nae bloodshed, if you please.'

'Well,' says Alan, 'as ye please; that'll be the dearer.'

'The dearer?' cries Ebenezer. 'Would ye fyle your hands wi' crime?'

'Hoot!' said Alan, 'they're baith crime, whatever! And the killing's easier, and quicker, and surer. Keeping the lad'll be a fashious* job, a fashious, kittle business.'

'I'll have him keepit, though,' returned my uncle. 'I never had

* Troublesome.

naething to do with onything morally wrong; and I'm no gaun to begin to pleasure a wild Hielandman.'

'Ye're unco scrupulous,' sneered Alan.

'I'm a man o' principle,' said Ebenezer simply; 'and if I have to pay for it, I'll have to pay for it. And besides,' says he, 'ye forget the lad's my brother's son.'

'Well, well,' said Alan, 'and now about the price. It's no very easy for me to set a name upon it; I would first have to ken some small matters. I would have to ken, for instance, what ye gave Hoseason at the first off-go?'

'Hoseason?' cries my uncle, struck aback. 'What for?'

'For kidnapping David,' says Alan.

'It's a lee, it's a black lee!' cried my uncle. 'He was never kidnapped. He leed in his throat that tauld ye that. Kidnapped? He never was!'

'That's no fault of mine nor yet of yours,' said Alan; 'nor yet of Hoseason's, if he's a man that can be trusted.'

'What do ye mean?' cried Ebenezer. 'Did Hoseason tell ye?'

'Why, ye donnered auld runt, how else would I ken?' cried Alan. 'Hoseason and I are partners; we gang shares; so ye can see for yoursel', what good ye can do leeing. And I must plainly say ye drove a fool's bargain when ye let a man like the sailor man so far forward in your private matters. But that's past praying for; and ye must lie on your bed the way ye made it. And the point in hand is just this: what did ye pay him?'

'Has he tauld ye himsel',' asked my uncle.

'That's my concern,' said Alan.

'Weel,' said my uncle, 'I dinnae care what he said, he leed, and the solemn God's truth is this, that I gave him twenty pound. But I'll be perfec'ly honest with ye: forby that, he was to have the selling of the lad in Caroliny, whilk would be as muckle mair, but no from my pocket, ye see.'

'Thank you, Mr Thomson. That will do excellently well,' said the lawyer, stepping forward; and then mighty civilly, 'Good evening, Mr Balfour,' said he.

And, 'Good evening, uncle Ebenezer,' said I.

And 'It's a braw nicht, Mr Balfour,' added Torrance.

Never a word said my uncle, neither black nor white; but

just sat where he was on the top doorstep and stared upon us like a man turned to stone. Alan filched away his blunderbuss; and the lawyer, taking him by the arm, plucked him up from the doorstep, led him into the kitchen, whither we all followed, and set him down in a chair beside the hearth, where the fire was out and only a rushlight burning.

There we all looked upon him for awhile, exulting greatly in our success, but yet with a sort of pity for the man's shame.

'Come, come, Mr Ebenezer,' said the lawyer, 'you must not be down-hearted, for I promise you we shall make easy terms. In the meanwhile give us the cellar key, and Torrance shall draw us a bottle of your father's wine in honour of the event.' Then, turning to me and taking me by the hand, 'Mr David,' says he, 'I wish you all joy in your good fortune, which I believe to be deserved.' And then to Alan, with a spice of drollery, 'Mr Thomson, I pay you my compliment; it was most artfully conducted; but in one point you somewhat outran my comprehension. Do I understand your name to be James? or Charles? or is it George perhaps?'

'And why should it be any of the three, sir?' quoth Alan, drawing himself up, like one who smelt an offence.

'Only, sir, that you mentioned a king's name,' replied Rankeillor; 'and as there has never yet been a King Thomson, or his fame at least has never come my way, I judged you must refer to that you had in baptism.'

This was just the stab that Alan would feel keenest, and I am free to confess he took it very ill. Not a word would he answer, but stept off to the far end of the kitchen, and sat down and sulked; and it was not till I stepped after him, and gave him my hand, and thanked him by title as the chief spring of my success, that he began to smile a bit, and was at last prevailed upon to join our party.

By that time we had the fire lighted, and a bottle of wine uncorked; a good supper came out of the basket, to which Torrance and I and Alan set ourselves down; while the lawyer and my uncle passed into the next chamber to consult. They stayed there closeted about an hour; at the end of which period they had come to a good understanding, and my uncle and

I set our hands to the agreement in a formal manner. By the terms of this, my uncle bound himself to satisfy Rankeillor as to his intromissions, and to pay me two clear thirds of the yearly income of Shaws.

So the beggar in the ballad had come home; and when I lay down that night on the kitchen chests, I was a man of means and had a name in the country. Alan and Torrance and Rankeillor slept and snored on their hard beds; but for me, who had lain out under heaven and upon dirt and stones, so many days and nights, and often with an empty belly, and in fear of death, this good change in my case unmanned me more than any of the former evil ones; and I lay till dawn, looking at the fire on the roof and planning the future.

CHAPTER XXX

Good-bye

So far as I was concerned myself, I had come to port; but I had still Alan, to whom I was so much beholden, on my hands; and I felt besides a heavy charge in the matter of the murder and James of the Glens. On both these heads I unbosomed to Rankeillor the next morning, walking to and fro about six of the clock before the house of Shaws, and with nothing in view but the fields and woods that had been my ancestors' and were now mine. Even as I spoke on these grave subjects, my eye would take a glad bit of a run over the prospect, and my heart jump with pride.

About my clear duty to my friend, the lawyer had no doubt; I must help him out of the county at whatever risk; but in the case of James, he was of a different mind.

'Mr Thomson,' says he, 'is one thing, Mr Thomson's kinsman quite another. I know little of the facts; but I gather that a great noble (whom we will call, if you like, the D. of A.)* has some concern and is even supposed to feel some animosity in the matter. The D. of A. is doubtless an excellent nobleman; but, Mr David, *timeo qui nocuere deos.*[54] If you interfere to baulk his vengeance, you should remember there is one way to shut your testimony out; and that is to put you in the dock. There, you would be in the same pickle as Mr Thomson's kinsman. You will object that you are innocent; well, but so is he. And to be tried for your life before a Highland jury, on a Highland quarrel, and with a Highland judge upon the bench, would be a brief transition to the gallows.'

* The Duke of Argyll.

Now I had made all these reasonings before and found no very good reply to them; so I put on all the simplicity I could. 'In that case, sir,' said I, 'I would just have to be hanged – would I not?'

'My dear boy,' cries he, 'go in God's name, and do what you think is right. It is a poor thought that at my time of life I should be advising you to choose the safe and shameful; and I take it back with an apology. Go and do your duty; and be hanged, if you must, like a gentleman. There are worse things in the world than to be hanged.'

'Not many, sir,' said I, smiling.

'Why, yes, sir,' he cried, 'very many. And it would be ten times better for your uncle (to go no farther afield) if he were dangling decently upon a gibbet.'

Thereupon he turned into the house (still in a great fervour of mind, so that I saw I had pleased him heartily) and there he wrote me two letters, making his comments on them as he wrote.

'This,' says he, 'is to my bankers, the British Linen Company,[55] placing a credit to your name. Consult Mr Thomson; he will know of ways; and you, with this credit, can supply the means. I trust you will be a good husband of your money; but in the affair of a friend like Mr Thomson, I would be even prodigal. Then, for his kinsman, there is no better way than that you should seek the Advocate, tell him your tale, and offer testimony; whether he may take it or not, is quite another matter, and will turn on the D. of A. Now that you may reach the Lord Advocate well recommended, I give you here a letter to a namesake of your own, the learned Mr Balfour of Pilrig,[56] a man whom I esteem. It will look better that you should be presented by one of your own name; and the laird of Pilrig is much looked up to in the Faculty and stands well with Lord Advocate Grant. I would not trouble him, if I were you, with any particulars; and (do you know?) I think it would be needless to refer to Mr Thomson. Form yourself upon the laird, he is a good model; when you deal with the Advocate, be discreet; and in all these matters, may the Lord guide you, Mr David!'

Thereupon he took his farewell, and set out with Torrance

for the Ferry, while Alan and I turned our faces for the city of Edinburgh. As we went by the footpath and beside the gateposts and the unfinished lodge, we kept looking back at the house of my fathers. It stood there, bare and great and smokeless, like a place not lived in; only in one of the top windows, there was the peak of a nightcap bobbing up and down and back and forward, like the head of a rabbit from a burrow. I had little welcome when I came, and less kindness while I stayed; but at least I was watched as I went away.

Alan and I went slowly forward upon our way, having little heart either to walk or speak. The same thought was uppermost in both, that we were near the time of our parting; and remembrance of all the bygone days sate upon us sorely. We talked indeed of what should be done; and it was resolved that Alan should keep to the county, biding now here, now there, but coming once in the day to a particular place where I might be able to communicate with him, either in my own person or by messenger. In the meanwhile, I was to seek out a lawyer, who was an Appin Stewart, and a man therefore to be wholly trusted; and it should be his part to find a ship and to arrange for Alan's safe embarkation. No sooner was this business done, than the words seemed to leave us; and though I would seek to jest with Alan under the name of Mr Thomson, and he with me on my new clothes and my estate, you could feel very well that we were nearer tears than laughter.

We came the by-way over the hill of Corstorphine; and when we got near to the place called Rest-and-be-Thankful, and looked down on Corstorphine bogs and over to the city and the castle on the hill, we both stopped, for we both knew without a word said, that we had come to where our ways parted. Here he repeated to me once again what had been agreed upon between us: the address of the lawyer, the daily hour at which Alan might be found, and the signals that were to be made by any that came seeking him. Then I gave what money I had (a guinea or two of Rankeillor's) so that he should not starve in the meanwhile; and then we stood a space, and looked over at Edinburgh in silence.

'Well, good bye,' said Alan, and held out his left hand.

'Good bye,' said I, and gave the hand a little grasp, and went off down hill.

Neither one of us looked the other in the face, nor so long as he was in my view did I take one back glance at the friend I was leaving. But as I went on my way to the city, I felt so lost and lonesome, that I could have found it in my heart to sit down by the dyke, and cry and weep like any baby.

It was coming near noon when I passed in by the West Kirk and the Grassmarket into the streets of the capital. The huge height of the buildings, running up to ten and fifteen storeys, the narrow arched entries that continually vomited passengers, the wares of the merchants in their windows, the hubbub and endless stir, the foul smells and the fine clothes, and a hundred other particulars too small to mention, struck me into a kind of stupor of surprise, so that I let the crowd carry me to and fro; and yet all the time what I was thinking of was Alan at Rest-and-be-Thankful; and all the time (although you would think I would not choose but be delighted with these braws and novelties) there was a cold gnawing in my inside like a remorse for something wrong.

The hand of Providence brought me in my drifting to the very doors of the British Linen Company's bank.

[Just there, with his hand upon his fortune, the present editor inclines for the time to say farewell to David. How Alan escaped, and what was done about the murder, with a variety of other delectable particulars, may be some day set forth. That is a thing, however, that hinges on the public fancy. The editor has a great kindness for both Alan and David, and would gladly spend much of his life in their society; but in this he may find himself to stand alone. In the fear of which, and lest any one should complain of scurvy usage, he hastens to protest that all went well with both, in the limited and human sense of the word 'well'; that whatever befell them, it was not dishonour, and whatever failed them, they were not found wanting to themselves.]

Notes

1. *erisypelitous*: A more conventional spelling would be 'erysipela-tous', pertaining to erysipelas, a virulent and painful inflammation of the skin.

2. Charles Baxter was one of Stevenson's earliest university friends who remained his constant correspondent and legal and financial adviser for life. After Stevenson left Edinburgh his correspondence with Baxter (by now an Edinburgh lawyer) seems to celebrate a pride and nostalgia in their shared Scottishness which puts their friendship on a different plane from that of Stevenson's other acquaintance. Stevenson's instincts were perhaps sound; without exception all of his English literary friends would in due course serve him ill. Of *Kidnapped* he wrote to Baxter, 'Sir, it's Scotch: no strong, for the sake o' they pork-puddens, but jist a kitchen o't, to leeven the wersh, sapless, fushionless, stotty, stytering South-Scotch they think sae muckle o'.'

3. For the historical events of the Appin murder and the character of Alan Breck Stewart, see Historical Note. While it is necessary to move the Torran rocks closer to the island of Earraid for the sake of the plot, there seems no clear reason to place the Appin murder in 1751 rather than the historical 1752.

4. *the old Speculative*: Stevenson and Baxter had both been members of the Speculative Society, a literary and debating club at Edinburgh University founded in 1764. Previous members had included Sir Walter Scott and Robert Emmet, the Irish patriot. William Macbean had been secretary of the Society from 1841 to 1842. Of the seven papers Stevenson gave there, the first was on 'The Influence of the Covenanting Persecution on the Scotch Mind' (1870).

5. *the L.J.R.*: The L.J.R. was a small and short-lived club which met in a public house in Advocate's Close, 357 High Street,

Edinburgh. The initials stood for 'Liberty, Justice, Reverence' and its constitution began, 'Disregard everything our parents have taught us'. As students, both Stevenson and Baxter were leading lights. The discovery of the club's constitution by Stevenson's father led to a deep rift between father and son over the latter's presumed atheist stance.

6. *Skerryvore*: See note 29 below.

7. *Balfours*: Balfour was Stevenson's mother's name and his own third given name. Balfour is from the Gaelic *bal* or *bail*, meaning a farm steading, and *puir*, meaning a pasture. The name is originally associated with the southern parts of the Kingdom of Fife on the east coast of Scotland. The name David comes from the Stevenson side of the family: '. . . you will see that both my families have been robbed to give a name'. (Letter to his cousin, David A. Stevenson, 1886.)

8. *Patrick Walker*: A seventeenth-century merchant who wrote inspirational biographies of the great and famous.

9. *'For it's my delight . . .'*: From 'The Lincolnshire Poacher' (anonymous). The introduction of the English idiom of the cabin-boy (the only English character in the tale) marks a distinct lurch in the diction of the novel. We get more than a whiff of the 'dull, neglected peasant, sunk in matter, insolent, gross and servile' of 'The Foreigner at Home'.

10. *my uncle had read the letter and sat thinking*: We have to assume that, unless Ebenezer somehow got a message to the outside world while David was musing over the chapbook, the intervention of the letter from Hoseason is pure chance and the kidnap is not premeditated.

11. *The Hawes Inn*: In 'A Gossip on Romance', first published in Longman's Magazine (November 1882), Stevenson wrote about his topographical inspirations:

> Some places speak distinctly. Certain dank gardens cry aloud for a murder; certain old houses demand to be haunted; certain coasts are set apart for shipwreck . . . The old Hawes Inn at the Queen's Ferry makes a similar call upon my fancy. There it stands, apart from the town, beside the pier, in a climate of its own, half inland, half marine – in front, the ferry bubbling with the tide and the guardship swinging to her anchor; behind, the old garden with the trees. Americans seek it already for the sake of Lovel and Oldbuck, who dined there at the beginning of the *Antiquary*. But you need not tell me – that is not all; there is some story, unrecorded or not

yet complete, which must express the meaning of that inn more fully.

12. *the* Covenant: Apart from the various biblical covenants between God and his people (e.g. at Mount Sinai), the name of the brig could refer to any one of three documents, all of which bound the signatories to uphold Presbyterianism in Scotland; the first in 1557, the National in 1638 and the Solemn League and Covenant in 1643. In any event we can be in little doubt as to Hoseason's religious sympathies and we learn later that, whatever his other faults, 'he was a great church-goer while on shore'.

13. *about twelve o'clock*: The first printings of the first edition give 'nine o'clock'. Stevenson later amended this to read 'twelve o'clock'.

14. *He was smallish in stature*: For a description of the historical Alan Breck Stewart, see Historical Note.

15. *A king's name is good enough for me*: The lines which produced the Stewart (or Stuart) kings and the Stewarts of Appin share a common ancestor in Alexander, Fourth Steward (or seneschal) of Scotland, who led the Scots against King Haakon IV of Norway at the Battle of Largs in 1263. The Appin Stewarts are descended from the Lords of Lorn who in turn trace their ancestry to Sir James Stewart, grandson of Alexander. Another grandson of Alexander, Walter, Sixth Steward, married Marjory, daughter of Robert 'The Bruce', and was father to Robert II of Scotland – the first Stewart monarch.

There is a fundamental cultural divide in this exchange. Alan would genuinely find David's reference to Shaws inconsequential and somewhat vulgar. The formal title to land would have been almost irrelevant under the loose arrangement known as the 'clan system'. The chief of a clan (*clann* = Gaelic 'family') would measure his wealth in terms of the number of loyal fighting men who would accept his authority, whether they were, strictly speaking, his tenants or not. In *Capital* Marx described the Highland chief as only 'the titular owner of this property, just as the Queen of England is the titular owner of all the national soil'. The clansmen in turn would believe that they owed their allegiance to their chief on the basis of a close consanguinity with him and his ancestors (both real and imagined).

Adam Smith, in a slightly bemused aside in *The Wealth of Nations*, comments that the Chief of the Clan Cameron, 'whose rent never exceeded five hundred pounds a year, carried, in 1745, eight hundred of his own people into the rebellion with him'. Bear in mind that Smith was a Lowland Scot and was writing only thirty years after the events in question.

The bitterness which resulted from the breaking-up of the clans was, at least to begin with, less to do with material disinheritance – they were probably no worse off anyway – but rather to do with the severance of dearly regarded ties of blood. Later, David is upbraided for being 'some kinless loon that didn't know his own father'. It is significant that here the speaker is a Macgregor – a clan which had had no territories since the 1590s.

16. *the reader would do well to look at a map*: Stevenson's confidence that his narrative will stand up to close topographical scrutiny is well founded. Apart from the moving of the Torran rocks referred to in the Dedication there is not a single navigational feature out of place between now and David's landfall on Earraid (or Erraid). 'Eriska' is more commonly given as Eriskay on modern maps and lies between Barra and South Uist at the southern end of the Outer Hebrides, as 'the Long Islands' would now be known. It was on the little island of Eriskay that the 'Young Pretender', Charles Edward Stuart, first set foot on Scottish soil in 1745.

17. *I am an Appin Stewart*: See Historical Note.

18. *Will ye bring me his brush*: Alan Breck is reputed to have used words very close to these. See Historical Note.

19. *Cantyre*: Now spelt Kintyre. The Mull (or headland) of Kintyre marks the most southerly point of West Highland culture.

20. *larboard*: Modern port, or left-hand side, of a ship. By the time of Stevenson's writing, the term 'larboard' would be already archaic.

21. *Torran Rocks*: In reality these are about three miles due south of Erraid, rather than to the south-west. In 'Memoirs of an Islet' in *Memories and Portraits*, Stevenson recalls three weeks spent on Erraid in 1870 when his father was supervising the construction of the Dubh Hirteach light, about fourteen miles to the west. The stone for the Dubh Hirteach was quarried on Erraid, which was used as the base for the whole operation. After many setbacks – at one point fourteen interlocking stones, set in concrete and each weighing over two tons, were washed away at a height of thirty-seven feet above high water by the force of the waves – the lighthouse was completed in 1872. Erraid is indeed a tidal islet, now once again uninhabited.

22. *In all the books I have read of people cast away*: Presumably a reference to Defoe's *Robinson Crusoe* (1719) in which the hero,

on being shipwrecked, draws up a 'balance sheet' of the evil and good in his circumstances. On the good side, the last entry reads, 'But God wonderfully sent the ship in near enough to the shore, that I have gotten out so many necessary things as will either supply my wants, or enable me to supply my self even as long as I live.' It is a book which would have been as familiar to David Balfour, as a good Calvinist, as it was to Stevenson. Because of its inherent metaphor of divine and human providence, it remains to this day one of the few secular works to find unmitigated approval in stricter Presbyterian households. Stevenson's father went one better by way of moral austerity and professed to prefer *The Serious Reflections of Robinson Crusoe* (also by Defoe) which consists of essays on honesty in business and divine providence. It is a work of such dryness that it had only one printing in Defoe's lifetime and was not reprinted until 1925.

Stevenson's first, privately published, work, *The Pentland Rising* (1866), a mildly fictionalized incident in Covenanting history, which he amended to please his father, is full of pious quotations from Defoe.

23. *the Highland dress being forbidden by law since the rebellion*: Although only a minority of the clans had taken part in the rebellion, that did not stop the whole clan structure being brutally suppressed and the authority of the chiefs taken from them including, ironically enough, that of the Duke of Argyll who had put his weight behind the Hanoverian cause throughout. The relatively mild Disarming Act which had followed the 1715 rebellion was stringently reimposed and the possession of Highland dress or bagpipes outlawed upon pain of transportation. As G. M. Trevelyan put it in his *History of England*, 'The King's writ must run in the glens. An Afghanistan could no longer be tolerated within fifty miles of the "modern Athens" [Edinburgh].' The government was later so confident that destruction of the threat of clan sentiment was complete that the ban on Highland dress was lifted as early as 1782. They were right. The full-blown romanticizing of the Highlands was just around the corner and the real grievances of the Highlander were by then of a different sort.

One exception to the ban on tartan was in the Highland regiments raised by Pitt in 1757 to fight the French in Canada and India. When questioned as to the wisdom of recruiting from some of the more disaffected clans, he replied that 'not many of them would return'.

24. *the chiefs kept no longer an open house*: Compare Adam Smith,
     The Wealth of Nations, Book 3, Chapter IV:

> In a country which has neither foreign commerce, nor any of the
> finer manufactures, a great proprietor, having nothing for which he
> can exchange the greater part of the produce of his lands which is
> over and above the maintenance of the cultivators, consumes the
> whole in rustic hospitality at home. If this surplus produce is suf-
> ficient to maintain a hundred or a thousand men, he can make use
> of it in no other way than by maintaining a hundred or a thousand
> men. He is at all times, therefore, surrounded with a multitude of
> retainers and dependants, who, having no equivalent to give in
> return for their maintenance, but being fed entirely by his bounty,
> must obey him, for the same reason that soldiers must obey the
> prince who pays them.

25. *an emigrant ship bound for the American colonies*: Although the
     phenomenon now known as the Highland Clearances did not
     begin in earnest until about forty years after the events of *Kid-
     napped*, there had been a steady drift of emigration since even
     before the '45. Most typically, small sub-sets of clans, possibly
     seeing the writing on the wall for the future of their way of life,
     would decide to emigrate as a unit – perhaps in the hope of
     preserving something of the close-knit clan values by starting
     afresh in a new continent. However, one suspects that Stevenson
     is conflating two slightly different periods of history in order to
     make a point.
26. *'Lochaber no more'*: Song attributed to Allan Ramsay (1685?–
     1758). Bookseller, publisher, founder of the first circulating lib-
     rary in Britain, theatrical manager: perhaps no one symbolizes
     more spectacularly the cultural confusion of eighteenth-century
     Scotland than Ramsay – indeed he probably did much to generate
     it. He founded the Easy Club in Edinburgh, which was overtly
     modelled on the Augustan values of the club of Addison's
     Spectator. In the same breath he was publishing collections of
     sentimental Jacobite ballads and reissuing antiquarian works of
     Scottish patriotism.
27. *the Edinburgh Society for Propagating Christian Knowledge*:
     The Scottish Society for Propagating (or Propagation of) Chris-
     tian Knowledge was founded in 1709 to teach 'religion and
     virtue' to young and old. Founded because of the Church of
     Scotland's concerns that the Reformation had not penetrated the

Highlands, the Society was Presbyterian in creed, and an affection for the Hanoverian succession (who helped to finance it) was implicit in its teaching. Stevenson may be guilty of an anachronism when he suggests that Henderland used Gaelic hymns and books. Because Gaelic was regarded as part of the problem of ignorance and backwardness, its use was officially banned by the Society until 1766.

This incident may have been introduced to please Stevenson's father. 'I quite agree with you, and had already planned a scene of religion in *Balfour* [*Kidnapped*]; the Society for the Propagation of Christian Knowledge furnishes me with a catechist whom I shall try to make the man.' (Letter to Thomas Stevenson, 25 January 1886.)

28. *ferny howes*: The first edition gives 'ferny dells'. Stevenson later amended this at the suggestion of Edmund Gosse.

29. *Skerryvore*: The Skerryvore rocks are about twelve miles west of the island of Tiree. The lighthouse there was designed by Stevenson's uncle Alan, and Stevenson's father was very much involved in its construction. It was completed in 1844.

30. *What the Camerons would think*: One of the enduring traditions of the Appin murder is that a Cameron who was a reputed shot crossed to Balachulish from Mamore on the morning of the murder. The motive would not be far to seek since the Camerons of Mamore had every reason to believe that they would be next in line to suffer as the Stewarts of Appin had suffered. See Historical Note.

31. *Cruachan*: As well as being 'the rallying-word of the Campbells', Ben Cruachan is one of the most prominent landmarks in Argyll. It rises to 3,689 feet between Loch Etive and Loch Awe.

32. *the massacre was in the time of King William*: Because of the tardiness of MacDonald of Glencoe in swearing an oath of allegiance to King William by the deadline of 1 January 1692 (he did in fact take the oath on 6 January, having been delayed by a blizzard on his way to Inveraray), two companies of the Earl of Argyll's regiment were dispatched to make an example of the MacDonalds. At dawn on Saturday, 13 February, having accepted quarters from the MacDonalds, the Campbell troops murdered thirty-six of the MacDonald men plus a handful of women and children. Far worse slaughters had occurred in the Highlands, but this one was regarded as particularly heinous because of the breach of the sacrosanct bond of hospitality.

33. *The moon by night . . .*: Psalm 121, verse 6. In the King James

version it reads, 'The sun shall not smite thee by day, nor the moon by night'.

34. *John Breck Maccoll*: The Maccolls are a sept, or junior branch, of the Stewarts of Appin.

35. *Cluny Macpherson*: Ewan Macpherson of Cluny, who died in France in 1756. The Macphersons had been particularly prominent in the rebellion and Ewan had been directly involved in helping Charles Edward to escape.

36. *General Cope's defeat at Preston Pans*: Prestonpans, about six miles to the east of Edinburgh on the Firth of Forth, was the scene on 21 September 1745 of one of the few routs of the Government army, under the command of Sir John Cope, by the Jacobite forces. Partly because of the publication in 1790 of a version by Robert Burns, 'Hey, Johnnie Cope' remains to this day one of the most familiar of Jacobite songs.

37. *clan of the Macgregors*: The name of Macgregor or Gregor was first proscribed (on pain of death) in a Privy Council ordinance of 1603 following a Macgregor raid on the Laird of Luss, Sir Humphrey Colquhoun, at Glen Fruin on the shores of Loch Lomond. This ordinance was reinforced by an Act of Parliament of 1617. On the Restoration, King Charles annulled the legislation against the Clan Gregor, but it was reintroduced, probably as a result of political pressure from nonconforming Presbyterians, in an Act for the Justiciary of the Highlands in 1693. The Macgregors had risen with the Jacobites in 1745 – though probably, as with many small clans on the fringes of Argyll, more out of hatred of the Campbells than loyalty to the House of Stuart. The Macgregors' civil rights and name were finally restored to them in 1774.

Rob Roy was an historical figure but is now largely known because of Scott's novel of that name. He was probably born in the mid-1660s and is said to have survived the year 1733.

38. *Robin Oig*: James More (or Mohr) and Robin Oig had in 1750 abducted a wealthy young widow, Jean Key, from her house at Edinbilly in the parish of Balfron in Stirlingshire with a view to forcibly marrying her to Robin. James was considered the instigator and was arrested in 1751 and tried in July 1752. The jury brought in a special verdict, finding James guilty of the abduction but that other charges of subsequent violence were not proven. However, this became rather academic as during the court's deliberations James had escaped from Edinburgh Castle to France. Robin Oig was eventually executed in February 1754 for his

part in the abduction. Alan Breck had some prescience in being suspicious of the Macgregors as James More attempted to kidnap him in France in 1753 in order to deliver him to the authorities in exchange for the freedom of Robin Oig.

39. *I can pipe like a Macrimmon*: The Macrimmons had been the hereditary pipers to the clan MacLeod of Skye since Donald Mor Macrimmon (born 1570).

40. *the Highland Line*: A cultural boundary (and, to a certain extent, a geological fault) between the predominantly Gaelic-speaking clan territories of the west and the Scotch-speaking lowlands to the east. Very roughly, it can be considered to start at the southern end of Loch Lomond and run northwards to Inverness.

41. *'Charlie is my darling'*: One of the best-known Jacobite airs; Charlie being Charles Edward Stuart.

42. *the 'Bonnie House of Airlie'*: This laments the destruction of the estates of James Ogilvy (*c.* 1593–1666), first Earl of Airlie, by the Earl of Argyll in 1640. This James Ogilvy was an ancestor of the David Ogilvy who commanded the Scottish regiments serving France at the time of *Kidnapped*.

43. *Nec gemino bellum Trojanum orditur ab ovo*: 'The Trojan War doesn't begin with the twin eggs' (Horace, *Ars Poetica*). The 'twin eggs' refer to Helen and Castor and Pollux. In other words, 'There's no need to go back to the very beginning.'

44. *in medias res*: in the middle of things.

45. *Fui, non sum*: I was, but am not now.

46. *imberbis juvenis custode remoto*: a beardless youth away from his guardian.

47. *Mr Thomson*: Stevenson and Charles Baxter were in the habit of corresponding with each other in the joke *personae* of two Edinburgh worthies – Thomson and Johnstone (or Johnson). In the first edition of *Kidnapped* there is a slip and Rankeillor later says, 'if any of your doings with your friend Mr Johnson [*sic*] were to come out'.

48. *quae regio in terris*: what part of the world.

49. *paribus curis vestigia figit*: 'Cui fidus Achates it comes, et paribus curis vestigia figit' (Virgil, *Aeneid*, VI, 158). 'With him the faithful Achates goes as a companion, setting his footsteps with equal care.'

50. *Odi te, qui bellus es, Sabelle*: 'I hate you, Sabellus, because you are handsome' (Martial, *Epigrams*, XII, 39).

51. *multum gementem*: complaining a great deal.

52. *majora canamus*: let us sing of greater things.

53. *dignus vindice nodus*: 'Nec deus intersit, nisi dignus vindice nodus' (Horace, *Ars Poetica*). 'A god should not interfere unless there is a cause worthy of his intervention.'

54. *timeo qui nocuere deos*: I fear the gods who have harmed me.

55. *the British Linen Company*: Linen-weaving was one of the economic staples of Scotland in the early eighteenth century. The British Linen Company was founded in 1746 to encourage the growth and manufacture of fine linens. It rapidly became involved in credit operations and to all intents and purposes functioned as a bank. It became the British Linen Company Bank in 1774 and was by then issuing its own banknotes. In 1906 it became simply the British Linen Bank and was one of Scotland's high-street clearing banks until its merger in 1971 with the Bank of Scotland, where its name lives on in the group's merchant banking arm. At the time of *Kidnapped* it would have been the natural bank for the forward-looking professional classes, the Bank of Scotland having been suspected of Jacobite sympathies.

56. *Mr Balfour of Pilrig*: Here Stevenson introduces one of his own ancestors – his maternal great-great-grandfather.

KIDNAPPED

BEING
MEMOIRS OF THE ADVENTURES OF
DAVID BALFOUR
IN THE YEAR 1751
HOW HE WAS KIDNAPPED AND CAST AWAY;
HIS SUFFERINGS IN A DESERT ISLE;
HIS JOURNEY IN THE WILD HIGHLANDS;
HIS ACQUAINTANCE WITH ALAN BRECK STEWART
AND OTHER NOTORIOUS HIGHLAND JACOBITES;
WITH ALL THAT HE SUFFERED
AT THE HANDS OF HIS UNCLE,
EBENEZER BALFOUR OF SHAWS,
FALSELY SO CALLED

WRITTEN BY HIMSELF AND NOW SET FORTH
BY
ROBERT LOUIS STEVENSON
WITH A PREFACE BY MRS STEVENSON

Preface to *Kidnapped* from the Biographical Edition of the Collected Works of Robert Louis Stevenson 1905–12

While my husband and Mr Henley were engaged in writing plays in Bournemouth they made a number of titles, hoping to use them in the future. Dramatic composition was not what my husband preferred, but the torrent of Mr Henley's enthusiasm swept him off his feet. However, after several plays had been finished, and his health seriously impaired by his endeavours to keep up with Mr Henley, play writing was abandoned forever, and my husband returned to his legitimate vocation. Having added one of the titles, *The Hanging Judge*, to the list of projected plays, now thrown aside, and emboldened by my husband's offer to give me any help needed, I concluded to try and write it myself.

As I wanted a trial scene in the Old Bailey, I chose the period of 1700 for my purpose; but being shamefully ignorant of my subject, and my husband confessing to little more knowledge than I possessed, a London bookseller was commissioned to send us everything he could procure bearing on Old Bailey trials. A great package came in response to our order, and very soon we were both absorbed, not so much in the trials as in following the brilliant career of a Mr Garrow, who appeared as counsel in many of the cases. We sent for more books, and yet more, still intent on Mr Garrow, whose subtle cross-examination of witnesses and masterly, if sometimes startling, methods of arriving at the truth seemed more thrilling to us than any novel.

Occasionally other trials than those of the Old Bailey would be included in the package of books we received from London; among these my husband found and read with avidity:–

THE,
TRIAL
OF
JAMES STEWART
in Aucharn in Duror of Appin
FOR THE
Murder of COLIN CAMPBELL of Glenure, Efq;
Factor for His Majefty on the forfeited
Eftate of Ardfhiel.

My husband was always interested in this period of his country's history, and had already the intention of writing a story that should turn on the Appin murder. The tale was to be of a boy, David Balfour, supposed to belong to my husband's own family, who should travel in Scotland as though it were a foreign country, meeting with various adventures and misadventures by the way. From the trial of James Stewart my husband gleaned much valuable material for his novel, the most important being the character of Alan Breck. Aside from having described him as 'smallish in stature', my husband seems to have taken Alan Breck's personal appearance, even to his clothing, from the book.

A letter from James Stewart to Mr John Macfarlane, introduced as evidence in the trial, says: 'There is one Alan Stewart, a distant friend of the late Ardshiel's, who is in the French service, and came over in March last, as he said to some, in order to settle at home; to others, that he was to go soon back; and was, as I hear, the day that the murder was committed, seen not far from the place where it happened, and is not now to be seen; by which it is believed he was the actor. He is a desperate foolish fellow; and if he is guilty, came to the country for that very purpose. He is a tall, pock-pitted lad, very black hair, and wore a blue coat and metal buttons, an old red vest, and breeches of the same colour.' A second witness testified to having seen him wearing 'a blue coat with silver buttons, a red waistcoat, black shag breeches, tartan hose, and a feathered hat, with a big coat, dun coloured', a costume referred to by one of the counsel as 'French cloathes which were remarkable'.

There are many incidents given in the trial that point to Alan's fiery spirit and Highland quickness to take offence. One witness 'declared also That the said Alan Breck threatened that he would challenge Ballieveolan and his sons to fight because of his removing the declarant last year from Glenduror.' On another page: 'Duncan Campbell, change-keeper at Annat, aged thirty-five years, married, witness cited, sworn, purged and examined ut supra, depones, That, in the month of April last, the deponent met with Alan Breck Stewart, with whom he was not acquainted, and John Stewart, in Auchnacoan, in the house of the walk miller of Auchofragan, and went on with them to the house: Alan Breck Stewart said, that he hated all the name of Campbell; and the deponent said, he had no reason for doing so: But Alan said, he had very good reason for it: that thereafter they left that house; and, after drinking a dram at another house, came to the deponent's house, where they went in, and drunk some drams, and Alan Breck renewed the former Conversation; and the deponent, making the same answer, Alan said, that, if the deponent had any respect for his friends, he would tell them, that if they offered to turn out the possessors of Ardshiel's estate, he would make black cocks of them, before they entered into possession by which the deponent understood shooting them, it being a common phrase in the country.'

Some time after the publication of *Kidnapped* we stopped for a short while in the Appin country, where we were surprised and interested to discover that the feeling concerning the murder of Glenure (the 'Red Fox', also called 'Colin Roy') was almost as keen as though the tragedy had taken place the day before. For several years my husband received letters of expostulation or commendation from members of the Campbell and Stewart clans. I have in my possession a paper, yellow with age, that was sent soon after the novel appeared, containing 'The Pedigree of the Family of Appine', wherein it is said that 'Alan 3rd Baron of Appine was not killed at Flowdoun, tho there, but lived to a great old age. He married Cameron Daughter to Ewen Cameron of Lochiel.' Following this is a paragraph stating that 'John Stewart 1st of Ardsheall of his descendants Alan Breck had better be omitted. Duncan Baan Stewart in Achindarroch his father was a Bastard.'

One day, while my husband was busily at work, I sat beside him reading an old cookery book called *The Compleat Housewife: or Accomplish'd Gentlewoman's Companion*. In the midst of receipts for 'Rabbits, and Chickens mumbled, Pickled Samphire, Skirret Pye, Baked Tansy', and other forgotten delicacies, there were directions for the preparation of several lotions for the preservation of beauty. One of these was so charming that I interrupted my husband to read it aloud. 'Just what I wanted!' he exclaimed; and the receipt for the 'Lilly of the Valley Water' was instantly incorporated into *Kidnapped*.

F. V. DE G. S.

Glossary

a' all
ae one
ain one
ance once
assoil acquit (Scots law)
aumry cupboard
aweel ah well
aye (adv.) always

bailie magistrate
bairn child
baith both
bee-skep beehive
begowk befool
bide stay
bield shelter
birling drinking
birstle roast, scorch
bizz bustle
blae cheerless
boddle coin worth two pence (Scots)
bonny beautiful, fine, handsome
brae brow of a hill
braw fine, handsome
breeks trousers
buckie obstinate person
burn stream
busk prepare
byke bee or wasp nest

byre cowshed
by-time spare time

callant lad, fellow
canny careful, astute
ceevil civil
chancy lucky
change-house inn, public house
chap knock
chield lad, fellow
clachan hamlet
clappermaclaw shrunken
coldrife cold in manner
collops slices of meat

daffing joking
daunton intimidate
deave pester, (literally) deafen
depone testify in court
dirl rattle
dod (euphemism) God! (as oath)
doit something of little value
dominie schoolmaster
donnered stupid
dour hard, sullen
dow do
dowie dismal
dram tot of liquor
drammach raw oatmeal with water

driegh dismal
dub small pool
dunch bump
dyke wall

eldritch unearthly
evite avoid

fash bother
feckless ineffective
fleech flatter
flit move
forby moreover
fyle defile

gang go
gant gape
gar cause something to be done
gaun gone, going
gear possessions
gentrice gentry
gey very
gillie male attendant
girdle griddle
girn complain, grimace
gloaming dusk
go-by miss, slip by
gomeral fool
gowl howl
guddle catch fish by groping
 under the bank of a river

hag bog
halesome wholesome
halfling half-grown
haw hawthorn berry
heugh steep bank, cliff
howe low-lying piece of ground
hunner hundred

intromission interfering with
 another's property (Scots law)

jeopard put in jeopardy
jing-bang [the whole] lot
jotter do something ineffectively

keek peep
keepit kept
ken know
kittle tricky, (literally) ticklish
kyte belly

laith loath
limmer woman (derogatory)
link travel briskly
loon scoundrel
lug ear

mair more
manse house of the parish
 minister
maun must
meenit minute
mind remember
mony many
morn, the tomorrow
muckle big, a great many
mull snuff-box (literally 'mill',
 meaning a snuff-box including
 the grinder)

nainsel literally 'one's own self'
neuk nook

ochone alas
orra superfluous, infrequent
out-by outside
ower over, excessively

parritch porridge
peewee peewit, lapwing
philabeg kilt (literally 'short
 plaid' to distinguish it from a
 full plaid)

pickle a few
pike thrust
pit put
plack coin worth four pence (Scots)
plenishing furniture
potato-bogle scarecrow
pretty [of men] courageous
probation the act of proving
pyat magpie
pyke pick

ranting spirited
redd up put in order
rickle disorganized heap
risp make a grating sound (particularly on an uneven bar on which a ring slides, used instead of a door-knocker)
roost tide-race
roup auction
rowt bellow

scrog scrub bushes
sept sub-division of a clan
shift himself change clothes
siller money

slocken slake (thirst, etc.)
sneck-draw deceitful person (literally 'one who pulls back latches')
snuff a fit of pique, huff
soople subtle, ingenious
speer make inquiries
sweir sluggish, unwilling, loth, depressed
syne since, ago

taigle move slowly, drag the feet
tass cup, goblet
thole endure with fortitude
tint lost
tirl rattle

unchancy unlucky
unco extremely

wame belly
wauk be awake
whaup curlew
wheen few
wheesht be silent!, shush!
whilk which
writer solicitor

PENGUIN CLASSICS

TRAVELS WITH A DONKEY AND THE AMATEUR EMIGRANT
ROBERT LOUIS STEVENSON

'I was not only travelling out of my country in latitude and longitude, but out of myself in diet, associates, and consideration'

In 1878, Robert Louis Stevenson escaped from his numerous troubles – poor health, tormented love, inadequate funds – by embarking on a journey through the Cévennes in France, accompanied by Modestine, a rather single-minded donkey. The notebook Stevenson kept during this time became *Travels with a Donkey*, a highly entertaining account of the French people and their country. *The Amateur Emigrant* is a vivid journal of his travels to and in America – describing the crowded weeks in steerage with the poor and sick, as well as stowaways – and the train journey he took across the country. Filled with sharp-eyed observations, this work brilliantly conveys Stevenson's perceptions of America and the Americans. Together, these two pieces are fascinating examples of nineteenth-century travel writing, revealing as much about the traveller as the places he travels to.

Christopher MacLachlan's introduction places the works in their biographical and literary context. This edition also includes pieces from Stevenson's original notebooks, a chronology, further reading, notes and maps of the journeys.

Edited with an introduction by Christopher MacLachlan

PENGUIN CLASSICS

KING SOLOMIN'S MINES
H. RIDER HAGGARD

'There at the end of the long stone table … sat Death himself'

Onboard a ship bound for Natal, adventurer Allan Quartermain meets Sir Henry Curtis and Captain John Good. His new friends have set out to find Sir Henry's younger brother, who vanished seeking King Solomon's legendary diamond mines in the African interior. By strange chance, Quartermain has a map to the mines, drawn in blood, and agrees to join the others on their perilous journey. The travellers face many dangers on their quest – the baking desert heat, the hostile lost tribe they discover and the evil 'wise woman' who holds the secret of the diamond mines. *King Solomon's Mines* (1885) is a brilliant work of adventure romance that has gripped readers for generations.

In his preface Giles Foden considers Haggard's treatment of the cultural stereotypes of the time, while Robert Hampson's introduction discusses the explorations and empire building that inspired Haggard's writing. This edition also includes further reading, an appendix and notes.

'Enchantment is just what Rider Haggard exercised … his books live today with undiminished vitality' Graham Greene

Edited with an introduction and notes by Robert Hampson
Preface by Giles Foden

PENGUIN CLASSICS

UNDER WESTERN EYES
JOSEPH CONRAD

'It was myself, after all, whom I have betrayed most basely'

Razumov is a university student of uncertain – possibly noble – parentage, who dreams of making his way in the academic world. But his solitary, industrious existence in St Petersburg is shattered by the appearance of his fellow student, the revolutionary terrorist Victor Haldin. Thrust into a world of state politics and espionage, Razumov is also brought into contact with Haldin's trusting sister Natalia in Geneva. When he falls in love with her he becomes caught in a tragic web and finds his identity torn apart. Exploring the conflict between East and West, this is a powerful and profound story of tyranny, guilt, loyalty and betrayal.

Part of a major series of new editions of Conrad's most famous works in Penguin Classics, this volume contains a chronology, further reading, notes and an introduction discussing the novel in the context of Conrad's troubled life, his mistrust of political institutions and his ambivalent attitude towards Russia's history and people.

Edited with notes and a glossary by Stephen Donovan
With an introduction by Allan H. Simmons
General editor J. H. Stape

PENGUIN CLASSICS

THE WONDERFUL ADVENTURES OF MRS SEACOLE IN MANY LANDS MARY SEACOLE

The Wonderful Adventures of Mrs Seacole in Many Lands (1857) is the autobiography of a Jamaican woman whose fame rivalled Florence Nightingale's during the Crimean War. Seacole travelled widely before eventually arriving in London, where her offer to volunteer as a nurse in the war was met with racism and refusal. Undaunted, Seacole set out independently to the Crimea where she acted as doctor and 'mother' to wounded soldiers while running her business, the 'British Hotel'. A witness to key battles, she gives vivid accounts of how she coped with disease, bombardment and other hardships at the Crimean battlefront. Told with energy, warmth and humour, her remarkable life story is a key work of nineteenth-literature that provides significant insights into the history of race politics.

This new Penguin Classic is accompanied by an introduction by Sara Salih, placing *Wonderful Adventures* in its historical and political contexts, and discussing Seacole's attitudes to race, slavery and war. This edition also includes suggestions for further reading, a chronology, appendices, notes and a map.

Edited with an introduction and notes by Sara Salih

PENGUIN CLASSICS

THE STORM
DANIEL DEFOE

'Horror and Confusion seiz'd upon all … No Pen can describe it, no Tongue can express it, no Thought conceive it'

On the evening of 26 November 1703, a hurricane from the north Atlantic hammered into Britain: it remains the worst storm the nation has ever experienced. Eyewitnesses saw cows thrown into trees and windmills ablaze from the friction of their whirling sails – and some 8,000 people lost their lives. For Defoe, bankrupt and just released from prison for his 'seditious' writings, the storm struck during one of his bleakest moments. But it also furnished him with material for his first book, and in this powerful depiction of suffering and survival played out against a backdrop of natural devastation, we can trace the outlines of Defoe's later masterpieces, *A Journal of the Plague Year* and *Robinson Crusoe*.

This new Penguin Classics edition marks the 300th anniversary of the first publication of The Storm. It also includes two other pieces by Defoe inspired by that momentous night, an introduction, chronology, further reading, notes and maps.

'Astonishing … a masterpiece of reportage' Sunday Telegraph

Edited with an introduction by Richard Hamblyn